PRAISE ~~...~~

VIN ~~...~~

~~WITHDRAWN FROM COLLECTION~~
~~OF SACRAMENTO PUBLIC LIBRARY~~

A Deadly Grind

"Has all the right ingredients: small-town setting, kitchen antiques, vintage cookery, and a bowlful of mystery. A perfect recipe for a cozy."

> —Susan Wittig Albert, national bestselling author of
> *The Darling Dahlias and the Texas Star*

"Smartly written and successfully plotted, the debut of this new cozy series . . . exudes authenticity."

> —*Library Journal*

"The first Vintage Kitchen Mystery is an exciting regional amateur sleuth . . . Fans will enjoy this fun Michigan cozy."
> —*Genre Go Round Reviews*

"*A Deadly Grind* is a fun debut in the new Vintage Kitchen Mystery series . . . Fans of Joanne Fluke or of Virginia Lowell's Cookie Cutter Shop Mysteries will feel right at home in Queenstown."   —*The Season*

"Victoria Hamilton's Vintage Kitchen Mystery series is off to a solid start . . . [A] fun cozy mystery."

> —*Novel Reflections*

"Hamilton's Jaymie Leighton completely captivated me . . . I'll be awaiting [her] return . . . in the next Vintage Kitchen Mystery."   ~~...~~ *Book Critiques* continued ...

Berkley Prime Crime titles by Victoria Hamilton

Vintage Kitchen Mysteries

A DEADLY GRIND
BOWLED OVER
FREEZER I'LL SHOOT

Merry Muffin Mysteries

BRAN NEW DEATH

FREEZER
I'LL SHOOT

VICTORIA HAMILTON

BERKLEY PRIME CRIME, NEW YORK

THE BERKLEY PUBLISHING GROUP
Published by the Penguin Group
Penguin Group (USA) LLC
375 Hudson Street, New York, New York 10014, USA

USA • Canada • UK • Ireland • Australia • New Zealand • India • South Africa • China

penguin.com

A Penguin Random House Company

FREEZER I'LL SHOOT

A Berkley Prime Crime Book / published by arrangement with the author

Berkley Prime Crime Books are published by The Berkley Publishing Group.
BERKLEY® PRIME CRIME and the PRIME CRIME logo are trademarks of
Penguin Group (USA) LLC.

For information, address: The Berkley Publishing Group,
a division of Penguin Group (USA) LLC,
375 Hudson Street, New York, New York 10014.

ISBN: 978-0-425-25237-6

PUBLISHING HISTORY
Berkley Prime Crime mass-market edition / November 2013

PRINTED IN THE UNITED STATES OF AMERICA

10 9 8 7 6 5 4 3 2 1

Cover illustration by Robert Crawford.
Cover design by Lesley Worrell.
Interior text design by Tiffany Estreicher.

❖ One ❖

HER EAR GLUED to the phone, Jaymie Leighton sat on the back porch of Rose Tree Cottage, listening to her mother while surveying the arriving merry band of plumbers that were set to rip up the cottage's entire backyard. The plumbers had to drive their excavator through the Redmonds' property, which faced the road behind the one Rose Tree Cottage was on, because it was the only way to access the Leightons' backyard with heavy equipment without taking down trees. The little Bobcat was negotiating the slope carefully, while one of the men guided the driver.

"Mom, I have to go because—"

"And another thing, Jaymie," the woman continued.

Jaymie covered her eyes with one hand. Ever since her parents had arrived in Queensville from Florida, Jaymie's mom had been complaining nonstop about the "junk" that Jaymie collected—her precious (to her) vintage kitchenware collection—and cluttered the kitchen in the Leighton Queensville home. Every time they were in the kitchen together doing something, her mom would sigh and glare at the old tins, vintage bowls, painted enamelware, and other things that lined the tops of the cupboards. Joy Leighton grudgingly admitted that the Hoosier cabinet Jaymie had bought earlier in the summer wasn't exactly in the way, but it was just another "junk magnet" and "dust catcher."

As if that wasn't bad enough, Jaymie's mom had found a new focus for her complaints. "That *woman* is going to drive me to an early grave," she said. "You've *got* to talk to Daniel and make him tell her to butt out of our family dinner plans! It's none of her business."

"That *woman*" was the mother of Daniel Collins, Jaymie's kinda-sorta boyfriend. Jaymie looked down at her chipped fingernail polish and blew out a puff of air on a deep sigh. How to handle this? Daniel had invited his parents to come from Phoenix to visit his historic home, Stowe House, in Queensville. Jaymie's parents had arrived at about the same time. Since the very first meeting, the men got along fine and golfed together often, but the women acted like cats, hissing and spitting each time they were forced to be together.

At first Jaymie had taken her mom's side; Mrs. Collins was sharp and cold, it seemed to her. But when the two were in company together, there was no choosing between them as to manipulative behavior and catty comments. With planning under way for the annual Leighton family dinner, to which Daniel's parents, as well as Becca's (Jaymie's sister) new beau, Kevin Brevard, had been invited, things were getting worse with every attempt to smooth things over.

Robin, the lead plumber and owner of the company, Robin Hood Plumbing, waved to her, then gathered his guys around, gesturing to the ravine part of the lot. Both the Leighton property and the Redmond property sloped down to a common area, a ravine that got soggy in spring, but was now, in August, dry and lush with green grass. The two properties were bound on both sides by a green belt of trees. Cottages and homes on either side were barely visible through the wooded lots.

"Mom, I don't know what else I can tell you. Mrs. Collins has a point," she said, going back to the argument from the day before. The two moms and Jaymie had gone on a disastrous shopping trip into Wolverhampton. The idea was shopping and lunch; what could be more soothing for three women? Instead the day had been a war of wills over whose vehicle to take, what shops to visit, and even where to have lunch. Jaymie was happy when it was over and they were on the way back to Queensville.

But they had one more stop, the grocery store. While strolling the brightly lit aisles, Joy Leighton started talking about buying ribs for the family dinner that they were planning to hold at Rose Tree Cottage. It was tradition; the Leightons had one dinner there altogether every summer, and this year the Collinses were attending. But Mrs. Collins said that with the upcoming plumbing work on the cottage being more extensive than originally thought, maybe they should move the dinner to Daniel's home, Stowe House.

You'd think the woman had made a unilateral declaration of war, because Joy Leighton's face had gone pinched and white. A hushed argument in the air-conditioned chill of the grocery store had taken place, followed by an icy ride home, where the chill in the air was *not* just from the air-conditioning. Mrs. Collins's round face had been set in a mulish expression, and her good-byes were perfunctory, to put it kindly. Abrupt, bordering on rude, was more accurate.

"Now you're taking *her* side?" Jaymie's mom said, her voice rising a decibel through the phone.

"I'm not taking Mrs. Collins's side, Mom. I'm just saying . . . Stowe House *is* a lot bigger, and who knows if we'll have the sewage system at Rose Tree Cottage back to functional. Robin told me just this morning that it's even worse than we thought. Not only do they have to put in a new septic tank, they have to lay out a whole new leaching field."

A week ago Jaymie had not even known what a "leaching field" was, and now she knew far too much. While her mother yammered on about the invidious Mrs. Collins, and why the "getting to know you" dinner Jaymie's mom was planning just *had* to be held at Rose Tree Cottage, her mind wandered . . .

To her first column for the *Wolverhampton Weekly Howler.* Her fledgling cookbook, *Recipes from the Vintage Kitchen*, was never far from her mind, and to that end she was following the advice of the urbane and kindly editor at Adelaide Publishing. He had declined to publish it, as it was in no way ready for publication; nor was she. He told her some hard truths about cookbook publishing. The recipes were vital, the writing was important, but an editor was going to want to know what kind of name Jaymie had in the cooking world. And would she/could she promote the heck out of her cookbook, should it be published? How was she going to publicize it? What contacts did she have?

It had set her back on her heels at first. She had pictured getting the cookbook published, holding it in her hands, even seeing it on a bookstore shelf, and she had imagined all the work building up to publication. What she had not realized was that the real effort would come *after* the publication. To be competitive in the cookbook industry, she would need to vigorously make appearances, do a tour, even, and appear on cooking shows, talk shows, and local and national news programs.

She pondered it for a few weeks, wondering whether she was cut out for the world of cookbook publishing. It wasn't that she was shy, exactly, but she was a small-town girl who liked a quiet life. She had gone away to college, but had returned to Queensville, Michigan, population a couple of thousand, at the first opportunity, before even testing the waters of career and/or job in the big city. It was her preference, but she had always supposed it made her rather cowardly, not to want what other girls seemed to want. After a few years, though, of soul searching, she had come to the conclusion that there was no shame in liking her life in Queensville, just as there would have been no shame in wanting something else. And so she had settled into a routine of holding down multiple jobs, with a jumbled schedule that would have driven some mad, and an unreliability of wages that was only tenable because beyond insurance, utilities and food, she had little else to pay for. She and her sister jointly owned the ancestral family home, and she managed the cottage rental.

Her cookbook venture was important to her, important enough that she must summon up all her courage and make her best attempt at success. To that end she had called the food editor, Nan Goodenough—also the owner's wife—at the *Wolverhampton Weekly Howler* to ask about writing for them. To Jaymie's delight, because she advertised in the *Howler*, Nan had heard of her as the innovative young businesswoman who had started Queensville Vintage Picnic, her basket rental business. It had started modestly enough as a simple service for tourists who could go to the Queensville Emporium and rent a picnic basket filled with vintage dishes and good food, everything they needed to enjoy an afternoon on the river, or a local day trip. It had rapidly expanded through the summer to include "destination" baskets to the local winery, a boat trip along the St. Clair, and an evening under the stars with the Queensville Quartet playing Scarlatti.

Nan had asked her to come in to her office in Wolverhampton to talk; after an hour chatting about the basket business, her vintage kitchenware collection and everything else under the sun—including the two murders that had occurred within a month or so of each other in quiet little Queensville—Jaymie was stunned and pleased to walk out of the *Howler* office with a tentative weekly column called "Vintage Eats."

"If you give me something worth printing, then we'll go

ahead," Nan said, in her brisk, New York pull-no-punches manner. She had "retired" when she married the owner of the *Howler*, and was now *just* the editor of the Lifestyles section, where once she had been the editor of a major lifestyle magazine in New York.

Jaymie wanted her first column to be perfect, but was afraid she'd gotten in over her head. What to write? She reluctantly admitted to herself that Nan intimidated her. How could she ever produce something good enough for Nan Goodenough?

"Jaymie, are you listening to me?" her mother asked.

Jaymie started, and Hoppy, her little three-legged Yorkie-Poo, yapped at her from inside the door of the cottage, where he was locked so he wouldn't get into trouble with the plumbers and heavy machinery. She had pretty much forgotten her mom was even on the line, the voice in her ear becoming the drone of a pesky mosquito. "Yes, of course I'm listening, Mom."

"Then what did I just say?"

Argh. Fess-up time. Or not. Confessing that she had not been listening would prolong the conversation, and she was not in the mood to be chastised. "Mom, I have to go. The plumbers are signaling me. Can we just see how this plumbing issue goes and resolve the family dinner thing later? I *really* gotta go! I'll see you tomorrow, when I come back to Queensville." She clicked off, heaving a deep sigh of relief that she was staying at the cottage overnight. Robin had promised that the work would be done in twenty-four hours. Maybe. He hoped.

She slid the screen door of the cottage open, to set the phone inside; Hoppy saw his chance and dashed out between her feet. Jaymie hopped back out, trying to catch hold of Hoppy's collar, but he thought that was a marvelous game, and dashed around the tiny deck, then down the steps to the patio below. Ruby Redmond, the vigorous fiftysomething co-owner (with her brother, Garnet) of the cottage behind the

Leightons' Rose Tree Cottage, as well as the Ice House restaurant, down near the marina, waved at Jaymie from her back porch. Hoppy saw his favorite woman in the whole world wave, and just knew she was inviting him over for treats!

He yipped a greeting to the biscuit lady, as he probably thought of Ruby, and dashed down the lawn, weaving around the machinery and giving Jaymie heart palpitations. "Hoppy, come back here," she yelled, racing after him, circling around the excavator that was moving to the center of the sloped back lawn, getting into position to start tearing up turf. Huffing a bit from the climb up the hill, Jaymie approached the Redmonds' back patio, where Hoppy danced and yapped at Ruby's feet.

"Sorry about that," Ruby said, fishing a biscuit out of her hoodie pocket, as Hoppy wobbled up to her, panting and wagging his whole body.

"Not your fault he's in doggie love," Jaymie said, watching Hoppy dance around for the biscuit.

"The way to a man's heart is through his stomach, right? Not that I know that from experience," she said, with a rueful chuckle.

Jaymie examined the woman while she made a fuss over Hoppy, who rolled around in the dewed grass, wriggling in glee, crunching on biscuit chunks that Ruby broke up for him. Ruby was tall and angular and had the deeply tanned face that came from being a sailor. Her short hair stood up in a shock of iron gray, and she never wore makeup. Her clothes were jean shorts and polo shirts most of the time, with a pair of Top-Siders. She and her brother, Garnet, the skipper of the *Heartbreak Kid*—Garnet resembled his sister in being tall and lanky, as well as deeply tanned—were the annual winners of the Heartbreak Island leg of the St. Clair River Regatta. She had never married, gossip had it, and Jaymie wondered, but didn't want to pry, whether there was some long-ago love that kept her from finding happiness. When the siblings arrived several years before, they seemed to ease into Heartbreak Island society with no ruffles, and they ran the renovated restaurant with competent grace.

Ruby straightened and said, "You can come and use our facilities anytime, Jaymie, I hope you know that. You're not staying at the cottage overnight, are you?"

"I am. Mom and Dad are in residence at the Queensville house, and for some reason it just seems . . . crowded." She shrugged, trying to ease the tension out of her shoulders that had built while talking to her mother.

Ruby chuckled, her weathered face creasing with laughter, and the morning sun glinting in her pale blue eyes. "Well, you're in for a challenge, then. Remember we had to have our leaching field torn up last year? It was a mess. Luckily, we have the restaurant, and can use those facilities night or day. I'll leave the back door unlatched. If you get caught short in the night, just come on over and use the head!"

"I appreciate that, Ruby. Come on, Hoppy," Jaymie said, snapping her fingers at the little dog. He ignored her, staring up at Ruby with adoration in his chocolate eyes. He watched her hands, hoping she would dig in her pocket for another biscuit, then dropped his nose to the ground, snuffling up crumbs. "Hoppy, come!"

"Coming down to the Ice House for dinner tonight?" Ruby said.

"I will. I hear you've got yellow perch on the menu, and I love perch. See you later!" Jaymie scooped Hoppy up and walked down the grassy slope to talk to Robin for a minute, before returning to the cottage. He was not so sure they would be done that day, he told her, and she sighed.

By late afternoon Jaymie was more discouraged than she had been that morning. She had a list of ideas for her first column, all of them crappy. They just sounded so darned dull! Maybe she wasn't cut out for this. Who told her she could be a cookbook author anyway? They weren't even her recipes. She was no fancy cook; she had just taken old recipes from her grandmother's cookbooks, rescued from the attic, and worked them over to suit modern cooks and modern ovens. It had kept her sane and upright during the long winter months when she was mourning the death of her relationship with Joel Anderson, who had moved on to blonder pastures with Heidi Lockland.

Jaymie had thought Joel was the love of her life. She would have married him if he'd asked, but of course, he never did. Strangely enough, she and Heidi had managed to construct an odd kind of friendship in the last couple of months. The girl from New York City was actually a sweetie, too good for Joel, Jaymie had decided. If he was such a gutless wonder as to walk out on her two weeks before Christmas without any explanation, then he didn't deserve the girl. Or *any* girl.

Looking at the torn-up mess that was her back lawn was too depressing, so Jaymie took her lunch to the cottage front porch. She was one road back from the riverfront, which was good when a storm swept along the river. The other cottages and trees along the riverfront sheltered Rose Tree Cottage from the worst of any storm. They were rarely in danger of flooding, another bonus of being on slightly higher ground. There was a long line of pines across the road surrounding the cottage across from theirs, but Jaymie could still see the glimmer of the St. Clair River as it slipped past, and they had access, if she wanted to walk down to it, alongside the neighbor's cottage.

But right now she needed to concentrate on the task at hand: a subject for her first column for "Vintage Eats." She lay on her back on the board porch and dropped her head off the edge of the first step, staring up at the blue sky as seen through the leafy green expanse of tree canopy. Hoppy turned in a complete circle and, with a little doggy sigh, settled beside her, nestled up against her thigh.

She closed her eyes. What to write about? Food history? Boring. Old dishes, maybe: Pyrex, Depression glass, etcetera? Not boring to her, but maybe to others.

She daydreamed, and may even have dropped off to sleep for a moment. Hoppy jumped up and wuffled a greeting to someone. When Jaymie opened her eyes, she saw hairy, tanned thighs. Good grief! She bolted up and whirled, finding herself face-to-face with dark-haired, gray-eyed and too-handsome Detective Zack Christian, one of the only two detectives on the Queensville police force. She'd had a few run-ins with him in the last months over a couple of murders that she had solved—from her aspect—or interfered in, from his viewpoint.

"Hi," she said, smoothing her ruffled hair. He was not in uniform. He was in swim trunks and a golf shirt, with a towel slung over his shoulder, and his dark hair was slicked back, wet from a recent dip. Yum.

"Hi, Jaymie," he said, reaching down to pet Hoppy, briefly, then straightening. "What are you doing out here on the island?"

"I was going to ask the same of you. This is my family's cottage," she said, gesturing behind her. "We're having some work done out back, so I'm staying here."

"Oh. I rent a cottage on the island." He watched her eyes, his expression inscrutable, as always.

"You live here year-round?"

"Yup, so far. Love the water." There was a brief silence, and he smiled. "I guess I'd better go. See you."

He strolled off, barefoot, down the sandy road. She watched him go. She'd never seen him so relaxed, and he was even more handsome that way than in his suit, investigating a crime. She took a deep breath and blew out the air. There was just something about him that attracted her, and she hadn't defeated it yet, though she was determined to. Her agitation in his presence was purely a physical response, just hormones jumping around at the sight of a guy so good-looking he could model for *GQ*.

Daniel Collins was the real deal, a great guy who genuinely liked her, and she had promised to give their relationship a fair shake. Six months, she had said to Daniel. She wanted six months to completely get past Joel's dumping her—she was pretty much over all but the last bit of anger now—and see how they felt about each other before taking their relationship to the next level.

And that included getting along with his mother, who didn't seem to like her too much, and making peace between their two moms, somehow. Zack Christian didn't figure into the equation at all. As Bernice "Bernie" Jenkins, one of the constables on the local force said, he was only in Queensville until something bigger came along. Then he'd be gone, leaving behind legions of sighing females. Daniel was as solid and trustworthy as the pine trees overhead; Zack was a leaf fluttering on a wayward wind.

He was wrong for her in every way, even if he *had* been interested in her, which he was not. He viewed her as the cute, provincial miss, a little sister, almost, like the older guy's ward in one of the historical romance novels she loved to read. Zack Christian had pinched her cheek once, for heaven's sake! There was no romantic sensibility in a man pinching your cheek.

"Come on, Hoppy," she said, scrambling to her feet. "I need to check in on the guys out back."

❧ Two ❧

JAYMIE WAS HELD up by a consultation with the plumber, who had to tell her at length about the problems they had run into that made laying the new leaching bed tricky. She phoned her dad, who was footing the bill, and put him on with Rob, of Robin Hood plumbing, and they sorted it all out. Then she had to walk Hoppy, feed him, lock up and walk the four blocks or so to the Redmonds' restaurant. The delay meant that she didn't get to the Ice House until well after six, prime time for the boating and cottage crowd. Mid-August in a touristy town meant that the restaurant was fairly full.

The Ice House was right on the river and had a long outdoor patio that lined the whole front, overlooking the river and facing Queensville, with benches for those who just wanted to sit and sip a glass of wine while they watched boats slip past. There was a larger patio at the back, where umbrella-covered tables were popular for the après boating crowd. It was just too hot to sit outside to drink or eat, though; she preferred the air-conditioned, dim interior.

As she opened the big oak door, the flood of noise disoriented her for a moment, until she sorted out the thump of music from an old-fashioned jukebox in the front corner, the sports bar section of the Ice House, and the chatter of tanned, relaxed vacationers who had spent an exhilarating day on the water, sailing, water-skiing and wakeboarding. There were a few folks she recognized, neighbors from the island crowd, but for the most part it was tourists who lined the bar and crowded around tables. She stood near the door, looking for a spot to sit, but didn't see anything. Ruby, talking to the Ice House manager, Marg, near the bar, caught her eye and waved her in.

"Hey, kiddo," she yelled, over the sound, "you're a little late to get a table!"

"I know," Jaymie said, leaning forward to talk into Ruby's ear. "You've got a crowd!"

"Come with me," Ruby said, grabbing her wrist and leading her through the bar section, back to the dining room proper, which was a little quieter, conversations calmer, the clink of silverware on china the only other sound. The jukebox noise was muted by a partial wall separating the two sections. There were quite a few couples and some families having dinner. "I've got one table that just has one guy at it. Do you mind sharing?"

"No, of course not," Jaymie said. She had begun to regret that she hadn't just stayed home and eaten another sandwich, and the regret became more pronounced when she saw who she would have to share a table with.

Zack Christian sat alone, a copy of the week's *Howler* in his hand.

"Hey, Zack, do you mind sharing your table?" Ruby said, clapping him on the shoulder.

He looked up, saw Jaymie and smiled. Standing, he

gestured to the other side of the table and said, "Be my guest. Didn't expect to see you again so soon, Jaymie!"

"You two know each other?" Garnet Redmond, who had materialized at his sister's elbow, asked.

"We do know each other," he said. "Quite well."

Jaymie felt herself flush pink, and bit her lip. It sounded more personal than it was, and she didn't know how to explain to Garnet and Ruby, who knew she was going out with Daniel Collins. Ruby glanced over at her with one eyebrow raised. Jaymie smiled and shrugged as she took that chair across from the detective and accepted the menu from Ruby.

"Lisa will take your order," Garnet said, indicating a waitress who sailed past with a giant tray holding five plates on it, which she expertly unloaded at the next table.

The brother and sister left, and Jaymie said, "Thanks for sharing your table."

"I expected I'd have to share, given how busy this place is. It's nice that it's with someone I know."

They chatted as they waited for their orders. Both of them were having the yellow perch dinner.

"So your family owns a cottage here. Why a cottage so close to home?"

"My great-grandfather Leighton built it way back as a retirement residence for him and my great-grandma. He gave the house in town to my grandpa and grandma, and moved to the island to spend the rest of his days fishing."

"And did he?"

"He sure did. Becca remembers him, but they were both gone by the time I was born." There was a fifteen-year gap between her and her older sister, who was forty-seven.

"So does it sit empty now?"

"No, we rent it out most of the summer, but we reserve a couple of weeks every year for Mom and Dad to stay in it. We had a cancellation this season—one of our regular guests had a family funeral—but it's a good thing because we need to replace the septic tank, and, I just found out, we have to have a new leaching bed laid."

He looked mystified, so she explained what that was. Because they were on a small island, every residence and business had to have a septic tank to handle waste, and the leaching bed was a necessity to process all that waste. "It's all natural," she finished.

"Wow, the things you take for granted," he said, shaking his head.

"I didn't know much about it myself until today. Now I know far too much!"

There was a moment of awkward silence, broken at last when their meals came. She wished it were Daniel across the table from her. They had established a relationship that was built on friendship first. Being with Daniel was easy; there was a comfortable silence, at times, an acknowledgment that they didn't need to fill every moment with chatter. But really, was it the detective who was making it awkward, or her?

As the waitress unloaded her tray and provided tartar sauce and condiments, Jaymie thought about that, and decided her own discomfort was driving her to fill every second with talk. So she'd stop. It was a little better after that. The perch was five small fillets pan-sautéed in butter, with a heap of home-cut fries and homemade coleslaw. It was delicious, and she ate enthusiastically, as did the detective. Zack; she had to start thinking of him by name, instead of as "the detective." Zack plowed through his meal faster than she did. He drank a microbrewery beer, while she had the Ice House's homemade iced tea.

She was still working on the problem of a topic for the first column of "Vintage Eats." She intended to blend articles on vintage cookware with vintage recipes. But inspiration was hard to come by when she was so afraid of making a misstep with her very first article.

Zack had excused himself momentarily, and Jaymie

finished her dinner, sat back and looked around. Along the wall behind the bar and dining lounge servery, vintage tools were hung. She got up to take a closer look. They looked lethal, many of them: poles with wicked hooks on the end, giant picks and saws, and many examples of what looked like a kind of claw. She remembered hearing that the Redmonds had preserved some of the history that went with the old building. They'd make great photos.

She took her digital camera from her purse and moved to the wall to take photos. Garnet came out from behind the bar and settled his lean form on a bar stool, arms crossed over his chest, chatting with her as she framed pictures carefully, playing with the options on her camera to get the best photo in the low light.

"You and Ruby renovated this place yourselves, didn't you?" Jaymie said over her shoulder. "When you moved here?"

"We did. It was a kind of warehouse for years, as I'm sure you know. Some folks from the marina were using it as a storage facility for machinery."

"Machinery?"

"Yeah, you know, for lifting boats out of the river, that kind of thing."

"So all of these tools were used back in the day?" Zack asked.

Jaymie jumped; he had approached without her noticing.

"Yup, from when this was a true ice storage facility. That there," he said, pointing to one of the tools that looked like a giant outside caliper, "was for lifting the blocks of ice out of the river."

Jaymie edged closer and stared. It was huge, but there were many of the same thing, right down to much smaller ones that she could imagine handling.

"And that," he continued, pointing to a large saw with a handle like a bicycle handle, "was for cutting the ice from the river. The big thing is an ice ax. With the ax and the tongs, a guy could manhandle a pretty big block of ice."

"What are those things?" she asked, pointing at a lethal-looking tool, a thin piece of steel with a green-painted wood handle.

"You don't know?" Garnet said, with a smile. "That's an ice pick." He pulled it down off its peg and handed it to her.

She turned it over in her hands; it was longish and came to a sharp point. "So this was for breaking up chunks of ice?" She laid it down on the wood bar top and took a close-up photo for research purposes.

"Yeah, for the housewife. If hubby wanted ice in his scotch, she'd go into the ice chest and chip some chunks off the big block."

"I'm not sure I get the whole system," Jaymie said, handing the ice pick back to Garnet. "How did they get ice chunks out of the river?"

"Ice cutting? It's pretty simple, really." He tossed the pick up in the air and caught it by the handle, making Jaymie wince, and Zack chuckle. "Of course, we're going back before refrigeration," he said, as Ruby approached. "Back in the day, ice was a necessity to keep your butter cool in your icebox and to make ice cream. Companies like Queensville Ice, which owned the Heartbreak Island Ice House until the mid-forties, would cut blocks of ice from the river in winter and store it in the storage locker, this icehouse. The delivery guy would take the chunks in the back of his cart and deliver them all over town. "

"But how did it stay frozen for so long?" Jaymie asked, getting her notebook out of her purse and scribbling some notes. She perched on a bar stool. An idea began to form in her brain, as she remembered a recipe for old-fashioned ice cream making from the early 1900s. She could blend local vintage resources, tools and methods with vintage recipes, starting with an article on ice cream making.

"Good question," Garnet said. "From what I've read, they

discovered that the thick walls of the basement of the icehouse, as well as lots of straw for insulation and ventilation to vent the warm air, would keep the ice good right up until winter, when they could start the process all over again."

"Wow," Jaymie said. "I never thought of all that." She surveyed the wall of tools: ice picks, saws, grapple hooks, tongs. She would need more info, and some photos of ice cream makers, maybe. Ruby hovered nearby, and Jaymie ran the idea past her, as Zack returned to their table and ordered another beer, picking up the *Howler* and folding it back to the Sudoku puzzle.

"What a great thought!" Ruby said. "Did you know that what we use as storage lockers at the back of the dining room are antique ice chests? You could use pictures of them to illustrate, maybe!" She grabbed Jaymie's wrist and tugged her back to a dim corner of the restaurant. They looked over the ice chests, beautiful lead-lined wood chests, with a place for the ice and a drip pipe to drain the water as it melted off the ice. The ice chests were full of plastic cups, take-out containers, paper towels and stacks of order pads. Ruby closed them back up, and Jaymie positioned herself to get the best photos.

Ruby ducked out of the way, and Jaymie said, "Hey, don't go! Let me get a photo of you by the ice chests!"

"No, no, I don't want to be in any pictures. I . . . I *hate* having my photo taken!" Her weather-beaten face stained a ruddy hue.

"Okay. I know the feeling. I cringe when I see pictures of myself." She lined up the shot, and the flash lit up the chrome handles on the doors. She looked down at the little glowing screen of her camera; good enough, since she didn't expect to use the ice chest photos for anything. She and Ruby threaded back between the tables, now emptier of patrons than they had been an hour before. Jaymie was going to go back to her table, but a shout near the front drew her attention.

A short, thickset man in his fifties was shouldering past

one of the waitstaff. "Redmond!" he shouted. "Where are you?"

Garnet, at the bar putting away clean glasses, turned and muttered a curse word under his breath. Ruby glanced around and saw the man.

"Darn it, what does *he* want?" she said.

"Who is that?" Jaymie asked.

"Urban Dobrinskie," Ruby said, following her brother toward the front of the bar. "He's the part owner of the marina. Owns the *Sea Urchin*."

"Right! The boat you and your brother beat in the race on July Fourth. What's his problem?" Jaymie asked, trotting along behind Ruby.

"This time? Who knows. He's always complaining."

Jaymie followed Ruby to the front out of curiosity, because the man's red face and pugnacious attitude was indicative of something more than a take-out order for perch. As they approached, she could hear him yelling at Garnet, as the two men stood toe-to-toe.

"I knew you two were crooked, but now I've got proof," the balding, pudgy man hollered, shaking his finger in Garnet's face.

It would have been comical, given the difference in the two men's heights, if not for the anger expressed in every choleric grimace on Dobrinskie's face.

"You're cheaters," he yelped. "You won last year by cheating, and you won *this* year by cheating. I'm gonna get you run out of the yacht club."

"What the hell are you complaining about now, Urban?" Redmond said, his pleasant voice pitched a tad louder than normal. He glanced around. Jaymie could see that the confrontation in front of patrons made him uneasy. "Look, I'll buy you a beer and we can discuss whatever it is—"

"The race, you jackass, the race!" Urban shouted. "I heard you ordered a sail from Switzerland, and bylaw 103, section A of the yacht club charter says no sail made in a country other than the United States is allowed."

"Switzerland? Why would I . . . Who told you *that* crap?"

The other man hesitated a second, but the temptation to name his source was too great. "It's not crap, Redmond. I got it from good authority. Sherm Woodrow don't lie."

Garnet's expression was becoming thunderous, as Ruby and Jaymie got closer. "Yeah, well, that's a load of horse manure, Dobrinskie. Sherm oughta shut his trap."

Jaymie looked over her shoulder and saw Zack get up and follow them to the front, weaving past the bar patrons, who were all quiet now, watching the confrontation.

"Why? So you can keep cheating?"

Garnet's face was flushed, a pulse throbbing in a vein in his neck. He shrugged his shoulder, as if working out some tension. Through gritted teeth, he said, "Dobrinskie, you old blowhard, you ought to be careful who you're accusing, or—"

"Garnet, temper!" Ruby said, taking her brother's wrist.

He shook off her grip, but shut his mouth. After a long minute, he said, his voice calmer, "You should leave now, Urb. If you think you've got a case, then take it up at the yacht club board meeting next week."

"You gonna listen to that she-male of a sister of yours? *Garnet, temper!*" he mimicked in a falsetto voice.

Someone among the bar patrons laughed. Jaymie's cheeks flamed with anger at the insult directed at Ruby, who gasped.

"Guess who wears the pants in that family," Dobrinskie said, turning and surveying the crowd. "*And* who has a pair o' balls hidden in there, prob'ly!" he finished, hitching his thumb over his shoulder in Ruby's direction.

Several of the drinkers gathered near the bar gasped, and one young guy said, "That's enough, now."

Garnet was done talking, but that didn't mean he was

done. He grabbed the shorter man, whirled him around, hauled back and let loose a punch that sent the fellow flying backward.

Zack, who had been lingering nearby watching the argument, lunged forward and blocked Garnet, who looked like he was going to drop on the fellow and deliver more punches. "Enough," he shouted, helping Dobrinskie to his feet with one hand and holding the other out toward Garnet in a "stop" gesture.

"I oughta sue you, Redmond," Dobrinskie whined, holding one hand over his nose, which was bleeding. "I'm calling the cops!"

"You want to file a complaint?" Zack asked, his glance steely.

"You're a cop, right?"

"Off duty, but yes, I'm a police detective. If you want to file a complaint, it's within your rights, but I am obliged to warn you that I heard everything you said, and what you said to Miss Redmond could be construed as . . . as hate speech," he said, avoiding Jaymie's glance.

Jaymie watched, openmouthed.

"Hate speech?" Dobrinskie shouted. "What the fu . . ."

The detective had him by the arm and steered him through the oak doors and outside to the wood deck, so the rest of his expletive was drowned out. Jaymie bolted out the door after them in time to hear Zack mutter, "Look, you little toad, I've had to warn you about your temper before. You are ruining people's dinner. Now, I *heard* Garnet say to you that you ought to take it up with the yacht club board if you have a problem—a reasonable suggestion in response to a base accusation—after which you gravely insulted his sister. That could be considered extenuating circumstances for him punching you, and I have to say, I'd have done the same if you insulted *my* sister."

Dobrinskie jerked his arm out of Zack's grip, his face red, spluttering in fury. "This ain't the end. You tell Garnet that I intend to take it up with the yacht club, all right, and I'll see him and his sister kicked out, pronto. I got a lot of pull, you know. I'm an important guy around here, and don't you forget it." With that he strutted away, down the board sidewalk muttering about big-shot cops, his own version of riding off into the sunset.

"Bravo, Detective," Jaymie said, as he turned back after watching the man walk away.

He shrugged and smoothed back his ruffled dark hair. "I'm eating the best dessert of my life and he ruined it. What else could I do?"

"Homemade vanilla ice cream on a Tansy Woodrow butter tart, right?"

He nodded. "I've got a shameful sweet tooth. Now you know my darkest secret." He held the door open for her and they entered the cooler interior.

"What did you mean, you've warned him about his temper before?" she asked, over her shoulder.

"The guy's a creep. I caught him down at the marina yelling at his kid last week, and warned him then. The boy's about seventeen, old enough to grow a pair, I guess, and stand up to the old man, but with a dad like Dobrinskie, he may never get a chance. That guy . . . If he doesn't calm down, he's going to have a heart attack before his next birthday."

"Or set someone off so bad they'll beat him to a pulp!"

❋ Three ❋

THE NEXT MORNING, Robin and his merry gang of plumbers woke Jaymie up early with the sound of the excavator chugging to life; she quickly got dressed in shorts and a sleeveless tee, and put the coffeepot on.

"You want to go over and see the love of your life?" Jaymie asked Hoppy, who sat staring up at her with his usual doggie intensity. He yapped. "I'll take that as a yes."

She grabbed a washcloth and towel, leashed Hoppy, and led him past the machinery, then dashed up the incline toward the Redmonds' to use their facilities. If this went on much longer, she'd have to rent a chemical toilet or go back to the mainland. It might just be worth the money to rent the toilet. She was supposed to go back home today for at least a few hours, but until her mom and Mrs. Collins settled their differences, it was a strain to listen to her mother's complaints.

"Mornin', Jaymie!" Ruby, who was sitting on the back porch in a wicker chair, stuck her thumb in her book to save her place. "And Hoppy, my little love!" she cried. The dog trotted up the three steps to the Redmonds' back porch and sat at her feet, gazing up at her with love in his eyes.

Jaymie could hear Garnet whistling in the kitchen, and the smell of bacon and eggs floated out the open window. "I need to use the washroom real bad," Jaymie said, hopping from foot to foot and rubbing sleep out of her eyes. "Can I leave Hoppy with you? I don't want him out among the workers alone."

"Sure," Ruby said, taking his leash and inviting Hoppy up to sit in her chair with her as she produced a biscuit out of her robe pocket.

Jaymie wandered through the back door and said hello to Garnet, who was at the stove.

"Hey, kiddo," he said, glancing over at her. "Want some breakfast?"

"No, thanks," she said. "I'm just here to use the washroom!"

"Be my guest."

She wandered down the hall, past Ruby's room, with its perfectly made-up bed, then past Garnet's, with the tumbled blankets half on the floor, to the washroom. Relieved of her worries and freshened by a good wash-up, she wove through the kitchen and waved good-bye to Garnet as she passed, then thanked Ruby, taking Hoppy's leash. She headed across the Redmonds' backyard to her own.

Rob the plumber caught up with her. "Jaymie, we've got a problem," he said.

She stopped, with a sigh, and turned. A "problem" usually had dollar signs attached. What was it now?

"Someone ripped us off last night, stole tools." His open, honest face, sunburned cheeks puffy like a chipmunk's, wore an unusual expression of anger.

"Really? Who would do that?" Her remark was not disingenuous, but honest astonishment. Thievery was not a huge problem on the island, especially not something so mundane as tools. Sometimes beer coolers were rifled dockside, and occasionally there was some drunken pilfering of boats, but tools? One of the machines fired up, and Hoppy yapped, so Jaymie picked him up.

"Damn weekenders, that's who!" he shouted, over the sound of the excavator, his cheeks getting redder. "Drink over their tolerance at the Ice House or the Boat House and can't keep their hands off stuff!"

Jaymie sighed. Rob's prejudice against the weekenders, those who rented slip space at the marina, or a cottage just for a week or two, was not his peculiarity alone. Many of those who called Heartbreak Island home felt the same way. The Boat House that he mentioned was the bar on the other half of the island, the Canadian side that faced the small Ontario town of Johnsonville. "Is it all replaceable?" she asked. "Why did you leave tools on the work site anyway?" She hoped he wasn't going to try to stick her father with the bill.

"Some of the stuff was locked up in the storage trailer. *It's* all okay, but one of my young guys . . . He didn't know to lock everything up. Someone made off with a pair of work boots, a pick-ax, a wheelbarrow and, of all the stupid things, a drill bit."

"A drill bit? Why would anyone take that?"

He shrugged. "You got me."

"I still don't understand why anyone would leave a pair of work boots on the site."

He shrugged. "That's Sammy for ya . . . He's just a kid, barely finished high school. He didn't think, I guess. He's the one left the drill bit out in the open, and the ax, too."

"So what do we do about it?"

"Suck it up, I guess. Nothing worth reporting to the cops or the insurance company."

"Okay. I'm sorry about that," Jaymie said.

"Not your fault. I'm just grumbling. Anyway, down to business . . . We've gotten down to the absorption trenches in the test area, so we know what we're doing now," he said, about the part of the leaching bed that worked as a natural system to control and absorb effluent from the cottage's wastewater system. He pointed to some PVC piping laid alongside the work area. "We're going to double or triple the size of the leaching field, so we have a lot of work with the excavator today; then tomorrow we lay the pipe and reroute the sump pump drainage. We think that's what was flooding the leaching field."

A sump pump was a necessity on the island because of the high water table. It would click on during rainy weather and pump water away from the cottage's footings, to keep them from washing out. Rob explained that because the sump pump piping was directed to the leaching field, it overwhelmed the system on occasion, which partly explained why the lowest part of the ravine got spongy in spring, and took forever to dry out after rainy weather.

"Okay. I'm here for the rest of the day. I might go over to Queensville, or I may just leave that until tomorrow," she said, thinking of her barely begun article. She was excited about it now that she had an idea. She *did* want to access her grandmother's old cookbooks, to see whether there were any ice cream recipes, but her mother's harassment would just put her off and irritate her.

She called Daniel before settling down to work, but he sounded harassed and frustrated, which, when she heard his mother's voice in the background saying, "Are you sure that ferry out to the island is safe? You know how I don't like boats, Daniel," she understood. He and his mother were having the discussion—again—about the Leighton family getting-to-know-you dinner at Rose Tree Cottage.

She told him about the continuing problems with the leaching bed, then hesitated, trying to figure out whether it would be disloyal to her mother to tell Daniel that she was trying to convince her mom that the world would not end if they had the family dinner somewhere other than Heartbreak Island. She decided to let it be, in the end, so she could think about it some more, and said good-bye.

"I miss you," Daniel said, with fervor.

Mrs. Collins's voice was strident in the background. "Who are you talking to, Daniel? Is that Mrs. Leighton? I'd like to speak to her, if I may!"

"Mom," Daniel said, his voice muffled as he turned his mouth away from the phone. "Do you really think I'd be telling Jaymie's mother that I miss her?"

Jaymie stifled a giggle. "I gotta go," she said, her voice gurgling with laughter. "I'm finally getting somewhere on the article for the *Howler*, and I want to get it mapped out today."

"Okay. Miss you. Consider yourself kissed."

She made a kissy-face sound and said, "I will. Hang tight!"

She then called Nan Goodenough with her idea for the story on ice harvesting and ice cream making, and got the okay to proceed. She was relieved to finally have an idea to work on.

By the end of the day, the plumbing workers had the whole backyard stripped of grass and dirt, and the anatomy of the leaching field had been laid bare. She supposed it was progress, of a sort, but it was like one of those tile puzzles where you had to tear apart what looked like progress to *really* make progress. There was nothing else they could do that day, since starting the next task would mean several hours of work, so the plumbers packed up, locking everything up tight this time, and headed home.

Though Hoppy usually had more freedom on the island than he did on the mainland, Jaymie hadn't been able to let him wander the joined sloping Redmond-Leighton backyards because of the plumbing work, so she felt she owed him a walk. It was getting on in the afternoon, the sun slanting low in the sky, but she just had time to go to Tansy's Tarts to get some pecan butter tarts to take home the next day.

She slipped her feet into flip-flops, grabbed a poop bag—just in case—clicked her Yorkie-Poo's leash on, and said, "C'mon, Hoppy, let's go get some sweeties!" She walked down the sandy road, thinking how simple life seemed when she was at the cottage. Just a fifteen-minute ferry ride and a ten-minute walk from her house, and yet it felt worlds away, thanks to the relaxed cottagers who at this time of day were just coming back from sailing the river, sunburned and laughing as they carried their life jackets back to dry in the sun, or over the porch railing of their cottages.

She took the long way around, skirting the river, the sun glistening on the water as a breeze skittered over the surface and a herring gull wheeled and screeched overhead. With a competent manager in Marg, the Redmonds were free to do what they wanted some days, and as she passed the marina she saw them just taking their sail down as they cruised closer to the island. They switched to motor power, pulling into the marina as Jaymie walked past the dock; she waved at them. Will Lindsay, the co-owner of the marina with Urban Dobrinskie, must have thought she was waving at him and shouted, "Hey, pretty lady, didn't even know you remembered me!" He finished tying off a sailboat and helping one young woman to the dock, then approached Jaymie. He bent over to scruff Hoppy's neck.

He was one of the members of the heritage society, and helped out at the Tea with the Queen event—known as the TQ by locals—every Victoria Day. Jaymie felt herself blush pink, but didn't want to correct his mistake. "Sure I remember you, Will. It's guys like you who make it possible to run the TQ event every May!" He was a cheerful, ruddy sailor type, so different from his business partner it was astounding.

He straightened and shaded his eyes, watching the Redmonds chug to their slip and pull close. Ruby leaped onto the dock and grabbed the rope, making an expert knot as she tied the bow of the *Heartbreak Kid* off. Her stringy muscles stood out on her arms, and her close-cropped hair was all askew. Garnet followed and tied off the stern end.

"Hey, Will," Garnet said, approaching and clapping the other man on the shoulder.

"Heard you had a run-in with Urb yesterday," Will said,

a rueful grimace on his tanned face. He waved at some other folks who were tying their sail craft up for the night, and another group that was firing up their dockside barbecue. "Sorry about that. He can be a pain in the ass sometimes, but he isn't always like that."

"You're not responsible for Urban, Will," Ruby said, approaching, but moving aside as a teenager squeezed past her down the dock. "He's his own worst enemy."

"Ain't that the truth!"

"Have you made any progress about the harbor dredging?" Garnet asked.

Jaymie knew they would soon slip into sailing talk—there had been some chatter about dredging the harbor mouth to allow bigger sail craft to enter—and excused herself, telling the Redmonds she'd be by the cottage later. "I have to get to Tansy's shop before she closes."

"Remember, the back door of the cottage will be open for you, Jaymie," Ruby called. "While we're at the restaurant, and even later, overnight!"

"I don't want to disturb you guys," she protested.

"Don't be silly. I don't want you to get caught short!"

"Thanks," Jaymie said, and walked on up the rising road with Hoppy, then cut back into the island, strolling the main road that bisected it into American and Canadian property.

There was a border, of course, and many roads that had crisscrossed the island in years gone by had now become dead-end streets. The thorny issue of border security had become a divisive subject on the island, with most saying they had for years been just fine with a virtually open border, so why tamper with perfection? On the other side of the issue were those who felt that security was more important than openness and convenience. Alien smuggling, drug smuggling, security; those were all good reasons to monitor who traveled back and forth. It didn't take long to cross, since most islanders now had a Nexus pass, which was for low risk/high usage trusted border crossers.

The old days of neighbors crossing back and forth with abandon was over, and most now obeyed the law. If they wanted to visit their backyard Canadian neighbor who was officially across the border, they had to go to one of the crossings, walk through, then go to their neighbor's home. That was what folks did officially, anyway, in the light of day. But after dark . . . it was well-known that drunks wove back and forth to the Ice House, then to the Boat House, and back, hopefully ending up on their own side of the border at closing time. Cottagers on both sides of the border were having to fence their yards to keep people from sneaking through.

The island was actually bisected by a channel that had been cut early on to divert springwater and excess river flow. In places, that channel was an actual stream; in others, it was covered by dirt over a culvert. There was talk of sensors being put in the length of the border, along that channel, to ensure that no one crossed illegally, but it was hung up in debate on both sides because of property rights issues.

Tansy Woodrow's shop, Tansy's Tarts, was a bakeshop on the American side of the island. Tansy made the most exquisite tarts and pies for miles. Her specialty was butter tarts, the recipe a well-guarded secret that had been handed down from her Canadian grandmother. When you bit into a Tansy Woodrow butter tart the filling gushed like liquid heaven, sweet and buttery, golden perfection. There weren't any like them in the whole rest of the United States and she was not sharing the recipe.

The shop took up much of the main floor of a white two-story frame structure with a big pink-and-white-striped awning over the front window and door with Tansy's shop name in script; beyond the shop was the bakery at the back. Tansy and her hubby, Sherm, lived in the upstairs apartment and had a deck out back from which they could see much of the island. Jaymie suddenly realized it was probably not the best plan to go to the bakery just before closing, when their stock would be depleted, but she tied Hoppy up to the doggie post outside the door, near the big bucket of water kept out there for the pooches, and slipped in as a couple of skinny girls in cut-offs darted out, mouths full, crumbs falling and the gooshy inside of a butter tart dripping down.

Sherm Woodrow, Tansy's husband, was staring out the window after the two girls, and turned to smile at Jaymie. "Hey, Jaymie, what can I do ya for?" he said.

She looked at the nearly empty glass case—the shop was lined with antique bakery cases, white porcelain and chrome, with huge glass expanses and wire shelves—and said, "I think I'm too late. I was going to buy a dozen pecan butter tarts to take back to the mainland tomorrow."

"None but a couple left," he said, as Tansy, her face red, came out through the swinging doors of the back bakery.

"Hey, Tans, how are you?"

"Good. You?"

"I'm good."

Sherm repeated what Jaymie had said, and Tansy blew her bangs off her forehead with her lower lip thrust out. "No can do," she said, "but I'm baking some more first thing tomorrow morning before it gets too warm, and I'll save you a dozen, nice and fresh!"

"How about half pecan and half regular butter tarts? I'm taking some over to Daniel's. His mother and father are in town and I don't know their stand on nuts versus raisins, so I'll buy both."

"Ah, you mean the future in-laws?" Sherm teased, winking at her. "Can't wait to 'butter' them up with Tansy's tarts?" he said.

Both women groaned.

Just then the doorbell rang and Zack Christian strolled in, still in his relaxed island mode, in baggy swim trunks and a polo shirt. "Hey," he said to Jaymie. "I thought I saw you go by, and then I saw Hoppy outside the shop."

"Oh. Hi!" Jaymie still wasn't sure what to make of the detective's friendliness, but it was good.

"Hey, friend," Sherm said, his greeting to anyone he didn't know by name. "What can I do ya for?"

"I just discovered a Tansy Tart at the Ice House last night, and I'm hooked," he said, with a wink at Jaymie.

Tansy was eyeing him and glanced over at Jaymie, raising her eyebrows.

"Sherm, Tansy, this is Zack Christian," Jaymie said. "He rents a cottage on the island, but he works for . . . Uh, he's a detective with the Queensville Police."

He greeted the bakery owners, then asked Jaymie, "How is the article going?"

"Good, actually. I may even be able to use a picture from the Ice House for it." She explained to Tansy and Sherm about the article on ice cream making for the *Wolverhampton Howler*. Then she said, "We had dinner there, and it was great until Urban Dobrinskie came in hollering about some illegal sail he claims the Redmonds are using in the race. You know anything about that?" She remembered what Dobrinskie said about Sherm having told him about the illegal sail.

Sherm had the grace to look embarrassed. "I might have accidently set him off," he said. "I heard from someone that the Redmonds were ordering their sails from Switzerland these days, and I just mentioned it while I was down at the marina yesterday, and he stormed off muttering."

"Sherm!" Tansy said, whacking him on the shoulder, "You should know better. Don't say anything to Urb, ever!"

"He's not such a bad guy," Sherm said with a shrug, "but he's got a couple of quirks."

"I'd better get going," Jaymie said. "I don't like to leave Hoppy tied up too long."

"Come by in the morning, Jaymie, and I'll have those tarts boxed up for you to take home," Tansy said, putting the two last ones in the case in individual boxes. "Here, both of you take one on the house for your dessert tonight."

"Thanks, Tans! See you tomorrow morning."

Zack said good-bye and dashed ahead, holding the door

open for her, and when she went through, she glanced back to see Tansy, eyebrows raised and a speculative look on her face. Uh-oh. She may get on Sherm's case about gossiping, but Tansy was known to like a good chinwag herself.

She would not let it bother her. Jaymie untied Hoppy and strolled back toward her cottage, accompanied by Zack, who seemed deep in thought. "Penny for your thoughts?" she said.

"I was just wondering, did Sherm Woodrow really just chat about the foreign sails accidentally, or did he intend to cause trouble between Dobrinskie and the Redmonds?"

"He wouldn't do that!" Jaymie said. "Would he?"

"I've seen my share of folks who enjoy stirring up trouble. I just don't know that guy well enough to know if he's one of them."

"Sherm and Tansy are gossips, but neither one of them is vicious."

They walked along in silence, and of course Hoppy chose that moment to do his business, so she had to stoop and scoop, while she was holding her tart. Zack, trying not to laugh, took her tart box from her.

"I'll carry this so you don't have two such conflicting packages."

"You could have offered to take the baggie," she said, and they both laughed. After a pause, she said, "Zack, what did you mean last night when you told Urban that you could charge him with a hate crime for what he said?"

He shrugged uneasily. "It's nothing."

"No, I want to know."

"I just blurted it out. I was in Canada a few weeks ago at a policing conference, and they were talking about hate speech and the law in Canada. If you say something cruel or libelous about someone's race or sexual orientation in Canada, you could be charged with a hate crime."

"Hmm. Really? Even though Canadians are supposed to be kinder and gentler than Americans, there still must be a lot of lawsuits. But how does that apply to Urban and Ruby?"

He looked uneasy.

"Be honest."

"Well, you know, his calling her a she-male, because . . . because she's gay. That's hate speech. Maybe not here, but in Canada."

"Why do you think she's gay?"

He looked flustered. They reached Rose Tree Cottage and Jaymie deposited Hoppy's little giftie in the trash can at the end of her sidewalk, then turned to regard Zack steadily.

"I guess I just assumed."

"Why? Because she can sail better than most of the men on the island? Because she doesn't wear a push-up bra?"

He shrugged.

"Or because she never married? Come on, you can do better than that!"

He took a deep breath and nodded. "You're right. I made an assumption and that wasn't fair."

"You don't know anyone's life unless you're in it," Jaymie said. "If I've learned anything this summer, it's that. Maybe she is, maybe she isn't, but it's not fair to speculate. Anyway, I've got to go." Hoppy tugged on the leash, anxious for his dinner.

"Hey," he said, as she walked toward the cottage.

She turned and waited.

"Do you want to go to the Ice House for dinner again?"

Dumbfounded, she paused, then said, "Uh, no, I don't think so." She was going to try to trot out some excuse, but decided it wasn't necessary.

"Okay. Talk to you later," he said, and walked away.

She watched him for a moment, wondering about the last-minute invitation. It must be boredom with his days off, she decided, and ascended the three steps to the cottage.

❋ Four ❋

S HE WROTE FOR a while, trying one more time to come
up with a suitable introduction for herself. Nan wanted
her to write a brief bio of herself to accompany the first
"Vintage Eats" column, and it was proving to be more difficult than anything else she had tried to write in the last
eight months. It also made her hyperaware of how little there
was to actually say about her and her fledgling career as a
food writer. Initially a respite from the heartbreak of Joel
Anderson's dumping her before Christmas the previous year,
rummaging around in her grandmother's old cookbooks had
been her refuge and solace.

Over the weeks, she had become fascinated. In a way it
was like the feminist social history class she had taken in
college, a view of one woman's life in the middle of the last
century. One old binder in particular was full of handwritten
recipes, and many more were snipped out of newspapers
from the forties and fifties. She started to buy vintage cookbooks in thrift stores and at auctions, and her love affair

with cooking from the recipes they contained blossomed. Though she had been collecting old cookware for years, now she was collecting cookbooks, too, and working out ways to explain old recipes to modern cooks.

But what was there to say about *herself*? She was just a woman, youngish, single, content in her small-town world. How could you make a bio out of that? She sat and tapped her pencil against the tabletop, then got up and went to the sink for a glass of water. The window over the sink overlooked the back deck and yard, a narrow strip that soon plunged down a decline to the ravine between their cottage and the Redmonds' home. On either side of the ravine were wooded glades separating them from the other cottages on their streets.

Would she ever live out here? Would there come a day, in the far future, when even Queensville felt too big or bustling, when the island would seem a welcome retreat from the world? Well, it already was that. But she felt no desire to live here. The Queensville house was home, and always had been.

With a sigh, she sat back down to try again to frame some kind of biography. When she got no further, she went back to what she really wanted to do, and that was work on the column. Now that she had thought of using the Ice House to talk about ice harvesting and ice cream making in the past, she saw a pattern emerging. Vintage equipment and vintage recipes, with photos to match, would make a continuing column possible. Would she run out of ideas eventually? Gosh, she hoped not.

The words came fast and furious, and before long she had the article roughed out. It wasn't bad, not bad at all. It moved from the fascination of the ice cutting procedure, through some background on how the homemaker of the past managed to keep and use the ice. She examined the photos she had taken, flipping through her digital camera and stopping at the green-handled ice pick. She'd thought she'd be able to use that as one of the illustrations for her article, but it was not the most interesting subject in the world, she supposed. The photo of the ice chests was cool, but the best one was ruined by Ruby's hastily moving out of the frame. And Jaymie thought of herself as camera shy! Ruby beat her at that.

As twilight snuggled in around the cottage, she moved out to the front porch with Hoppy, clipboard in hand, tea mug beside her, but her thoughts wandered far afield from the article to Zack Christian. Why did he ask her to dinner? Was it intended as a date request? Friendly dinner offer? But she was "going" with Daniel Collins and he knew it. There was no way she and Zack were *quite* friends. Acquaintances, yes; friends, no.

Her instincts said Zack Christian—relatively new in town, attached now to a police force that was small and prosaic compared to the big-city police force he once was a part of—was just bored and lonely, and that the dinner invitation was a passing impulse. Had he made any friends in the months he had been working for the Queensville force? Officer Bernie Jenkins, a deputy on the same police force, had told Jaymie that the detective was rumored to have been fired from his last post after an incident involving a witness. If that was true, it must have left him angry, and maybe unsure of his future in his chosen career. As much as she liked Bernie—Bernice—gossip was unreliable at best, damaging and hurtful at worst. Until she knew the truth, she would not speculate.

She watched the shadows lengthen as Hoppy curled up next to her in the Adirondack chair with a sigh, falling into that profound doggie sleep that was the aftermath of contentedness. The line of pines across from her cottage darkened to a deep hunter green as shadows crept into their branches to nestle for the night. Darkness stole over the island and cottage lights came on; the sound of laughter from back patios and front porches waned, quieting as weary folks drifted off to their beds, but Jaymie still sat and thought.

How peaceful life was on the front porch, she reflected, ruffling Hoppy's fur. She was not the kind of girl to look for excitement from life. Joy didn't come at ninety miles per hour. Joy, which had little to do with pleasure, stole through you in moments of hope, feelings of tenderness for the good friends and loving family who surrounded you, and gratitude for life, she firmly believed. Pleasure was transitory; joy was lasting.

Her grandma Leighton had once said that Jaymie was an old soul in a new body. Maybe that was true. When Joel told her that living with her was like living with an old woman and a toddler all at once, she took umbrage. But he explained that he meant that she was sometimes wise, always patient, and yet at times she viewed the world as if it were all new to her, and took delight in the most unexpected things. It was the nicest thing he ever said to her, and yet for all that, he still preferred the company of Heidi Lockland. Heidi, while a truly sweet person despite cultivating a blond bimbo exterior, held a view of the world that was sometimes gratingly out of sync with reality, perhaps the result of being born wealthy and beautiful.

Her eyes drifted closed, but Jaymie awoke with a gasp, having fallen into a dream of tumult and fear, one of those half-waking, half-sleeping worlds of chase and capture that dotted one's night life. "It's time for bed, little dog," she said, heaving herself up out of the chair and picking up her clipboard from the porch floor, where it had dropped when she fell asleep. "Tomorrow we have to go back to the mainland, no matter what. I need a shower."

But of course, as sleepy as she had been just minutes before, when she locked up the cottage and headed to bed, she couldn't sleep. So after a half hour of tossing and turning, she gave up, made a pot of tea, and sat at the kitchen table writing her article by the weak yellowish light of an incandescent bulb. She was writing longhand, since there was no computer at the cottage, and she had several sheets scribbled with wandering text by the time another two hours had passed. She had thought she had a handle on it, but now it seemed lacking: dull, flat and unoriginal. She was beginning to experience a bad case of midnight desperation, the certainty that not only was she not a writer; she never would be. She had no talent. Every opening line she tried came out sounding trite and overused.

Tapping her pencil on the clipboard, she felt that pressure in the lower regions that comes from too many cups of tea late at night and no bathroom facilities. She glanced up at the old clock, an electric rooster-shaped clock that had been in the cottage as long as she could remember. It was one o'clock in the morning, and sleep seemed an elusive chimera. If she could just go to the bathroom, she'd be fine.

She looked out the back window that topped the kitchen sink and stared through the gloom toward the Redmonds' home. No lights. Darn! Ruby had said that the back door would be open, and to come on over whenever she needed to, but it would feel weirdly invasive to just walk in. Maybe she should just do what she had done as a kid on rare camping trips, and go in the bushes. That gave her the creeps, though, since she was so close to neighbors. It was definitely a last resort.

Hoppy trotted out to the kitchen, took a long slurp of water, and then scratched at the back door to go out. If only it was that easy for humans, she thought, as she stepped out on the back porch to wait for him to cock his leg and come back in. Not that he actually did cock his leg, exactly. He was three-legged, and wobbly, but he was still a boy dog and gamely tried. His late-night ventures were never long, just enough time to piddle, so it was a surprise when he suddenly bounded out into the lawn and began to bark.

"Hoppy!" she hissed, going to the edge of the deck and searching what was left of the grassy area behind the cottage. "Come back here!"

Barking again.

"Hoppy!" Darn it! She did not want him wandering out onto the mucky leaching bed, because that would mean having to bathe him. She ducked back into the cottage and grabbed the flashlight that was attached to the wall by the back door. She turned it on and swept it around the mess of her backyard. Hoppy was on alert, his quivering nose pointed toward the small grove of crab apple trees that puddled around one small spot in the hollow between the Leighton yard and the Redmonds'.

Please don't let it be a skunk, Jaymie prayed! She tripped and skidded down the slope and across the mucky backyard, then pounced on her Yorkie-Poo, grabbing his collar. "Hoppy Leighton, you are *not* going be skunked tonight," she whispered. She carried him back in, hoping he had done his business, and wishing it were so easy for her.

It took a good ten minutes to wash his paws and her own, and then she was left wanting a cup of tea but not daring to drink one more ounce of fluid, and sitting at the table drumming her pencil while Hoppy stared at the back door with wistful eyes. She *still* had to go! She paced and glanced out the back window again, hoping to see a light on in the Redmonds' kitchen. She thought she saw a flash, but it was gone in an instant.

Okay, ignore the urgent need to relieve yourself, she thought, as she settled down to work. An article on ice harvesting and ice cream making. *Ice, ice, baby,* she hummed; it caught in her brain, repeating like a manic refrain. She had to think of a way to start her article.

In the beginning, there was the ice age . . .

Or . . .

I scream, you scream, we all scream for ice cream . . .

Rotten beginnings, both of them.

*Summertime, and the livin' is easy . . . but it wasn't
always so far as making that delicious summertime
treat, ice cream. Today we head to the supermarket and
buy a quart, but not so very long ago if you wanted ice
cream to go with your cherry pie, you depended on a
ready supply of ice and hours of hand churning. But
where could you go to get ice in the age before mechani-
cal refrigeration?*

Not *too* terrible. Maybe she could do something with
that. As she sat cudgeling her brain, noise erupted in the
backyard, a loud shout and clang of metal. Then Jaymie
clearly heard, through the open back window, *"Get off my
property!"*

The voice was loud and harsh, not one she recognized.
Jaymie bolted up out of her chair and hustled out to the back
deck, but couldn't see anything. There was a light on in the
Redmonds' kitchen now, but there didn't appear to be any
movement. Hoppy started barking, and Jaymie was stunned
into inaction for a moment. That voice had been clear as a
bell, floating in her back window. If it was from the street
in front of the cottage, she wouldn't have heard a thing.

She reached back in, pushing Hoppy away with her foot
as she grabbed the flashlight again, and played it across the
yard. There was a dark hump down the slope, in the gully
between her and the Redmonds' backyard. She slipped flip-
flops on her feet and trotted down the hill as her neighbors'
back porch light came on.

"Jaymie, is that you? Everything all right?" came Garnet's voice floating down to her.

"I don't know. There's something down here. Did you
just yell at someone to get off your property?"

"No! What's going on?"

"Is everything okay?" That was Ruby's voice, thick with
sleep.

A dog barked in the distance, then yelped; it sounded

like someone had thrown something at it. Jaymie stumbled down the slope and across the muddy ravine, over the ruts of dirt, to the clear space that the plumbers were working in. She stepped over PVC piping, and played her flashlight over the grass as Hoppy barked at the back door. Other lights were beginning to flicker on through the woods that separated their cottages from others.

Where was that dark spot she had noticed, the one that hadn't been there earlier? There! She approached and the flashlight pinned on the dark spot, which quickly became a human form. "Garnet, call 911!" she cried.

"Jaymie, are you okay?" Ruby shouted, as Garnet said, "What's going on?"

"Someone's hurt," Jaymie yelled, and, gasping for breath, approached the figure. She played the flashlight over the man, beginning at the feet, shod in sand-clogged, deep-treaded work boots. As the light moved up the paunchy body, she wondered at the stillness. "Mister, are you okay? Can I get some he . . ." She stopped talking. The glassy eyes, wide-open and staring, as well as the bloodred stain drenching his golf shirt left no doubt that help would be too late. She sobbed, her voice clogged and unnatural sounding. "It's Urban Dobrinskie," she yelled. "And he's . . ." She paused as her stomach heaved. She reached out and touched him; he was cold! She retched, then cried, "He's dead!"

Not again, not again, not again; the refrain thrummed through her brain. Another body?

"What? Impossible," Garnet said, his voice coming closer as he spoke, echoing her own thoughts.

It *was* impossible. And yet . . . there was Urban. Garnet came up to Jaymie and hovered over her shoulder as she trained the flashlight on the remains of what was once the marina co-owner.

"Damn!" Garnet yelled, backing away, stumbling a bit. "It *is* Urban."

"What's going on?" Ruby hollered.

"Call 911, and don't come down here, Ruby," Garnet said. "It's Urban. He's . . . damn! Just call 911!"

Garnet stayed with Jaymie while Ruby made the call, but unlike the last couple of times she had found a body, now there were no sirens, no onslaught of cops swarming the place. They were on an island, after all, and one with very few motor vehicles and no physical police presence. Neighbors began to gather, and some even trudged through the dirt of the bared leaching bed toward Jaymie and Garnet before being warned to stay away.

Fifteen minutes later the bobbing stream of light from another flashlight played across the slope and the ridges of dirt. "What's going on here?" a voice called out.

Zack Christian! Well, of course the police would call their very own eyes on the island, Detective Christian. It was comforting, in a way, that he was the one arriving to take charge.

He approached, cautiously, and said, "I understand you've found a body, Jaymie. Again."

She slumped in weariness on a mound of dirt and covered her face with her dirty hands.

"This is no time to be caustic," Garnet said, his voice hard with anger. "This young lady is ready to collapse. She wouldn't leave poor Urban alone, though, and I wouldn't leave *her*!"

"I know, I know." The detective cautiously stepped closer to them and bent over the body, shining his flashlight over Urban. "Have either of you touched him?"

"No," they both said in chorus.

"Well, yes," Jaymie said. "I had to be sure, that he was . . . *you* know. And he was . . . is. He's dead!"

"But this is exactly how you found him?" The detective reached out and touched the man's gray skin, his quick eyes scanning Urban's face. "You two need to go to your homes and wait, while the Queensville team gets here."

"They're coming to the island?" Jaymie asked.

He nodded.

"Police boat," Garnet murmured and Zack again nodded.

Of course! Every riverside municipal police force had a boat or two. Just as she thought of that, the thrum of a heavy outboard motor sounded, echoing in the quiet night as it approached the Heartbreak Island marina.

"Jaymie, will you go back to your cottage, please? And no phoning *anyone*, either of you!" Zack said.

Jaymie picked her way back across the dirt toward her cottage, slipped off her flip-flops and went in, putting on the kettle for a cup of tea as Hoppy danced around her. She gave him some kibble and tried to settle down, blearily reading through what she had written. It was just a jumble of letters in front of her eyes, and she gave up. She got up to look out the back window every few seconds, it seemed, as the cops stood talking at the perimeter of her property, then made their cautious way toward the body of Urban Dobrinskie.

There were no doubt other things going on, other cops doing things: notifying Mrs. Dobrinskie, who Jaymie vaguely knew as a mousy little woman, apple-shaped, with soft brown hair going to gray. There was a son, too, she remembered hearing; Zack had said he had to stop Urban from berating his son. She could also see a uniformed officer questioning the neighbors who stood in housecoats and pajamas on the perimeter of Jaymie's backyard. Flashlights arced beams around her yard and into the wooded copses on either side of the ravine.

As much as she tried, Jaymie could not stop wondering, though: Who had killed the man, and right beneath her cottage? The blood had saturated the chest of his short-sleeved sports shirt, so there was some kind of chest wound, but she hadn't seen a knife or any other weapon. She glanced out at the commotion on her back lawn again; a floodlight had been set up, the area tented with a quickly set up canopy and tarps to keep it from the eyes of the curious.

She knew the drill; soon she would be asked to recount

every moment of the last few hours, and she had best be prepared. She thought it over, and remembered the shouts of what she thought sounded like an argument. Then "Get off my property!"

Who would have said that but Garnet? It hadn't sounded like Garnet, but if he was angry, and from a distance?

She was actually beginning to feel nauseous from needing to go to the bathroom so badly, but it would still be hours before she could intrude on anyone to borrow their facilities. And going in the bushes was definitely out now, unless she wanted a police officer's flashlight shining on her behind. She looked up at the Redmonds' cottage. Surely it wouldn't hurt to go there. She skirted the murder scene and found Zack. "Look, I really need to use the bathroom, but with the plumbing work being done on my property, I can't flush the toilet. I've been depending on the Redmonds. Can I *please* go and use their bathroom? I won't stay, I promise."

He looked harassed and tired, and swiped one hand over his eyes, scrubbing them with his thumb and forefinger. "Okay, all right. Look, go and use their bathroom, but do not—and I mean this, Jaymie—do *not* speak of this to them. I've got a cop at their cottage, and I need to manage this scene properly, given the circumstances."

She was so relieved already she felt like kissing his scruffy cheek, but she sketched a wave and trotted up the hill toward the cottage.

Coincidentally, the officer on duty at the cottage was Bernie. "I was just thinking of you," she said to the other woman.

Bernice was in uniform, and grim-faced. "You okay?" she asked. "I couldn't believe it when I heard the detective say your name. Girl, you have got to stay out of trouble!"

"I'm trying to," Jaymie said. "But it keeps finding me!" She explained, briefly, about her family's cottage and what she was doing on the island, and told Bernie about the leaching field and her inability to use her own bathroom right then. "Zack said I could use the Redmonds' bathroom if I just went in and came out."

"All right, but be sure you just go straight to the bathroom and out!"

Jaymie tiptoed in the back door. She heard voices, and caught a glimpse of Garnet and Ruby quietly talking in the small pantry off their kitchen. She headed toward them to let them know she was using their facilities, but paused, feeling a little awkward. Ruby was weeping; how could one interrupt that?

"I didn't mean to do it, Garnet. You *know* that!" she sobbed.

❅ Five ❅

*D*IDN'T MEAN TO *do what?* Jaymie wondered, as she began to back up, and tripped over something, making an awful clattering noise in the process.

Garnet poked his head out and saw her. His expression wary, he eyed her as he said, "Jaymie. What's up?"

"Uh, I just came over to . . . I mean, I asked the police and they . . . He . . . Detective Christian said I could come over to use your washroom," she said, practically dancing in place, she had to go so badly.

"Oh yeah, go ahead," he said, as Ruby hid her face in her brother's shoulder.

Jaymie scooted down the hall. Relief! She scrubbed her hands and her face, drying them on the pretty finger towel on the rack by the sink. It was an almost blissful moment, and she felt human again, until she remembered what she had overheard and wondered what it had to do with Urban Dobrinskie's murder. Or maybe it wasn't murder; maybe . . . Oh, who was she kidding? It was murder. She went back to the Redmonds' kitchen to find them both sitting at the table, composed and stoic.

"I have to go right back," Jaymie said, feeling awkward for any number of reasons.

"Are you okay?" Garnet asked her, his eyebrows slanting over his gray eyes.

Bernie came to the back door. "You done, Jaymie?" she asked.

"Yeah, I'm leaving. I just . . . I'll be right out."

The officer nodded, her gaze darting between Jaymie and the siblings.

Jaymie glanced out the Redmond back kitchen window to the ravine, where the white tent glowed from the floodlights within it. It was a surreal scene, like some secret government operation in one of those alien life-form movies Joel had always been fond of. Glancing back to the Redmonds, she whispered, "The cops let me come over here on the promise that I wouldn't stay, or talk about this."

"I understand," Garnet said, getting up and walking her to the back door. But he grabbed her arm with a steely grip when they got there. "Jaymie, I don't want you to misinterpret what you heard just now," he muttered, glancing over her shoulder at his sister, who still sat at the table, looking tired and worried. "Ruby was talking about something else, not . . . not that," he said, motioning down the hill with a nod of his head.

Jaymie nodded. "Of course. I know that, Garnet," she said. There was no way Ruby Redmond could kill someone, even Urban Dobrinskie, who had been so rude to her.

He squeezed her arm and released her.

"Who do you think did this?" she whispered, looking over his shoulder at Bernie just outside the door. She was on her radio, talking intently to someone.

He shook his head. "I just don't know."

Jaymie exited, nodded to Bernie, who was still talking to someone, and walked down the slope and across the lawn, avoiding the tented area. Dawn was just beginning to break, the pearly light making everything gray and sage, as mist rolled over the landscape from the river. She was so tired, and yet on edge. Just knowing there was a body there, behind the tent, was unnerving. It didn't matter that what she had seen of the man she had not liked; Urban was a human being. And the fact that such violence had happened right there in her own backyard was awful.

Her torn-up, muddy backyard; what about the plumbers! Oh Lord, she was going to have to call them and tell them not to come. There was no way the area would be clear for them until later in the day, at best, or the next day, even. She looked up the slope to her back deck. It seemed so long a climb, the weariness she was feeling burrowing right down to her soul. How could cops deal with such cases day in and day out?

Zack came out of the tented area just then. She felt a sudden pang; he looked as tired as she felt, so maybe it affected the police, even as they did their job. Ruby's statement, "I didn't mean to do it," echoed in Jaymie's brain. Should she tell Zack about that? How would he take it? Well, how *else* would he take it? She was so torn! But deep in her gut she did not believe that Ruby could kill anyone.

"Jaymie, can we talk for a moment?"

She nodded, motioned to her cottage, and he followed her. She led him in the back door, and Hoppy skittered around him, wuffling and sniffing his shoes, which he removed at the door and left on the rubber mat, as they were caked with mud.

He gently pushed the little dog away. "Nice cottage."

She smiled and glanced around at the blue painted cupboards and natural wood countertops. She had resisted Becca's desire to modernize the cabin. It was a cottage, not a house, she insisted. When people rented it, they wanted the rustic cottage feel. Secretly, she wondered whether she was right about that. Lots of cottages on the island had been remodeled or rebuilt with gorgeous glass enclosures, modern openness, and there was a certain grace about them that made pokey little Rose Tree Cottage, with its flaking blue paint, seem more worn-looking than rustic.

"I like it," she said, and it was true. Despite its flaws it was quaint and charming; they never had a week during the late spring, summer and early autumn when it wasn't rented out. "I always come here in summer for a few days, but I really like it best in the fall, when the leaves are all beautiful colors. And Hoppy loves it; he has more freedom here." Her smile died. "Usually, anyway. When I don't have plumbers and dead bodies."

"Look, speaking of that . . ." He took her elbow and guided her to a chair.

It reminded her of Garnet's steely hand on her elbow, and she wondered about that. His grip had been positively iron-fisted, the clutch of a worried man. If his sister's words truly had nothing to do with the murder, why was he so worried about Jaymie overhearing and misunderstanding? And why hadn't he just explained what she meant?

"You need to give a statement, of course, but I don't think it's appropriate that I take it," Zack said.

"Why not?" she asked, looking up at him. He turned away and stared out the back window at the scene below.

He shrugged and eased some tension out of his shoulders by flexing them. "Because when you give it, I'll be in it. We walked back here last night and I asked you to go to dinner with me. That makes me a part of your last twenty-four hours." He turned back and regarded her solemnly. "I've been through this before," he said, his tone hard, "and I won't let it happen again. Ever. I won't let my objectivity be put in question."

She was taken aback by his harshness, but nodded. So, what Bernie had told her was very likely true; he was gun-shy after being fired for involvement with a witness. "It doesn't really matter who I give my statement to."

He watched her eyes, and she could see he was torn. "Okay, then," he said. "I have to tell my chief everything, but maybe I'll leave it up to him to decide who questions you."

So now it was not a definite "no" that he would take her statement. In a way she hoped it *was* someone else, because she hated having to lie, and not telling him what she had overheard Ruby say felt like a lie by omission. It would be far easier if it were a stranger she was talking to.

Confused by his wavering, she said, "I don't care, Zack. I just want to do it and get it over with. I'm hoping to go back over to the mainland." She was weary to the bone. Hoppy pawed at her lap and she picked him up, cradling him in her arms. "Look, I have to call my plumbers and tell them not to come today to finish the leaching bed. At least, I'm assuming we won't be able to finish the work right now?"

He nodded. "I think the body will probably, given the circumstances, be here for a few hours more. Tell them tomorrow, and I think you'll be safe." He headed for the door, slipping his muddy shoes back on. "Just sit tight, and I'll find out about the statement."

She set Hoppy down and made a pot of coffee, needing the jolt of caffeine.

The phone rang and it was Valetta, town gossip and Jaymie's best friend. "Jaymie, I heard you killed someone in your backyard, a burglar or something. What's going on?"

The Queensville telegraph was working as wonkily as usual; some of the facts, plus speculation, plus gossip, plus a wild bit of imagination, all heaped together, whipped into a frenzy, and baked until piping, crazy hot. She explained, in unadorned terms, that she had found the body of Urban Dobrinskie in her backyard. "And now, if you don't mind, I'd better call my mom before she gets the same whacky message and believes it!"

Valetta's laugh cackled across the river. "Okay, but are you coming in today? We have some basket returns," she said, mentioning the vintage picnic basket rental business Jaymie operated with the Emporium, where Valetta worked as a pharmacist.

"I hope so. I have to wait here until I give my statement to the police."

"That's becoming a bad habit," she said.

"I know." Jaymie spotted Zack and a tired-looking older man coming to her back porch. "I've got to go. Looks like the cops are coming."

Zack deferred to the older man, who rapped peremptorily on her back door and stepped in without waiting for her okay. Of course Hoppy promptly went nuts, and tackled his pant leg. Jaymie grabbed her little dog by the collar, and smiled up at the two, noting that Zack was compressing his lips in an attempt not to smile.

"I'm so sorry. He thinks he's a Doberman. He wouldn't have done that if I had asked you in," she said, pointedly, "but right now he thinks you're an intruder."

"Jaymie Leighton, this is Chief Horace Ledbetter," Zack said. "Chief of the Queensville Police Department."

"Hi, Chief Ledbetter," Jaymie said, letting go of Hoppy, who, now that he knew these were not intruders but invited guests, sniffed politely around their feet and waggled his body.

The man observed her for a long moment, then said, "You're the little lady who keeps finding bodies. Our best bet for peace in Queensville is exiling you, it seems."

She stood still for a moment, hand stuck out to shake, and mouth open. Then the big man's face wrinkled in what could be mistaken for a smile, and she relaxed. He was joking. "Wrong place, wrong time." She dropped her hand to her side.

He bent down, grunting and puffing over his belly while he scratched Hoppy's neck and got a hand licking for his efforts. Straightening with an effort, his shrewd eyes took in her cottage and he nodded. "This is the kinda place I'd like to retire to."

"I like it. It's been in our family for a long time." She glanced between the two men, still wondering what was going on. Were they there officially, or what?

"Why don't we have a seat, Miss Leighton?" he said.

"Would you like a coffee?" she asked, taking them both in.

"No," Zack said, and at the same instant Chief Ledbetter said, "Yes."

"Okay, have a seat at the kitchen table. Just swipe that stuff away," she said, about the papers and clipboard.

The chief glanced at the heading on the paper, which read "Column Ideas for *Howler*." "Ah, you're a writer?"

"Not really," she said, getting some mugs down from the cupboard. "Or . . . well, I'm trying to write a first column. I'm . . . I want to be a food writer, I guess you'd call it. I'm going to have a column in the *Howler* called 'Vintage Eats.' *If* I can ever write it. That's a big 'if.'" She sighed and got the cream out of the fridge, adding it to the tray that she then brought over to the table.

"'Vintage Eats'? What would that encompass?"

Warming up, now that she was on familiar ground, she poured both men coffee and talked a little about her idea for a column on vintage recipes and kitchen utensils.

"My wife would read that," the chief said. "She loves cooking. She's almost as good a cook as my mom was," he said and patted his belly. "As you can tell. You and your family had this cottage long?"

"Always," she said, sitting down opposite him. "My great-grandfather built it, back when this was all just woods."

"When I was a kid, the Ice House here on the island was a spooky abandoned building. We used to row over here at night and hide out in it smoking cigars we'd stolen from my dad," he said, his bulbous nose becoming red as he chuckled.

"I was just there the other night, at the restaurant! I was thinking of doing my first article on the Ice House, and ice harvesting, with a recipe for old-fashioned ice cream!"

"Young Zachary, here, says he was there, too! You two shared a table, so I understand," the chief said, his broad face wreathed in a smile. "So you really find that stuff interesting? My wife and I had our thirtieth anniversary party there in the spring. They've got quite the display of tools and implements!"

Zack, despite saying he didn't want coffee, busied himself with fixing a cup.

"Actually, Garnet and Ruby were explaining it all to me, the ice cutting and harvesting, and ice chests, and all that."

"Really? I can't say I know a lot about it. Especially the tools and all that. Before my time, though you wouldn't know it to look at me!" he said, and let out a bellowing laugh.

Jaymie eyed him, entranced by his larger-than-life character. "They've got those old ice chests at the back; they use them for storage. Ruby was telling me all about it."

"Hey, d'you know, my wife and I love the old movies. Just watching one the other night, *Some Like It Hot* . . . Marilyn Monroe and Tony Curtis, you know? There's a scene in that where Marilyn Monroe's character is breaking ice chips off a block for drinks. What is that thing they use for that, chipping ice off a block?"

"An ice pick!" Jaymie said, delighted by the reference. "Garnet took one down off the wall to show me! Very cool."

"It's like a long steel thing, right, kind of like a stiletto?"

"Yeah."

"Bet he was happy to put that back up on the wall; not the kind of thing you'd want to leave lying around in a bar."

"I guess . . ." She frowned and took a sip of coffee. "I don't remember him putting it up on the wall, now that I think of it."

"Really? That's odd. What did he do with it?"

"I don't know." She shrugged. It didn't matter.

"Well, he was probably distracted from putting it back in place when that Dobrinskie fellow stormed in and started insulting his sister, right?"

"Not exactly," she said, wrinkling her nose. She glanced

over at Zack; he was stirring his cup and staring out the back window. Something was not right. "What's going on here?" she asked, meeting the chief's gaze.

"We're investigating the death of Urban Dobrinskie, who was found by you in your backyard at"—he consulted the small notebook that had, until that moment, been concealed in his ham-sized fist—"approximately two twenty a.m."

"Yes. I don't think I follow."

"It's important to establish who would have had a run-in with Mr. Dobrinskie in the hours preceding his death. Both the Redmonds fall into that category."

It still didn't make any sense, and Zack was still not meeting her eyes. "Not exactly . . . not in the hours before his . . . his death. That was night before last, that they had that confrontation. And then it was just an argument over sails," she said. "No one murders anyone over a sail!"

"But Mr. Dobrinskie then insulted Miss Redmond rather gravely, and Mr. Redmond punched him in the face."

She was silent, but shook her head.

"No, he didn't punch Dobrinskie? Is that what you're saying?"

"Yes, he did punch the guy, but . . . that doesn't mean anything."

"I understand that while in the restaurant you took photos of the wall of tools and of the ice pick that Mr. Redmond took down. I am officially requesting your camera for forensic purposes. If you tell me where it is, Detective Christian will retrieve it."

"I don't understand," she said, a cold chill shaking her.

"I'd like to compare your photo against the old green handled ice pick that was found on the scene. Under the body of Urban Dobrinskie."

❖ Six ❖

S HE HAD SEEN and handled the murder weapon? The green-handled ice pick had killed Urban Dobrinskie? It wasn't possible. But if they said they found one under the body, it *had* to be the same one; there just couldn't be two. Not that they were rare, really, but it would have to be an awful coincidence, if it was *another* green handled vintage ice pick. Numb with horror, Jaymie told Zack where to find the digital camera and he impounded it, giving her a receipt.

"How well do you know the Redmonds, Miss Leighton?" the chief asked, all pretense of friendly conversation now over.

"Uh, I've known them seven years or so, since they bought the cottage behind ours."

He sat back in his chair, and it creaked a warning. "I asked how *well* you know them, not how *long* you've known them."

She frowned and tried to push away the awful feeling that her world had just tipped on its axis. Nothing was what it seemed. She needed to think, but to be able to do that, she needed to send the chief and his minion on their way. "Uh . . ."

Zack took a long slurp of his coffee, and pushed his chair out, going to gaze out the back window again.

"Never mind; we'll come back to that," the chief said, with a glance at his inferior officer. He read his notes, murmuring aloud, and then asked, "What about Mr. Dobrinskie, the victim . . . How long have you known him?"

"I don't really know him at all. I know he co-owns the marina, but we don't have a boat, so I've got no cause to deal with him. I see the other partner, Will Lindsay, more often in the day-to-day running of the marina. And Will helps out at the Tea with the Queen event every May."

"Would you say you're good friends with the Redmonds?"

So he was back to that; same question, different wording. "I wouldn't say I'm *good* friends with them." She thought about it. "No, we're not really close."

"But friendly enough for them to leave their door open for you to use their washroom whenever you need to?"

She was silent while he watched her eyes. What was he implying? She had no clue. Maybe nothing. The silence dragged on, but she had seen this method before; let the silence continue until, being a social animal, as humans are, she would feel compelled to fill it with nervous chatter of the confessional variety. Her will hardened and her chin went up.

The chief watched her, while Zack rejoined them at the table and sat down. "Okay, let's go over the last twenty-four hours or so, beginning with night before last."

She recounted her last two days—including how she just happened to be seated with Zack at the restaurant—and came down to the night before, and her restlessness. She told them about her dilemma, not really wanting to burst in on the Redmonds while they were sleeping, but keeping an eye out while she paced and tried to write, just in case she saw their light go on. "I thought I saw a *flash* of light at one point, but I don't know what it was."

"What time was that?" Zack asked, exchanging a glance with the chief.

She squinted and thought. "I'm not sure."

"Was it a long time before finding the body?"

"I don't know. Let's see . . . It was around one a.m. when I let Hoppy out to piddle, and he took off, barking at some animal in the woods."

"Wait—Hoppy was barking? At something in the woods. Are you *sure* he was barking at an animal? Did you see one?" Zack asked.

"No. I—I don't know," Jaymie said, startled by his sudden intensity. "I *assumed*, because he's been in trouble with skunks before, but it was something . . . or someone . . . in that little grove of crab apple trees near the ravine between our properties."

"Show me!" he said, getting up and heading toward the back door.

"What, now?"

Zack met the chief's gaze, and slewed his look back to Jaymie. "Just point," he said.

She got up, went to the back door, and pointed to the little copse of crab apple trees. Zack scribbled in his notebook.

The chief took over. "So that was around one a.m., and then what happened?"

Jaymie came back and sat down at the table. "Let's see . . . I came in, cleaned Hoppy up, and it wasn't long after that that I saw a flash of light. I was hoping it was at the Redmonds, but it wasn't."

"Are you sure of that?"

"That it wasn't in the Redmonds' cottage? Yes, I'm sure."

"Okay, and then?"

"I wrote for a while before I heard some commotion, and got up."

"What did you hear?"

This wasn't going to sound good, but she had to say it. She looked down at her folded hands in her lap and mumbled, "I heard a voice; then someone yelled, 'Get off my property.'"

"Excuse me?" Zack asked, catching her glance. "I want to make sure I heard you right. Someone said, 'Get off my property'?"

She nodded.

"Whose voice was it?" the chief asked.

"I didn't recognize it."

"Are you *sure* about that?" Zack asked.

"I'm sure," she said, feeling like she was being ganged up on. She looked back and forth between the two of them, and Hoppy sat at her feet and grumbled.

"It wasn't one of the Redmonds?" the chief asked.

"No," she said, defiantly. "It was *not* one of them."

"How can you be sure?" Zack said.

"It just didn't sound like either one of them."

Both men were silent and stared at her.

Ruby's words rang in her head: "I didn't mean to do it." Jaymie *should* tell Zack and the chief, but it felt as if she would be turning her in, sealing poor Ruby's fate, if she did. It wasn't right. Ruby could have meant *anything*, anything at all.

It wasn't her job to do their work for them anyway. She swallowed hard. "So . . . you obviously think that Garnet or Ruby murdered Urban Dobrinskie. But really . . . over a little tiff and an insult?" Miss Ruby in the ravine with an ice pick . . . It was like a Clue game.

Both men shuttered like a Venetian blind, their eyes going cold and empty. It was a weird moment, and Jaymie felt a shudder pass over her.

"We're exploring all possibilities," Zack said.

There was silence.

"I have to go back to the mainland. Can I go now?" she asked.

Zack watched her eyes, as the chief said, "We have your address and phone number in Queensville?"

Sighing, Jaymie said, "Oh, you do indeed!"

AGAINST ALL ODDS, the day was bright and beautiful, an example of Michigan, which in spring could be surly, in autumn, sullen, and in winter, a veritable termagant, at its most pacific. Exhaustion made her quiver, but Jaymie could not stop. She had to go home and make sure everyone knew the truth of what was going on, not some half-baked theories or speculation.

On her way out, Jaymie headed over to Tansy's Tarts. She tied Hoppy outside the shop and entered, the little bell over the door jingling, bringing Sherm out of the back room. He looked troubled, but swiftly erased the expression of worry on his face as he saw Jaymie.

"Jaymie, howarye?" Sherm said it automatically, but without the heartiness he usually had in his voice.

"I'm okay. I'm going back to the mainland, and I was wondering if Tansy made the tarts yet?"

"Lemme check," he said. He ducked into the back room and came back carrying the trademark turquoise Tansy's Tarts box. "Here ya go," he said, sliding them across the glass counter. "Say, Jaymie, did I hear right? Was Urb Dobrinskie killed?"

She nodded, and sketched for him the bare details.

"Poor Sammy and Evelyn!" he said. "I don't know what they're gonna do. Urb had his faults, but he was a good provider."

"That's the wife and son, right? I heard that he bullied his son," she said, getting a ten out of her wallet and glancing outside to make sure Hoppy was okay. "Did he bully his wife, too?"

He shrugged and looked away. "He had a temper; I'm not saying he didn't."

An awful idea occurred to her. "Are you saying he . . . Did he hit her?" In her idyllic vision of her town, including Heartbreak Island, such things did not happen, but the realist in her knew that there was a dark underbelly to even the prettiest scene. There were bound to be families in her beloved town struggling with violence and pain.

"I don't know anything!" he said, his hands up in a shocked expression of horror.

She watched Sherm for a moment. "Do you know Garnet and Ruby very well?"

"Sure. Tansy and I are on a darts league at the Legion with the Redmonds. Garnet is a crackerjack shot. Ruby's pretty damn good, too. They weren't at darts last night, though; don't know why."

"I know them as neighbors, but not really as friends. Isn't it a little unusual for a brother and sister to be so close?"

He shook his head, clicking his tongue against his teeth. "Garnet was married, but his wife died about ten years ago, from what I understand. Tragic situation . . . She died down in Jamaica; fell off of their sailboat. He's never remarried."

"Wow. I never knew that! What about Ruby?"

"She's never been married, I guess. Leastways, I never heard her talk about a husband. I kinda thought she was . . . you know." He waggled his eyebrows and winked.

"Gay?"

He nodded and his cheeks colored up red. "I never cared, you know, 'cause they're good folks."

That was Sherm Woodrow's charm; he was a gossip, but not judgmental. He liked everyone, and talked about them, but there was never a mean spirit in his chatter. "Just because she never married doesn't mean she's gay," Jaymie said, repeating what she had said to Zack when he made the same judgment.

"I guess. I say, if it walks like a duck and quacks like a duck, it's a duck. I like Ruby—she's a real sweetheart—but I never seen any woman handle a sailboat like her."

Tansy came out, and her eyes lit up. "Jaymie! You okay? I heard about the trouble over at your cottage."

Just then the door chimes sounded and a woman entered the shop. Sherm's eyes widened. "Evelyn!" he said, and rushed out from behind the counter. "Oh, honey, are you okay? Well, of course you're not, but . . . let me get you a chair."

Evelyn . . . Urban Dobrinskie's wife? Jaymie was stunned. What was she doing in the bakery? She must have been told about her husband's murder just hours before.

Tansy joined her husband, who was helping the new widow sit down on the retro vinyl café chair Sherm had hauled over from a little café table near the window. Jaymie watched. Evelyn was a small woman, with a round face and fluffy dark hair streaked with gray; she was dressed in a skirt and sleeveless blouse, exposing white, thin arms, one with a purple bruise. Was that bruise a result of Urb's temper flaring? Jaymie's mind kicked into questioning mode, something that had not happened up until now. She had been in shock, she supposed, but now she was truly curious. Who killed Urban, and why behind her house? It seemed an odd place for him to be.

"I . . . I'm so sorry, Mrs. Dobrinskie, about your husband," Jaymie said.

She looked up, a question in her vivid cornflower blue eyes, the only real color on her face other than the dark smudges under her eyes. "I'm sorry. Do I know you?"

"No," Jaymie admitted.

"This is Jaymie Leighton. Poor Urb was found behind her cottage; you know, Rose Tree Cottage, on the River Road? The pretty little blue clapboard one?" Sherm helpfully supplied.

The new widow's eyes teared up. "What was he doing there?" she whispered, and one fat tear trembled and overflowed down her pale cheek.

"I don't know," Jaymie said, crouching by the woman. "Do you have any idea?"

She shook her head and looked to Tansy. "He didn't come home last night, but I thought he just had a meeting, or . . . or was at the Boat House. I . . . I just came in to . . . Tansy, what am I going to do? Urb's family is going to come down from Canada . . . his mother . . . I don't know if I can . . ." She trailed off, shaking her head.

The baker seemed to know exactly what she was saying. "Look, hon, don't you worry about it. I'll call the business association . . . Urb was active in it, and the Polish-Canadian club over in Johnsonville, right?"

"Urb was Canadian?" Jaymie interjected.

"He was born in Poland, and came over to Canada," Evelyn Dobrinskie said, the tears in her eyes gleaming in the sun streaming in the window. "Then he came here, to the island, and that's when we met, and got married. He was so handsome. My parents didn't like him, but I knew he was the one for me."

Evelyn colored, faintly, and Jaymie could see that when young, she had probably been one of those pretty women, frail and a little needy, who appeal to the big, burly guys.

"We'll make sure you don't need to worry about food, and if you have an overflow, I know a couple of empty cottages where we can put folks up. Don't you worry about a thing," Tansy said, patting the other woman's shoulder. "Come on back and we'll talk about it over tea."

The baker pulled the other woman to her feet and led her back behind the counter toward the kitchen.

"I have to go," Jaymie said to Sherm, glancing down at her watch. "The ferry leaves in five minutes or so. I'll be back, maybe even tomorrow."

She walked down to the dock in a thoughtful frame of mind. Seeing the widow gave her a different view of the awful event, and she wondered whether this case was going to be an easy one, or difficult. For all she knew the police could have someone in their sights already, but if they did, it was likely Garnet or Ruby Redmond.

As the ferry pulled away from the marina, Jaymie looked back at her pretty island. She could *almost* see Rose Tree Cottage through the trees that lined the riverbank. She was torn, in her feelings; on one hand, she wanted to go back to the bosom of her home in Queensville, but on the other, she knew what awaited her there. Her mother was on a tear, and nagged constantly about what she called "the state of the kitchen." But she had to face her. She loved her mother, truly, but sometimes they didn't see eye to eye.

So she'd stop at the Emporium first, since she had business to take care of there. She put Hoppy in the puppy pen beside the store, where he could consort with Roary, an asthmatic pug that belonged to Mrs. Trelawney Bellwood. Mrs. B. played Queen Victoria in the annual Tea with the Queen event in Queensville, and carried her regal bearing with her throughout the rest of the year, mostly to drive her nemesis, Imogene Frump, wild with envy. As far as Jaymie could tell, the two women had been competing ever since they were both pigtailed girls in school, back in the 1930s. Hoppy and Roary bounded about in the puppy pen for a moment, before Roary was stopped by a fit of sneezes and coughs.

Jaymie entered the Emporium, the chimes above the door dancing and jingling merrily. "Hi, Mr. Klausner," she said to the ninety-year-old owner, who sat behind the cash desk reading his paper. He looked up, one eye huge behind the magnifying glass he used to read, and nodded. Jaymie circled the desk and picked up the reservation, rental and return book for her thriving vintage basket rental business.

Valetta, the combination pharmacist catalog order clerk for all of Queensville, closed her window at the back of the store with a bang, and locked the door, hustling to the front. "Jaymie! You have to tell me . . . have they made an arrest, yet?"

"No. Why?"

She looked around, and moved closer. "I hear that Ruby

Redmond is going to be arrested!" she whispered, her hiss urgent. "I can't believe it! Ruby?"

"Who told you that?" Jaymie exclaimed.

Brock, Valetta's brother, wandered up from the back. That explained that. Brock Nibley, unlike Sherm Woodrow, was a gossip of the vicious and unreliable type.

"Ruby did *not* kill Urban Dobrinskie," Jaymie stated firmly. Wouldn't she look like a fool if it turned out that she did? But she didn't care about that right now. It was most important to stop Brock in his tracks. "And as far as I know, no arrest is imminent; isn't that how the paper puts it?"

He shrugged. "It's what I heard. She was his mistress, and found out he was poking some other woman, so she did him in."

❧ Seven ❧

JAYMIE WAS STUNNED. "Urban and Ruby? Wow, Brock, how wrong can you be? Where on earth did you hear that?"

He shrugged, but his expression was smug, as if he knew what no one else would admit to knowing. It was infuriating!

"For your information," Jaymie said, "Ruby Redmond would not have done *anything* with Urb Dobrinskie. In fact, she couldn't stand Urban. You know, he was really rude to her the other night at the Ice House. He had the nerve to call her a 'she-male'!" Oops! She clapped her hand over her mouth.

Brock smirked, and Jaymie felt her stomach churn. The last thing he needed was more fuel for his gossip line.

Jaymie whirled toward her friend and moaned, "I didn't mean to let that slip."

Valetta glanced swiftly from her friend to her brother, and said, shaking her finger in his face, "Brock, if I hear anyone else say that, I'll know it came directly from you. *Please* be a better person than that!"

He sniffed and shrugged, rolling his eyes. "Whatever. Urb had a girlfriend; that's all I know. Thought it might be Ruby. Lovers' quarrel, and all that."

"I don't know who did it," Jaymie said, a headache forming like a tight band across her forehead. "All I know is, I found his body in the gully between our two properties."

"You poor kid," Valetta said, squeezing Jaymie's shoulder. "Another body!"

"Our very own grim reaper," Brock said, heading for the door. "I gotta go. Gotta show a house to a couple."

"Someone new in town?" Valetta asked.

"Yeah," he said, over his shoulder. "Daniel Collins' parents are thinking of buying a place here." He left, the chimes over the door ringing a death knell on Jaymie's future peace in her hometown.

Jaymie's heart dropped. Daniel's parents, moving to Queensville?

"Did you know that?" Valetta said.

"I did *not*," she said, grimly.

"Your mom and his mom don't get along, do they?"

She sighed. "Like two territorial Chihuahuas, not that I'm calling either one of them a bitch. I don't know why they don't get along. They're so similar, in a lot of ways."

"That's why," Valetta said, with a laugh. "Two strong-minded women will never be able to get along if their son and daughter are dating." She grabbed Jaymie's elbow, and led her behind the counter, "Anyway, settle down. It'll all work out. Better look at the book for the basket rentals."

They did some business, and Jaymie went to the back room to wash a few sets of the melamine dishes for the baskets, then restocked the basket rental shelf. Finally, she couldn't put it off any longer, and retrieved Hoppy. She headed home, dragging her feet as much as she had as a kid coming home from school, swinging the box of Tansy Tarts and letting Hoppy sniff everything.

She went down the back alley behind her beloved home, unlatching the gate. The back door was open, and there were mats and rugs lined up over the fence. Mom was cleaning, surprise, surprise. Oddly enough, while home in Florida, her mother employed a local woman to clean for them, but as soon as she got to Queensville it was as if a cleaning demon possessed her, and she fell to scrubbing and dusting.

Jaymie let Hoppy off his leash so he could stay in the yard. As she strolled up the flagstone walk she heard a low growl, and glanced over at the holly bushes. Denver was hiding in the shadows, and he was glaring at her. In his mind, no doubt, she had abandoned him to the not-so-tender mercies of Jaymie's mother, who did not like cats at all. Joy Leighton tolerated Hoppy, but Denver was sneaky and gave her the evil eye, she said.

Poor fellow. It must be hard to live in a household where you weren't appreciated. Jaymie crouched down by the bushes, and Denver slunk out, hunkering down in her shadow and letting her pet him. "I know, old boy," she murmured. "Mom is a little high-maintenance, isn't she?"

He grumbled and slunk back into the shadows, but this time he curled up for a snooze, appeased by her sympathy. Time to face the music. As Jaymie approached the house, she could hear shouting. Her folks were bickering again.

"Joy, where's the instant coffee? I can't find a thing in this jumble. I don't know why the hell you feel the need to pull everything out of the cupboards like that. Can't we come here and just relax?"

"I'm cleaning!" she said. "Jaymie said it was clean already, but it sure doesn't look like it to me."

"You should give that kid a break," her dad said. "It's her house now, isn't it?"

"It's Becca's, too, and all this junk irritates her."

"Let the girls sort it out on their own!"

"I'm home," Jaymie called out, coming up the steps to the summer porch.

"Honey, are you okay?" Alan Leighton came out to greet her, and took her into a bear hug.

Jaymie had been out at the cottage for only a couple of days, but with all that had happened, one of her dad's tight hugs felt good. "I'm okay, Dad," she said, her voice muffled against his shoulder. The sun beamed through the open door of the summer porch, warming her back as her dad rubbed her shoulder blades.

Jaymie's mom came out to the summer porch, watching them. There was a tentative expression on her heart-shaped face, as there often was when she watched her husband with his daughters. Joy Leighton at sixty-eight seemed to defy her age. She was slight, the kind of woman who will always be described as "tiny," with fluffy auburn hair that curled in light bangs over her smooth forehead. She suited to a tee the bluff squareness of Alan Leighton. But the two, as firmly united as they usually appeared, had once come close to divorcing; Jaymie remembered a bleak period of her childhood that was a time of bitter and loud quarrels. Becca, her elder sister by fifteen years, had become almost a second mother to Jaymie, telling her stories and singing songs that masked some of the acrimony from below.

"Jaymie, darling, are you okay?" Joy asked, her blue eyes full of worry.

Her mom *did* love her; that Jaymie knew, even if they didn't understand each other or always get along. Both of the Leighton girls had taken after their father in physical looks, both solid, where Joy was slight, but Becca at least seemed to have inherited their mother's clean gene, while Jaymie reveled in disarray. "I'm fine, Mom," Jaymie said, pulling her mother into a three-way hug with her dad.

They all released, and Jaymie entered the kitchen to find it pretty much as she expected. Everything was pulled down from the tops of the cupboards, and the whole place smelled of pine cleaner. She stifled her reaction, which was to gripe at her mother about the disruption. Instead, she carefully said, "When you're done, I'll put it all back, Mom. I don't want you having to climb the ladder or step stool."

"I thought we'd go through it first, dear," her mother said, moving over to the long trestle table where the array of vintage tins, bowls and utensils was lined up in military fashion. "Now, look at this baking powder tin," she said, picking up the tall round container. "It's all rusty! You don't want something that rusty in the house, do you?"

The rusty piece was a vintage Calumet baking powder tin that Jaymie had paid ten dollars for at a vintage store, one of her more pricey acquisitions, besides the old Emporium scales. The tin was tall and red, and offered a striking contrast to the other more muted silver and steel items. "Mom, I could double my money on that now, if I sold it online."

Her mother's eyes lit up. "Great! I'll get our camera and we can post it right away."

"Mom, no!" Jaymie, exasperated, looked over at her father, but he wasn't going to be any help at all, since he was shaking with silent laughter. "I'm not selling it," she said, taking it from the woman's hands and putting it back down on the table. She cast about for another topic, as she coaxed her mother past the kitchen toward the parlor. "If you really want to clean, why don't you take down the books in the library? That room hasn't been dusted in a dog's age. Hoppy starts sneezing every time he goes in there."

"Okay," she said, doubtfully. "But we need to talk about Mrs. Collins and the family supper, and soon!"

"We will, I promise." Jaymie returned to the kitchen. "Dad, what am I going to do?"

"About your mother? Or about Mrs. Collins?"

"Both!" Jaymie plunked down on a chair and covered her eyes with her hands. "It's all a mess. But all I can think of is . . ." She trailed off and shook her head.

She felt her father's arm over her shoulders, and he pulled her close.

"I don't know how you've managed these last few months, and then to find another body! My poor girl."

She sank into the hug for a long minute. Her dad always smelled of mints and wool and shoe polish, for some reason, even in midsummer.

He released her and examined her face. "Jaymie, there's something I've been meaning to tell you for a while."

She looked into his blue eyes, the very color of her own. "What's up?"

"Do you remember back in the winter, when your mom told you I was in the hospital for a few days?"

"Yeah. You had a hernia operation, right?"

"Not exactly. Your mother felt . . . We *both* worried that telling you something difficult at a distance would upset you, especially since you were going through that thing with Joel at the time."

She felt her stomach drop. "Dad, what's going on?" she asked, staring into his eyes. Her voice trembled, and she felt like her stomach was quivering.

"Damn," he said, and shook his head. "I should have waited. Honey, it's nothing, really. I'm good now. I really am!"

"You're good *now*? What do you mean?"

"I mean that I had a prostate exam, and it showed up some anomalies."

"Was it . . ." Her words choked off. She couldn't say it.

"It was *not* cancer!"

She searched his eyes. Was he telling the truth?

"Honest, honey, it was *not* cancer. There's a medical name, but I basically had an infection. They weren't sure at first, but that's what it turned out to be. I took an antibiotic, and it cleared up."

"Why didn't you tell us?"

He looked away and frowned. Hoppy bounced into the

room and begged at her father's knee for attention. He leaned over and petted the little dog's head, and said, "Well, actually, we did tell Becca."

Jaymie sat, stunned, for a long moment. "Becca went down to stay with you guys in March. Was that when . . . ?"

He nodded. "She came down to help your mother. You know your mom; she was a basket case for a while. Once we knew the truth, that it wasn't cancer, and that I was going to be just fine, Becca left."

"Why didn't you tell *me*?" Jaymie said, tears clogging her voice and trembling in her eyes.

"Because we didn't want to worry you, dear," her mother said, from the kitchen door.

Jaymie twisted to meet her mother's gaze. "But that didn't occur to you with Becca?"

"When we saw you last Christmas you were so hurt by that jerk, Joel, and . . ." She shrugged. "We worried that it would be too much for you."

She stood, and her glance went back and forth between them. "I'm real happy that you're okay, Dad. I don't know what I'd do without you. Either of you," she said, looking to her mother, who still paused, elegant hand on the door-frame. "But when, in the last ten years, have I ever struck you as someone who couldn't handle the truth?"

Neither answered, and Jaymie walked out the back door, down the flagged walk, through the gate and then into Anna Jones's backyard. It was the same old problem; her parents just refused to see her as a grown-up. But at thirty-two, maybe they never would. She should just let it go, she supposed, even though it rankled. It wasn't as if they were around all the time. Maybe they *needed* to still see her as their "baby."

But the fact that they didn't tell her about her father's health scare was both saddening and maddening. What if it had been something much worse? How long would she have been in the dark? Maybe Becca would understand and could explain to her parents why Jaymie was hurt by it.

She let herself in to the B and B and found Anna in the kitchen, sitting with her head in her hands. Forgetting about her own concerns, she sat down next to her friend. "What's wrong, Anna?"

"Oh! Jaymie." She looked up, the dark rings under her eyes signaling another sleepless night. "I didn't hear you come in. Nothing's wrong. I'm fine."

"Liar. Talk to me," she commanded, putting her arm over her friend's shoulders.

She sniffed and shook her head. "I'm all right. Really!"

Anna was a few months pregnant with her second child, something she hadn't planned when she and her Jamaican-born husband, Clive, sunk her entire inheritance into a bed-and-breakfast. Lately she had been suffering morning sickness, so Jaymie had been making the eggs part of the breakfast for her, since it was the one thing that turned her stomach.

If she wasn't going to fess up, then Jaymie would just have to guess. "Has my mom been working out okay?" she asked. Jaymie's mother had promised to do the cooking for Anna for the few days Jaymie was tied up with the cottage plumbing.

"Yeah, she's been great! She made me mint tea this morning and was really so sweet! I . . . I . . ." Tears puddled in her green eyes and ran down her freckled cheeks, as Tabitha wandered in and stood by her mom. The toddler put her hand on her mother's knee with an expression of concern in her dark eyes.

"Please, Anna, talk to me! I'll just worry if you don't."

"I have to go back to Toronto," Anna said. "We just can't afford to pay for my prenatal health care down here, not when I have free universal in Canada! And I need to go back anyway, at some point, to spend enough time there to keep my OHIP up-to-date," she said, naming her provincial health insurance plan. "I've been having some trouble, and last week, when I went back to TO to have a checkup, they were concerned about my glucose levels."

"Are they worried about diabetes?"

She nodded. "And my blood pressure. Anyway," she said, with a sniff. "I might have to get someone to look after the B and B for the fall and winter a little earlier than I thought I'd have to. That's all. It's just . . . none of this has turned out like I thought it would. It's my own fault for being careless." Careless, as in missing days with her birth control.

"But you don't regret the baby coming?"

"Oh no!" Anna said, her smile breaking out like sunshine, warming Jaymie and relieving some of her anxiety.

"So it just means you'll have someone take over a little earlier than you had planned, that's all." Anna had always planned to have someone else look after the B and B for the winter while she went back to Canada. She needed to stay there for at least six months to keep her eligibility for their universal health care. Jaymie still wasn't quite clear on why Anna had felt opening a bed-and-breakfast in Michigan was a good idea. "Do you have someone in mind?" Jaymie asked, half afraid of the answer.

Jaymie just did *not* have time to run the B and B, not with the basket rental business—though that would slow down over the winter—the (hopefully) new column for the *Howler*, working at the Emporium and some of the other main street stores and, most important, writing her cookbook. But if it was necessary, she would definitely fill in for her friend until she found someone to take over the Shady Rest.

Anna nodded, even as her expression held a hint of doubt. "My cousin Pam lives in Rochester, and she needs to get away for a while. I told her she could come here to stay, and she's going to arrive in the next week or so." She sniffed. "If she works out, she can take over. I can teach her what to do, and go back to Toronto."

"Problem solved, then!"

Anna nodded. "I know, but . . . Jaymie, I'm going to miss you so much!"

"Oh, honey, me, too!" They hugged.

"Halloo?"

Jaymie looked toward the door to see Heidi standing there, waving and smiling.

"Your mom told me you were here," she said to Jaymie. "She was kind of weird, like she didn't even want to look at me. Why is that?"

Jaymie sighed. Sometimes it was as if everyone else in her life was holding the grudge against Joel and Heidi longer than she had. Joel had a new girlfriend; Jaymie was over it. In fact, she liked Heidi a lot, and they got along just fine. So it was odd, considering everyone had been telling her for months to get over it, that they still treated Heidi like a pariah much of the time. "I'm sorry, Heidi. We had a bit of a quarrel just now. It's probably that."

Heidi sat down on the floor to play with Tabitha, then looked up and said, "I can't believe what I heard happened over at the island!"

In muted tones and oblique language, avoiding the M-word (murder) and the D-word (dead) around Tabitha, they discussed it.

Jaymie had to dispel some of the weirder rumors, and wondered yet again at the Queensville telegraph, and how they got things very, *very* wrong much more often than they got them right. "I saw Bernie at the scene. I'm assuming she's working on the case?" Jaymie asked. Bernice Jenkins and Heidi had forged a friendship begun when they discovered their common interest in mid-century modern furniture.

"Yeah. I just talked to her. She has a day off two days from now, and we're going to an auction. You want to come?"

Given the state of her kitchen, and how her mother was dealing with her collection, she probably shouldn't. "I'd love to," Jaymie said. With Bernie on the case, as she was, maybe she'd be able to tell Jaymie was what going on, because Mr. Detective Zack would be no use at all, she knew from experience. It hit her suddenly that she assumed she'd get to know the details, that she just figured she'd be involved somehow, even though she really didn't know the victim this time.

Maybe she was as big a nosy parker as the rest of Queensville; she just didn't like to admit it. But she didn't gossip; she "exchanged information." And that was what gossip was, she realized, information given and received. So she was really every bit a Queensville gossip. She supposed that admission meant she could no longer criticize the rest of the town.

After a few moments more of chat, Anna asked something Jaymie had been wondering for a couple of weeks. "So, Heidi, have you told your folks yet about getting engaged?"

Heidi blushed, and a faint expression of irritation crossed her pretty, pale face. She shrugged and rolled her eyes. "Gosh, you and everyone else wants to know! I swear, if it gets back to Joel that I haven't told my family yet, he'll be so hurt."

"I didn't tell anyone," Jaymie said. "Honest!"

"You haven't told Joel that your folks don't know you're getting married? Hey, Brock Nibley was the one who told me," Anna said, her hands up, palms out. "Don't ask me how *he* knows."

"That's the thing about gossip," Jaymie mused. "It seems that once a rumor starts, there is no stopping it. You'd better either tell your folks, or let Joel know you haven't yet told them."

"Will *you* tell Joel for me?" Heidi asked Jaymie, with a hopeful expression.

Astounded, Jaymie gaped at her while Anna snickered.

"Did I say something wrong?" Heidi asked, looking from one of them to the other.

"Doesn't it strike you the least bit odd to ask your fiancé's ex-girlfriend to tell him that you haven't let your parents in on your engagement?" Jaymie carefully asked. Between the two of them, Joel and Heidi seemed determined to drag her into their relationship, the one place she did not, as his ex, belong.

Her expression blanked; then she turned pink. "I did it again, didn't I?" she asked. "I was insensitive. Oh, Jaymsie, I'm so sorry!"

"Jaymsie?" Anna said, eyes wide, staring at her friend, then eyeing the blonde.

Jaymie shrugged. "Heidi, my feelings aren't hurt, but it is *completely* unthinkable that I should break that kind of news to Joel. That's your job."

She sighed. "I'd better tell him when he comes back from his sales trip on Friday."

"You had better!" Jaymie sighed and got up. "And speaking of parents and boyfriends, I have dinner tonight with Mom, Dad, Daniel and his parents. Oh, joy."

"It'll all turn out, Jaymie," Heidi said, jumping to her feet. "They're gonna love you!"

❋ Eight ❋

JAYMIE HAD STARTED a foodie blog online even before deciding to try to get her "Vintage Eats" column in the *Howler*. It was good experience, and had gotten her in the habit of writing every day, sometimes about recipes, and sometimes about vintage cookware. It was past time to update it, so she spent a few hours scanning old cookbook pages and recipes, wrote some blog entries, and postdated them to launch over the next several days.

As she hit "publish" on the last one, it occurred to her there was no way she could continue with the article on ice harvesting and ice cream making for the *Wolverhampton Howler*. How could she blithely talk about wickedly sharp and lethal ice picks, when one had been used, quite possibly, to murder someone on the island, right in the backyard she shared with the owners of the Ice House? What a mess!

She had to call Nan Goodenough, her prospective editor at the *Howler*. Wasn't this wonderful? She didn't even really have the job yet, but she had to phone her editor and change her article subject. It just wouldn't do to use the Ice House and have photos of ice picks, not with the murder so raw and recent. And unsolved.

It was late afternoon, but she hoped she'd catch the woman at the office. She dialed the *Howler*, and got Nan on the phone. She explained her dilemma, and said, "So I think I should change it, don't you?"

"Yeah. It's too bad in a way; if we were a different kind of paper . . . but we're not. We don't want to have to tiptoe around people's sensitivities. You can do the Ice House story later, unless Garnet or Ruby are arrested, of course."

Jaymie sat back in her office chair, and it squealed in protest. "Do you think one of them will be?"

"I've heard things," Nan said. "The paper is covering it, of course, and my hubby has some tips he's running with. Garnet's prints are all over the ice pick, of course, and after that fight between him and Urban . . . Well, I wouldn't be surprised."

For the first time Jaymie wondered, if Garnet *did* do it, then it was easy to figure his access to the ice pick. But if he didn't commit the murder—and Jaymie still could not imagine him doing something so heinous—then how did someone else get the pick?

"So what other idea did you have in mind for the article?"

Too late, Jaymie realized she should have been prepared for this. "Uh . . . I . . ."

"You don't have a clue, do you?" Nan said, her brash voice holding an amused note. "Honey, you should always be ready with spare ideas." So spoke the New York journalist who had retired, married a widower, and moved to a small town in Michigan to help run a weekly newspaper.

"How about an article on vintage picnics?" Jaymie blurted.

"Not to tout your own business, is it?"

"No!" Jaymie's face flamed; what an idiot! Of course the

woman wouldn't want to do an article that was so clearly self-promoting. "No, not at all, I—"

"Jaymie, I'm just kidding you. Honey, you have *got* to stop taking things so seriously. Look, just do it, already. The picnic idea is great, and you probably already know a lot about it, so you can hurry the story along. I need it soon, in case I want to use it for this week's *Howler*. Photograph some of your vintage picnic rigs, and we'll include your business in the article. Cross promotion is what it's all about, and it'll save me feeling bad about not paying you. Gotta go, kiddo."

The dial tone woke Jaymie up to the fact that Nan had hung up on her. As always, when she was done talking to Nan Goodenough she felt like a limp dishrag. The woman, at sixty-seven, had more energy than most twenty-year-olds Jaymie knew. But she felt lucky to have such a valuable contact, and sat down to write her article with a much better handle on it than she had before.

DINNER WITH HER parents, Daniel, and his parents, Roger and Debbie, was an event not so much to be looked forward to, but to be gotten through. If she could keep her mother and Daniel's mother from becoming implacable foes, that was about the best she could hope to manage. Why did the romance novels she loved so much never deal with that particular peril? Danger was not in highwaymen or roving bands of pirates, but in the social intricacies of dealing with your boyfriend's family.

Jaymie dressed carefully, a new skirt and wrap blouse bought just for its suitability for dining with parents. The thought that the Collinses might buy a house in Queensville and stay was like a dark cloud on an already gloomy day.

"Are you ready, Jaymie?" her mother yelled up the stairs to her.

She glanced at herself in the mirror over her chest of drawers and grimaced. Not at her looks, which were fine;

her longish light brown hair was pulled up off her neck and coiled into a roll, and she wore a light coating of makeup, just enough to make her look happy, as her grandma Leighton would say. Her frown was brought on by the memories instigated by her mom hollering up the stairs to her. It had never been an easy relationship, between her and her mother, even though they loved each other.

Now, many years later, all it took for her to retreat to being a snarly teenager was to have her parents—especially her mother—in the same house with her. She took a deep breath and straightened her posture, practicing a placid smile in the mirror, hoping it reached her blue eyes; she was an adult, and she would find a way to make peace between her mother and Daniel's.

The sun was setting, gilding every white surface with a layer of shiny gold, and lengthening shadows until they created long, dark patterns across the grassy yard. Jaymie locked up and they strolled down the long, flagstone path to the parking lane behind their house. It was already ten to eight, and they were to meet the Collinses at eight o'clock at Ambrosio, a new restaurant just outside of town on the highway; her dad was driving his car, since her vehicle was a rusting white van with room for only two people, and no air-conditioning. It had turned hot and dry, in a late-August kind of way, the kind of heat that makes any northerner long for the cool, crisp days and nights of autumn. Jaymie was already regretting the three-quarter sleeves on her blouse, but the car was air-conditioned and the restaurant would be, too.

They rushed from the coolness of the car to the coolness of Ambrosio, and followed the waitress through the murk to where the Collinses had reserved a table. Roger and Debbie Collins were younger than Alan and Joy Leighton by a few years, but still contemporaries. The men got along fine, and Roger and Jaymie's dad greeted each other with firm handshakes and a comment on the possible matchups for the World Series. Joy and Debbie made polite noises while smiling on the surface, icy-cool expressions that did not reach their eyes. Daniel rose and took Jaymie aside, kissing her and giving her a very satisfying hug. Debbie watched from her seat with a neutral look on her plain, round face.

"I've been so worried about you," he said. "For that to happen to you again, finding a body!"

It was much the same as he had said in their phone conversation earlier in the day. He had wanted to rush to her side, but she had reassured him that she was all right. Pretty much, anyway. He was comforting in every way, she thought, inhaling his soapy scent, fresh and vigorous. She looked up into his plain face, eyes set just the right distance on either side of a beaky nose, and a gaunt, rather lanternish jaw. "I'm fine," she said, smiling up at him and squeezing his shoulders. "It was terrible, but it has nothing to do with me."

He searched her face and nodded. "Good."

"Let's order soon. I'm starving!"

They sat down side by side and all chatted politely, until a waitress came and handed them each a menu. Jaymie glanced up at her, recognizing her immediately.

"Hey, Lisa," she said, reading her name tag. "You also work at the Ice House, on the island, right?"

"I sure do. Oh! I recognize you; I saw you there the other night. You were sitting with a hot dude, that cop."

Jaymie felt Daniel's searching gaze fasten on her face as her cheeks reddened. "We weren't *really* sitting together, at least not . . . It was just because it was crowded and there was nowhere else to sit," Jaymie stuttered. She met Daniel's gaze and said, "Zack Christian rents a cottage on the island. I didn't know that until Ruby Redmond sat me at his table. There really was no other place."

"It was hopping," the waitress agreed.

Daniel smiled, crookedly, but his mother looked confused and concerned. For some, no explanation was necessary, and for others, no explanation would suffice; Jaymie repeated that to herself, and brightly looked up at the waitress. "So, do you work out there much?"

She shrugged. "Mostly in summer. I need the money for school, so I've got, like, four jobs in the summer."

"Me, too," Jaymie said.

"Oh, honey, that's not quite true," her mom said.

Jaymie closed her eyes and counted to five, then opened them and calmly said, "I work at the Emporium a couple of days a week, and substitute at Jewel's Junk whenever she needs me. I cook breakfast for the B and B, and now I have the basket rental business, and in my spare time, such as it is, I'm working on that column for the *Howler* while writing a cookbook."

"That's not the same as a real job," Daniel's mother chimed in, agreeing with Joy Leighton. "You try being on your feet as much as this young girl is; you'll soon see the difference."

Daniel said, "Mom, you can't—"

"It's okay," Jaymie said, touching his hand, keeping him from launching into a defense of her work ethic. "Let's look at our menus."

Lisa listed off the specials, and said she'd give them a few minutes. Jaymie stared at the menu, but didn't really see it until she forced herself to relax. Ambrosio was a nice place, Jaymie thought, as she breathed deeply and looked out the huge picture window overlooking the river. Sparkling lights on the other side showed where a town was, and one slow-moving light was a mast top on a sailboat, slipping along the St. Clair.

She decided on her dinner choice, folded her menu and put it down. "I understand you have been looking at houses for sale in Queensville," she said, brightly, taking both Roger and Debbie Collins in her glance.

Daniel glanced at her quickly. "Mom and Dad love looking at houses wherever they go," he said. "Don't you?"

His mother sniffed, her eyes still on the menu. "If you're

going to spend so much time here, Daniel, we may just *have* to buy a house. I haven't seen hardly anything of you this summer."

"Now, Deb, that isn't true," Roger said, heartily. "He came back for a couple o' weeks in July, there."

"Just to fix that trouble at Collins Inc.," she replied. She looked over at Jaymie's father. "He's our only son, you see, and we miss him terribly."

Alan Leighton, diplomat, said, "I can understand that, Debbie. He's a fine young man."

"And a good son," she said. "It's too bad that work and . . . *other* things, keep him busy so much, but you don't get as wealthy and successful as he is without a great deal of hard work."

There was a moment of silence, perhaps to mourn the death of any hope of subtlety behind Debbie Collin's dislike for her son's girlfriend, and Daniel sighed.

"I'm ready to order," Jaymie's mom said, slapping her menu closed. "Everyone else?"

Lisa came back and took everyone's order, ending with Jaymie. "You had the perch at the Ice House, too, right?" she said.

"I did. Loved it."

"It's better there than here," she said in a whisper, glancing around. "You didn't hear it from me, but the fish at Ambrosio is not the best. You're better off with pasta."

That changed a couple of orders, including Jaymie's, and Lisa gathered up the menus. But still she lingered for a long moment, and leaned over to talk to Jaymie. "Say, I need to know ahead of time . . . do you think Miss Redmond is going to be arrested? Or Mr. Redmond?"

Jaymie quickly said, "I really don't believe so. Neither one of them killed Urban Dobrinskie. You know them better than that, don't you?"

Lisa looked doubtful. "I don't know. Mr. Redmond hit Mr. Dobrinskie pretty hard the other night. And the cops came back this afternoon to search the restaurant. Had to close down early. That's why I'm doing a shift here."

"Really?"

"Nonsense," Jaymie's dad said. "We've known them for years. Garnet Redmond is A-OK in my books, and so is his sister."

"You never know what people are capable of," Debbie Collins said, a dark expression on her face. "I thought Trish Brandon was a really nice girl until she dumped my Daniel."

Jaymie glanced over at Daniel, who was turning red.

"Mom, not here, please."

"Didn't you tell Jaymie about Trish?"

"He did, Mrs. Collins," Jaymie said, folding her hands on her lap. "He told me all about her. And that he now thinks it was for the best." Some of the triumph left the woman's face.

"So you don't think they'll be arrested, or the Ice House will close down?" Lisa asked, bringing the conversation back to the matter at hand. She glanced over her shoulder, at one of her other tables. "I really like my job there, better than this one. You know, I wouldn't think anything of it— the Redmonds being guilty, you know—except for those phone calls that evening."

"Phone calls?"

"Yeah. Garnet and Ruby both kept getting phone calls, and a couple of times they left the restaurant."

"Really. Were they gone long?"

"Ruby was gone for a good half an hour or more, at one point. Maybe more like three-quarters of an hour."

"So you don't mean they were gone together?"

"No!" Lisa said. "No, I didn't mean that. They were gone separately, at different times, and not to dart league, either, because I asked Marg about that. It was weird. Usually once they're there, they're there."

Separately, at different times. You could get anywhere

on Heartbreak Island in twenty-five minutes or less. If you had a bicycle, which everyone did, even faster. If one of them wanted to kill Urban, and knew where he was, Jaymie supposed Garnet or Ruby could have done it.

But their absences from the restaurant didn't matter a jot, since the killing had happened right behind the Redmonds' and Leightons' homes in the wee hours of the morning. "What did Ruby say when she came back?" Jaymie asked. "Anything?"

Lisa shrugged. "I was busy. Didn't see Ruby again until a while later. It was nothing, I guess, but some bored kids prank calling. That's what I heard Garnet telling Marg about the stupid phone calls, anyway."

"What's this all about?" Jaymie's mom asked, her brow furrowed.

Jaymie had hoped the others were involved in their chatter and hadn't been listening in on the conversation. She was silent, but Lisa was the original Chatty Cathy. "Jaymie found Urban's body behind you guys' cottage, right? Creepy! I'd be really weirded out by that, but she's a trooper."

Daniel's mother had a look of horror on her face. "You found a body? Is this about that terrible murder out on the island? And it was behind the cottage where you all want to have dinner?"

Joy opened her mouth to reply, but Daniel and his father started to both talk at once, and Lisa, her face blanked into puzzlement, seemed to get that maybe—just maybe—she had put a foot wrong. The restaurant manager was looking over at them, frowning, so the waitress excused herself to see to her other customers and hustled off. Daniel's mother had been soothed into calmness again, but Jaymie's mother still looked ruffled.

Jaymie wondered whether she should raise the family dinner issue. As laden with emotion as it had been, it might just be a less fraught subject for conversation than the murder and her discovery of the body. Of course, even the dinner party at the cottage had violent overtones, now that it had been revealed where the body had been found. Fortunately, the men began talking golf, and proposed a foursome for the next day at the country club, at which the Collinses had a temporary membership while they were in Michigan, and the conversation wandered off in another direction.

As the others chatted, Jaymie began to wonder about something she hadn't thought of before: there didn't seem to be a lot of blood on the scene for someone who was stabbed, even though his shirt was soaked. She closed her eyes for a moment, the image of the body popping into her head. The bloodstain on his short-sleeved summer shirt had been an elongated oval, spreading down to his left side, even though he was flat on his back.

And Urban had been cold to the touch. Her eyes popped open, and she stared blindly down at the glossy wood surface of the table. Now she wondered not only *who* had killed him, but *when*? If Ruby was gone for a good while, that evening, could she have killed him earlier? It didn't seem likely. Jaymie knew she would have noticed his body lying in the ravine when she looked out at some point, before the light was completely gone, or later, when she went looking for Hoppy. No, his body had not been there earlier; she was sure of it.

When Jaymie tuned back in, Daniel was observing her with a puzzled frown on his face, but the conversation among the parents had turned to the neutral ground of gardening. Debbie Collins was an enthusiastic gardener, it seemed, and had taken on the task of revamping the Stowe House gardens.

"I really miss gardening," she said with a sigh. "It's just not the same in Phoenix."

"Bakersfield wasn't much better," Daniel said, with a grin, referring to his hometown of Bakersfield, California. "Dry and dusty, too."

"It is different here," Debbie Collins admitted. Her round

face was alight with pleasure, for once, and she spoke enthusiastically of her trips to a local garden nursery, and her purchase of three new trees for the lawn of Stowe House.

Roger Collins grinned. "Yeah, and of course who gets to move them?" The others laughed as he raised his hand. "I had to get the wheelbarrow out. One of those things, with the root ball, is about two hundred pounds!"

"It is not *that* heavy," Debbie demurred.

"I'll help you out, Roger," Jaymie's dad said. "You and I can manhandle those babies into place. I've done that before."

Joy Leighton, a look of alarm on her face, said, "Alan, you will do no such thing. I won't have you straining something!"

Their dinners came just then, and they ate, agreeing that the food was not as good as the name Ambrosio promised. But the evening ended pleasantly enough, and Jaymie was relieved. The older couples made conversation in the parking lot while Daniel and Jaymie said their good-byes on the riverfront walkway. It reminded Jaymie of the Seven Minutes in Heaven game she played as a curious eleven-year-old, when she got her first kiss from Josh Burney; it was awkward, and yet oddly stimulating. They kissed for a couple of minutes; Daniel was a rather good kisser, not too hard, not too mushy.

"I'm sorry about my mom," Daniel said, holding Jaymie close in the warm evening air.

"Are you kidding? My mom is no picnic either, Daniel. I was going to bring up the family thing out at Rose Tree Cottage, but there was already enough tension. I just wanted dinner to go okay. I think it did; don't you?" She looked up at him.

"It went just fine," he said. "You seemed a little distracted, though. Is everything okay? Despite finding a dead body in your backyard?"

She appreciated his delicacy. He never made her feel

weak, or like he thought she couldn't handle something difficult. "No, it's okay. Troubling, and scary—I mean, there's a murderer on the island somewhere, probably, unless he or she is already gone—but I'm all right."

"C'mon, you two," Roger Collins said from the parking lot. "Get done and let's get going."

"I don't think your mom likes me," Jaymie said, as they walked arm in arm back to their parents.

He shrugged, but she felt a thread of tension in his wiry body.

"She's still holding a grudge against Trish," he said. "She'll come around. How could she not?" He gave her a quick kiss and the Collins family moved toward Roger Collins's rented Beemer.

The Leightons returned home, and her parents turned in. She fed Hoppy the doggie bag she had brought home, then sat out on the back step while he took his piddle and Denver prowled the perimeter. She was going to do breakfast for Anna tomorrow morning, work four hours at the Emporium, then head back out to the island, hopefully, from her earlier conversation with the police liaison office, to supervise the plumbers as they finished their work.

Something that was said that evening should mean something to her, but what? She went over her conversation with Lisa. Was it about Ruby being gone from the restaurant? Or was it something someone else said? Finally, hopelessly confused, she called the animals in and retired, to dream of ice cream and Daniel's kisses, not necessarily in that order.

❧ Nine ❧

JAYMIE BUZZED THROUGH her morning, taking care of Anna's breakfast service for her, then spending a few hours working at the Emporium, filling in as cashier for the elderly but fairly spry Klausners, who both had medical appointments. The Emporium was a big, square clapboard building with a Victorian false front. The porch spanned the entire width, and had been a gathering place, of sorts, for over a hundred years, from a time when the newest shapes in bustles were available at the dry goods counter, to the present, when boxes of water weenies and boogie boards were lined up along the huge old windows. At one end of the wooden porch a newly reinforced wheelchair ramp gave access, but at the front, by the road, three wood steps ascended, and that was where Jaymie and Valetta took their midmorning tea, partially shaded from the glare of the sun that was traversing the cerulean sky.

"So they haven't made an arrest yet," Valetta said, sipping

out of her mug emblazoned with the saying "Drug Dealer" in big red letters.

"No."

"Do you think it could be Garnet or Ruby who did it?"

"I really don't, Valetta," Jaymie said, sipping her cooling tea. "What idiot would kill someone on their own property?"

Her friend shrugged. "It happens all the time. I don't think if you're killing someone you think of that. At least, not at that moment." She had shed her lab coat, and tugged at the neck of her T-shirt, which sported a design of playful kittens in neckerchiefs.

What she said was true, but Jaymie didn't *want* it to be Ruby or Garnet. She liked them both. Valetta was someone whose opinion mattered to her, so she tried to give it a fair chance in her brain. "Do *you* think it was one of them? Have you heard anything?"

Valetta chuckled. "No, not at all. I just think we have to keep an open mind."

"You must know them both, right?"

"And like them." She frowned off into the distance, and screwed up her mouth, suddenly serious.

"What is it?" Jaymie asked, watching her.

"There's just something there, and I can't put my finger on it. I've always felt like they're hiding something."

"Do you mean about the murder?"

"Good Lord, no. I haven't seen either of them since the murder. But I've always felt there was something there that just . . ." She shook her head and shrugged. "I don't know. Just something not quite right."

Jaymie pondered what different people had said about Ruby, in particular. A couple of people assumed she was gay, and then Valetta's brother was convinced that she was having an affair with Urban Dobrinskie. In a town like Queensville, rumors and gossip bubbled up through most conversation like magma, and Jaymie had long ago learned to ignore 90 percent of what people said. But could it be true? Was Ruby having an affair with Urban? Even an idiot like Brock Nibley had to be right *some* of the time.

She shook her head. Not about this; it just didn't add up. Ruby was smart and even-tempered, and Dobrinskie had been an angry twerp. Still, Ruby's words haunted her; she had said, "I didn't mean to do it." Do what?

After lunch Mr. Klausner came back from his doctor's appointment, and Jaymie headed home a roundabout way, reluctant to return home immediately. As she passed Jewel's Junk, she noticed the store next door—it had been a bungalow once, but had become a store since, a bookstore in its last incarnation—with the door wide-open and a sign leaning against the railing. She had heard about a new shop opening, but when it didn't happen by Memorial Day weekend, she had put that down to unsubstantiated rumor.

She peeked in, curious.

"Hi there!"

Jaymie started, but then realized that the disembodied voice was floating down from the top of a ladder, and it was someone she knew. "Cynthia!" she said, to Cynthia Turbridge, transplanted big-city yoga instructor. "What are you putting in here? Your yoga studio?"

"Nope, I'm opening a junk store," she said, with a laugh. "My cottage is too crowded with shabby chic, so I decided to open the Cottage Shoppe. Check out the sign outside when you leave."

Jaymie glanced around at the boxes piled high with linens and white-painted furnishings lined up along the walls. "What a great idea! Can't wait till you open."

"About a week. Actually, you could do me a favor," Cynthia said, climbing down from her perch, where she had been hanging white and gold drapes. She dusted her hands off and stared at the drapes, adjusting them slightly. "I hear you know all there is about vintage kitchen junk. My vision for this place is the complete shabby chic cottage, and I need some advice on the kitchen." She explained that each room was going to have stuff for sale related to that room, like bed linens and furniture in the bedroom, china in the dining room, etcetera. "But when it comes to the kitchen, I'm stumped."

Shabby chic, Jaymie mused. She wasn't quite sure what it would entail. Cynthia, maybe seeing her puzzlement, rooted around in one of the boxes and produced some magazines. "Here, this will show you what I mean, at least as far as the bedroom goes. I just can't figure out how to apply shabby chic to the kitchen."

"Okay, I'll see what I can come up with."

"You've already inspired me, without even knowing it!" the older woman said. "For the front porch, I'm going to have some Adirondack chairs, of course, and a porch swing, but for the backyard, I was thinking of something like your picnic rigs!"

Jaymie returned home in a thoughtful mood. The Cottage Shoppe was going to be her kind of store, it sounded like, except she was thrifty, and Cynthia was likely going to charge an arm and a leg for her artistic vision of cottage life, planning to milk the tourists for their vacation shopping bucks.

Jaymie's mom and dad were out with the Collinses golfing, their note said, so she settled down to her computer in her office to try to work on the article while she had the house to herself. It was no good. Her attention just wasn't there, not with this murder hanging over them all, and her beloved cottage right in the middle of it. She picked up the phone; she needed answers.

First the police department. She gave her name and asked for Zack Christian. He was not available, but surprisingly, she was put through to Chief Ledbetter.

"H'lo," he said, ending the word on a harrumph.

She apologized for taking up his time, then asked about

her property, and whether she could arrange for the plumbers to do their work.

"Yeah, okay. We're finished with your property, Miss Leighton," he said. "But I do have a few questions." Without waiting, he charged on: "You said you saw a flash of light. Can you describe it for me a little better, where it came from?"

She thought back, and said, "It was kind of like when you're in the woods, and someone has a flashlight, and they play it around an area, you know?"

He grunted; then there was silence for a minute. "When you saw the body, did you know who it was?"

"Yes, of course! I had seen him not too long before, after all."

"What about before that? Would you have recognized him before the argument at the restaurant?"

"I don't think so."

"But your family has had the cottage there a long time, right?"

"Sure, but I don't spend that much time out there now, you know. And Dobrinskie had only been a part owner of the marina for . . . a few years? I'm just guessing. I don't really know a thing about him."

He grunted again, and again there was a long pause. "Okay. You can tell your plumbers they can go ahead."

"Chief Ledbetter," she shouted, before he could hang up. "When can I get my digital camera back?"

He was silent for a moment. "Come in tomorrow and get it. I'll make sure they have it for you at the desk."

"Chief, are you close to an arrest?"

"No comment." Click.

Jaymie cuddled Denver and fed him, then snapped a leash on Hoppy, and headed down to the marina. Usually she loved the trip. The ferry's approach to the island was done from the tip of the heart shape of Heartbreak Island, and on the bluff overlooking the river was a lonely cottage that Jaymie always watched, trying to imagine the view. It looked uninhabited, to her, but it was probably just used by vacationers, like many of the cottages, including her own.

As the ferry chugged toward the marina, her stomach did a few flip-flops that she knew were not motion sickness. Though she spent only a short while there every year, Rose Tree Cottage was her refuge. To get it back to being that, she had to hope the police solved Urban Dobrinskie's murder, and erased all the bad feelings associated with Heartbreak Island.

"Hey, there, howarye?" Will Lindsay asked, as she disembarked with Hoppy. He looked a little harassed, his hair askew and his eyes underlined by dark circles.

"I'm good, Will. How are *you*? You look tired."

He shrugged. "You never know how much there is to a business until you have to do it all on your own. I miss Urb. He could be an ass, but he sure know how to get stuff done."

Heavy machinery rumbled down the hill, and he looked over his shoulder, as Hoppy yapped and growled at the noise. It was Robin driving a tractor, pulling a generator. Jaymie waved, but Robin didn't see her, and turned, continuing on to the far end of the marina. He was followed by a couple of other guys on bigger machines.

"Wow. Something going on?"

"We're finally getting the much-needed dredging done. The ferry port is being done first; I'm always so afraid of the ferry getting grounded. Then we'll be doing the harbor mouth and some of the marina."

Hoping it didn't set her own project back, now that she had the okay from the police to continue, Jaymie said good-bye to Will, picked up Hoppy, and hustled to talk to Robin before he got down to work. She scuffed over the gravel and huffed and puffed her way over to Robin, Hoppy bouncing on her hip and her shoulder bag swinging wildly and whacking her on the back. The plumber had hopped off his tractor and was talking to one of his big machine operators.

"Robin!" she called.

"Oh, hey, Jaymie."

"I just got the okay to finish the plumbing on the cottage property," she said, gasping from sprinting the distance. "Are you going to be available?"

His round face wore an annoyed expression and he rolled his eyes, as if he saw dollar bills fluttering away, but he nodded. "I didn't know when we could continue, and Will finally got the go-ahead to do the harbor work. But I promise I'll personally come back this aft and finish up. There really isn't that much, and a couple of my unskilled guys can do some of the heavy labor."

"That's why you're the best," she said, clapping him on the shoulder.

"I gotta go," he said.

She caught her breath and walked Hoppy back to the cottage. As she ascended the steps up to the cottage, keys in hand, she tried not to let the events of the past days ruin her haven. All was safe and sound, and she poured some water in a bowl for Hoppy, then glanced out the back. Garnet was glaring at the mess, hands on his hips. Jaymie exited, scaled the slope and stepped carefully past the muddy hole, moving steadily toward him.

"Hey, Garnet," she said, keeping her tone chipper. He looked a little gray, but pretty much as he always looked. "I just talked to Robin. I've got the okay from the police chief, so Robin is going to come back and finish up this afternoon. I hope. If he doesn't get done, though, may I borrow your bathroom tonight again?"

"Sure, Jaymie," he said, a worried expression on his long face.

"Everything okay? I mean, besides the obvious?"

"The obvious being everyone in town is whispering that either Ruby or I killed Urban?"

"No one really believes that. I've been through this myself, last month, when folks thought I killed Kathy,"

Jaymie said, about the whispers that she had murdered her longtime foe, Kathy Cooper, at the Fourth of July picnic. "Trust me, your friends don't think that, and even those who might believe it will be proved wrong as soon as the police figure out who *did* do it."

He smiled. "I appreciate it, Jaymie. I forgot about your trouble last month."

They looked over the mucky terrain. Jaymie had never realized how important the unseen and unnoticed leaching bed and septic system was until it was no longer functioning as it should. She suspected, after talking to Robin, that the failure of their septic system was due to their renters trying to defray the cost of renting by having additional family and friends come and bunk in with them, despite the written agreement, which stated no additional guests not on the rental agreement. Too many people overwhelmed the system. It didn't help that their sump pump was draining into the leaching bed, too, though.

But now they were putting in a system that would handle it all, something that Robin told her was a necessity if she wanted to keep renting out the cottage. The Redmonds had had to do it the summer before, she knew, and it was only the two of them. Now, that was odd. She glanced over at Garnet. She had never pondered that before, their lack of visitors. As far as Jaymie knew, the Redmonds never had family or friends bunking in with them. In general, once folks knew you lived in a tourist area they started dropping hints about coming to visit dear cousin so-and-so.

"I'm relieved we can go ahead and get this done, anyway," Jaymie said. Once it was done, it was done, and it was good to go—other than an occasional pumping out of the solid waste from the septic tank—for thirty years or more.

"So what are you going to do with the property, once the leaching bed and septic system is done?" Garnet asked.

"What do you mean?"

"I just assumed that you'd do what we did, take the opportunity to reimagine the landscaping."

He had a point, Jaymie thought, scanning the landscape. It had always been just a grassy slope, but if she looked at it as an opportunity, as the Redmonds had, it could be so much more. When the Redmonds did their septic system and leaching bed, they had built in some terraced gardens dotted over the slope, and now had a gazebo in the shade of the copse of pine trees on their side of the ravine.

"You guys did such a great job. I'd love your opinion. What do you think we should do?"

She walked around the muddy open pit with him, and he elaborated on the terrace idea, showing her where there could be a natural fieldstone patio, a kind of open-air living room, halfway down the slope. He mentioned patio furniture, and she tried to picture different kinds, natural rattan, or wicker, or synthetic versions. "And a swing," she said, picturing soft summer nights and a swing set in the privacy of the grove of trees.

"Hello?" Zack Christian approached from the side of the cottage just then.

"Hey!" Jaymie said. She glanced over at Garnet, but he was looking down at the mud at the edge of the new leaching field, and didn't acknowledge the detective.

"Chief Ledbetter told me you'd be here," he said. He was dressed in his off-duty clothes, a towel slung over his neck.

"Yeah. He gave me the go-ahead to have the plumbers finish the septic system."

Her neighbor knelt at the edge of the muck looking at something. Jaymie glanced over at him, and said, "Garnet, what are you looking at?"

He pointed. "There's something wedged in the mud, something metal. What is it?"

Zack snapped into cop mode, the difference like that between a blazing hot day and a freezer. "Don't touch it!"

he said. He whipped his cell phone out of his pocket as he knelt down to look. But he didn't make a call; he took a photo. "It's a drill bit," he said, finally, as he used the end of a key to dislodge it from the muck.

Jaymie squinted, and could see the blue steel and nodded. "You're right! What's it doing in the mud?"

The detective was noncommittal, but was on the phone calling for a forensic team. Jaymie groaned. Would this put her plumbing work on hold again? Garnet shrugged and grimaced, mouthing, "Sorry." He climbed the hill to his cottage.

A half hour later the team had swarmed her property, after photographing and extricating the drill bit. It would be sent to forensic, Zack said, in case it was the murder weapon.

"But I thought the ice pick was the murder weapon?"

"It probably is, but we can't be too careful. We are going to have to search again, just in case," he said. "Better now than when you've laid sod. Have you thought of anything else regarding the ice pick yet? When you last saw it?"

"I told you in my statement; I last saw it when Garnet had it."

"Okay, all right."

The team cordoned off the area again. Darn! Just when she thought they'd make headway and get the plumbing job finished. There was no point in staying on the island that night, and Jaymie didn't think she could face another lonely night with no toilet, so she went back to Queensville, after calling Robin and telling him that finishing the job had to be put off for another day or two. He was relieved, Jaymie could tell.

That evening she and Daniel went for a long walk, since both of their homes were off-limits, due to the parents being in residence. It felt like a high school date, and they shared a laugh over the annoyances attendant upon being thirty-something and living, however briefly, with one's parents.

The evening ended with a very satisfying make-out session in the back alley of her home, interrupted at last by Trip Findley, her backyard neighbor, turning on his light and letting out his little dog, Skip. It started barking, setting off Hoppy in her own backyard.

"Good night," she said to Daniel, softly. She took his glasses off, ran her fingers through his thick hair and kissed him. She felt him sigh, and smiled to herself, as she carefully placed his glasses back on his nose.

"Good night, sweetheart," he said, kissing her forehead and ambling off.

Sweetheart? She felt like she had retreated to the 1950s. Kind of appropriate, given her fondness for all things vintage!

The next morning she helped Anna out at the bed-and-breakfast, giving her mom time to get ready for another day of golfing, and then updated her blog—she had three whole followers and no comments—and wrote for a while, clearing her mind of all the extraneous garbage that was plaguing her and concentrating on the words. The article on vintage picnics was coming together very well now, and she even found some recipes she was interested in trying. It was a subject, after all, that she had researched thoroughly for her thriving business.

Then she drove her van out to the police station to retrieve her camera. She now needed to photograph some of her vintage picnic baskets for the article on picnicking the old-fashioned way. There was a bit of a holdup, but she did get her digital camera back. She stood at the desk in the bustling office for a moment—phones rang and printers chattered to life, dispatchers talked and officers escorted the odd arrestee through the station—thumbing through the slide show of photos.

So, the ice pick photos had been removed. Interesting. Why remove them from her camera? Shuddering, she decided that was just fine; she didn't really want to be reminded of

Urban's death anyway, and even though she had not actually seen the pick in the man's chest, she could imagine it all too well. She frowned and stared at the other photos, one a blurry image of the ice chests at the back, with Ruby moving out of frame. The ice pick was likely the murder weapon, but now there was the complication of the drill bit. On the other hand, it was possible that the drill bit had nothing to do with anything, and had just been dropped, not stolen.

She turned away from the counter to leave, but just then Chief Ledbetter lumbered out from his office and yelped her name, then beckoned her back. Almost out. Oh, well. She threaded through cubicles and entered his office, a bland glass and metal box with a big picture window overlooking the back parking lot, and a desk facing away from it, with two hard chairs facing the desk. She sat down in one of them, as he circled to sit behind his desk.

He plunked down in his chair with a grunt of relief. "You've been a busy little bee the last few months, haven't you, Miss Leighton? First that body on your back porch, then that girl dead at the park with your bowl as the murder weapon, and now this, out at your cottage. You don't have any other properties I should be aware of, do you? Anywhere else you're hiding dead bodies?"

As an example of gallows humor, it failed miserably, Jaymie thought, and she didn't smile. Stiffening, she said, "A series of unfortunate coincidences."

"Hmph," he grunted. "Don't really believe in coincidences. But Detective Christian seems to believe in 'em. Says you're an innocent victim in all this."

Her cheeks warmed, but she merely said, "Technically, Urban Dobrinskie's body was not on my property, but on the Redmonds'. It was only chance that I happened to be out there that night and found Urban."

"Yeah, we know that. Technically." He sat and stared at Jaymie for a long few minutes.

"I have to go," she said, standing. "Now that I have my

camera back, I need to take photos of the subject of my newspaper article."

"You're not writing about the Ice House, right?"

"No. I decided to go with something else. Vintage picnics, actually."

He squinted up at her. "Me and some buddies used to swim out to the island to hang around the rich girls, the ones whose families had cottages out there. We'd mooch a hot dog off someone, and go fishing off the dock. Guess that's not the kind of vintage picnic you had in mind."

"No," she said, a little peeved. If he was trying to imply that she was a "rich girl" and a snob because her family owned a cottage on Heartbreak Island, then he was barking up the wrong tree. "You'll have to read the *Howler* to see my article."

"Sure. I'll tell m' wife about it. Don't go finding any more dead bodies, right?"

She ignored him, merely asking, "I hope I can now have the plumbers finish my septic system?"

"Yup. Work away. That's what I asked you back here to tell you. You are free to finish your plumbing adventure. Good luck."

She returned home, parked the van and escaped, with Hoppy, back to the island. When she strode up the road toward Rose Tree Cottage, though, she saw that her sloping laneway was covered in muck, and some of the neighbors were standing around, examining it.

"What now?" she muttered, approaching.

❈ Ten ❈

THE "WHAT NOW" turned out to be the wreckage left by an excavator brought in by the police to dig up what had already been done by Robin's men, in search of any missed clues. They had blithely mowed down several saplings, part of a row of young poplar trees at the top of the Leighton cottage laneway. That row of saplings was the very reason Jaymie had had the plumbers access the joint backyard from the Redmonds' property in the first place.

With Hoppy securely locked inside, Jaymie examined the mess and fumed.

Ruby descended their sloped, terraced backyard, surveying the damage from her side of the devastation. "I'm so sorry, Jaymie!" she called out. "What a mess!"

"I suppose I should just be thankful that Robin and the guys hadn't laid all the pipe yet, so really, it's just a little extra mud moving they'll have to do. *If* I can get them away from Will, down at the marina."

Ruby circled the muddy expanse and approached. Jaymie

was shocked at how wan she looked, a ghostly gray, when usually she was healthy, if a little too tanned from hours on their sailboat, the *Heartbreak Kid*. "They've started work on the dredging, haven't they?"

"Yeah, I saw them moving the equipment in," Jaymie said. "How am I going to get them back for our piddly little job?"

"Garnet might be able to help," she said. "I'll have him call Will. I know they need to get moving with the harbor dredging and slip expansion, but you have to have this finished first. Especially if your future in-laws are going to come out here, eh?"

"Future in-laws?" Jaymie blurted. "Daniel and I don't have any plans."

Ruby smiled, a slightly sad expression. "Don't let him get away. I've met him, and he seems like the real deal."

Jaymie had the sense that there was a sad story behind Ruby's eyes. She wondered whether there was a lost love in her past. But still, her life was her life, and no one else's sad story could impact her. "I'm not rushing into anything. Not after Joel. I like Daniel a lot, but he's not my future husband. Not yet, anyway."

"I'll get Garnet to call the marina," Ruby said, squeezing her shoulder again. "And have Will send Robin and the guys back to finish up here."

"That would be great, Ruby," Jaymie said, at the same time wondering how the woman just *knew* that Garnet would have so much pull with Will. "I guess you guys are close?"

Ruby, who was heading back to her cottage, turned around and cocked her head. "What do you mean?"

"You must be close to Will Lindsay, if you figure Garnet can sway him." Jaymie remembered what Valetta had said; she felt like there was something about Ruby, or Garnet, or both of them, something they weren't revealing.

The other woman looked uneasy. "No, not particularly

close. But we do keep our boat in the marina, and Will is the one we deal with most."

"Understandable, with the way Urban behaved toward you, that you'd want to deal with Will more than that jerk. Was he always that hostile toward you and Garnet?"

She shrugged. "Urban was like that with everyone. We didn't avoid him, but we didn't seek him out. I had a feeling he was going to be moving on, anyway. The owner of the Boat House said Urban was in there talking to someone about buying the marina on the Canadian side of the island. That guy was always full of plans, though, and most of them didn't go anywhere. I've got to go if I'm going to catch Garnet and get him to talk to Will and Robin."

Ruby was as good as her word, and the plumbers were back that afternoon. They worked fiercely, with Robin shouting orders. One of the workers was a slim boy who looked to be working even harder than the older men. Jaymie was a little uncomfortable, knowing they were only working so hard to get done with her less profitable work and on to the big job, the marina. But darn it, she needed to have the leaching bed and septic system up and running. In another ten days or so they'd have more renters in the cottage; that was far more important a reason to hurry than her mother's wish to have the family dinner at the cottage.

Robin came up to talk to her late in the day, to tell her they were working overtime, and would be done that evening.

"Thank you so much, Rob. I really appreciate it."

"Hey, if we can get this off our schedule, I can get all of these guys working on the harbor and marina project."

"That young fellow, the teenager, looks like he's working harder than everyone else!"

"Yeah, he's a good kid. You know who that is?"

She shook her head. "But he looks familiar. He's one of your crew, right?"

"Yeah, but that's Urban Dobrinskie's son, Sammy."

"Really?" She was shocked. "How long has he been working for you?"

"All summer. He's going to college in September."

"He wasn't . . . Was he working here the day his dad . . . I mean, before his dad . . . ?" She let the question hang.

"Yup."

"Does he know his dad was killed here?"

Robin grimaced. "I *think* he knows, vaguely, but he probably doesn't know exactly where. And I'm not going to tell him."

Jaymie appreciated Robin's tact. "It must be hard on him right now, though, with his dad just murdered."

Robin glanced over at her, with a wry grin on his lips. "Urban was an asshole, and no one suffered more at his hands than Sammy. I had it out with the jerk once, told him to leave the kid alone. Urb didn't listen, of course. The kid is probably secretly doing the dance of joy."

Jaymie was shocked to her core. Her father was so important to her, she couldn't imagine being happy he was gone. Just the news that he'd had a cancer scare that he hadn't told her about was frightening. But for all anyone knew, Sammy was deeply saddened. Abused kids still loved their parents, some of them right up to the day they snapped and committed patricide. She was shocked by her train of thought, but she couldn't help it. Until the murder was solved, everyone was a potential suspect.

"Should he even be working today?"

"I told him to go home, but he didn't want to."

The boy was skinny, but wiry. After a summer of working for Robin, his bony arms were clothed in impressive biceps for one so slim. She remembered what Zack had said about having to tell Urban to back off from browbeating his son, and now Robin had added his independent testimony to the fact that Sammy and his dad had a troubled relationship. Had

Sammy had enough that fateful night, and done his dad in? The police would certainly be looking into that.

The day wore on, the sun beginning to descend in the sky; the workers took a dinner break. Garnet had sent food over for all of them from the restaurant, one of his many kind and generous gestures. Jaymie sat out on the grassy border of the muddy area with them, and listened to Robin describe what was left to be done. It was taking longer because of the damage done by the police team. Sammy Dobrinskie sat near Robin, wolfing down his burger and onion rings, and draining a large bottle of water.

"I was thinking of doing some landscaping, since we have the opportunity now," Jaymie said to Robin.

"As long as you don't run over the septic area with excavators once we're done, you'll be okay," Robin said. "The weight of the machine can crush pipes, even the new ones. Once the turf has packed in around them it'll be okay, but at first the area will be a little fragile."

"I have no clue what to do, but something like Garnet and Ruby's maybe." She gestured to their terraced lawn and seating area, gilded by the sun, which now hung low in the sky, casting a golden glow over everything.

"What do you think, Sammy?" Robin said, nudging the younger guy. "You're the landscape guy."

"You're into landscaping?" Jaymie asked.

The boy flushed scarlet, tossed his flop of sandy hair off his forehead, and ducked his head. "I did our backyard. D-Dad said it looked like shit."

"Your dad was wrong," Robin said. "I've seen it, and you did a great job." He turned to Jaymie. "His mom is into Asian influences, so he designed her a rock garden. Real Zen looking. It even has one of those areas where you rake patterns into the sand, you know?"

"Our property is k-kind of on a ravine, too," Sammy said, sitting up straight, his thin face lighting up with enthusiasm.

"The whole island is really a moraine left when the ice age receded, so there are these long grooves, and gravel deposits. I built a rock slope, with pockets of soil for plants, and we brought in all these mosses and alpines. I made her a waterfall to trickle through it, and found a kind of Chinese pagoda for the top."

"It sounds awesome," Jaymie said.

"Are you and your mom still thinking of leaving Heartbreak Island?" Robin asked, searching the boy's face.

He sighed and looked down at his muddy boots, scraping one against the other. The setting sun lit up streaks of bleached-out blond in his hair. "I don't know. If Mr. Redmond buys our share of the marina, like he wants, then Mom says she'll move to Oakland so she can be near me while I go to school. I'm registered at Oakland Community College for the Landscape Tech course this fall. But if things don't work out, I might not go for another year. I just can't leave her alone right now."

Jaymie was silent, but her mind was whirling. Garnet wanted to buy Dobrinskie's part of the marina?

Robin asked the question Jaymie was thinking. "Since when did Garnet Redmond want to buy out the marina?"

The boy said, "I don't know, but I heard him talking to Mr. Lindsay, and he said he was preparing an offer for Mom's lawyer."

"That's happening awful fast, isn't it?" Robin said.

Jaymie's thoughts exactly.

"Well, *I* don't want to run it, and Mom *can't*. It would kill her."

"I'd wait, if I was your mom," Robin advised. "Garnet may push for it to be resolved quickly—he's a good businessman, and sees an opportunity, I guess—but Will could get some help, and your mom could hold on to her share. Just my two cents." He stood, and put two fingers to his mouth, whistling. "C'mon, guys. We gotta get this done tonight so we can get back to the marina in the morning."

Some of the fellows groaned, as they stood, stretching out aching muscles, but they got back to work and two hours later, it was done. Jaymie had been working on her article on vintage picnics—and in fact she was pretty much done—but when she saw them packing up, she went outside and caught up with Sammy Dobrinskie.

"Hey, Sam," she said. "I'd be really interested in any ideas you might have for my backyard, now that the plumbing is done. Can we talk about it some time?"

"Yeah, sure," he said, a smile wreathing his face. "I've been thinking about it all day. I'll make a couple of sketches tonight, if you like."

That was more than she had hoped for. "Great. If you're going to be working at the marina tomorrow, can I come by there and bring you lunch, and you can show me your ideas?"

"S-sounds good."

"I'll pay you for your input," she said, suddenly. If this was going to be his profession, she ought not to expect his help for free.

He flushed and ducked his head. "Naw, that's okay."

Robin, coming up behind them, overheard and clapped him on the shoulder. "Never turn down money, son. You can use the sketches for course work at Oakland. Even better, I'll give you a little time free, if you want to work on it *with* Jaymie."

This was all going too fast. Jaymie had just planned to sod the area and *think* about landscaping, at some future point in time.

"Naw. I'll do some sketches, but she doesn't have to pay me."

"Let's talk about it tomorrow," Jaymie said. "Show me your ideas, and we'll take it from there."

They left it at that, but as darkness enfolded the cottage and Hoppy sniffed around the perimeter of the newly smoothed dirt along the slope of the yard, Jaymie sat on the back step and called her dad. He was all for giving the kid a shot at designing them a landscape scheme, and told her he trusted her judgment. He was adamant about one thing, and that was paying Sammy Dobrinskie for his work. No one should work for nothing, he said. She didn't tell him she was probably doing just that for the *Wolverhampton Howler.*

The next morning dawned gloomy, with an enervating tension in the air that was usually the precursor to a massive thunderstorm. It was such a relief that she could now use the cottage bathroom, that she cleaned it in celebration. The backyard still looked awful to her, a long muddy expanse that needed a lot of work. She was curious to see what Sammy Dobrinskie would come up with, and she was even more curious about Garnet Redmond's push to buy part ownership of the marina.

Did that give him a motive for murder? Or was it the insult to his sister, on top of his dislike of the man and the fellow's threats, that made murder seem like a viable option for the calm, cerebral Garnet Redmond? She pondered that, but just couldn't picture Garnet killing a man in cold blood. Maybe when he jumped in and offered to buy the Dobrinskie share of the marina, he was just taking advantage of the opportunity presented by the man's death. Perhaps he even thought he was helping out the widow and her son.

Jaymie made some salad, sandwiches and a batch of real lemonade, and piled it all in a basket, then, just after noon, leashed Hoppy, grabbed the basket and took a walk along the sandy beach that lined the river side of the island. Hoppy barked and dashed at the herring gulls that swooped overhead and bobbed upon the river. She approached the marina, where Robin's men were already working, crunching across the gravel that covered the slope up to the dock area. From what she understood, the whole affair of dredging the harbor and marina was complicated by the fact that on a small island, getting big equipment over was difficult, and sometimes impossible. They had to innovate, using the equipment on hand and a lot of backbreaking manual labor.

It was a busy place, and she saw that Garnet was there, standing with Will Lindsay and Robin, pointing and gesturing, as men do when they are intent on the important task at hand, whether it be building a barbecue or a skyscraper. Hoppy, with his long leash, bounced over to them and begged for attention at their feet, his one front paw stroking the air like a friendly wave hello. Garnet reached down to scratch the Yorkie-Poo behind the ear. Jaymie approached.

Robin grinned as she walked up to them. "Hey, Jaymie. Sammy is excited about your landscaping project. He won't tell you that himself, but take it from me, he is. It's nice that he has something to look forward to right now, with all this crap about his dad happening."

"My dad okayed paying him for any design work he does, and you mentioned he could use the project for his course work. Is that true?"

"Sure is. I went to see his mom last night, and she has pretty much decided to go with him to Bloomfield Hills, where the Oakland Community College campus is. She wants to get the hell out of here."

"Bad associations?"

He shrugged. "I just don't know. She's so upset and frazzled. I don't know what to make of it."

Will and Garnet had been talking as Robin spoke to her, but they called him back to their conference. "I'll tell Sammy to take his lunch break and show you his sketches," Robin called back to her, as he walked away with the other two men.

Jaymie chose a picnic table, as a rumble of thunder rolled across the sky. The air had that languid kind of humidity that often accompanies a low cloud cover, and she was glad she had dressed in shorts and a sleeveless tee. She put down a bowl of water for Hoppy, and spread a cloth on the rickety picnic table, unloading the plastic containers of food. Sammy Dobrinskie, his face and hair damp from washing up, approached the table shyly, looking off into the distance as he walked toward her with his clipboard under his arm.

"Hey, Sam," Jaymie called out. "I'm looking forward to seeing your sketches."

"It's not much," he said, tossing down the clipboard.

"Eat," Jaymie said, pushing the container of sandwiches and salad over to him, and waving her hand at the plates, paper towels and cutlery.

While he dove in, she examined his sketches, orienting herself first and figuring out his symbols. He had done a couple of different plans, and to her untutored eye, they looked remarkably professional. But she didn't completely understand.

He wolfed down a sandwich, eschewing the salad and taking another sandwich instead—Jaymie hadn't realized how much one skinny teenage boy could eat—and bounced around to sit beside her on the picnic table bench. The table squeaked in protest and shifted under them.

"Look, it's not to scale, because I didn't take measurements," he mumbled around a mouthful of chicken salad sandwich. "But here is your cottage, and there is Mr. and Miss Redmond's cottage. I roughed in their terraces—I know you think they look good, but they should have done something a little different; doesn't matter, though—and then showed your property. You've got this cool opportunity here," he said, pointing with the end of a pencil, "to add a water feature, before you lay sod . . . you know, the piping and electric. And you said something about a seating area. Down here near that grouping of trees, you could do a flagstone patio—you don't need a gazebo because you've got natural shelter—with the water feature near it. You'd want a path snaking around to a low stone wall," he added, "so people can sit by the fountain."

"A fountain?"

"Yeah, the water feature . . . I see a fountain. You could

either have one coming out of a stone wall, or a freestanding one in the middle of a small patio. It would be like a grotto . . . you know, back in the day rich folks had a grotto on their property. You could do, like, a miniature version."

It appealed to her. She read historical romances, and she pictured the grottos where romantic couples often got frisky. "Isn't that a lot of work?" she asked. And expensive, she thought.

He shrugged and swallowed a long gulp of lemonade. "I say, do some of this now," he said, pointing to the patio and landscaping, "and work in the other aspects as you have time. But you should lay in the electricity and water pipes now, cap them, and they'll be ready to put in a water feature."

"What about winter? Won't they freeze?"

"You'd have to winterize it. Robin can tell you how."

"That's a good idea." She looked over the drawings, and noticed that he had worked up a couple of plans, one with, and one without, the water feature. He saw her land sloping down to a terrace, with a circular stone patio in the shade of the copse of alders. The crab apple trees were gone, she noticed. He used gentle curving lines for gardens, and had sketched in some perennial plants. At the edge of the sketches was a list of suggested plantings, many of which she had never heard of.

When she asked him about that, he colored faintly. "I did a lot of research, when mom and I were doing the garden. Some of these we used; some we didn't. You've got more shade than we do."

Jaymie considered the nervous, frail Evelyn Dobrinskie, and tried to imagine her and her slim son working on a garden together, bonded by their mutual love of landscaping. And bonded also by their fear of Urban Dobrinskie?

Shouting down by the marina made them both focus on the workers, those who were already back to work. Robin had run over, and several others, including Will Lindsay, joined them. "I wonder what's going on?" Jaymie said aloud.

"I don't know, but I'll find out." Sammy sprinted off.

Hoppy yapped excitedly, and Jaymie untied his leash and followed the teenager at a more sedate pace, with Hoppy dancing and tugging at the end of the leash.

She approached the small crowd, and saw them pulling something out of the harbor.

"That's my wheelbarrow," Robin shouted, one hand on his hip, the other thrust into his mop of reddish brown hair. "Who the hell dropped it into the harbor?"

❧ Eleven ❧

JAYMIE WAS STILL puzzling over that, as she caught the ferry for home. The easiest explanation was that some drunken weekender had seen the wheelbarrow, taken a joy ride in it, and ended up down at the marina. Dumping it in the drink may have seemed like fun, to an alcohol-fuzzed brain. But the wheelbarrow was taken from her job site, which was *behind* her cottage. It was private property; what had someone been doing wandering around there?

It made her shiver. It was weird that a veritable crime wave—first thefts, and then murder—had been happening in her backyard, while she slept just yards away.

As she disembarked at the ferry landing in the marina on the Queensville side, she had Sammy's sketches in her bag, as well as her almost finished article on vintage picnics. She was heading home eventually, but her first stop, digital camera in hand, was the Emporium.

She put Hoppy in the puppy pen—the little protective pen between Jewel's Junk and the Emporium—with his best buddy, Junk Jr., a bichon mix who belonged to Jewel, owner of the upscale, boutiquey junk shop next to the Emporium, then entered the dim old grocery variety store, the wood floors making their usual *thunk* sound with each footstep. She said hello to Mrs. Klausner, who nodded and knitted on, wordless, and checked out the vintage picnic basket rental book. The weekend was coming; there were several rentals that she had to prepare for. She used the store phone to call over to the Queensville Inn, and arranged for the appropriate food to be delivered, and called, also, for reservations at the Wolver-hampton Winery, where one of the basket renters wanted to have their picnic.

She rearranged the basket display and stood back, gazing at the checked red cloth spilling out of the vintage wicker basket, as she swiped some tendrils of hair off her sweaty neck. The afternoon was hot and close, the kind of humid air that makes everyone jumpy in their own skin. Too many days of heat and high humidity made her think about autumn with longing, so the occasional cooler breeze was exciting, a sensory warning of nature's plans to shut down leaf production and bring vivid color to their green and blue world. Jaymie had already started thinking about autumn picnics, since there were those day trippers in the area who liked to do a color tour. Baskets could feature the chef at the inn's Brie en Croute, and Tarte aux Pommes, and the winery's maple wine. Yum!

After a sweaty summer, she also looked forward to autumnal sweater weather because that would mean her mom and dad, and presumably Daniel's parents—unless they bought a house and stayed in Queensville, dread thought— would all have departed for warmer climes, and she could get on with the tasks at hand: building a career as a food writer and figuring out what there was between her and Daniel. She had until Christmas or so, the deadline they had given themselves to figure out what they both wanted. More properly, what *she* wanted. Daniel had been quite clear about what *he* wanted, a relationship, with all the trimmings.

Valetta closed her pharmacy office and joined Jaymie, staring at the picnic basket displayed on the shelf behind the cashier's counter. Finally, she said, "Is there a reason we are glaring at these poor baskets as if they've done something dastardly?"

Jaymie laughed, and even dour Mrs. Klausner smiled.

"I'm just lost in thought, I guess." She related her musings regarding autumnal baskets, and Daniel, and their parents. "Once they go back to Florida, I won't see them until we all meet up at Grandma Leighton's and Becca's for Canadian Thanksgiving."

"That's October, right?"

"Yeah. Second Monday."

"So . . . are you going to stare at the baskets all day?"

Jaymie shook herself and smiled. "No. I'm actually here for a purpose." She explained having to rethink her first article for the *Howler*, and said, "So, Nan Goodenough okayed me using the vintage picnic baskets idea. I need to do this quickly, though, because I have to turn it in as soon as possible, pictures and all."

"I've got a few minutes to help. What do we do?"

Jaymie said, "I think I'll use that picnic table behind the Emporium, the one in the shade of the oak, as a staging area."

Valetta helped her lug out picnic baskets, linens and a couple of sets of melamine dishes. Starting with the vintage wicker basket that she used only for display—it was too fragile for renters to use, and too valuable—she laid out a scene at the base of the old oak tree, with a red-and-white-checked tablecloth spilling out of the basket. She retrieved the lacquered fake "baguette" and wine bottle she used for display, and set up the red and white melamine in a "picnic for two: display. She photographed it, then set to work setting up a second display on the old wood picnic table, using one of the red-and-black plaid tin picnic baskets.

"It needs something," she said, staring at it. She raced back to the store and grabbed a beach ball, sand buckets, and a few more kid's toys. Finally, when she was happy, she photographed the family picnic scene.

"So, you're happy with the article?"

Jaymie shrugged. "It still needs work."

"What food are you going to use for the story?"

"You'll see!"

"In other words," Valetta said, "you have no idea yet."

As they packed the stuff up to take back inside, Valetta asked her about the cottage plumbing, and Jaymie told her it was done, and explained Sammy's sketches. They took a break on the Emporium veranda and had a cup of tea, while Valetta looked over the sketches. She pronounced herself impressed.

"Something else odd happened," Jaymie said, sticking out her bare feet and wiggling them in the sunshine. "Garnet Redmond is pressuring Urban Dobrinskie's widow to sell him their half share of the marina."

Valetta's eyes widened. "Really? Didn't know he was ever interested in *that*."

"Me neither," Jaymie mused. "Robin says she should keep it. Will Lindsay could get someone to help him run the marina, he says. But I guess Garnet wants it pretty bad."

Valetta chewed her lip and tapped her fingernails on her tea mug. "Did he ever try to buy it from Urban?"

"Good question," Jaymie said. "I don't know." It made her feel a little hinky inside, wondering whether her pleasant backyard neighbor at the cottage was really a scheming killer. She was suspecting Garnet, but she just couldn't overlook Ruby's words that night.

Why had Ruby said, "I didn't mean to do it"? Jaymie hadn't told anyone about that, not even Valetta. She just couldn't, and she didn't quite understand why, except that she knew what it was like to have the police examining your every move, thinking you'd killed someone when you hadn't. She just could not believe Ruby was a murderer, and it didn't feel right to expose her to the police for something Jaymie had accidentally overheard. If she was the murderer, which Jaymie doubted, there would be other evidence.

After her tea break with Valetta, Jaymie retrieved Hoppy and headed home, to find that the war between the moms was heating up. Her mother was stiff with anger and slamming dishes around in the kitchen, but it took some prying to get the source of the trouble out of her. It was a phone call, she said, from Mrs. Collins, in which that woman not-so-subtly implied (according to her mother) that the Leightons should accede to her wishes and have the family dinner at Stowe House because Daniel had a lot of money.

"Mom, she can't have said that."

"It's not what she said; it's what she meant," her mother said, drying the last dish and shoving it into the cupboard.

Jaymie cringed at the cupboard door slamming, and exited to the backyard to find her dad.

He shrugged helplessly when asked about it. "I don't know, honey. I wasn't even here," he said, as he put the lawn mower away in the garage. "We came back from our foursome this morning," he said, and rolled his eyes. Alan Leighton did not like golfers who weren't serious about the game, and neither Jaymie's mom nor Daniel's was a serious golfer. "Then Roger and I went back to the club to play nine holes with Grant Watson." Mimi and Grant Watson were the Leightons' next-door neighbors and best friends both in Queensville and Boca Raton, where they wintered, like the Leightons did. "The women seemed to get along fine on the golf course this morning, but I came back in just as she slammed the phone down after talking to Debbie Collins. She's been like that ever since. She won't tell me what's wrong."

"But you know how she gets. Is Mom getting bent out of shape over nothing? I just don't know," Jaymie said.

"Don't talk about me as if I'm automatically in the wrong," her mother said.

Jaymie whirled around to find her mother standing on the flagstone path, her arms folded over her chest. "Mom,

I don't automatically think you're wrong. Mrs. Collins can be difficult."

"Difficult? Ha! You don't know the half of it. You should have heard her this morning. Your father thinks everything went swimmingly? You should have *heard* how condescending that woman was, how . . . how *snippy*! Mrs. Butter-wouldn't-melt-on-her-tongue! She has no intention of doing anything but *exactly* what she wants."

"I know that. But I'm trying to figure out what to do about it."

"There's nothing *to* do. We will have the family dinner at Rose Tree Cottage, as always. They can come or not; I don't really care." She turned and started up the walk.

"Mom, we need to find a compromise!"

"That ship has sailed!" she said, with a flippant wave of her hand.

Jaymie rolled her eyes and turned back to her father. "Dad, you have no clue what our cottage looks like right now. It's awful! If we plan to have a family dinner out there, I'd really like to make it look at least . . . I don't know, passable? But Mom doesn't seem to care."

"You know your mother; once she gets a bee in her bonnet." He shook his head. "She can't give in now, or she'll lose face."

"She's not a samurai warrior, and she won't have to commit hara-kiri if we don't do dinner at Rose Tree Cottage."

She went up to her room and called Daniel's house, praying that he answered, and not his mom. He did. "Daniel, we need to talk," she said, tersely.

"Is everything okay?" he asked, panic in his voice.

"Yeah, fine, but we need to talk family dinner. Can we meet somewhere? After dinner?"

They agreed to meet up at the park band shell much later, after Jaymie got back from the auction she was attending with Bernie and Heidi. "I'll call you when I get home," she said, and hung up. Sitting cross-legged on her bed, she reflected on the many times over the years that she had holed up in her room after a fight with her mother. She was thirty-two, not twelve, but when her parents were back in their room down the hall, twenty years seemed to disappear like a handful of feathers blown away by a puff of air.

SHE WAS SET to meet Bernie and Heidi at an auction house in the country. It was once a barn, but MacKenzie and Sons had purchased it a few years before, and had renovated it to use as their auction house. It was big enough, and with huge sliding doors above a ramp, so it could be used even for farm machinery and recreation vehicles.

She pulled her beat-up van into place in the muddy parking lot, which was really just a field near the barn. It must have rained out here, not unusual in Michigan; it could be sunny and bright in one spot, and a few miles away could pour. Given the heat and humidity, it was only a miracle it hadn't poured over Queensville, too.

The place was not that busy, which might mean she'd get something for a decent price. She signed in, got her buyer number, then entered the vast barn and scanned the widely dispersed crowd for her friends. They stood together near the auctioneer's podium. Bernie and Heidi were as physically contrasting a pair as ever there was. Bernie was round-faced and stocky, with close-cropped unstraightened hair, chunky gold earrings and little makeup on her mocha skin. Heidi was slim and pale, with blushed cheeks, mascaraed lashes and chandelier earrings dangling in the midst of blond, straight hair.

Jaymie waved hello to them, but then raced up and down the long tables of box lots and around the perimeter where the larger items sat, to do a quick scan of the auction items. It seemed to be a mishmash of estate relics and garage sale leavings. There was nothing for her kitchen, which was a good thing, but there *was* a collection of patio furniture from the sixties and later. She stopped to examine it more closely.

There were quite a few items in one lot, several white-painted wrought iron chairs and a table; the paint was flaking, but the whole lot, with intricate roses in the ironwork, had an authentic shabby chic look that she loved. She thought of Cynthia Turbridge's store, the Cottage Shoppe; this was just the kind of thing she'd love for the backyard! But Jaymie wasn't going to give it up. *Mine,* she thought. *All mine.* She practically rubbed her hands together over it.

There was a newer double glider that was made to look like an antique, and some random chairs and small tables, too. If she could get it for a good price, she'd buy the lot for the cottage and the new patio. She might not be able to use it all, but she could think about that later. Whatever she didn't want could easily be sold to Cynthia. Jaymie wrote down the lot number.

As she was getting ready to walk away, she spotted a box piled high with what looked like china dishes. When she got closer, though, she saw that they were really all made of enameled tin, pretty bowls and mugs and plates in white enamel with pale sky blue edging and bunches of painted posies in the center. She took some out; made in Mexico! Interesting. There was another box with larger pieces in it, mostly white with a red rim, big bowls and basins and a pitcher, as well as a coffeepot and kettle.

She had spent some time with the magazines Cynthia had loaned her, and noted that shabby chic seemed to be embodied by lots of white and pastels, or pops of vivid color; overall the style was characterized by a pretty airiness. For the kitchen, Jaymie was going to advise Cynthia to use dotted Swiss for the curtains, and furnish it with a vintage Arborite dinette set, but until this moment she hadn't really figured out about the dishes. These enamelware dishes would be perfect! She could see an enamel coffeepot on the stove, and as she dug in the box she found even more stuff . . . canisters and bowls, many with a gingham print design in enamel paint. The blues and pinks were so pretty, it was impossible to resist. She'd have to see whether she could get the stuff cheap. She already knew she had a stack of vintage linens that Cynthia could sell in her Cottage Shoppe kitchen.

As the auctioneer started on a box lot of tools, she moved to join Heidi and Bernie. "Hey, guys, how's it going?" They exchanged brief hugs and chatted, since the items up for bids at that moment were not interesting to them yet.

"You see anything you want?" Bernie asked Jaymie.

She told them about her need for patio furniture, that the lot she was going to bid on would satisfy, and mentioned the new vintage store soon to open, and how she was buying up some stuff for it. It wasn't the kind of place Heidi or Bernie was interested in, though, since their style was more sleek and modern than cottagey. They tuned back in to the auctioneer's spiel. Bernie was bidding on a teak sideboard for her dining room. She and Heidi were both collectors of mid-century modern, though Heidi, as a trust fund baby, could afford to shop at a much higher level than Bernie. When the teak piece came up, it escalated fairly quickly, and Jaymie thought for sure Bernie would drop out; instead, she hung back, bidding only at the last moment. Jaymie watched as competing bidders covertly examined Bernie, who ignored them, appearing calm and determined. One by one the others dropped out. She got the sideboard, and at a decent price.

"Congrats, Bernie!" Heidi said, leaning toward her friend and patting her shoulder.

The police officer was flushed with happiness. "I got it!" She hopped in place. "Now I need to get a few hours of overtime to afford it!"

"How is the murder case going?" Heidi asked, glancing sideways at Jaymie, eyebrows raised.

Jaymie held her breath and listened in.

"The detectives definitely have a suspect in mind,"

Bernie said. "But you know I can't say who; don't ask me. I can't gossip about that stuff. It's worth my job!"

Jaymie thought quickly. "Well, the spouse is *always* a suspect. But I've met Evelyn Dobrinskie; she couldn't hurt a flea."

"Never be taken in by a frail-looking lady," Bernie replied, with raised brows and a quirky grin. "A determined woman can do anything she wants."

That could equally as well go for Ruby Redmond. Was Bernie hinting at who the police suspected? Jaymie turned her attention back to the auction stage; her first lot was coming up. She scanned the crowd quickly, and unfortunately recognized a few other cottage owners from the island. Were they there for the patio furniture? She hadn't even had time to really evaluate the furniture, but she had a feeling about it, and bid aggressively, quickly upping the price, hoping that discouraged others. It seemed to work, and though she paid more than she had wanted, for the amount of furniture there was, she got a good price. She got the enamelware, too, for a pittance.

"Good for you!" Heidi said, and Bernie high-fived her.

"I'll see if I've done well when I get the furniture delivered. That's going to cost me, too, considering I have to find someone to take it all over to the island."

The auction moved on, but nothing interested them and after another half hour, all three women were done.

"There's nothing there for me," Heidi said, and they all headed out.

Jaymie and Bernie paid for their purchases, and the three walked out into the misty, humid night to their vehicles. Bernie and Heidi had come together in Bernie's silver sedan. The police officer had carried one of Jaymie's boxes for her, so she shoved the one she was carrying in first, then took the box from Bernie, clunking it down in the back of the van by the other one. She slammed the doors shut and turned back to her friends.

"Come out for a drink with us," Heidi said to Jaymie,

touching her arm. "The bar at Ambrosio serves mai tais!" She and Bernie were into retro drinks and barware, and their newest kick was drinks from the fifties and sixties.

"I can't. I asked Daniel to take a walk with me later. I need to talk to him about the family dinner and our moms. There is a war brewing." She explained what she meant to Bernie, who looked mystified.

"Yikes," she said, making a face. "I don't envy you. I broke up with a guy once because my mother hated him."

"At least Mom and Dad like Daniel, but Mrs. Collins is difficult, and my mom isn't much better. They're like a couple of mob bosses, competing for territory. I feel like going into hiding."

They parted ways, and Jaymie drove back to Queensville. She decided to leave the enamelware in the back of the van until she had time to deliver it to Cynthia's store.

The house was empty; her parents were next door playing euchre with the Watsons. She could hear their voices floating out of the kitchen window of the Watsons' home. Jaymie stopped only long enough to call Daniel, grab Sammy's plans for the cottage and leash her pooch. Darkness had fully enveloped the town by the time she started out toward Boardwalk Park. Hoppy tugged at the leash, sniffing at the peemail he had missed over the last few days of island hopping. She made her way to the band shell, and tied Hoppy's leash off, letting him wander around on a long lead, while she sat and examined Sammy's plans for the cottage landscaping by the band shell light.

"Hey," Daniel said, from the bottom of the steps.

"Hey," she replied, examining his face, the overhead light glinting in his glasses lenses. She saw the same exasperated "My parents are driving me insane" look that she saw when she looked in the mirror.

He joined her, gave her a quick kiss, then sat beside her and slung his arm around her over the bench back. "Whatcha got?"

She explained the landscape designs that Sammy had drawn up, and he looked them over. His mathematical, neat mind seemed to grasp the complexities immediately, and though he pointed out a couple of problems with Sammy's design, overall he praised it. "The kid's got potential, it looks like. His sketching is really good. I'll bet he's taken drafting."

"And he's so enthusiastic. It's clear he loves this stuff. His dad apparently was not too supportive." She explained about Urban Dobrinskie, and what Sammy had said about his father ridiculing his work. Hesitantly, she also told him what Zack Christian had said, about intervening when the man was bullying his son.

There was silence between them for a long moment. Did Daniel know that the detective had an annoying ability to send her heart rate into the triple digits? She sure hoped not; it was her guilty secret. The response was purely physical—the detective was extremely good-looking—but that would not be reassuring for the slightly awkward, gawky, beaky computer software mogul. She had never thought of herself as shallow, but clearly she was, at least in some ways. Luckily, it seemed that she was beginning to be immune to Zack Christian's presence. In time, the effect would wear off completely.

Finally, she said, "What I can't decide is, would Sammy Dobrinskie have the strength and the anger and the . . . I don't know . . . guts? To kill his father."

A look of alarm narrowed Daniel's eyes and set two exclamation marks between his sandy brows. He examined her face over the top of his glasses, then pushed them up on his nose. "Jaymie, you're not investigating again, are you?"

"Of course not. You make it sound like I've taken up a Nancy Drew obsession. But I can't exactly ignore it; it happened right in the backyard of one of my two favorite places in the world!"

"I know," he said, hugging her to him.

She turned around on the bench and looked up into his eyes. He had a calmness about him. Daniel Collins was one of those no-nonsense individuals who are endowed with an expansive heart and compassionate nature. She appreciated his rationality and ability to examine any problem and come up with a solution. "Change of subject. What *are* we going to do about our mothers, Daniel?"

"Mine doesn't really have a problem," said compassionate, rational Daniel. "It's *yours* that is causing all the trouble."

"*My* mother? She's just reacting to . . ." She stopped, took a deep breath and let it out slowly. "I don't think you meant that how it sounded," she said, carefully.

"I don't know, Jaymie," he said, with an exasperated sigh. "All I'm hearing is how stubborn your mom is being. I mean, why *does* the dinner have to be at the cottage? Why not my place? Or even *your* house here in town?"

"Or 'even' my house? You make it sound like a barn!" Although this was much the conversation she had had with her parents, from him, it was annoying. "Okay, I'm going to ignore that word 'even.' The reason my mom is adamant, is that it's always been that way. She's a stickler for tradition, and why shouldn't she be? She only gets up here a few times a year, so why *shouldn't* we do the family dinner out at the cottage, like we always do?"

"Maybe because, by your own reckoning, the backyard of the cottage looks like a strip mining site."

"I'm looking for solutions, Daniel, not reasons to crush my mom's wishes!"

"Be reasonable, Jaymie. She has to be realistic. Why knock yourself out when we could just as easily do the dinner at Stowe House?"

"Thus giving your mom *her* way!"

"That's not my intent," he said at last. He pulled her back into the circle of his arms. "Look, if this is a big deal to you, let's work it out."

She thought about it. It *was* a big deal, and she did want to work it out. All of it, including her relationship with Daniel. Taking her wishes into consideration, Daniel finally started helping her brainstorm solutions. Compromise, in Jaymie's book, was extremely important.

After another hour or so of chat and a little kissing, they walked home along darkened streets, with a weary Hoppy tucked up in Daniel's arms. "So we'll go over to the island tomorrow morning, and survey the damage," he said, confirming the plan they had finally worked out. "I'll call the guys who do my landscaping and ask for quote on sod, and if they'll include delivery over to the island."

"And I'll enlist my dad and Grant Watson, if I can, to help with some of the other stuff," she added. "We ought to know in a couple of days if we'll be able to get the place up to scratch to hold a family dinner there."

"I'll see if my dad wants to help."

They stopped in front of Jaymie's home and she turned around in his arms. "Thanks, Daniel. I really appreciate your support." She threaded her fingers through his thick sandy hair, and they kissed good night. Then she took her sleepy little doggie off his hands, and went into her house.

❊ Twelve ❊

THE NEXT MORNING Jaymie called Daniel to arrange what time to meet him at the ferry dock, but he was in crisis containment mode. There was some kind of big blow-up at his company headquarters, and he was actually in the middle of a Skype conference with his management team in Phoenix. As the owner and president of a software development corporation, he should not really be living so far away from the head office, but with the sophistication of modern technology, his "office" was just a video conference or Skype call away.

So Jaymie was once more on her way down to the marina, with just Hoppy for company, to catch the ferry over to Heart-break Island. She had decided that some of the enamelware would fit in perfectly at the cottage, so she had a shopping bag full of the pretty dishes, and they clanked against her leg as she walked. Waiting on the dock for the ferry were Heidi and Joel. Not long ago the sight of them together would have crushed Jaymie's heart into little pieces. Heidi was the kind of girl who had once intimidated a younger Jaymie. Her clothes were fashionable, though understated, and her makeup was impeccable. She came from money; one look told the casual observer that, from the solid gold bangles on her slim wrist, to the pricey footwear on her feet.

Her family had once been Queensvillians. Her great-great-some number of times-grandfather, Homer Lockland, had been the owner of the hardware store that was now an Ace Hardware. Homer moved to New York City and made his millions in real estate, and the rest was history. A fuzzier, more recent history was Heidi's odd decision to buy a house in Queensville. Why had she decided to perch in such a backwater, when she was clearly accustomed to the finer things in life, like mani-pedis and shopping at Barneys? Not that Queensville was hopelessly rustic; it was as sophisticated as a smallish touristy Michigan town could be, but it was no New York City.

Her "theft" of Jaymie's live-in boyfriend, Joel, was by now ancient history to many, though it had happened less than a year before. Finding out two things helped the process of Jaymie's recovery from the wretchedness of heartbreak. One: Heidi was a truly sweet girl; good-natured, bubbly, not a mean bone in her body. Two: Joel was kind of a jerk; self-centered, conceited and most definitely condescending. Without the blinders of love Jaymie saw his feet of clay, and was grateful to be out of his circle of influence. Given another six months with him, she probably would have come to the same conclusion, that he was not the dreamboat she had thought him. His attraction to Heidi may partly have been because they both worshipped the same object, *him*, and his "brilliance."

"Hey, Jaymie!" Heidi called out, waving.

As soon as he saw Joel, Hoppy whined and yapped. His complete adoration for Joel was still a mystery to Jaymie. She took the sloping walk down to the dock and let her little dog have a long lead; he wriggled over to Joel, who squatted down and petted the little dog's head while his current girl-friend and ex-girlfriend chatted.

"What are you two doing down here?" Jaymie asked. When she had seen Heidi the night before, the girl hadn't said anything about going out to the island.

Heidi gave a little hop, and said, "Guess what? Joel planned this big surprise. We're going over to the island to look at a sailboat that's for sale."

"Really? I didn't know you sailed."

Heidi colored, prettily. "Actually, my boarding school had a sailing team. It's the one sport I'm good at."

"Why am I not surprised?" Jaymie said, drily. Joel looked up at her sharply, but she smiled down at him.

"Yeah, Brewster has a great curriculum!"

"So now you're going to buy a sailboat?"

Joel stood. "The owner died, and the widow needs the money. I told Heidi it could be our good deed for the day!"

"Wait . . . are you going to look at the *Sea Urchin*? Urban Dobrinskie's boat?"

Heidi looked down at Joel, a question in her eyes.

"Yeah," Joel acknowledged. "It must be a good boat; it almost beat the Redmonds this year. With a better crew, it may just do it next year."

The ferry, aptly named the *Ferry Queene* by its erudite owner, pulled into the marina and disgorged the few passengers near the small boathouse that held the customs office. Jaymie, Heidi and Joel strolled down to line up with the ten or so other passengers going to Heartbreak Island or Johnsonville, Ontario.

The day was getting warm already; the stormy weather of the previous day had been cleared out by a heavy thunderstorm in the night, so the humidity had eased, even as the wet earth perfumed the air. "I didn't know you were such a sailor, Joel," Jaymie remarked, shading her eyes and watching him.

"He was first in his class in college, right, honey?" Heidi said.

"Sure," Joel said, heartily. "Say, heard you had a little trouble out at the cottage?"

"Yeah, I guess you could call murder 'a little trouble,'" Jaymie said, sharply. She looked away, feeling a slow flush rise in her cheeks. Mention of the cottage from Joel reminded her of when things were better between them. Last summer, Joel and her parents had enjoyed the annual family dinner at Rose Tree Cottage. After that, everything seemed to go bad, and now she knew why. Heidi moved to Queensville in September, and she and Joel had met some time that month. He had made some excuse not to go to Canada with her for Canadian Thanksgiving, in October, and she surmised that he and Heidi had had their first real intimate "date" that weekend. By American Thanksgiving it was finished between her and Joel, though she didn't learn that until a couple of weeks before Christmas. She was over it, and over him, but preferred to forget the whole episode.

They climbed aboard the ferry, Hoppy staggering a bit on the ramp. Jaymie picked him up and found a seat on the prow, which was lined with benches, setting her clunky bag down under the seat. Heidi and Joel followed. Jaymie didn't talk much on the way over, though she did haltingly comment on the Dobrinskies' selling of the *Sea Urchin*. As they pulled into the marina she saw Sammy there, along with Will Lindsay, both dressed in better-than-average clothes. It soon became apparent that Will was helping Sammy in the potential sale of the boat. Sammy smiled at Jaymie and waved, shyly.

"Can we talk in a while, Sam?" she said. "About the landscaping?"

He nodded, and turned back to Will, who was talking to Joel and Heidi. They all walked down to a slip where the Sea Urchin bobbed in serene beauty. Jaymie strolled over to Robin, who was leaning against an excavator looking at a clipboard. She let Hoppy have a length of his lead, and he happily sniffed at a clump of bushes where dock doggies would have left peemail.

"Hey, Robin."

"Hey, Jaymie."

"I came over on the ferry with Joel Anderson and Heidi Lockland. So Sammy and his mom are selling the *Sea Urchin*? I guess Joel and Heidi are looking at it today."

Robin looked up and smiled. "Yeah. Sammy never really liked sailing anyway. If they can sell the *Sea Urchin*, it'll help with his college costs."

"You've known Sammy for a while," Jaymie said. "He seems like such a nice kid, but with a dad like Urban . . . that can't have been easy on him. Or his mother!"

"He *is* a nice kid, and a hard worker, but his mom . . . She's a little odd. I know she loves her son, but . . ."

"How do you mean, 'odd'?"

He shook his head, then glanced around, hunkered closer to her, and said, "I've never told this to anyone, but from what I understand, Evelyn used to follow Urban when he went on his little 'dates,' you know?" He waggled his unruly eyebrows.

"Why is that 'odd'?" Jaymie asked, not surprised that Urban was widely known to have outside interests. The island was small, and people talk. But who was he cheating with? Ruby, as Brock Nibley had asserted?

Robin's brown eyes widened and he reared back. "You mean you're not surprised?"

"That a woman would tail her cheating louse of a spouse? No." An unacknowledged ribbon of anger in the pit of her stomach, left over from Joel's cheating on her, surfaced. "Maybe she wasn't sure. Maybe she wanted details." Maybe she was planning on divorcing him, but murder seemed simpler?

Zack Christian walked toward them, that moment, in just his swim trunks and with his towel over his shoulders. Just then a shout from his men called Robin away, and Jaymie was left with a shirtless Zack.

"How is the investigation going?" she asked, trying not to stare at his chest, chiseled abs and all.

"Why? You want to come work for us?" he joked, using the towel to dry his arms and stomach.

Sweat or river water, she wondered, distracted; what liquid was racing in droplets down his chest? *Focus, Jaymie,* she commanded herself. "Zack, this is important to me. That cottage is my . . . my haven."

"You need a getaway from the hustle and bustle of Queensville, Michigan, so you cross a few yards of water and camp out?"

She eyed him speculatively. Was he distracting her from the investigation by throwing bon mots her way? Not-so-witty repartee as a diversion? "So, was Urban murdered with that ice pick or not?"

"You know I can't give you that information," he said. Hoppy trotted over to sniff his leg and the detective watched him, warily. "He won't pee on my leg, will he?"

She rolled her eyes. Good grief. "He doesn't cock his leg and pee against things like most male dogs. Not very well, anyway. He's a little wobbly, being a 'tripod' as one of my friends calls him." She was not going to be deflected. "Okay, assuming it was the ice pick, how much strength would it take to push that thing in deep enough to kill him? Would a woman be able to do it?"

"Depends on the woman," he said, shifting impatiently. "Look, Jaymie, I have to go. This was just a break, and I'm late for work." He whirled and strode away, his shoulders set in an angry line.

What had she done to set him off? She shook her head; no telling. She pondered her ice pick query. The tool was sharp, even though it was old, so surely it wouldn't take that much strength to push it in, as long as one didn't hit bone. She shuddered, a little alarmed at the way her mind was working these days. Heck, if she was home, she'd do a little research on the Internet—she was becoming quite proficient at finding out esoteric information—or ask around, but out here, she was Internet-less. It occurred to her in that moment, though, that if the ice pick was the weapon, it really did limit the number of people who had access to it. The last she had seen it, it was in Garnet's hand, so Garnet and Ruby were the most obvious. Would Evelyn Dobrinskie or her son even have been able to get ahold of it?

That was the sticking point for her, the one thing that kept her coming back to Garnet and Ruby Redmond. How could the murderer be anyone else, if the ice pick was the weapon?

Hoppy whined, so she moved along, the heavy bag bumping against her leg, clanking like a bag of tin cans; she let Hoppy sniff farther afield along a line of ornamental shrubs that bordered the customs shed, while she pondered the possible murder weapon. What had Garnet done with the ice pick when she was done photographing it? She couldn't just assume the murder weapon was the ice pick. With all the fuss over the drill bit that was found near where Urban's body lay, she had to wonder, could the same damage come from a drill bit as an ice pick?

It was all too confusing, and she didn't know the folks involved well enough. But one thing she was sure of: to kill someone with either the drill bit or the ice pick would require close quarters and a cool, brutal side to one's personality. It wasn't like a shooting, where the perpetrator could commit the crime from some distance, or poison, where you didn't need to see the victim die. No, this was up close and personal.

Sammy and the others wandered back to the dock area and stood talking for a few minutes. Heidi saw Jaymie, and said something to Joel, then sprinted over to join her.

"Are you buying the boat?" Jaymie asked.

"I think so!" she said, bouncing up and down, her silky

hair flying out in a wave. Hoppy yapped and danced around, and she laughed. "It depends on Joel. He's making the deal now. It's so exciting!"

Jaymie had known Joel awhile, and never once had he expressed any interest in, or even any acquaintance with, sailing, but it wasn't up to her to break that news to Heidi. "Well, good luck."

"It's been a couple of years since I sailed. I think I'll need a refresher, some lessons or something. I asked the kid if he would take us out so I could see how she handles." She glanced back at the guys. "He looked a little hesitant."

"I don't think he's fond of sailing," Jaymie said. "Robin—that's the owner of the plumbing company that's excavating the harbor; Sammy has worked for him all summer—said as much. His dad used to bully and berate him, and maybe that's his only memory of sailing."

"Aw, poor kid!" Heidi said, quick to empathize, as always. She picked Hoppy up and cuddled him against her cheek. "Why would any daddy do that to his 'ittle boy," she said, her voice skirting dangerously close to baby talk territory. Hoppy, of course, loved it and wriggled, licking her face. She giggled.

"Heidi, if you guys are going back to the Dobrinskies to do anything—sign papers, or hand over money—can I come? I . . . I'd like to see the landscape work that Sammy has done."

Her head cocked to one side, Heidi asked, "Why don't you just ask to see his work?"

The straightforward approach; it had its merits. "I never thought of that until now." The guys were coming toward them. She knew Heidi was eyeing her with curiosity, and she realized that Heidi was likely not up to speed on all the relationships, but it was too late to explain.

"Hey, sweetie, it's all set," Joel said, putting his arm around Heidi and squeezing, scruffing Hoppy's head with his free hand. "We are the proud new owners of the *Sea Urchin*!"

"Congrats, Joel, on achieving your lifelong dream," Jaymie said, her tone laden with sarcasm. "Didn't you always talk about sailing the seven seas, or . . . something?"

He shot her a quelling look. "When I found out how much Heidi loves sailing, well . . . this seemed perfect. It'll be a wedding present."

A wedding present. Confused, Jaymie said, "From whom to whom?"

Will Lindsay glanced back and forth between the two of them, a question in his eyes. But Joel ignored her. As Heidi gently set Hoppy down, Joel turned to Sammy, who was pink with embarrassment and shifting from foot to foot. "If you were older, I'd buy you a drink to celebrate," he said.

Heidi was about to speak, but Jaymie beat her to it. "Sammy, I'd like to talk to you about your landscape ideas, but I wondered if I could see what you and your mom did in your backyard? Just as a reference."

"Uh, sure. Okay. I'll let my mom know we're coming." He pulled a cell phone out of his pocket and called home, hunching his shoulder and moving away from the group.

Too late, Jaymie realized how rude it was to blurt it out, like that. She had interrupted the celebration, and could have been more delicate in her approach. Should she even be butting in on his mother, especially given that she had lost her husband and was in mourning? Will Lindsay was staring at her as if she were a ghoul, and she shifted, uncomfortably aware of her lack of sensitivity. They hadn't even had the funeral yet, for crying out loud. She felt bad, but the knowledge that someone had killed Urban Dobrinskie in her backyard—and was so far getting away with it—fueled her.

"I . . . I told her ab-bout selling the sailboat, and everything, and she said for you *all* to come over for lemonade." Sammy slipped the phone back in his cargo pants pocket.

"Great," Joel said. "I'd like to meet your mom, assure her we'll take good care of the *Sea Urchin*."

Sammy gave him a startled look. Jaymie surmised that his mom had little or nothing to do with the sailboat and couldn't care less about it, except as a source of revenue for her boy to go to college. They all hustled off, an ill-assorted group—Will Lindsay went with them, probably feeling protective of Sammy, with such a group of ghoulish hangers-on—headed for a visit with a woman Robin had called "odd."

It took only ten minutes to walk there. The Dobrinskie house was a white clapboard two-story, a little run-down, one of the bigger houses near the center of the island, close to the border between the Canadian and US sides of Heartbreak Island. It was on a hill, the walkway up to it punctuated with several runs of three or four steps with black-painted plumbing pipes as railings. Sammy raced up the steps and dashed ahead of them, into the house. Hoppy yapped and strained at the leash to follow. The rest of them followed at a more sedate pace, and were greeted at the door by Evelyn Dobrinskie.

Jaymie was startled by the difference in the woman she knew only from her brief encounter with her at Tansy's Tarts. There she had been wan, pale and nervous. But now her cheeks were pink, and she was smiling as she held the door open and asked them to come through to the back garden. The big house echoed with their footsteps. They followed her through a dim hallway to a sunny, modern kitchen that smelled of fresh herbs, then out sliding doors to a garden.

The garden; Jaymie stared at it, her mouth open. Sammy had not done justice to his and his mother's project. Up near the patio there was a normal kind of garden that held a tumult of flowers and herbs breathtaking in their variety. Dotted among the exotic were plants that Jaymie knew: rosemary beside geraniums, varicolored thyme accompanied by dwarf daisies, and assorted other herbs alongside more prosy flowers, and all interspersed with some plants Jaymie didn't recognize.

But the vista that opened out below the patio area and beyond was enchanting. There was a gully, with steps down into it, and pathways cutting through sections that held a pagoda surrounded by leafy ferns. There was, partially shaded by overhanging bushes, a lovely water feature, the whole garden walled by casual-looking but beautifully planned rockery plants, interspersed by outcroppings of lichen-covered rocks.

"This is lovely," Jaymie breathed, standing and staring, stupefied.

"Mom, this is Jaymie Leighton. She's the one I was doing the garden sketches for."

The woman turned knowing eyes toward her, and there was some fleeting expression of worry on her face. "We met at the bakery on . . . on *that* day."

Joel and Will were talking, off to one side, but Will was watching her, Jaymie knew.

Heidi clapped her hands. "Oh, Sammy, this is lovely! I had no idea you were so talented!"

He flushed and shuffled his feet. Evelyn took Heidi by the arm and guided her around the garden. Jaymie, after tying Hoppy to a deck railing and stowing her noisy bag of enamelware under the table, followed in their wake, and Sammy trailed behind, punctuating his mother's running commentary with his own explanations. They made an odd little train.

Upon returning to the patio area, Evelyn offered everyone cold drinks in the shade of the deck pergola. The day was heating up, and refreshment was welcome.

"So," Evelyn Dobrinskie said, when everyone had a cold lemonade in their hands. Her voice seemed brittle, as if she were on the edge of cracking. "How about a toast to the memory of my husband? My *dear*, departed husband?"

❧ Thirteen ❧

THERE WAS AN awkward silence; then everyone got that hearty "We're uncomfortable but we'll pretend not to be" expression and clicked glasses of lemonade. Hoppy, seeming to sense the tension in the air, looked around, his tail wagging intermittently, like a windshield wiper in a drizzle.

"Mom, that's messed up." Sammy shrugged and looked away.

Her expression softened. She reached over and caressed his shoulder, saying, "It's okay, Sammy, we're with friends. Everyone knows that your father and I didn't . . ." She shook her head, tears gleaming in her pale eyes.

Robin's comment on Evelyn's "oddness" came back to Jaymie. How many people would make that kind of a toast with virtual strangers? Did that qualify as "odd" behavior? And she had called them "friends." Did that mean she had no real friends, or was she being facetious?

Sammy said, his voice taut with strain, "Just let it go,

willya?" He scuffed at the deck with his Adidas, staring down at his feet the whole time.

"No one's pretending he was a prince among men," she said, an edge to her voice. Two spots of color bloomed on her cheeks, and a frown pulled her mouth down as tears formed in her eyes. "He could be an ass, and everyone on the island and in Queensville knew it."

There was a moment of shocked silence.

"You must be looking forward to college, Sammy," Heidi said quickly. "I mean . . . I know it's a difficult time, but you are really talented." She waved her hand over the garden, like a garden fairy sprinkling magic dust. "Your dad would have been proud."

"I wouldn't even be going to college, if D-dad was still here," Sammy blurted out, then shut his mouth, his eyes wide, his gaze now fixed on his mother. Tears were rolling down her cheeks, drying without her so much as swiping them away.

"What do you mean?" Jaymie asked.

"N-nothing."

"His father wanted him to go to business school, not college for landscaping, right, Sammy?" Will said. "He just wanted you to explore all your options, don't you think?"

"What he *really* wanted was for Sammy to make a million dollars," Evelyn said, harsh lines bracketing her pinched mouth. The salty tears were dry now, leaving faintly puckered trails down the fragile skin of her cheeks. The brilliant sunlight filtering through the top of the pergola made her look older than she was, and wan. She had been chipper, at first, but the turn of the conversation had left her bitter. "All he cared about was money. He made fun of Sammy for wanting to work with his hands, said no son of his was going to grub around in the muck for a living!"

"Mom!"

"It's true," she cried, her hands gripping each other on

her lap, anguish throaty in her voice. "He tried to kill your talent!"

So Evelyn killed him, instead? How far would a mother go, especially one who was clearly abused by her husband? But this was not an unplanned crime, Jaymie thought, her gaze shifting from mother to son. Who was to say how long Evelyn's anger had festered, though, and how it might have fueled a plot to kill her difficult husband. But would she then leave his body in a place where Sammy had been working? That didn't make sense, unless there was some kind of message there.

Sammy hung his head, not meeting anyone's gaze. It was one of those silent, intensely uncomfortable moments, and Joel pulled Heidi to him, circling her in his protective embrace.

"That's why the morning after he died, I called the college up right away and made sure Sammy could get in for the fall semester!" Evelyn finally said, her voice softening as she gazed at her son.

The very morning after she had just learned her husband had been murdered? The same morning Jaymie saw her at Tansy's Tarts looking like she was grief stricken?

"No one's saying he was perfect, Evelyn," Will Lindsay said, his tone soothing. "Urb was a tough nut to crack, but he meant well."

"Don't give me that," Evelyn said, her cheeks pink. "He never saw anything but his own way, and if you thought differently, well . . ." She caressed her arm, where a faint bruise still colored the skin.

There was another longish silence. Hoppy begged for attention, and as Jaymie picked up her little dog, she began to wonder where both Evelyn *and* Sammy were on the night in question. As the wife and son of the victim, the police must be looking at them as possible culprits, but Jaymie had not seriously considered either. Sammy seemed too skinny to do such a heinous deed, and Evelyn too weak-willed, given Urban Dobrinskie's hefty power and dominating will.

But she had seen for herself that Sammy was thin, but strong, a summer of hard physical work toughening him. And as far as Evelyn being weak-willed? There was a simmering anger burning in her. She may have accepted abuse as her due. But if Urb was denying his son the chance to go to the school of his choice for the career of his choice, how deep may a mother's anger have gone?

"So, what do you think happened?" Jaymie asked, suddenly, looking around. She agitatedly scruffed her Yorkie-Poo's tufted fur.

Silence, for another longish moment. Their uneasy little gathering seemed to be punctuated with awkward silences.

"Jaymie, no one wants to talk about that," Joel admonished, frowning.

Heidi pulled away and straightened, sitting up tall. "I think maybe people do, Joel. You all must be terribly upset about it," she said, gently, scanning the others. Her gaze lingered on Sammy and his mother. "It must be a little . . . frightening."

"Frightening?" Evelyn asked.

"I mean, whoever did it must live on the island, right? And to have a killer right near you . . ." Heidi shuddered and huddled into Joel's embrace again. "I'd be worried."

"We never used to lock our doors at night," Will said. "But we do now! My wife, Barb, is really upset."

"I can't believe I was so close to it all," Jaymie said. "It scares the *heck* out of me." She glanced between Sammy and his mom; Evelyn had gone even paler, and looked about ready to faint. "I'm sorry . . . We're discussing all of this, and you . . ." She shook her head. "You're still suffering the shock and loss. You were probably sleeping soundly in your bed, that night, not knowing what was going on."

"Sammy was at a sleepover with his pals that night!" Evelyn said, her gaze defiant.

Hmmm, odd reaction. Unless Evelyn thought Jaymie was implying Sammy may have committed the murder. Was the sleepover story true? The boy had glanced at his mother with a furrowed brow.

"So you were all alone?" she asked Evelyn point-blank. "Was Urban at home and left? Or did he get any phone calls or anything that evening?"

There was a kind of collective gasp.

"Jaymie!" Joel said, giving her a disgusted look.

Okay, maybe she had gone too far in her consuming need to find out what had happened in her backyard that night. "I mean, that must be hard to remember," Jaymie added, glancing around, "that you were alone when . . ." There was no way to continue that; she had boxed herself in, and Evelyn Dobrinskie would be within her right to ask her to leave. "I'm sorry," Jaymie said, surprised by her emotion, her voice thick. How did cops do it, probe open wounds, expose people's raw emotions, without getting tangled up in them? "It's been a really difficult time, finding Urban like . . . like I did, but even more so for you, Evelyn, Sammy. I'm so sorry."

Heidi put one hand on her arm. Jaymie glanced at her, grateful for her supportive gesture.

"You've had *your* share of dead bodies," Evelyn said, her voice brittle. Her chin went up, in a combative expression. "Sherm says you're a regular Jessica Fletcher."

Will stared at Evelyn, his eyes wide. He had probably never seen his partner's wife so outspoken as she had been today. How the worm had turned! "I, uh, have to go," he said, standing and looking around at the rest of them. "I've gotta . . . do some things."

"It must be a busy time, with no partner to help run the day–to–day business. Robin told me that Garnet Redmond is buying out the Dobrinskies' share of the marina," Jaymie said.

"He's talking about it," Will said, cautiously, glancing over at Evelyn. "We don't know if that's what Evelyn and

Sammy want yet. I don't want them to rush into anything. I really gotta go. I've got a customer coming to look at a boat."

"Not the *Sea Urchin*, though, right?" Joel said, standing and thrusting out his hand.

"Nope. You guys and Sammy have a deal on that. We can't do the paperwork until the will is probated, but as soon as that happens, I'll let you know." Will shook his hand, and said to Evelyn, "I'll let myself out, okay?"

Joel turned to Jaymie and said, "We ought to leave these people be, and let them get back to . . . to whatever."

"Sammy," Jaymie said, turning to the teenager. "I like your sketches and plans, and we—my family and I—would like to work on it with you. My dad thinks it would be a good investment. Robin said he can spare you to work for a few days on the landscaping. Do you *want* to do that? I mean, I'll understand if you don't." Given that his father had died right there, and that she had been a bit aggressive with his mother, it seemed even odds that he would turn down the work.

He exchanged a glance with his mom, who nodded, and he turned back to her. "I'd like to help. Will I be able to take photos along the way, so I can make a project out of it when I get to school?"

"Absolutely!" Jaymie said, sighing with relief. "You can take as many photos as you want."

She trailed out after Joel and Heidi, lugging her shopping bag and accompanied by Sammy. Evelyn stayed behind, gathering glasses onto a tray. Sammy scooted ahead of them, guided them around the side of the house, and let them out a gate. Jaymie was wondering, all the while, about Evelyn's assertion that Sammy was at a "sleepover." Surely a guy in his late teens didn't still do "sleepovers"? But maybe she meant he was hanging out at a friend's place, and sacked out on his couch.

Or was that what he told his mother? Who knew her job

site better than Sammy, who had been working on it for
Robin? At that moment, something else occurred to her, and
she stopped stock-still on the sloping lane. She eyed the
teenager, as he talked to Joel and Heidi.

Means, motive, opportunity.

Who knew the plumbing job site, where Urban's body
was found? Robin, Garnet, Ruby and Sammy.

Who would gain from Urban's death? Evelyn, Garnet
(indirectly, if he was cheating in the sailing race) and
Sammy.

And who had opportunity? Garnet and Ruby, if they were
working together, but otherwise it would be risky for either
of them to go it alone. Evelyn, if she was alone, as she
appeared to be, but then there was the problem of knowing
the site. And Sammy.

A terrible idea occurred to her. Had the intention been
to *bury* Urban in her backyard, in the mud of the leaching
field? Sammy would have known they were not finished yet,
but he may have intended to bury Urban in a part of the site
that would not be disturbed by the work. Was he interrupted
midplan?

Sammy was the common thread, it seemed, among those
with a motive to want Urban Dobrinskie dead, and those who
had the means and opportunity. She thought of all the famous
cases of the last twenty years of sons killing their fathers in
a fit of rage, or sometimes coldly calculated fury. Abuse was
a common thread in those trials, and she had an eyewitness
account that Sammy was his father's victim, in that sense.

It was more important than ever to find out what Sammy
was up to that night, and the only way to do that was to get
him to talk. As Heidi and Joel finalized their plans with the
kid, Jaymie approached and said, "So, Sam, if I clear it with
Robin, can you start tomorrow morning? My boyfriend is
calling the company that provides him with sod, to see if
they can bring it over here, but I should have asked first if
you knew any suppliers that served the island."

"Sure, I'd be happy to start tomorrow. There aren't any sod suppliers on the island. If you want to use my plans, we'll need to take measurements first, and then I can tell you how much you'll need." He seemed surer of himself away from his mother, more confident already, with his father out of his life.

"I hadn't thought of that," Jaymie said about the measurements, stricken by how much work this could turn out to be. What had she pictured? She had just thought she'd sod over the whole area and be done with it, a couple of hours, and presto, a new lawn. "Can you swing by later to do that? I need to call my dad and boyfriend to see what's going on, on their end."

"Sure."

Sammy walked back to the marina with Joel and Heidi. He had agreed to take them out, with Will's help, to see how the *Sea Urchin* worked. As they walked away, Joel was enthusing about her "clean lines," and asking about the shrouds, and Sammy was just listening, his shoulders hunched, hands in his pockets.

Jaymie returned to the cottage even more confused about the murder, and the possible guilty parties. She unpacked the bag and put the enamelware in the sink to wash. While Hoppy noisily ate a bowl of crunchies, she made a cup of tea and some phone calls. First, Valetta.

"Hey, kiddo, what's up?" Valetta said.

Jaymie related the details of her afternoon, then asked, "So, what do you think? Is Sammy Dobrinskie even capable of killing his dad?"

"Now, you know my thoughts on that," Valetta said. She had often asserted her belief that anyone could commit murder, given the right circumstances. "I don't know the Dobrinskies that well, but Sammy has always seemed such a quiet kid, to me. He's babysat for Brock a couple of times."

Brock Nibley was a widower and the proud father of two

kids Jaymie nicknamed Evil and Wicked. Their real names were Eva and William.

"I'm trying to figure out how the ice pick—if it's the murder weapon—got from the bar into Urban Dobrinskie if the murderer wasn't Ruby or Garnet."

"Do you know for sure it was the murder weapon?"

"No, and that's the frustrating part. Detective Zack won't say. Guess I can't blame him for that. But he acted kind of weird when I saw him today. I asked a few questions about the murder, and he got huffy and walked away."

"Hmm. Huffy in what way?"

Jaymie described what happened.

"Maybe just for once you should try talking to him as a friend. He probably doesn't know that many people here, and he's lonely. Don't tackle him with murder questions every time you see him."

Jaymie thought about it for a long minute. "He wasn't in work clothes. I guess it wasn't fair to attack him with work-related questions in his off time."

"Heidi may be right about him. He does seem to like you. A *lot*."

"Uh, no! She's *way* off base about that."

"Okay. Well, you know best. Hey, do you need a hand getting things ready for the family dinner at the cottage, with everything else you've got going on?"

"Maybe," Jaymie said. "Look, you want to paint that back room of yours this fall, right? Well, I'll trade you help with that, for some work here."

"Agreed. No landscaping, though, and no mud."

Jaymie laughed. "Interior work only. Now I just have to convince Daniel's mother that having the dinner out here won't be a dangerous event. She and my mom are driving me nuts."

"What about a compromise?"

"That's what I've been trying to get to the whole time,

but nobody is going along with me. I wonder what I can offer her?"

"What does she want?"

Gloomily, Jaymie said, "Good question. For Daniel to break up with me, it seems. I can't do anything right for her, nor can my mother. What does she want? Complete control?"

"Doesn't every woman want control? Give her a little, and see if it helps."

"But that just puts her in charge, and we end up having dinner at Stowe House!" Jaymie wailed. "I don't know where this thing with Daniel is going, but if it's long-term, I think giving in to his mom is a bad precedent."

"I don't mean give up total control. You just have to make it *look* like you are. Let her handle some key part of it so you can do what you want for the rest. Make a deal."

Thinking about it for a long moment, Jaymie said, "Like, if I said she could choose the menu, as long as we hold the dinner at Rose Tree Cottage."

"Now you're thinking!"

"Valetta, you're a lifesaver. But I gotta go and arrange for sod and backbreaking work, if we're going to be able to do that."

She called Daniel, who said that he had spoken to the supplier who provided his landscaping needs, and they could indeed supply sod to the island. She told him she'd call him with the amount, once Sammy told her, and then she asked to speak to his mother.

"Why?" he asked.

Taken aback, she said, "Why not?"

"Okay. Uh, I'll get her."

"Thank you."

When Debbie Collins came on the line, Jaymie made polite chitchat for a minute, then said, "Mrs. Collins, I have a proposition for you. If you will agree to come to the Leighton family dinner at Rose Tree Cottage on Heartbreak Island, I will be pleased if you would help me plan the menu.

Daniel has said what a wonderful cook you are, and I'd be happy to have the help."

She was silent for a moment, then said, "All right. But why don't you let me take care of all the food? You just worry about getting the cottage ready, and I'll plan the menu and cook."

Jaymie held her breath for a moment. Was she making a mistake? Their dinner had always been corn on the cob, ribs and salads. But surely that was pretty much what Mrs. Collins would plan, knowing this was a summer dinner. And did it matter what they ate? The most important detail for her and her family was upholding tradition by having the meal at Rose Tree Cottage.

Her own mom had too much on her plate, with helping Anna and other assorted activities, and truth be told, she wasn't really much of a cook anyway. Jaymie had been looking forward to investigating some old recipes and trying them, but with all the landscaping to do yet . . . She made a sudden decision. "Great. Do we have a deal?"

"Absolutely. I'll put Daniel back on, dear."

Dear?

"What did you say to her?" Daniel said, his tone full of awe. "She looks like the cat that swallowed a canary."

Uh-oh. "Is that a good thing?"

"If you knew my mother really well, you might not think so."

She told him what she had done. "It's all in the name of compromise, right?"

"Well, that ought to be okay. Call me when you find out the sod requirements, and we'll get to work."

The moment she hung up, Sammy called and said he was on his way over. Ten minutes later they were standing on the slope of her backyard, and he had out his measuring tape, a heavy industrial-looking affair. He directed her with all the confidence of an accomplished landscaper, and she thought how well he was going to do in his life's work. But this blossoming of confidence . . . had it required Urban Dobrinskie's death to bring it to fruition? And which of them was more likely the culprit, he or his mother?

"Sammy, I really am sorry about your father," she said, as he sat on the deck writing down some figures.

He did some quick sums and looked up. "Don't worry about it." His tanned face set in a hard expression. "He tried to ruin my life, you know, like I was never good enough to be his son. Well, he can't ruin it now." He bent his head back down, did a final sum and ripped off a piece of paper. "This is how much sod you need. I'll be back first thing tomorrow to start working on the landscaping, okay?"

In an instant he was back to looking like the thoughtful seventeen-year-old young man she knew him as; gone was the hard and sullen boy. It was like a persona that flickered on and off.

"Okay. See you tomorrow."

❧ Fourteen ❧

SHE PIDDLED AROUND for a while, still trying to write her bio for the newspaper, wretchedly aware that it wasn't going at all well. She needed to send the article to Nan, and soon, but she wanted to look it over one more time, make sure it was as good as she could make it. It was difficult to focus when all she could think about was that a murder had happened in her backyard. It was bad enough that she'd been caught up in that at her Queensville home—she had just gotten over feeling squeamish about the summer porch from the incident in May—and now it had happened out here. Was she some kind of doom magnet? It was disturbing. If it kept happening, the villagers would gather and it would be pitchforks or the river for her.

But while her mother was resident in the Queensville house, the cottage was still her preferred nest, despite the horrid happening. Now that she had her bathroom privileges back, she could drink tea to her heart's content. For her supper she was about to use the recipe that she was writing about for the article, a "sandwich loaf" in miniature.

A sandwich loaf was an amazing fifties concoction that was served at bridal showers, picnics, club luncheons and the like. It looked pretty (in the old photos she had seen, anyway) but might be a challenge to make. She took a whole loaf of bread, sliced it into four pieces with three long horizontal slices, then filled it with three sandwich fillings. She chose ham salad, egg salad and, for the center, cream cheese with chopped olives. When it was stacked, she frosted the whole with some thinned cream cheese colored pale pink. Standing back from the table she thought how pretty it looked, like a loaf cake; she finished it with a decoration of olive "flowers" and parsley leaves on the top.

Before consuming it she needed to photograph it, so she took it out to the front porch, and set up a vignette with her Adirondack chair, a side table, and a frosty glass of lemonade with a cocktail umbrella in it. She tucked some pink roses from the vine that climbed the front porch into a mason jar, and set it on the little table, then carefully sliced the sandwich loaf and laid two pretty striped pieces on one of the enamelware plates, leaving the rest on a decorative tray. The blue siding of her cottage made a lovely background for the blue and white enamelware dishes, and the pink roses picked up the posies in the middle of the dishes. She hoped this was going to be good enough. She took several photos from different angles, moving things around, trying to find an arrangement that she liked.

After a couple of slices of the sandwich loaf for supper, she wrapped the remainder, put it in the fridge, and wrote the rest of the article in longhand. It was simple enough once she got going. Then she took a mug of tea out onto the front porch, sitting with her feet up on the porch railing, as Hoppy settled in next to her, with a contented doggie sigh. The sun sank behind Queensville, and the trees across the road from the cottage took on that brilliant green glow that comes from slanting sunlight.

Closing her eyes, she put her head back, trying to let go of the anxiety that spiraled through her, making her antsy and uncomfortable. Heartbreak Island had always been, to her, a peaceful place, despite the dramatic name and its history as the center of a tug-of-war between nations that finally ended in a peaceful resolution, and the splitting of the island in two. But maybe she just hadn't spent enough time at the cottage lately to notice all the tensions and anger that swirled around among the islanders. The Dobrinskie marriage, so full of violence, and the hard-nosed competition between Urban Dobrinskie and the Redmonds were examples. Urban seemed like the kind of guy who was the center of a lot of controversy.

But what had contributed to it was the gossipy nature of such a closed environment. Everybody seemed to belong to the same clubs and go to the same places. Sherm Woodrow had wasted no time in passing on to Urban what he had heard about Garnet and Ruby buying a sail from overseas, one that was against regatta rules. But who had told Sherm that? Jaymie couldn't remember whether he had mentioned where the information came from. She opened her eyes and watched the last rays of the slanting sunset gild the trees.

A dark figure trudged up the road from the direction of the marina, and in a moment Jaymie identified the figure as Will Lindsay. "Hi, Will!" she called out.

"Oh, hi, Jaymie," he said. He looked down in the dumps, his boots scuffing along the gravel road like he didn't have the energy to lift his feet.

"How's it going?" she asked. "You all right?"

"I'm just tired," he said, approaching her porch.

Hoppy jumped down from the chair and wriggled toward Will. The marina owner sat down on the bottom step and took Hoppy up on his lap. The little dog licked his chin and panted happily.

"On your way home?"

He scruffed Hoppy under the chin, and said, "What? Oh, no, that's in the opposite direction. I'm actually on my way to see Garnet. I'm hoping he'll back off a bit on the marina deal. I don't want Evelyn and Sammy to rush into selling their share."

"Is Garnet pressuring you to get them to sell?" she asked, alarmed.

He shrugged and looked down at Hoppy. "It depends on what you call pressure, I guess. I really like the guy, but I just don't know how to tell him to lay off."

"I don't know if either of them will be home right now, but if they are, why don't you try talking to Ruby about it?"

He stilled and cocked his head to one side. "That's a good idea, actually." He touched Hoppy's wet nose and smiled. "That's a *great* idea. I never did understand what Urban had against her. She's such a *nice* woman. But he said she was not who she seemed."

Something Valetta said teased the back of Jaymie's brain, something about Garnet and Ruby. What was it? She couldn't remember; she'd have to ask her friend. "What did he mean by that?"

"I don't know. I guess we'll *never* know now, right?" He put Hoppy gently on the porch, and stood, stretching. "Thanks for the chat, Jaymie. I'll see if I can get Ruby on my side."

"Good idea. Try not to worry, Will; you're doing the right thing."

"That's what Robin says. Evelyn and Sammy might need that income in a few years, if he's going to start a landscape business."

He trudged off into the darkness, and Jaymie pondered his problem. How much did she really know about Garnet Redmond? She spent very little time on the island, as a rule, generally making flying visits to clean the place, and make sure it was ready for guests, a few hours each time. But with the plumbing woes she had spent a lot more time in contact with the Redmonds in the last week or so. They both seemed very nice to her, but how would Garnet be if he was crossed? He had certainly cleaned Urban's clock for what he said about Ruby, hadn't he?

She just couldn't believe Garnet would *kill* the man, though, and leave him in their own shared back area. That made not one speck of sense. Unless Garnet was counting on *everyone* thinking that way. It would take a particular kind of cool courage to be bold and leave the body right on your own property, to deflect suspicion in a kind of reverse psychology way. Having watched him sail, Jaymie knew Garnet was indeed decisive and bold.

Okay, so it could be Garnet. She had to admit it was possible. But to play devil's advocate, if not him, who? Who killed Urban Dobrinskie in her backyard? She squinted into the gathering gloom. Or . . . wait . . . *Did* someone kill Urban Dobrinskie in her backyard?

The more she thought about it, the more it felt like a staged set. The body in the mud. The "murder weapon"—the vintage ice pick—placed under the body. Whatever it was in the trees that made Hoppy go nuts that night. And the voice, saying, "Get off my property." All had been designed to point toward Garnet Redmond.

But some stuff didn't fit. The items that had been stolen from the work site; what were they again? Boots. Wheelbarrow. The drill bit . . . though that may have been a coincidence and perhaps was just lost in the muck by a careless workman.

The wheelbarrow.

Hoppy, after investigating the perimeter of the steps and sniffing out any messages he may have missed, begged to come back up on the comfy chair, and Jaymie picked him up, scratching behind his ears.

The *wheelbarrow.*

Of course! She held her breath, close to a breakthrough.

If Urban was killed elsewhere and his body moved, it would need to be carried in something, and what was more useful to move a heavy object than a wheelbarrow? It was a tool in the staging of the "murder" scene!

One detail—one pointed, particular detail—came back to her in that moment. She could picture the boots Urban had been wearing, deep-treaded boots common to many men; the treads had been clogged, but not with mud, as they would have been if he had walked across her work site. The treads were clogged by fine-grained sand. That was the final detail that proved her theory, that he had been killed elsewhere, was accurate. She had no doubt that she was late to that conclusion, though. The police would already know that.

So . . . sand. How would the treads of his boots get clogged with sand? If it was fine dry sand, it would have just fallen out of the treads, so it was damp sand, like that found on a beach, or down by the river's edge. There was only one spot on the island that had that particular area of damp sand, and that was down by the Ice House.

She heard a noise on the road, and Will Lindsay trudged along, head down, back toward the marina.

"Hey, Will, what did they say? Did you talk to Ruby?"

"Neither of them was home," he said, strolling up the walk to her step again, and putting one foot up on the bottom step. "They're probably both at the restaurant until closing."

"I thought they might be. Are you going to go down there to talk to them?"

"The restaurant's not a good place to talk about this. And I'm so tired," he said, scrubbing his eyes with his thumb and forefinger. "I think I'll just leave it until tomorrow morning."

Realizing she didn't know much about Will Lindsay's private life, she asked, "Do you ever go to the Ice House?"

"My wife, Barb, doesn't like going out much," he said. "She's a good cook. We eat at home most nights."

"Is she a local?"

"Yup. We met in high school. We split up for a while, but we got back together again and got married."

"Does she like the marina business?"

"Hates it! She'd be happy if I sold it and got a regular nine-to-five job. Says she doesn't see me enough."

What about the night of the murder, Jaymie wondered. He and Urban were business partners; could he have gotten sick of Urban's behavior and wanted him out of the way? She examined what she could see of his face in the shadowy evening gloom. The porch light cast a faint glow, but not enough to see his eyes. "I guess you work late a lot?"

"I try not to, but when you're in the leisure business, you have to stick around if the customers want you, you know? But boaters don't stay out late, so I'm always home by eight or so, regular as clockwork . . . dinner at eight thirty, TV, then lights out. Barb says she can't sleep unless I'm snoring beside her."

Jaymie sighed. The police had probably already established where he was, given he was Urban's business partner. "Is everything going all right with the marina? At least you're starting work on the dredging. I heard that Urban was not willing to go ahead with that."

He frowned. "Who told you that?"

"I don't remember. Why? Isn't it true?"

"Uh-uh. He was just careful is all, making sure we took it step by step. I didn't blame him. It's a big financial commitment. And you really have to have all your T's crossed and your I's dotted, when it comes to the environmental agencies. We're right on schedule with how he wanted to handle it."

He frowned and looked down at his feet, scuffing his boot on the bottom step. "I miss the old asshole, pardon my French." He cleared his throat and looked up, with a quirky grin on his shadowed face. "He'd hate even thinking that Garnet was going to buy out his share. Another reason I guess I'm a little wary of selling out. I gotta go. I called Barb and told her I'd be a little late, but I don't want to keep dinner waiting. It's nachos night!"

After another hour on the porch, Jaymie headed to bed and slept soundly.

The next morning, Jaymie called Daniel and gave him the measurements for the sod. He said he'd call his supplier.

"Do you want me to come over and have a look at the area?"

"Would you?" Jaymie said. "I looked out there this morning, and I'm a little overwhelmed. It just seems like so much work. Sammy is due here in a half hour."

"I'll catch the next ferry," he said.

Jaymie then called her dad, but he was already golfing with Roger Collins and Grant Watson, the Leightons' next-door neighbor. "Have him call me when he gets home, Mom," Jaymie said.

"So, have you talked to that woman yet, about the family dinner at the cottage?" her mother said.

Jaymie hesitated, but ultimately, her mom needed to know. "Dinner out here is a go," she said. "You're pleased with that, right?"

"How did you manage that?"

"Uh, well . . . I gave her menu control, and she offered to cook, too. I figured, with all you and I have on our plates, that would work out for everyone."

"Well, okay," she said, doubt in her tone. She sighed. "At least we can do dinner at Rose Tree Cottage."

"How is Anna doing?" Jaymie said, not ashamed to change the subject while she was ahead.

"She wasn't feeling well this morning. Her cousin is coming in on the Greyhound this afternoon, and I said I'd watch the bed-and-breakfast and babysit Tabby while she goes to pick her up in Wolverhampton."

"I'm sorry this has ended up on your shoulders, Mom. I really didn't think the plumbing thing at the cottage would be such a big deal."

"It's okay, honey. I feel for Anna. I remember how I was when I was pregnant with you . . . sick as a dog!"

Reminded of all her mother's sterling qualities, among them a generosity of spirit when someone was ailing or troubled, Jaymie said, "I'm so happy you and Dad are here, Mom. Really."

There was a pause, and her mother said, "Have you heard from Becca? She called me last night. I think we might be hearing an announcement at the family dinner."

Jaymie strolled out to the front porch to wait for Sammy. "She and Kevin are getting serious real fast. I just hope she knows what she's doing."

"So how about you? I may not care for his mother, but Daniel seems like a really nice young man."

"We're giving it a little while, Mom. I'm just over Joel, and I need to take my time."

"Joel was never good enough for you. I always knew that."

"Funny, last summer you were saying the same things about him you're now saying about Daniel."

There was a chuckle at the other end of the line. "I guess that's true. But I want grandchildren, darn it! And you're my only hope."

Great. So nice to be the only hope for a future generation of Leighton progeny. "I have to go, Mom. Tell Dad to give me a call. If I don't answer, it's because I'm up to my knees in mud." She looked up at the lowering sky. "I sure hope it doesn't rain."

As she clicked the off button on the cordless handset, Zack Christian jogged past, then backed up and stopped, his breathing barely faster than normal. She sat down on the top step.

"How are you doing?" he asked, strolling toward the steps.

"Good, I guess." She thought about what Valetta had said, to for once just talk to him about other things than the crime du jour. "It must be a little strange, adjusting to life in Queensville after the big city. How long have you been here?"

"Since March." He stretched and flexed his shoulders. "It is different, but I like it."

"Do you have any family nearby?" She realized she knew virtually nothing about him, whether he had family or not.

"My folks live in Montana."

"Is that where you're from?" She could totally picture him in western gear and on a horse.

"Actually, I lived most of my life in Chicago, but my folks moved to my grandparents' ranch in Montana when they retired. Granddad needed help running the place."

"Do you ever go there?"

He frowned, his brow furrowed. "What's up, Jaymie?" he asked, wiping his forehead on the edge of his T-shirt. "Why all the questions?"

So maybe Valetta was wrong? He seemed uneasy with the personal touch. "Just trying to keep my mind off things." She took a deep breath, and said, "Zack, I've been thinking a lot, and I'm wondering if you guys have considered that Urban wasn't killed in my backyard, but was moved there. Maybe with the stolen wheelbarrow?"

He didn't say a word, just stared with his eyebrows arched.

"Okay, so that *is* what you're thinking. That means he was killed somewhere else and brought to my backyard. There was sand clogged in his boot treads, so that means the riverbank, and I'm thinking the only patch nearby is down by the Ice House restaurant."

"That's not the only spot on the island with that kind of sand," he said, then grimaced. "Forget I said that."

Jaymie thought for a long minute and said, slowly, "It is the only spot on the American side, but there's the marina on the Canadian side of the island, and it has the same kind of sand." She frowned. "But the Canadian side? Why would . . . Wait! Urban was born in Poland and emigrated to Canada; that's what his wife said. So he likely still has Canadian citizenship. And, in fact, their backyard is probably one of those that lie on the border! He could just cut through, and there wouldn't even be any record of him crossing the border."

Zack looked conflicted, but then said, "Look, I shouldn't be saying anything at all, but sometimes a local perspective is helpful to me."

"That's what I've told you many times," Jaymie said, with a smug smile.

"You're really irritating sometimes, you know that?" He glared at her in mock ferocity. "Anyway, we're still investigating everyone involved. I can't comment, of course. But I can ask you questions."

"Haven't you already done that? A thousand or so of them?"

"But these questions may be more interesting to you. Like . . . do you know any reason why Urban Dobrinskie would be poking around the marina on the Canadian side of the island late at night?"

She stared at him. "No. Not offhand." But she sure would be pondering that now.

"I've heard that he had a girlfriend. Do you know who she was?"

Darn. Slowly, reluctantly, she said, "Brock Nibley said that he had heard Ruby was involved with Urban, but that's ridiculous." She paused. "I also heard that Urban's wife would follow him. Maybe *she* knows who he was involved with."

Just then, Sammy came down the road on his bike and skidded to a halt. He eyed Zack, his expression somber.

"Hey, Sam," the detective said. "How are you and your mom doing?"

"You were at our place yesterday, so you know how we're doing." Sammy cast Jaymie a suspicious look.

"Jaymie and I are friends, Sam. I just stopped on my way around the island."

Jaymie cast the detective a surprised look. They were friends? Hmm. They'd had dinner together, so she supposed they could call themselves that.

"Yeah, well, maybe you should try a little harder to find out who killed my dad, instead of hanging out talking to girls." He flung his bike to one side and stomped along the walkway toward the backyard, disappearing past the line of young trees that topped the lane, the same one damaged by the police excavator.

"Wow," Jaymie said, watching him go. "Poor kid! He's here to do some landscaping for me. I guess I've underestimated how losing his dad is affecting him. I hope he's going to be okay."

Zack shook his head. "Maybe he didn't realize himself how much he'd miss his dad until it was too late. Gotta go. Bye, Jaymie."

Fifteen

SHE STOOD STARING after Zack as he returned to the road and jogged away, his athlete's tread pounding out a steady rhythm in the quiet morning. He disappeared down around the bend, heading toward the marina. He'd take the loop, which wreathed the point of the island, rising up to a cliff, where one house sat in solitary splendor, then down back to the heart of the island. Or maybe he'd go through the marina and take the stairs that rose from it to the road above, as some energetic joggers did.

She stared off down the road, her gaze unfocused as she pondered his words. What did he mean, "until it was too late"? Did he think Sammy might have killed his father? She had considered the kid as a suspect; it wouldn't be the first patricide she'd heard of. Or maybe Zack just meant it the way everyone did when they said something like that, that you never knew what you had until it was gone.

One thing had become clear to her over the past few days . . . Whoever killed Urban Dobrinskie was not a stranger, not to the island, and not to herself. He or she had stolen the wheelbarrow the night before the murder; that indicated planning, and that he or she was likely present on the island as someone who owned or rented a home, not someone who went back and forth from the mainland. They then killed Urban, probably with the ice pick from the Ice House restaurant, and brought the body from the riverside area of the Canadian side of the island or the US side to her backyard, dumped it, then created the scene that implicated Garnet or Ruby Redmond. That person then managed to take the wheelbarrow away, dump it in the river and get away. Not the perfect crime, but proving to be tougher to solve than it had first looked. The cops hadn't made an arrest yet, but that didn't necessarily mean they were stumped. For all she knew they could have a theory and be watching someone, ready to pounce.

It was irritating that she just didn't know, and she was no closer to knowing than she was the night of the murder. It was creepy, knowing there was a murderer out there. Garnet and/or Ruby could not be the guilty parties. They were just too sane. But if that was true, then what did Ruby mean when she said to her brother, "I didn't mean to do it"? The logical solution to her puzzlement was to just ask the woman, and she would do just that.

But first she needed to go back and handle Sammy. The boy was drawing something on a clipboard when she joined him behind the house, after confining Hoppy to the cottage. She didn't want her exuberant three-legged Yorkie-Poo lurching around the mucky work site.

Putting herself in Sammy's shoes, she empathized with how overwhelming everything must seem for him at that moment. "You okay, Sam?" she asked, watching his face.

He nodded, but didn't answer. His lower lip trembled, and huge tears welled in his eyes, splashing down on the clipboard.

"Come and sit," Jaymie said, grabbing his arm and tugging him to the steps up to the deck. "If this is a bad day and you want to go home, it's okay. I should never have expected you to do this, not while . . . not while you're grieving." She took the clipboard from his quivering grasp and set it aside. She then pushed him to sit, and sat on the step beside him. "Talk to me, Sam."

"I just . . . I looked down at that field of dirt, and I thought, that's where my dad died." His shoulders shook and he buried his face in his hands.

"I can't imagine what you're going through," Jaymie said, gently. She rubbed his shoulder.

Just then, Daniel came around the corner of the cottage and approached the deck. His expression sobered when he saw the teenager sitting by Jaymie. "Hey, guys. Did I come at a bad time?"

Jaymie said, "No, it's okay. Sam, this is Daniel Collins, my . . . my boyfriend."

Daniel caught her hesitation and eyed her, gravely.

"You're Sam Dobrinskie, right? I'm so sorry. I heard about your loss." He stuck out his hand, and the teenager took it and shook. "I know how you feel . . . well, kinda. I lost my dad when I was younger than you. It hurt bad."

"You lost your dad?" Jaymie asked, puzzled. "What do you mean?"

He met her gaze and said, "Roger Collins married my mom three years after dad was killed. I took his name. He's been a great father to me."

How did she not know this about him? She stared at Daniel, her head swimming. What else didn't she know?

"Thanks," Sammy said. "It's just . . ." He waved a hand helplessly over the ridged dirt of the backyard. "This was where he died. I've managed to shut it out until now, but . . . it's hitting me how awful it is."

"But he *didn't* die here," Jaymie blurted out, then wished she had kept her mouth shut.

"What?" Daniel gazed at her in astonishment. "How do you know that?"

"Did that cop tell you that?" Sammy demanded. "That detective who was here this morning?"

"Zack was on his way past the cottage, jogging, and stopped to talk," Jaymie explained to Daniel, then turned back to Sammy, so she didn't have to see the questions in Daniel's eyes. "No, he didn't tell me anything. I figured that out on my own." She explained how she knew, citing the sand in the boot treads as proof. "If your father had been killed here, there would have been mud in the boot treads, not sand."

The information had helped; she could see that as she regarded Sammy's face. He was relieved, and heaved a deep breath, steadying himself as he looked out over the dirt gully. "So . . . where was he killed? And why bring him here?"

Those were questions she couldn't answer. "Your mom said you were at a sleepover that night. Were you?"

Daniel flashed her a questioning look, but Sammy answered without hesitation or guile. "Nah, I was home. I don't know why she said what she did. I was in my room on my computer."

"Did your dad come home at any point?"

"I think so." He squinted toward the Redmonds' place, across the gully. "I heard him and Mom argue; then he left, and I think Mom . . ." His eyes widened and he shook his head. With sudden energy he stood, shifting his baggy cut-off shorts. "Look, if we're going to do this stuff, we need to get at it."

Had he been about to say that his mom followed his dad that night? Jaymie wondered. She tried to figure out a way to ask, but how did you ask a kid to incriminate his mother in his father's murder? "Sammy, did you, uh, see your mom later that night, or—"

"So, have you got the sod coming?" Sammy asked, grabbing his clipboard and glaring down at it.

Daniel exchanged a glance with Jaymie, behind Sammy's

back, then said, "Yes, it should be coming anytime now. My dad is coming over to help lay it."

"Then we need to get moving to prepare the site," Sammy said, hustling off and trudging down to the muddy gully.

"What was that all about?" Daniel asked Jaymie. "Am I hearing what I think I'm hearing? Do you *really* think his mother killed his father?"

Jaymie shrugged. "I just don't know. You haven't met her, Daniel. She's . . . odd." She told him about the exchange at the Dobrinskie home. "She's got to be glad Urban is gone."

"Don't bet on it," he said.

"What do you mean?"

"Love's not a fairy tale, Jaymie," he said, impatiently, shoving his glasses up on his beaky nose and pushing back his sandy hair. "I think you'd better stop reading those romance books. Just because the guy was a jerk sometimes doesn't mean his wife wanted him dead."

She bridled. "I know that! Do you think because I read romance novels I'm not realistic about love?"

He regarded her steadily, as the sun peeped above the peak of the house and beamed down on them. "I don't know what you think." He turned and joined Sammy and the two began gesturing and planning out the day's work.

Back at you, buddy, she thought. "I'm not sure I know much about *you* at all," she muttered, still wondering how she could not know that Roger Collins was his stepdad. What else hadn't come up in the two months or so they had been dating?

The day was backbreaking, and the work hot and miserable. Roger Collins did arrive, and he had his new golfing buddies Grant Watson and Jaymie's dad in tow. With all the turmoil of the past week, Jaymie had not foreseen how much work simply laying the sod would be. Sammy was invaluable. Because he had done his mom's garden and yard so recently, he knew exactly who to call for estimates on patio stones and water piping for the water feature she still wasn't sure about. He consulted with the various specialists who arrived to give quotes, and gravely wrote down figures.

Jaymie was glad her father was there, because he could help her make decisions. It was almost noon, and she stood with him in the shade of the copse of trees at the bottom of the gully and looked around. Her brain was mush, the heat having simmered it like a snail in a shell. "What do you think, Dad? Fountain? No fountain? I need to figure this out. Help!"

Sammy joined them, pulling up the bottom edge of his filthy T-shirt to wipe the sweat off his face.

"What's *your* vision, son?" Alan Leighton asked, his bluff face red and his sparse white hair standing up in a corona around his head. "You've probably spent more time thinking about this than any of us."

When Sammy began to talk, Jaymie was mesmerized.

"This place," he said, waving his hand at the grove of alder trees around them, "is like a staging area, you know? You look at everything else *from* it. But for a minute, picture this spot where we're standing after a hot day like today, a stone terrace here, some nice furniture, and the splashing water from a fountain. Did you know that even the sound of running water cools people off? It's, like, psychological."

The way he said it, Jaymie could almost picture the fountain and the stone terrace, a seating area for them and their guests after a hot day on the water or out golfing.

"Now look toward the house."

Jaymie obeyed, turning toward the back of the cottage on the rise above them, the scruffy wooden deck, which had definitely seen better days, and the PVC patio furniture, which needed to be replaced. She wasn't sure whether the stuff she had bought at auction would be enough now.

"This fall you could take that deck off the back, and build a two-level stone patio that overlooks the gully. I'd plant some scattered trees along the slope, instead of terracing like the Redmonds have done. If you plant some poplars, you'll have good fast growth, and soil retention. You'll have to avoid the leaching bed—you don't want tree roots interfering with that—but if we mark the perimeter, we should be able to do it. It wouldn't hurt to give your property some privacy with a copse of evergreens at the far edge.

"Now, if you want to make the patio a covered deck instead, and do a railing," he continued, "you might even be able to put an outdoor heater on it and rent the cottage out in fall, right up to Christmas. You're close to the river, and some folks come to Queensville for Dickens Days between Thanksgiving and Christmas."

"Wow. You've given us a lot to think about, Sam. You seem to have thought this through," Jaymie marveled, examining the teenager. He had chosen the right profession.

Her dad said, "It's about time we invested in this old place, don't you think, hon?" He put his arm over Jaymie's shoulder and squeezed. "Sammy, I was wondering about sound. Can we wire up the patio with speakers?"

The boy's brown eyes lit up, and he swiped shaggy bangs off his forehead. "That would be off the chain, Mr. Leighton. Do you want me to price it out for you? We can lay the wiring at the same time as laying the waterlines for the fountain. It'll take an electrician, but if we have one out for the fountain wiring, he could do it at the same time. I know just the guy, and he could do a small job like this in two hours."

"If you do me the quotes, I'll be able to make a decision right away."

"That would be *awesome*!" He bounced off a ways, and whipped his cell phone out and started making calls.

"Speakers? Dad, are you serious?" Jaymie asked.

"Why not? It's about time we started fixing this place up."

A sudden idea twisted her stomach. "You don't want to sell it, do you?"

"What? No way!" He grabbed her around the waist and

squeezed. "I'd never do something like that without consulting you girls first. I just think the old place needs something. Next year we can talk about the inside."

He trotted off to consult with Roger, Daniel and Grant, leaving Jaymie in the shade, watching the hubbub. She retreated inside, made stacks of sandwiches and wraps for lunch, also cutting the rest of the sandwich loaf into slices, and brought them out with a dozen or so bottles of water and cans of pop. They ate lunch; then everyone went back to the task at hand.

Many hands make light work, it is said, and that turned out to be true. By late afternoon, with Sammy's excellent direction, the sod was mostly done, and the water, electrical and sound wiring was planned and the trench dug, waiting for the professionals. The last bit of sod would be laid after the wiring was done, and trees and perennial plants to implement Sammy's vision were to be delivered the next day. Daniel suggested they order dinner in for everyone, and Jaymie suggested they go to the Ice House instead.

Daniel eyed her, with a question in his eyes, but agreed. Jaymie invited Sammy, and he said yes, if he could bring his mom.

Her voice clogged with emotion, Jaymie squeezed his shoulder and said, "Of course. You're a nice kid, to think of your mom like that."

He squinted up at the descending sun, the freckles across his nose standing out and the sunlight picking golden highlights out in his sandy hair. His expression serious, he said, "I'm all she's got now. Dad wasn't much good, but at least he was someone to look after, you know? She lives for that kind of stuff, cooking and cleaning. That's why she wants to move to be near me when I go to college next month."

Jaymie still believed, despite Daniel's doubt, that Evelyn would enjoy life a lot better now. Her beloved son was able to do what he wanted, and she now had the freedom to take care of him near his college of choice. It had to be better than staying on the island looking after an insufferable ass of a husband, while worrying that her son wasn't being allowed to pursue his passion. But she wasn't about to make such a comment. "We'll meet you and your mom at the restaurant, okay?"

Everyone parted ways to clean up, Daniel, the dads and Jaymie using the cottage. Grant Watson refused the dinner offer. He was going back to the mainland, he said, to find out what trouble his wife, Mimi, and Jaymie's mom had gotten into. Jaymie called her mom, to see whether she wanted to come over to the island and join them for dinner, but she was taken up with Anna, Tabitha and Anna's cousin, Pam, and told them to go ahead and have dinner at the Ice House, as long as her husband made the last ferry back.

Jaymie walked Hoppy, then, at about eight, locked him up in the cottage with a bowl of crunchies. The four of them walked down to the marina before heading to the restaurant, where they were going to meet Sammy and his mother. Daniel wanted to show his dad the marina, and he pointed out the path on the Queensville side of the river, where he and Jaymie had watched the July Fourth sailboat race, and where they often walked.

It was a lovely evening. From looking like it was going to storm again, the late-day mugginess had eased off. A breeze now scooted along the river, blowing away the clouds that had been so ominous earlier.

Roger and Jaymie's dad walked down the pier that cradled the marina. "I want to show Roger the Redmonds' boat, the *Heartbreak Kid*," he called back to his daughter. The Redmond siblings' boat was gorgeous, all sleek, polished wood and brass. Many people took the walk to admire it, where it sat in the last slip near the ferry dock.

"Sure, you guys go ahead."

Daniel took her hand and led her to a bench by the marina. "Sit. You look tired."

They sat for a few minutes, while the sky turned a pinky-orange color to the west, over the rooftops of Queensville.

"Jaymie, I'm sorry about that crack this morning, about romance novels."

"It bugged me," she admitted, turning on the bench to look into his brown eyes. "Why does everyone believe that if you read romance novels, you must have your head in the clouds and believe that the world is full of rainbows and unicorns? I'd never make assumptions about someone who . . . I don't know . . . read spy novels or murder mysteries. I don't figure that folks who read murder mysteries are bloodthirsty!"

"I know. I was wrong."

She smiled over at him. One of his many charms was the ability to truly apologize with sincerity and absolutely no irony or subtext. "Forgiven, and it's forgotten."

"You have seemed a little distracted lately, though," he added, his smile dying.

Aha. So maybe he was still brooding about the Zack problem. Her little slip that morning, the hesitation in calling Daniel her boyfriend to Sammy, had not gone unnoticed. "It's the murder. Finding a body—especially when it's your third in three months—is upsetting. Am I some kind of trouble magnet all of a sudden?"

"Just bad luck," he said, rubbing her shoulder.

"There's something I haven't told anyone yet," she said. She felt him stiffen, and looked up at him. His expression was blank, but his posture was stiff. "Why do you do that?" she asked.

"Do what?"

"Every time I say anything like I want to talk, or I have something to say, you stiffen up and get this look, like you're going to be a strong little soldier and not cry."

"I don't do that." He frowned and looked down at her. "Do I?"

"You do."

He rolled his shoulders and moved his neck, as if he was holding tension there. "I guess it's just a reflex. Whenever

Trish would say that, it would mean she was about to drop a bomb. I guess it's just reflexive."

"Daniel, your mom said that the trouble with Trish happened five years ago. Are you *ever* going to get over being dumped? Was she the love of your life or something?" Jaymie was a little exasperated, and it showed in her voice.

"I don't think so."

"You don't *think* so?"

"No, of *course* she wasn't. I didn't mean to express any doubt, Jaymie. It's just a word."

Just a word. Words held meaning, she had always believed, so why should this be any different? "Let's get going to the restaurant," Jaymie said, standing. She was being irrational and she knew it. What was wrong with her? As she watched Roger Collins walking back toward them, deep in conversation with her father, she knew what it was.

How could she not even have known Daniel's natural dad died when he was young? It had thrown her for a loop. It might not be the kind of information you led with—*Hi, I'm Daniel Collins and I lost my father at a young age*—but it was certainly something that should have come up in the last several months they had been dating. It led her to wonder what else she didn't know about him. She was an open book, but was he?

She walked toward the fathers, near the marina office. Just then the door to the office flung open. Garnet Redmond stormed out, and shouted back in the door, "I won't be jerked around, Will. I mean it!" He stomped off toward the stairs that led up to the road above the marina, not even noticing Jaymie and the others.

Will Lindsay came out, locked the office, then noticed Jaymie and Daniel. Jaymie walked over to him. "What was up with Garnet?"

The marina owner shook his head. "I just flat-out told him I was advising Sammy and Evelyn not to sell right away, to give it some time."

"He didn't take it well."

"No. Garnet Redmond doesn't like being crossed. I'd better get home; my wife's expecting me." He hustled away, walking up the hill away from the marina.

"What was that all about?" Jaymie's dad asked, as he and Roger Collins approached.

Jaymie explained, lightly, as they walked along the riverbank in the golden glow of the setting sun, then up the deck steps to the Ice House restaurant. As they entered, Jaymie saw Sammy right away, sitting with his mom and a group of older people. Evelyn Dobrinskie looked ill at ease.

When Jaymie approached and took Sammy aside, she said, "So . . . who are all these people?"

The teenager rolled his eyes. "When I got home, Dad's family was there. They came over from Canada to talk to Mom about the memorial service. I only see them once every couple of years, but Mom couldn't really say no. I mean, they're my grandma and aunts and uncles."

"Uh . . . Sam, when Daniel invited you and your mom to dinner—"

"No, no, don't worry about it!" the kid said, his cheeks glowing red. He shoved his hands in his pockets and hunched his narrow shoulders. "We're eating here; then we gotta get going . . . find them all places to stay. But I'm . . . I mean, my mom is paying. For our family, I mean."

Placing her hands on his shoulders, Jaymie shook him slightly and said, "Sam, you've done a great job today. I really appreciate how you took charge and helped us out. Especially with all you're dealing with right now." She impulsively drew him into a hug, and when she released him she saw how the red cheeks had spread to red ears and neck. "You'll get through this. Will we see you tomorrow, or . . . You should spend time with your family, I guess. We can go on without you, right?"

"I want to help," he said, fervently. "Unless my mom needs me, I'll be at your place tomorrow morning."

"Does your mom have family? Will they be coming, too?"

"I sure hope not. I just want to get this all over with."

As he went to sit down, Jaymie saw Ruby and waved, but the restaurant owner didn't appear to see her. Just then, the waitress they'd had at Ambrosio approached.

"Hey, guys, can I find you a table?" she said.

"You go on ahead," Jaymie said to Daniel and the dads. "I want to talk to Ruby." She followed her island neighbor as the woman headed down a private hallway behind the bar area, trotting to catch up with her, but when she turned a corner, it was to find Ruby crumpled into ball beyond a bend in the hall, huddled on the floor, her head on her knees. "Ruby! What's wrong?"

"He did it . . . I know he did it. Garnet killed Urban Dobrinskie for *me*!"

❧ Sixteen ❧

"**G**ARNET KILLED URBAN?" Jaymie gasped.

Shivering, her tear-streaked, ashen face turned up to Jaymie, Ruby grabbed the short sleeve of her T-shirt and scrubbed at her eyes, leaving a trail of mascara on her cheek. "I don't know what to think. He says he didn't, and I believe him . . . Really, I do. He's just not a violent guy."

"But?" There had to be a "but"; it was unspoken, and yet Jaymie could feel it lingering in the air between them like an odor.

"*But* he was gone from the restaurant that evening for a long time, and when he came back, he was upset. If Urban was killed behind your cottage, then Garnet couldn't have done it. He was inside the whole time." She hugged herself. "But if it was earlier, like the detective is implying . . ." Tears streamed down her cheeks and she shook her head.

"But you say you really don't believe he did it," Jaymie said, confused by Ruby's vacillation.

"I know, I know. I'm not making sense. I think . . . I think I'm breaking down!" she sobbed.

Jaymie helped Ruby stand and walked her back to the employee break room, what used to be the Ice House office, and sat her down, got her a cup of black coffee from an urn by a microwave, then sat beside her at the scarred wooden table, turning the rickety plastic chair to face her neighbor. She was thinking quickly, trying to decide what to say, what to ask, how to handle an emotionally fragile Ruby.

Regarding the woman with a critical eye, she saw someone who was worried, frightened, even. Her skin was ashen, where usually she was ruddy with good health. Wrinkles had appeared that hadn't been apparent before. Dissecting the crucial parts of Ruby's assertions, she asked, "Why was Garnet gone from the restaurant that evening? Did he tell you what he was doing?"

Ruby's gaze flickered away, and she took a sip of coffee. "It's ridiculous. Of course Garnet didn't do it! He's not a killer."

"Of *course* not," Jaymie said, keeping her tone soft and soothing. "But you must be worried the police will think he did. Why do you think that?"

She shrugged and looked down at the table. "He hit him; then Urban was dead the very next night. I'm just worried they'll see something that's not there."

"What was Garnet doing that evening?"

"We had some prank calls. Someone kept calling and asking for Garnet, but he was busy, so I answered, and they hung up."

Sounded a bit like an evasion. Watching Ruby, Jaymie prodded, "You said 'calls,' so did Garnet finally answer?"

Ruby shuddered, and nodded.

"And then what?"

"Nothing. Nothing!"

Jaymie pondered, watching Ruby fiddle with her coffee cup. "Did Garnet go out to meet the caller?"

She shrugged. Carefully, she said, "If he did, he didn't tell me. I mean, why would he?"

"Have you guys talked about that evening at all?"

Ruby shrugged yet again. She was retreating back into her shell; Jaymie could feel it. "Why are you upset if you are so sure Garnet didn't do anything?"

"I'm just worried about what that detective thinks, I guess," the woman said, her voice steadier. "He basically said to me that he thought Urban called Garnet to settle their argument, and that they met, quarreled again, and Garnet killed him. He's getting the restaurant's phone records. Said if the calls were from Urban, he'd be able to prove it."

Jaymie thought it through. "He's fishing, Ruby, trying to fit the facts with a theory, trying to frighten a confession out of one of you. Don't let it rattle you. What do *you* believe? *Could* Garnet have killed Urban? I mean, what if Urban attacked him and it was self-defense?"

"He's not a killer," she repeated, her tone stubborn. She turned her coffee cup around and around, sloshing dark liquid over the side.

Was she stating that, or trying to convince herself? Jaymie pondered the idea that Garnet met Urban, as the result of a phone call, and killed him as she had speculated. But it didn't seem right. What about the wheelbarrow? The theft of the wheelbarrow the night before implied planning, not a crime of passion. She could believe that Garnet might accidently kill someone when angry, but not that he would cold-bloodedly plan a murder.

Would Garnet kill Urban down at the river's edge and transport the body to his own backyard? It made no sense at all. Though Jaymie didn't fill Ruby in on the reasoning— she didn't want to spoil the detective's investigation by spilling details she knew or surmised—she tried to reassure her. "*You* know you're right, and *I* know you're right. Your brother did not do this, and I would bet on it. After an argument over a sail? That's ridiculous."

Ruby still looked haunted. "Who called, though?" she asked, her tone plaintive. "Garnet said he didn't recognize the voice, but the person asked him to meet him to discuss . . . something."

Jaymie caught hesitation in Ruby's demeanor, suddenly. There was something she wasn't saying. "So what did he do?"

"He . . ." She trailed off.

"He did what?"

"He says he went down to the dock, but no one was there. He waited around awhile, then came back."

Jaymie decided it was now or never to ask the other woman what had been on her mind since the morning of the murder. "Ruby, I heard you, the morning after the murder; you said, 'I didn't mean to do it.' What were you talking about?"

The older woman shook her head slightly, and was silent. Jaymie's stomach clenched. She had waited too long; Ruby had regained her composure. There was something, some mystery that Ruby was not revealing. If it had nothing to do with the murder, why didn't she just tell Jaymie what it was? "Ruby, what did it mean?" she asked.

"It . . . it was nothing. I didn't mean . . . Obviously it had nothing to do with the murder."

"Then just tell me what—"

Lisa, the waitress who had guided Daniel and the dads to their table, poked her head in the break room. "*There* you are!" she said to Jaymie. She drummed her fingers on the door, curiosity in her intelligent eyes. Her gaze flicked over to Ruby, who had her head down, then back to Jaymie. "I thought I saw you going this way. Your dad is wondering if you want to order appetizers? They're starving out there."

"Can I just have a moment, Lisa?" Jaymie said. "I'll come out in a sec."

But Ruby rose and said, "We're done. You shouldn't keep your father waiting." She swept past Lisa and down the hall, past the public washrooms and through the door to the restaurant.

Jaymie stood, staring after her.

"What is up with her?" Lisa said. "Her and Garnet have been fighting, and I've never seen that happen."

"What do they fight about?"

"I don't know. But it's like they've got some kind of secret, because all of a sudden, they're fighting in whispers and whenever anyone gets close, they shut up." The waitress shook her head. "I have this awful feeling like . . . I don't know, like Ruby is getting ready to leave or something."

"Leave? What do you mean?"

Lisa checked behind her, down the hall, then came into the break room and shut the door, leaning back against it. "You didn't hear this from me," she said in a confidential tone, "but I saw Ruby at the bank in Wolverhampton, and she took out ten thousand dollars in cash. In *cash*! Why else would someone take that kind of cash out of the bank? She's got to be planning to take off for some reason." She was silent for a beat, then added, "Please don't say that to anyone! I don't want to get Ruby in trouble. I'd better get back to work."

As Jaymie made her way through the restaurant to her table, she thought that despite Lisa's assertion, there *were* more explanations for taking cash out of the bank than just leaving town. Was Ruby paying someone off? Planning a secret purchase? Or was she giving the money to someone else to get out of town, someone like . . . Garnet?

"What took you so long, honey?" her dad said when she got to the table and sat down. "We're starving here, after a long day of working hard."

"Sorry. Just . . . just a girl thing," she said, the first thing that came to her mind. It effectively shut the guys up, but Daniel raised his brows. She mouthed "later" to him, and he nodded.

Dinner was uneventful and good. But Jaymie was

distracted, wondering about what she had learned, and more important, what she hadn't learned. What was Ruby Redmond hiding?

THERE WAS SOME awkwardness, later, as they got ready to leave the restaurant. Daniel's father seemed to think that his son would be staying on the island overnight. Jaymie's face flamed at the idea. She and Daniel were not to that point yet in their relationship, and she didn't know when they would be. So far he hadn't pushed it, and she was grateful. She was silent for a moment, not sure what to say, as she walked with them all down the board deck toward the road that wound along the river to the marina.

Daniel stepped in to save Jaymie embarrassment, saying, "I'll go back to Queensville with you, Dad, and come back out here tomorrow morning. I have to, uh, check my email, and stuff."

Not true, because he had his cell phone with him and had checked it on and off all day. But she squeezed his arm in gratitude and walked them to the ferry dock. She never did have a chance to share with Daniel what she had learned and *not* learned, but figured they'd have time the next day.

She returned alone to the cottage. It was late. While Hoppy had his evening piddle and sniffed around at the new grass and trees in the dark, near the back deck, Jaymie sat on the step watching the stars. What had she learned over the last few hours? For one thing, she would swear that Sammy did not know that his father was killed elsewhere and brought to the property after death. If she was right, that, of course, eliminated him as a suspect in the killing of his father, but did not clear his mother. She had lied about her son being home, probably because she wanted him to have some kind of alibi, but why did she not just say he was home all evening, just as she was?

Was it because at some point in the evening on the night

her husband died she was *not* home? Sammy had almost said something like that that very morning; he had been on the brink, it had seemed, of saying that after his dad went out, his mom followed. Was it physically possible for a woman like Evelyn to move a heavy body? Not likely, and not easily, but it was possible, she supposed, especially if she had planned ahead and had the wheelbarrow stashed somewhere.

And the nagging questions still lingered; with whom was Urban having an affair? And did that unknown woman have anything to do with his death? What if she was married, and her husband found out about them? Hmm. Zack's implication that Urban could have been on the Canadian side of the island that night threaded through her mind, too, and she wondered whether it was true.

Jaymie was deeply disturbed by her conversation with Ruby, and could not ignore it. The woman was scared, and it had something to do with Garnet. Why else would she blurt out that her brother killed the man? If it was true that she was having an affair with Urban, maybe Garnet didn't approve, or maybe Urban, given his propensity for domestic violence, hurt her at some point, and Garnet stepped in. What brother wouldn't? But she kept coming back to one firm conviction: Garnet would not deliberately bring a dead body to his own doorstep, especially not the body of a man he had punched just hours before.

It was confusing, a tangled web of deceit and violence.

She slept fitfully, and awoke the next morning hoping to figure out some of the mysteries that were swallowing up her and the peace of her island haven. After a quick shower and a little walk to let Hoppy piddle, she called Valetta, knowing that her friend would be having her pre-work cup of tea on her front porch. A dedicated gossip, Valetta never missed an opportunity to watch the neighborhood, just to keep her eye on what was what, though gossip was more often delivered to her via the shoppers who came into the Emporium.

"Hey, kiddo, what's shaking?" Valetta said, her tone chipper as usual.

Jaymie filled her friend in on some of her suspicions and new knowledge. "What was it that you said about Garnet and Ruby?"

"Me? Nothing, really. I just said there was something off about them."

"What do you mean by that?"

"I can't explain it. Just . . . off."

"Is it more one than the other? And what kind of 'off' do you mean?"

Valetta was silent for a long minute, and Jaymie could hear her slurping tea.

"I *just* don't know. Let me think on it. You coming back to Queensville?"

"I have to come back sometime today. My article for the *Howler* is due, and I just have to email it over to Nan. I hope it's good enough. I'm so nervous about it!"

"You'll be just fine. Talk to you later. Let me know when you need help with cleaning up the cottage, and I'll take a day off."

The phone rang as soon as she hung up; it was Daniel. He and his dad were ready to go, with trees already ordered for Sammy's reimagining of the cottage back lawn, and the pair willing to help.

"My mom wants to talk to you," he said, with an odd tone in his voice.

"Uh, okay," she said.

Debbie Collins came on the line. "I must admit, Jaymie, I'm curious about Heartbreak Island after the boys came back talking about it last night. Let's set a date for the family dinner right now."

With a sigh of relief at the woman's conciliatory attitude, Jaymie set the next Saturday for the dinner.

"And do any of you have food allergies? Our Daniel can't eat shellfish, did you know?"

"No, none of us have food allergies. Uh . . . I hope this isn't putting you out too much, Mrs. Collins?"

"It's fine. See you next Saturday."

And, dial tone.

After that, everything kicked into high gear. She fed Hoppy, made some sandwich fillings, stuck them in the fridge and did dishes, and then the men arrived. Roger, Jaymie's dad and Daniel all worked to Sammy's direction. It was kind of funny to see an eighteen-year-old bossing around two retired businessmen and a multimillionaire software company owner, but to their credit, the guys were all good-humored about it. Late in the morning, Jaymie saw Garnet sitting on his back porch watching the work. She made a quick decision, and climbed the hill to his house to talk to him. She needed answers.

"How are you doing, Garnet?" she asked.

He waved to a chair. "Sit down, Jaymie. Ruby says you all were at the restaurant for dinner yesterday."

"We were," she said, sitting in one of the Adirondack chairs that lined the back patio of the Redmonds' home. "What were you up to?"

"I was down talking to Will at the marina. Seems that the Dobrinskies have decided not to sell after all."

She watched him in profile, the tightening of his jaw, and didn't mention seeing him storm from the office. "I was surprised you were even interested. I didn't know you wanted to buy into the marina."

"I tried to buy half of it seven years ago, when Ruby and I first settled here. Urban sold a half share to Will instead."

That was interesting. She hadn't known that Urban once owned the whole thing. "Really? You must have been angry."

He shrugged. "At first, but we found the Ice House and built a great restaurant out of it. I always did want to own a marina. With Urban gone, and Evelyn Dobrinskie wanting to sell, it seemed like the right time."

"I'm surprised you and Ruby didn't settle down in Florida. I mean, you're practically professional sailors, and that's where sailing is at its best, right? On the ocean?"

His jaw flexed and his brown eyes held a faraway look. "We like the north better. I like to ski in winter. It's a compromise, really. I would have been happy with Florida, but Ruby wanted to be close to family in Canada."

"I didn't know you had family in Canada. Whereabouts?"

"Uh, up near Montreal." He shifted and looked over his shoulder, through the kitchen window of the cottage, then back to Jaymie. "Look, I don't want you to misinterpret anything you may have . . . uh . . . heard the morning after the murder."

She watched him. "You mean what Ruby said? About not meaning to do it?"

"Yeah. There's, uh, a very simple explanation for that."

Garnet had never been the kind to stammer, so the repetition of "uh" in his speech pattern was suspicious in and of itself. "And the explanation is . . . ?"

He looked down at his feet. "She said after we had that confrontation outside of the restaurant that she wished he was dead. That's it."

She eyed him with a frown. "But why did she say, 'I didn't mean to do it'? That doesn't make sense."

"She's superstitious, like, the wish becomes the reality, you know?"

"What?" It felt like he was making it up as he went along.

"You know . . . if you wish someone harm, and it comes true," he said impatiently, looking over his shoulder again, "wouldn't you feel bad if that happened to you?"

She looked down, and noticed that his hands were clenched on the seat of his chair so hard, his knuckles were white. Did that much tension really go with telling the truth? She wanted to ask him about how angry he was the evening before, storming out of Will's office, when he found out he wasn't getting the marina after all. She wanted to ask him why both he and Ruby were telling different tales, and about what Ruby had said about him the evening before, that she was afraid he had killed Urban. Where did he go that evening, she wanted to ask.

But she needed to think about it first. If she was talking to a killer, she didn't want to tip her hand, as had happened in the past. She couldn't keep blundering around into murder cases, not looking where she was going, so she was going to be more cautious this time around.

"You and Ruby have always been great neighbors, Garnet, and we've always been friends. I never believed for a second that either one of you could kill someone." That much was true; it was impossible to conceive of either sibling as a murderer. But *someone* had killed Urban Dobrinskie. Was it going to be her task to believe something impossible that day? "I've got to go back and pitch in," she said, standing. "The guys are working hard, and I'd better make some lunch for them."

"Jaymie," he said, grabbing her wrist and staring up at her. "I hope you believe what you just said, that neither of us killed Urban. I know it looks bad, but we didn't do it."

She looked into his eyes, noting the dark circles under them, and that they were bloodshot. It didn't look like he was sleeping well. "Can you think of anyone with a grudge against you? Someone who also knew about your tiff with Urban? Maybe someone was trying to make you look guilty."

His steely grip relaxed and he let her go as his expression changed, becoming thoughtful. His eyes widened and his mouth dropped open.

"Did you think of something?"

But his open expression shuttered, like a blind going down. "No. I just never thought of that . . . someone setting us up. I'll think about it. I'd better get going, too," he said, shoving himself up out of his chair. Jaymie stood, too. "Supplies coming in to the Ice House today."

He trotted into the house, and through the window she

saw him grab the phone in the kitchen and call someone. When he saw her still standing there, he waved good-bye, and she had to leave. But he thought of someone, she was sure of it. Unless . . . unless what he suddenly thought of was a way to deflect police suspicion from them by throwing it on someone else?

She started down the hill, pausing partway to overlook the work so far. The sod was down, and some trees were planted, with another load still sitting, root balls in burlap, to one side. This was getting expensive, but her dad considered it an investment. She didn't know what she thought of his suggestion to modernize the cottage, though. Becca had been talking about that for years. Jaymie was kind of a traditionalist, and liked the cottagey feel of their cottage.

She was just an old-fashioned girl, stuck in the past. She loved vintage anything, but it seemed that the rest of the world wanted shiny and new, convenient, modern. Boring. Sighing, she put that broody thought to one side, and focused on the new look of the backyard. Daniel was helping Sammy with the hard work of laying out the stone patio in the shade of the alders, while Roger and Jaymie's dad planted yet another tree. The scene of the crime was now just a sod covered grassy valley. Or . . . not really the scene of any crime, but the dumping of a body, as sad and horrible as that was.

She still thought the body placement was an attempt to implicate Garnet or Ruby by someone who knew about the tension between them and Urban. It appeared to be working, and she worried that gossip would condemn them as guilty, even if they weren't. Would their reputations suffer? If the murder was never solved, would they be ostracized, or had they made enough friends in the last seven years that they could weather it out? Jaymie didn't know.

As she slowly descended the slope to the gully, she turned her mind to the murder, and wondered, instead of trying to think of who benefited from Urban's death, maybe she should turn it around. Who suffered?

Sammy had lost a father and, no doubt, some financial stability.

Will Lindsay had lost a competent, if difficult, partner.

Evelyn had lost a husband and therefore some stability in her world. Heck, she may even have loved the jerk, for all Jaymie knew.

So that little exercise got her exactly nowhere. Confused by her conversation with Garnet and his evasiveness, Jaymie decided that lunch was what she needed.

❧ Seventeen ❧

S HE WAVED AT the guys as she passed, then climbed
the steps up to the sliding back door. Hoppy was at the
door, begging to go out, but there was no way she was going
to let the little Yorkie-Poo out when there were holes being
dug. It might give him the wrong idea, or he might fall in
one and get planted under a birch.

"You, my friend, are going to have to wait," she said,
throwing him a crunchie from the treat bag on the counter.
"I'll let you out while we eat lunch, and not a moment before."
The phone chimed just then, and she grabbed it.

"Jaymie! Oh, thank God I got you." It was her mother.
"Anna is not well, and Clive came and picked her up this
morning to take her back to Toronto, and Pam is doing the
best she can, but she doesn't know how to work the computer
and I don't, either, so I don't know what people are coming
in this afternoon, and Pam is freaking out, but I don't want
to call and worry Anna and Clive."

Jaymie glommed onto the one thing that worried her most in the stream of chatter. "Anna's not well?"

"Her blood pressure has been a little high. Could be pre-eclampsia. It was important that she get to her specialist in Toronto to have it checked out."

"But is she okay?"

"She's going to be fine. But, Jaymie . . . did you hear me? Pam and I can't figure out this computer thingie and I don't know what to do."

"Mom, you've worked with computers before." Her mother emailed regularly, had a Facebook page and had even figured out things like attaching photos and download-ing movies.

"But she's on some kind of bed-and-breakfast network, and I have her password—or at least I think I do—but . . . I'm lost!"

"You sound harried. Isn't there some kind of support phone number for the software?"

"I tried that. They won't help me, since I don't know Anna's PIN. Can you come?"

"Let me make lunch for the guys, and I'll come. Sit tight, and I'll be there in an hour or so." Well, she had said to Valetta that she needed to go home to email the article, so she'd do that at the same time.

A half hour later, after making a speedy lunch of sand-wich wraps, salad and cold drinks for her eclectic work crew, she and Hoppy were heading down to the marina. Robin and his guys were taking a lunch break, sitting and lying in the shade along the river's edge with lunch boxes open and a radio blaring FM rock radio. "Born to Be Wild" was play-ing, and one guy was playing air guitar while lying on his back.

Zack was at the marina talking to Will, who held a clean-ing cloth and a bucket, which he set down at his feet. The detective seemed distracted, and just sketched a wave to Jaymie before heading off up the road toward the cottager's section of the island. While she waited for the ferry, she headed toward Will, who was scrubbing down a sailboat, a "For Sail" sign, misspelling intended, lying on the wooden deck.

Hoppy went to the end of his lead and barked at some seagulls floating on the waves. "Another sailboat up for grabs?" Jaymie said. "That's the third one this week. Is everyone leaving Heartbreak Island?"

He shrugged and went back to work, using a stiff brush to scrub the greenish line off the hull. "Pretty normal this time of year. Now that we're dredging the harbor and fixing up the slips, we won't lose any more. I'm pretty sure I can add another ten slips, actually, and we can move ahead, instead of backward."

"What did the detective want?"

Will frowned and paused in his work, wiping sweat off his forehead with the sleeve of his shirt. "He wanted to know how long I'd known Garnet and Ruby. I don't understand it. It was like . . . he seemed suspicious."

"Of you?"

"No. Of Garnet and Ruby."

"Why?"

Will's gaze shuttered. "I . . . I don't know. Look, Garnet is a friend, and I won't gossip about him."

He was the only one of the Redmonds' friends who seemed so reserved, and she appreciated that. "They're lucky to have you as a friend, Will." She hesitated, but then said, "But I have to say . . . the other night, when you told him finally that you were advising Evelyn and Sammy not to sell, he stormed out of your office kind of angry, right?"

"Yeah, but at least he apologized this morning. Called me right up and said he was sorry about getting bent out of shape. That's a true friend." He swiped at his eyes, then scruffed Hoppy under the chin, while the little dog panted and danced, trying to get more attention. "I will never believe that either one of those people had anything to do with Urban's death.

Couldn't it have been an . . . I don't know, an accident or something?"

"No one ends up stabbed though the heart with an ice pick accidentally," she said.

"Stabbed? Oh my gosh! I . . . I didn't know. Poor Evelyn!"

He really *didn't* listen to gossip, she guessed, because Urban's manner of death was common knowledge. The ferry chugged into the marina, pulled up to the dock, lowered the gangplank and disembarked passengers. Jaymie tugged at Hoppy's lead, picked him up and then walked onto the ferry, settling on a bench near the railing with her little pooch in her arms. As she gazed back at the marina, she saw Will sitting on the overturned bucket, head in hands, looking for all the world as if he'd lost his only friend.

When she got home, her mother was in a dither. As Jaymie let Hoppy off his leash in the yard and walked up to the back door, Joy Leighton charged out onto the summer porch, saying, "Oh, Jaymie, thank goodness you're here. Let's go over to the bed-and-breakfast right now and see if you can help poor Pam."

"Give me a minute, will you?" Jaymie said, squeezing past her mom and into the kitchen. "I just need to go online and . . . and check my email."

Her mother followed her and folded her arms across her chest, looking put out. "I thought you were only coming back to help poor Pam. But if your email is more important . . ."

Her mother had a habit of saying something irritating, and letting it trail off. In the past it had elicited instant obedience from Jaymie, because guilt would overwhelm her. This time was going to be different; she'd react as an adult. "Mom, it won't take long, I promise. This is important to me. I have to email my article to Nan Goodenough, the editor at the *Howler*."

Her stomach growled. She was nervous about the editor's

reaction. She had been assailed by doubts in the middle of the night, sure that her wording was trite, her subject matter boring, and her grammar horrendous. After all, she was no writer. She had even woken up in a cold sweat thinking that she had forgotten to list a key ingredient in her recipe. That was another thing: she wanted to check her article over before sending it out, just to make sure she hadn't left out a key ingredient in the recipe.

"All right," her mom said. "But hurry up!"

First, she typed and checked the article, reading it through and checking the vintage sandwich loaf recipe. It was exactly right, but she adjusted it a little, having now made the loaf, with some tips to make spreading the cream cheese "icing" easier. With a sigh of relief she realized she had not forgotten a thing, and the article sounded okay. Not great, but okay, except she had misspelled "picnicking." Darn. Why hadn't spellcheck caught that? She made the correction. She got the memory card out of her camera and uploaded the sandwich loaf photos, choosing the two best, as well as the vintage picnic settings she had photographed. Then she logged on to her email, attached the document and the photographs, and held her breath, pushing "send."

Done. No going back. It was in Nan's in-box.

Now she would handle her mother and Anna's cousin's crisis. She was interested to meet Anna's cousin Pam, who would be taking over the running of the bed-and-breakfast for the winter months, while Anna spent at least six months in Canada making sure her baby would be healthy and safe. All Anna had said about Pam was that she needed the job, and she would be happy to live in a small town after living in Rochester.

Jaymie and her mom went next door, where a harried-looking blond woman with her straggly hair pulled back in a ponytail stood on the sidewalk peering at the door, a frown on her thin face. "Oh, Joy, I'm so glad you came back!" she said, throwing her arms around Jaymie's mom.

Jaymie's brows inched up. Really? Pam had just met Jaymie's mom and was acting like the long-lost best friend?

"You must be Jaymie," she said, turning with a nervous smile. She touched her hair and tucked a stray wisp behind her ear. "I'm sorry to be so much bother already; I'm such a dunce! Anna ran me through the computer program, but I'm such a dolt I can't remember stuff like that. It just goes in one ear and out the other."

"Pam, don't talk about yourself like that," Jaymie's mom said. "I didn't have any more luck than you did with the software."

"But I'm the one Anna is depending on! I *knew* I couldn't do this. I just knew it, but Anna said she had faith in me. I'm going to let her down and ruin her business." A tear welled up in one eye and slid down her cheek.

"Let me see the trouble," Jaymie said, to stem the tide of self-abuse.

They went upstairs to the office, and Jaymie noted, on the way, that the house was cleaner than it was even when Anna was present. It gave her pause, because she wondered whether her mom had been helping Anna out more than she was supposed to. Her mom seemed to like cleaning other people's homes, even though she hired a woman to clean the Leighton condo in Florida.

Jaymie sat down at the computer and familiarized herself with Anna's setup, while Pam chattered nervously to Joy, babbling about her son, Noah, who was going to go to school at Wolverhampton High, and how she hoped the kid would fit in, and how sorry she was to cause so much trouble.

"It's no trouble, Pam," Joy said, touching the other woman's arm. "Jaymie has time. She helps Anna all the time, you know, so it's no imposition at all."

Jaymie gritted her teeth. Oh no, her time wasn't worth anything at all . . . She was *only* pulled away from landscaping the cottage yard that she was slaving over because her mother insisted that they have the dinner at the cottage, and so Mrs.

Collins wouldn't look down her nose at them for having a mud yard, as if they were a bunch of poor relations. Jaymie took a deep, cleansing breath and tuned out the chatter.

Anna used a software called InnKeeper. It tracked bookings, and held a wealth of information about past, present and future guests of the Shady Rest Bed and Breakfast. Anna had slowly been adding to her InnKeeper database, entering information on all of the clients the former three landlords had compiled on paper. That way Anna could send out email and paper invitations to visit the Joneses, the new landlords of the Shady Rest. They had a website, with Clive and Anna's smiling faces, cradling Tabitha between them, in their arms.

There was a log-in button in the corner, and Jaymie clicked on it, but it came up with a window for a PIN. How was she supposed to magically guess Anna's PIN? It appeared that the software required both the password they already had, and a PIN, something that had been missed in the hurry of Anna's leaving. Of course, she could always phone or email Anna to ask, but they were trying not to upset her friend, and there would, no doubt, be more pressing concerns in the days ahead, if this first day was any indication.

As she thought about it, she listened in on Pam's stream of self-deprecating chatter.

"I'm so lucky Anna had this idea, for me to work here. I was at my wit's end, you know, because with Jack after me, and running out of money, I had to get out of town but I just didn't know what I was going to do." She touched her cheekbone.

When Jaymie glanced up, she could see a faint purpling of the area.

"I just hope he doesn't find me. I don't know what I'll do if he does! I can't leave now, not with Anna depending on me."

Yikes, there was a lot of drama in this woman's life. Had Anna made the right decision for her business, or had she let her heart and family loyalty sway her? Would Pam prove to be the B and B's undoing? Jaymie sat and stared at the screen for a minute. Anna must have her password and PIN information stored somewhere. She rummaged around on the messy desk and found a little booklet that Jaymie had seen Anna consult before. Flipping through it, she came upon a list of words. Aha! Such a random list could only mean one thing. She methodically started entering words, one after another, but nothing worked. She sat back and thought about it.

"Do you think your ex will follow you?" Jaymie's mom said to Pam, alarm in her voice.

"No, I covered my tracks. I never told him my real name. He knows me as Lana Jones."

Jaymie had a moment of worry . . . Lana Jones? That was pretty close to Anna Jones. What if this violent Jack made the connection, or figured it out?

She shook her head, clearing it. She was down to the last word on the list, and when it didn't work, Jaymie sat back, puzzled. She looked at the list and squinted. As she stared, a pattern emerged. The second letter of each word, in the column of words, spelled *another* word. "Yes! I've got it," she said, and typed in "TabbysMom." Up popped the welcome screen, and when she clicked on the Guests tab, a booking page popped up, and two names of the guests who would arrive later that day. "There we go."

"You're a lifesaver," Pam said, with a sigh of relief. A boy stomped down the hall without a look in to the three women in the office.

"Noah . . . Noah! Why don't you say hi, or . . . Okay, you go to your room for a while, then, honey," Pam said. She lowered her voice and said, "I just don't know what I'm going to do with him. I sure hope he fits in okay in his new school. The last one didn't turn out so well; then he and Jack got into it, and he ended up in the hospital . . . Noah, not Jack. That's when I knew I had to leave."

At that moment, Jaymie realized how much she was going to miss Anna. Sometimes her friend was scattered, and sometimes she needed help, but she had never been so down-trodden and yet fulsomely forthcoming as Pam. A second later, she felt bad for her thoughts, as she watched the worried face of Pam. For Anna's sake she would try to help this woman cope. She really did feel sorry for Pam, and wanted to help her, but she sure did miss Anna!

"At least now you'll know who to expect to arrive this afternoon," she said, standing.

"Thank goodness! One of the guests has been here two weeks, and he's left the room in a mess—Anna said he was gone half the time, sometimes for a couple of days, but while he was here he sure generated enough laundry to sink a barge—but now I know who is coming and I can concentrate on getting it clean. I just hope . . . Oh, I *hope* I don't mess things up too bad!"

"You'll do fine, Pam. But . . ." She paused; to speak or not to speak? "I hope this isn't out of line, but . . . you won't talk too much about your trouble with Jack, especially with your guests, right?"

Pam's eyes welled up and her lip trembled. What had she said that was so bad? Jaymie wondered.

"Jaymie, I'm sure Pam just trusted us," her mom said, with a note of rebuke in her voice. "She knew she could confide in us."

Restraining the urge to roll her eyes, Jaymie replied, "Good. I'm just thinking of her. She was saying she worries that Jack will find her."

"I'm sure she *meant* well, Mrs. Leighton," the other woman said, her tone filled with affront. The emphasis in her words showed exactly what she thought of Jaymie's concern. "I know she's just looking out for her new friend, the cousin I've loved my whole entire life. Jaymie, I promise I won't *shame* Anna in Queensville."

"I didn't mean that!" Jaymie said, shocked to her core by the construct the other woman had placed on her words. "Honest. *You* know that, Mom; I would never say something like that." She watched the other woman's face, and glanced over at her mother, who raised her eyebrows. Turning back to her friend's cousin, she said, "I'm sorry, Pam, if it came across like that. It would honestly never occur to me that any woman should be ashamed of being abused! I just want your safety."

"It's all right. I'm sure you didn't mean it how it *sounded.*"

Jaymie stifled her natural response, and simply said, "I have to get back out to the island. I'm going to check in with Valetta at the store first, but other than that, I'll be gone the rest of the day, Mom. Are we good here?"

"Yes, thank you for adding in your little bit."

She stifled the urge to scream and smiled. "Good. Mom, are you coming home?"

"No, I'm going to stay here for a bit and help out Pam."

Teary eyed, the younger woman hugged her. "Thank you, Joy! I'm a little nervous, meeting new people."

Oh, now, *there* was a good trait for an aspiring innkeeper! This had disaster written all over it. What had Anna been thinking, choosing Pam to stand in? But then, maybe she hadn't had many options. How many people could drop their whole life and move cities?

And how soon would Pam's past catch up to her?

That question haunted her as she returned to the house. But she had her own life to think of, and was not going to let Pam's troubles overwhelm her!

She went back in to check her email. It had been more than an hour; Nan was always on top of her email, and would have received the article by now. Jaymie hit the log-in button and held her breath and . . . nothing. No answer at all? Maybe Nan had hated it. Maybe it was so awful, she couldn't even be bothered to comment. Maybe her article was even now being sent around the Internet as a meme for how awful a beginning writer could be.

She took a deep breath and let it out. Or maybe—just maybe—Nan was busy. She logged off.

Jaymie headed back out, with Hoppy on a long tether, and briskly strode the short walk toward the dock, caught the ferry, and then headed back toward the cottage. It had been wrong, she decided, as she walked, to be so judgmental of Pam. It actually took incredible courage to leave your life behind and make a whole new one. Next time she saw Pam, she'd cut her some slack and try to befriend her.

In the cottage kitchen she put down a bowl of crunchies for Hoppy, and walked out the back door. The guys were all sitting in the shaded copse on the new flagstone patio. The whole yard still had a raw, new look, but what a transformation in the few hours she had been gone! There were clusters of young trees, and a planting of three birches, surrounded by low-growing shrubs, their red leaves brilliantly offset by the white bark of the birch. Down in the shade of the grove of alders, there was a lovely irregularly shaped seating area surrounded by lush, new grass.

Daniel waved to her, and Sammy grinned at her stunned expression. The two dads just sat, exhausted, dirty and obviously weary to the bone.

"You guys!" she said, dashing down the deck steps and hurrying across the new, lush sod, toward them. She had tears welling in her eyes, and she wondered whether she was just tired, or was she just so thrilled at how Daniel and the dads had worked together to make such a wonderful transformation to a place she loved so much? "This is amazing!"

Daniel stood and put his arm around her shoulder, pointing out all the fine points of the patio, what stones he had done, what he had learned and how helpful Sammy had been.

"I give you an A on this project!" she said to the teenager.

He ducked his head, and said he ought to get home, since he shouldn't leave his mom to deal with his dad's relatives alone all day.

Roger and Jaymie's dad, Alan, both stood and stretched with identical looks of weariness.

"Do you guys want to clean up here and go to dinner? Or something?" Jaymie asked.

"Honey, all I want is to go home and collapse," her dad said, putting his hands on her shoulders.

"Dad, I'm so sorry I put you to this kind of work. And Mr. Collins . . . you've been so kind about this, but it's probably the last thing you wanted to do."

Roger Collins, his broad, weather-beaten face wreathed in a weary smile, clapped his son on the shoulder. "Don't worry on it, sweetie. It was a good day's work, and now I look forward to coming out here to relax, next time." He paused, but then said, "Jaymie, can I talk to you for a minute?"

Daniel looked a little alarmed, but Jaymie followed Roger a little ways away.

"I just wanted to say how much I appreciate how you handled Debbie, compromising, and all that. She doesn't mean to be difficult. It's just her way."

"Mr. Collins—"

"Call me Roger."

"Okay, Roger, I didn't want it to become a tug-of-war. My mom can be stubborn, too, and I thought if we gave a little, it would work out better." What she didn't add was that she and her mom were both so busy, Debbie was actually performing a valuable service. She left it unsaid because in this case, she didn't mind Daniel's parents thinking she had given in to promote their happiness.

"Truer words were never spoken. Now I'm going to go back to Danny's, and let a hot shower beat the pain out of my muscles." He limped back to the group. "I just hope I'll have enough energy for my golf game tomorrow, right, Al? You ready to skedaddle?" he said, to Jaymie's dad.

The fathers left, but Daniel stayed. He wanted to go with Jaymie to the Ice House for dinner to celebrate the completion of the work, and her turning in her first article, but first, he needed a hot shower. While the water ran, Jaymie tried to keep her mind off the thought that this was the first time she and Daniel had been in the same house alone while one of them was naked. She pondered the differences between Daniel and Zack. Daniel was not the kind to unselfconsciously strip off his shirt and work naked to the waist, but she had noticed that he was not unimpressive, wiry, rather than bulky, in the muscularity department.

The two men epitomized the differences in romance novels heroes. Zack was the brooding alpha male hero, an action guy, a little mysterious, dangerous, tough and ready to handle any situation with a well-placed fist. Daniel was the beta hero, the witty, funny, smart guy who could be your friend and your lover at the same time.

But she knew better than to simplify the two men into romance fiction archetypes. The trouble was, she was attracted to them both for different reasons. She had thought her attraction to the detective was simply physical, but talking to him over dinner she had seen the human side of him, and he was really a very nice guy. Unfortunately.

But Daniel . . . he was the real deal, right? That was what everyone kept saying. He was someone who would stick around for the long run, someone she could count on in difficult situations. And she liked him. She was mildly attracted to him. He was a good kisser, and physically they seemed compatible. And he was naked in her shower right that minute. She thought of all the sexy moves women made in romance novels, how one of the heroines of a contemporary would probably strip down and hop into the shower with Daniel, which would lead to hot lovemaking.

Except, that just wasn't her.

Instead, she took Hoppy outside and sat on the porch, watching as day turned to evening. Then Daniel came out dressed in clean clothes and they walked to the marina, then to the restaurant. She was taking it slow, she knew, compared to some women, but that was her. And it felt right.

❈ Eighteen ❈

R UBY AND GARNET were both there, but busy. The waitress who took their order was not one she recognized, and Jaymie thought Lisa was probably working at Ambrosio that night. She talked about the murder investigation with Daniel. "I feel like I don't know the players well enough. I've been coming to the cottage my whole life, but I only spend a few days here, at the most, and don't really interact with the islanders as much as I thought I did."

"What do you think, so far?"

She outlined what she knew, what she guessed, and sighed over what she didn't know. "For all I know, the police could be preparing to arrest someone right now." She glanced over at Garnet, who was pouring a beer for one of the locals. "Maybe even one of the Redmonds."

"Who else is there?"

"I don't know. You want me to name everyone I've considered?" He nodded, so she took a deep breath and named them all, counting them off on her fingers. "Garnet and

Ruby," she said, throwing Ruby a glance. The woman looked deeply uneasy, and kept glancing toward the door. What was that all about? "Evelyn and Sam, Will Lindsay, Sherm Woodrow, and then there are the unknowns, like whomever was dating Urban."

"Sherm Woodrow?" he asked. "He's the tart baker's husband, right? Why him?"

Jaymie frowned off into the distance, trying to solidify her thoughts. "I wouldn't say this to anyone but you, but . . . well, I just wondered about him tattling about the Redmonds' sail to Urban. Was he trying to cause a problem between them? And did he use that trouble to . . . I don't know, make Garnet look guilty?"

"I see what you mean. But if you put Sherm on there, don't you have to put his wife on, too?"

"I don't think so."

"You must have an idea who seems most likely to you, though." Daniel eyed her and squinted, behind the glinting lenses of his glasses. "I know you do. Who is it?"

She watched him a moment, and said, "I know this is going to sound awful, but Evelyn seems almost the most likely to me. She's just . . . I don't know. She seems odd. I hope, for Sammy's sake, that it's not her."

"Me, too. I really like that kid. He's got a great future ahead of him. I'd hate for the way his dad died to become a burden."

"Daniel, speaking of fathers, I have a serious question. Why didn't you ever tell me that your father died, and that Roger was your stepdad?"

Daniel drummed his fingers on the surface of the table. "I should have, I guess. It's just not something I talk about a lot."

"Shouldn't we talk about everything? If we're . . . if we plan to get serious, I mean?"

"But are we? Are we serious? Are we *planning* on getting serious? And how do you 'plan' to get serious?"

Jaymie edged away from the topic, nervous about it for

some reason. She had to make some decisions, and she didn't feel ready yet. Maybe she should just let it go.

Fortunately, their food came just then, and silence fell as the edge of hunger was sated. The attentive waitress, not as chatty as Lisa but better at her job, refilled Jaymie's iced tea and Daniel's beer. The conversation, when it resumed, was about food, and then the upcoming family dinner.

Daniel dipped a French fry in a pool of ketchup. "What did my dad want to say to you, when he drew you aside?"

"He's just happy I talked to your mom and worked out a compromise. We're going to supply the venue, and she can plan the menu. She seemed happy with that."

"I'm surprised you would let go of the food side. You like to cook; I figured that would be one thing you'd want to do."

"What I *want* is for my mom and your mom to get along."

He rolled his eyes.

"Daniel, I'm serious. If I can facilitate that by giving in on something, while they hold fast, then so be it. This way my mom got what she really wanted, which was to have the dinner at the cottage, and your mom got to control some aspect of it, the food."

He chuckled. "We both come from families with stubborn women."

She was happy he didn't use some other adjective that many used to describe stubborn women; all too often, men called woman like that difficult, or even bitchy. Not that Daniel would use that word. He and his mom seemed to be close. She adored him, her only child.

As Jaymie finished her meal, the house special of the night—an exceptional ground sirloin burger and mixed greens salad—she told Daniel about Pam, though she didn't go into detail about the woman's tale of fleeing abuse. "It's all going to be different. I'm so used to Anna being there, and running over to her place for coffee. I miss her already!"

"I know. You'll still see her when she comes down to check on Pam. You said she plans to come down, right?"

"That's her plan. She's going to stay overnight once or twice a month just to give Pam a break and make sure things are going all right."

Daniel excused himself to go to the washroom, and as he moved toward the hallway, out of the corner of her eye Jaymie saw Ruby glance around, and slip out the door, a large bag over her shoulder. Everything in her demeanor suggested stealth. She followed the woman out the door to the wooden deck, but Ruby was speeding off toward the marina, not looking either way, but hurrying. Maybe she was taking the ferry to Queensville for something. It was a mystery, but not one she could figure out an answer to. She couldn't exactly gallop after Ruby and demand to know where she was going, and it was really none of her business, she reminded herself with some severity. She had to stop thinking that she could solve every problem that came along.

Even if the curiosity tugged at her brain until she was cross-eyed.

Jaymie returned and they finished dinner; then she walked Daniel down to the ferry. In the darkness something splashed and a duck, awoken from its rest, quacked indignantly. While they waited, Daniel took her in his arms and kissed her gently, rocking her back and forth; it was kind of like dancing. Then he held her away from him, looking down into her eyes with a serious expression. Uh-oh. When men looked like he did, they had something on their mind; she knew that from experience. She smiled up at him in the halo of light from the dockside lanterns. "What's up?"

"Jaymie, we're taking this slowly, I know, but . . . are you still interested? In me? In *us*? I don't want to be anyone's safe choice, or second choice."

She felt a shudder pass through him, and looked up into his questioning eyes, partially hidden behind his glinting lenses. "Where is this coming from, Daniel? What's going on?"

"Nothing." He was silent for a moment, squinting off to the horizon. "I just need a little security, I guess."

"Security? What, like a guarantee? There are no guarantees in life; you know that." She could see by his expression that she had not reassured him; nor did she really intend to. She wasn't sure of her own feelings yet, and couldn't promise anything. "You've never struck me as insecure."

"I care more now, I guess. And when I heard that you had dinner with that cop . . ." He shrugged and gazed down into her eyes. "I've just got a feeling, I guess. Promise me you don't . . . don't have feelings for him?"

Uh-oh. How to put this without lying, hurting his feelings, or ruining everything that was so good between them? "I explained why I ended up having dinner with Zack. He's just a casual acquaintance, Daniel, nothing more. Honest. He asked me to have dinner with him another night, and I said no. Would I do that if I was interested in him?"

"He asked you to have dinner? Doesn't he know we're dating? Why would he do that?"

His panicked tone suggested she had gone wrong. Why was he focusing on the one part of the statement that wasn't important? She sighed in exasperation. "Daniel, I said *no*! He's just new in town and doesn't have a lot of friends, that's all." Why on earth was she having to reassure him about Zack's nonexistent feelings? Surely that was the least important part of it all. It was what *she* felt and did that was important! She pulled away from Daniel. "We talked, and were friendly, but nothing more. Honest."

The ferry chugged up to the dock and several people disembarked. Daniel looked torn, but finally said, "I guess I'd better get going. Just ignore what I said, Jaymie. I was just . . . I think I'm going a little crazy, with Mom and Dad here." He kissed her quickly, ran to the ferry and hopped aboard, waving at her from the railing as it chugged over to Queensville.

She stood and watched as the ferry disappeared into the dark, then appeared again by the lights of the Queensville dock as it approached shore. Was his sudden insecurity completely about Zack, or something to do with his mother? She clearly did not like Jaymie, and who knew what the woman was saying to him when she wasn't around? And now she was being paranoid. She was going to cut Daniel some slack and stop obsessing. In a thoughtful mood, she returned to the cottage and leashed Hoppy.

"C'mon, fella . . . let's go for a walk. You need to pee and I need to think."

She walked through the village part of the island first. Tansy's Tarts was locked up tight, and Jaymie saw in the windows of the apartment above the unmistakable flickering of a television set. Were her faint suspicions of Sherm just lingering questions? Hard to say. She looped around and walked past the Dobrinskie house, but it was dark. Where had Evelyn and Sammy put her numerous houseguests? She remembered Evelyn's panicked state in Tansy's Tarts the morning after the murder; Tansy said she'd help her find vacancies, but if the Dobrinskie family members had come from Canada, they could just as easily stay on the Canadian side of the island.

She looped around and past the Ice House restaurant, then cut down an alleyway and past a Dumpster, where Hoppy had to stop and sniff. "C'mon, fella. This place reeks of fish."

Movement caught her eye, and she saw Garnet stealthily slipping into the back door of his restaurant. Why the secrecy? Or . . . was he just being quiet for some reason? It was odd, but she shook her head and let it go.

As she walked down toward the marina and dock, though, she pondered the mysterious phone calls and what Lisa, the waitress, had said about the Redmonds' actions the evening of the murder. Both had been missing for a portion of the evening, it seemed. Both, therefore, had the opportunity to slip out for the necessary length of time to kill Urban Dobrin-skie. Ruby had outright said she worried that Garnet had done it. This *had* to indicate something much more serious between them and the marina owner than an insult to Ruby. Did it have to do with Garnet's desire to buy the marina? Even that seemed ridiculous. Killing Urban did not assure that Garnet would be able to buy the marina, as had been proven true just recently.

There had to be something more.

Little, niggling details, things she had noticed, came back to her. She paused and let Hoppy sniff a light standard. Why was Ruby so camera shy? The woman had positively blanched and skittered away when Jaymie was taking photos, and would not allow herself to be in a picture with the ice chests. Was that normal? Was she really that shy? What could account for that?

She pressed on, waiting for Hoppy to do his job, plastic bag in hand at the ready. Nothing yet. He was prolonging the walk, as he always did, and would probably not stop to poop until they were on their way back to the cottage. As she walked along the dock, she saw a shadowy figure near the marina office, and realized it was Will Lindsay. "Hey, Will," she said.

He yelped and spun around. "Gosh, you scared me, Jaymie!"

"What are you doing here this late? I thought you were always home by eight?"

"I just forgot some papers."

She pointedly looked at his empty hands.

"I thought I left them here, but they *must* be in my home office. That's what happens when you have two offices; you can never remember where you left things." He bent over, petted Hoppy, then straightened. "What are you doing . . . catching the last ferry back to town?"

"No, I'm staying out on the island another couple of nights. Now that the landscaping is done, I need to clean up the cottage. Valetta is coming out to help. And my new patio furniture is coming over tomorrow."

"Nice. Well, I told the wifey I'd only be a few minutes, so I'd better get going home." He strode off whistling, his hands shoved in his shorts pockets.

"Say, Will? Did you see Ruby down here earlier? Did she catch the ferry over to the mainland?"

He turned back, frowning, his face illuminated by the security lighting near the marina office. "Ruby Redmond? No. Why?"

"Just thought I saw her heading for the marina, that's all."

"Nope . . . can't help you there." He turned to walk away, but then turned back toward her, with a perplexed frown on his face. "Now, that's odd. I didn't see Ruby, but . . ." He shook his head.

"But what?" she prodded.

"I *thought* I saw Garnet. I could be mistaken. I just caught a glimpse, you know, and it is getting dark."

"Garnet? Really? How long ago was this?"

He shook his head. "I don't know . . . twenty minutes, half an hour? Maybe more. Gosh, I'm terrible with time, especially when I'm busy! It was when I got here, and I don't know how long I've been looking for that darned paper. I must be wrong. It was just a quick glance, you know, and then the guy was gone." He waved one hand in dismissal. "Nah . . . he'd be at the restaurant all evening. Forget I said anything."

He headed off, and she led Hoppy down to the dock and sat on a bench, while Hoppy sniffed around and growled. She gave him a little more lead, and he pulled all the way to the end of it.

The thought that had been in the back of her mind all day as she went about her business came back to her. Who had killed Urban Dobrinskie and dumped him on her property? And why there? It made no sense at all, unless the killer was Evelyn or Sammy Dobrinskie. Sammy, especially, would know about the wheelbarrow and the muck and might think burying him would just make the problem of his father disappear. Was he capable of the coolheadedness necessary to think fast enough to shout, "Get off my property," making it seem like Garnet was speaking? The more she thought about it, the less likely that seemed.

Something struck her in that moment. She was automatically eliminating Garnet from the pool of folks who committed the murder *because* of that voice, and her assumption that he had been in his house at that moment, along with her feeling that he wouldn't plant the body in his own backyard.

But she really only had Ruby's word for that. How could Ruby be so sure her brother was in the house? If she shut her bedroom door, she would never know if he crept out. It would be a clever double bluff to yell that phrase, and Garnet was clever; she knew that. She got a weird feeling that crept up her back. Valetta had said there was something "off" about Garnet and Ruby, but she couldn't put her finger on it. She needed to pin her friend down on that feeling, see whether she'd thought of what it was that made her say that.

"C'mon, Hoppy, let's get back," she said, tugging on the leash.

But the little dog was on the edge of the dock peering down into the water and could not be pulled.

"Hoppy, come *on*!"

He growled, but didn't obey. It was probably a big fish at the water's edge. He hated carp, for some strange reason, and would bark ceaselessly at carp, goldfish, suckers, any kind of big, slow fish. What was he glaring at this time?

She inched to the edge of the dock, and saw something floating, something blue. Blue? Not a fish, then, at least not the kind that frequented the dull waters of the St. Clair. There was too much shadow for the light overhead along the dock to help, so she dropped her dog's leash, scooted off the edge of the dock near the shore, shed her sandals and waded out, the squishy muck on the bottom of the river oozing up through her toes. She caught hold of the blue cloth, but it was fixed to the dock support. She pulled harder, with Hoppy barking at her from the edge.

Just then she heard a commotion from up the beach.

"Ruby!" a voice called. "Ruby, is that you?"

Jaymie's stomach lurched, and she grabbed hold of the blue cloth and pulled harder. The figure pulled free and floated toward her. A face moved into the light. "Oh my G— Help! Help me!" Jaymie cried, as she stared down at the body of Ruby Redmond.

❋ Nineteen ❋

GARNET REDMOND CAME clumping toward Jaymie, and when he saw who she was holding on to, he cried out in anguish, "Ruby! My God, what happened! *Ruby!*" He leaped off the edge of the dock, grabbed her up in both arms and carried her to the edge of the river, his shadowy figure appearing and disappearing by the dock lights as he splashed toward shore. Another dog started barking in response to Hoppy's yapping, and in the distance someone shouted, trying to make it shut up. Jaymie waded ashore behind Garnet. He gently laid his sister on the muddy shore and tilted her head back, trying to breathe into her mouth to give her mouth-to-mouth resuscitation, but fumbling. It was a surreal scene, like some waterlogged love scene made even stranger by the fact that they were brother and sister.

Soon others joined them on the shore in the spill of light from the dock lamps, but one man in shorts and a T-shirt elbowed his way through the crowd. "I'm a doctor; let me through!" Garnet surrendered his spot, and the man knelt by her and began CPR. In two minutes, miracle of miracles, she sputtered and he turned her over, as a rock fell out of her sweater pocket. A gush of water flooded from her and she coughed, choking and gasping.

Garnet wept with relief, then collapsed to the mucky shore, clutching his sister to his chest. Tears streamed down Jaymie's face as Zack raced down the beach toward her and Hoppy, who was dancing around her feet, yapped nonstop.

"What the hell is going on here?" Zack said.

Jaymie picked up Hoppy as she explained.

Will Lindsay raced toward Jaymie, too. "What's going on? What happened to Ruby?"

As Zack whipped out his cell phone and called for an ambulance, Jaymie quickly told the marina owner about her discovery.

"Oh my God!" Will whispered, his glance slewing toward Garnet, who held Ruby while the doctor checked her pulse. Tears glimmered in the corners of Will's eyes. "I was just down here, and I didn't . . . What happened? How . . . ?" He choked back a sob and pushed his fingers through his hair. "She could have *died*!"

"I know. Thank heavens for Hoppy!" Jaymie hugged the pup to her and gave him a kiss. He wriggled, wanting down, so she set him gently on the gravel that lined the approach to the dock.

"What is going on in this place?" Will said, still staring at Garnet.

The marina owner then joined a knot of curious, chattering onlookers, while Zack directed a local, who was one of the township's volunteer firemen, to fire up his motor boat and take Garnet and Ruby over to Queensville. The fireman was a trained paramedic, but the doctor who had revived Ruby insisted on going along. The detective then strode off and made another cell phone call, as an ambulance roared up to the dock on the Queensville side, along with a police car.

Zack walked back toward Jaymie, still talking on his cell phone, then clicked it off.

"What could have happened? How did Ruby get down almost under the dock?" Jaymie shivered, the night air cool on her wet skin. Hoppy whined at her feet, and she picked him up again, cradling him to her as she retrieved her sandals and slipped them on.

"I don't know," Zack said, "but I am sure going to find out. And you are going to stay put and tell me everything that happened."

He supervised the moving of Ruby onto the boat, and clapped Garnet on the shoulder, saying something to him. Garnet looked around and spotted Jaymie; he tossed her a set of keys and called out, "Can you tell the staff at the Ice House what's going on—not everything; make something up—and lock up the cottage for me? I . . . I don't know what else to say!" His patrician face held a look of confusion and agony.

"Don't worry, Garnet. I'll take care of it." Even as she said that she wondered, should she be telling Zack immediately what Will said about thinking he saw Garnet on the dock earlier, and her witnessing him sneaking into the restaurant? Ruby was safe in the protective embrace of the law and the paramedics, but Jaymie would *have* to tell Zack what she had heard and seen.

The crowd abated, walking away from the marina in groups, heads together, telling and retelling all the known and unknown details. Will began to walk away, but Jaymie called out to him, "Hold on, Will!" She jogged over to him. "I think you should tell Zack that you saw Garnet earlier, down on the dock."

His face was shadowed, but she could see his dismay.

"Look, Jaymie, I appreciate that you're trying to help, but . . . I don't think it was Garnet I saw. It can't have been! You saw how he was; his sister is the most important person in the world to him. If you're thinking he did anything to her, you're dead wrong!"

"Look, I know you're friends, but . . ."

"I imagined it, okay? Just drop it!" He whirled and stalked away.

She watched him go. She understood his reluctance to implicate a friend in any kind of wrongdoing, but Ruby was his friend, too. Wasn't it best to let the police sort it out? Her mind was in turmoil, and she was caught in a dilemma.

When Zack was done on his cell phone, and the ambulance left the dock on the other side, he came over to her and said, "Let's talk." He took her arm and guided her to a bench on the gravel approach to the dock.

But she was too anxious to sit, and so she paced, as Hoppy sat and watched her. She told the detective, minute by minute, exactly what happened. Kicking at a sizable rock that sat on the smooth beach almost where Ruby had lain, she finally finished her story and looked up at the detective. "There's one more thing I have to tell you," she said.

He was alerted by her tone and watched her. She sat down beside him.

"While I was down here, Will Lindsay was just coming out of his office. He asked me if I had seen Garnet. He said he thought he saw Garnet down by the dock, but then, just now, he said he couldn't swear to it, and he was clearly upset. I think he did see him—in fact, it felt like he may have been *more* sure now, not less sure—but he's afraid you'll think Garnet did something to his sister." She told him what she saw, too, Garnet sneaking into the back door of his own restaurant.

"Excuse me for a minute." He walked a ways away and pulled out his cell phone, making a quick call, no doubt to police headquarters. He came back and sat down. "Thanks for being honest, Jaymie. I appreciate it."

"I couldn't handle it if I didn't say something and anything happened. But I just can't believe Garnet could have done that to his sister. They're so close!" She paused and looked off toward Queensville, the Victorian-style lamp-posts lining the walkway across the river invisible except for the faint glowing blobs of yellowy light in the humid night air. "How the heck did Ruby end up in the water?" she muttered. "I just don't understand."

"I don't know, either," Zack said, rising. "But before the night is out, I intend to."

As he strode away, no doubt headed for a sleepless night, Jaymie walked to the restaurant. Her little dog was getting weary, so she carried Hoppy in just to the cash desk where Margaret, the bar manager, stood tallying the night's receipts. Jaymie had known Marg for years from her high school days working part-time at the Queensville Inn, where the older woman had been the housekeeping manager.

"Marg, can I talk to you outside?" Jaymie asked.

She locked up the cash desk and followed Jaymie out to the board sidewalk, their heels clattering and echoing in the quiet night. They stood in the lemony pool of light cast by the restaurant's outdoor bug lamps. "What's up, hon?" Marg asked, her whisky voice gruff, but soothing. "You look upset." She reached out and scruffed Hoppy's chin whiskers.

"Have you seen Ruby or Garnet in the last while?" Jaymie asked.

"Haven't seen Ruby all evening, and Garnet . . . Well, he was here; then he was out of sight. I assumed he was working in the office, but maybe he's gone home."

"Do they do that often?"

"What, leave me to lock up? Sure. Usually they tell me, but not always. I check the offices and all around the place before I lock up."

Jaymie took a deep breath. "There's been an accident. Ruby fell into the river. They're taking her to Wolverhampton General to check her out, and Garnet went with her. He just wanted you to know so you could take care of things."

"Oh, *no!*" the woman said with a gasp. Her lipstick-stained mouth formed an O; then she asked, "Is she okay?"

"I sure hope so," Jaymie said.

"I'm shocked!" she said, one hand on her bosom. "Will Garnet be here for opening tomorrow?"

"I don't know. Can you be here to open, just in case?"

"Sure. What's *really* going on, Jaymie?" the woman said, searching Jaymie's eyes. She swiped a hank of her frizzy blond hair out of her eyes. "I mean, first Urban gets himself killed, and now this. Do you think the murderer tried to kill Ruby, too?"

It wasn't anything Jaymie hadn't already thought of. Will at the dock came back to her. Could *he* have been involved? Why would he have killed Urban, and tried to kill Ruby? But it was possible, she supposed; she needed to think about that some more. She could see by the look in the older woman's eyes that she had taken too long to answer. "I don't know, Marg. I really don't. As far as I know it was just an accident. Please don't say anything else to anyone!"

"I wouldn't. I've been friends with Garnet and Ruby for seven years."

"That's as long as they've been here, right?"

"Yeah. I met them when they came to stay at the Queensville Inn when they were researching business opportunities here. Then they bought and started renovating the Ice House, and asked me if I wanted a job as assistant manager."

"But Garnet tried to buy into the marina first, right, before they settled on the Ice House restaurant?"

"Yeah. Fancy you knowing that! I thought that was a well-kept secret."

"Well, he's been trying to buy it again, since Urban died. He wasn't too pleased when Evelyn, on Will Lindsay's advice, turned him down."

Marg's eyebrows rose, but she just shook her head, looking puzzled.

"Where did they live before Heartbreak Island? Ruby and Garnet, I mean."

"Uh, Florida, right? I think so, anyway."

"You don't know for sure? Haven't they ever had family staying, or gone to visit friends?"

Marg frowned. "Jaymie, I don't poke my nose into their business." She shifted and looked back toward the restaurant. "I gotta go. The rest of the staff is done tallying tips and sharing out, and I have to make sure everything is ready for morning if I'm going to open."

Jaymie headed back around to the Redmond cottage in a thoughtful frame of mind. She let herself in the front door, and put Hoppy down, expecting that the Yorkie-Poo would head to the kitchen, where he knew Ruby kept the treats in a jar by the back door. She wanted to make sure all the doors were locked. On the island, people were lax. They often left their back doors unlocked for convenience during the day-time, but folks usually locked up at bedtime. Garnet and Ruby had gotten into the habit of leaving theirs unlocked while Jaymie was there, though, for when she needed their toilet.

She did a circle check of windows and doors; the back door was, indeed, unlocked. She made sure the basement sump pump was off—if it rained, she'd make sure it was turned back on—the coffeepot was unplugged, and she was done. But where was Hoppy? Not in the kitchen, that she could see. "Darn you, little dog, where are you? Hoppy! Where are you, fella?"

No bark, no skitter of claws on hardwood, nothing. "Where *are* you?" She moved through the dim cottage, back to the bathroom, then Garnet's messy room, then Ruby's pristine bedroom. Hoppy was up on Ruby's bed, paws on the side table, sniffing at an envelope that was propped against a digital clock. In printed block letters it read "Garnet."

Her stomach lurched. She shouldn't look, but . . . if there was something here that could help answer the questions that plagued them, it was important to find it out. She reached out, took the envelope and saw that it was not sealed. She opened it with trembling hands. The note was written in a generous, looping hand that Jaymie recognized as Ruby's. She read the letter, then wished she hadn't.

Garnet

> *I tried to make it all work. I was hoping everything would be all right, but it's not turning out that way. I'm scared and unhappy and tired of it all, and I'm taking the easy way out. I hope you won't be too hurt, and I'll see you again, I know. I love you.*

R.

Gently, Jaymie put the letter back in the envelope and propped it where it had been. Aching with a deep sadness, she grabbed Hoppy and took him back to her cottage, then picked up the phone. This was not how she wanted things to turn out, but how else to construe it but as a confession and suicide note?

In her purse she had a card with Zack's cell number on it. She phoned him directly, and got his voice mail. "Zack, I know by now you're probably at the hospital, but there's something at the Redmonds' that I think you need to see. Call me."

So, did Ruby kill Urban alone, or did she and Garnet conspire? It was likely the two of them. There had to be more to it than just the confrontation and trouble over the sail controversy. The more she thought about it, the more she wondered, where had the Redmonds come from? What was their story? They had arrived in Queensville as if out of nowhere, had the wherewithal to buy their cottage and what would become the Ice House with no mortgage, it was rumored, and had never seemed to want for anything. Where did anyone get that kind of cash?

She tried to sleep, but tossed and turned all night. As dawn broke, she called Valetta.

"M-yeah?"

"I woke you up, didn't I. Sorry, Valetta, but I needed to talk to someone."

"What's up, kiddo? Hey, I saw the ambulance go down to the dock last night. That means someone from the island needed it. What gives?"

"Well, that's what I wanted to talk to you about." She sketched out what had happened the night before, then said, "You're coming out here today, right?"

"I can leave in ten minutes."

"Okay. See you in a few."

Overnight, shock had been replaced by anger. The Redmonds were hiding something dire from those who had befriended them over the years, people who had trusted them in their homes and been nothing but open. Zack phoned just a couple of minutes after she and Valetta hung up. She told him what she had found when she went over to close up for Garnet.

"So he didn't know the note was there, if he sent you over to lock up," he mused. "Unless . . ." He stopped himself, and went silent.

"He couldn't have known it was there, or it would have been opened, but it's sitting on her night stand, envelope closed, with his name on the outside. I saw her leaving the restaurant while I was having dinner there with Daniel. I wonder if she left it there before or after that? She could easily have stopped there, before heading down to the marina."

"I need to see it," he said, "but I have to ask Garnet's permission, or get a warrant. I'm still in Wolverhampton at the hospital."

"Zack, I really think there's something hinky about the Redmonds." He was silent. It occurred to her that he knew much that she didn't know, and of course, with the power and resources of the police department behind him, he was likely ten steps ahead of her. "You know something, and you're not going to tell me."

"So sorry not to be able to share info with my fellow peace officer," he said, "but it's privileged information."

She got the sarcasm. He was telling her to butt out. "How is Ruby doing?"

"She's still unconscious. Gotta go," he said. "Thanks for the call, Jaymie. I do appreciate it."

"Right."

She had coffee waiting for Valetta, who settled on one of the farm chairs at the kitchenette table and opened the box of Tansy's Tarts she had brought with her. "Breakfast," she said, and took one, biting into it with gusto. Runny, sugary goodness dripped down her chin and she grabbed a napkin.

"So, what's going on with the Redmonds?" she asked.

"I wish I knew." Jaymie looked out the back door toward the Redmonds' place. "You know," she said slowly, with heavy emphasis, "I'm not quite sure I locked up *securely* last night, like Garnet asked."

"What do you mean? You went over there to lock up but didn't lock u—*Oooh*! I get it." Valetta nodded. And took a slurp of coffee. "Well, you know, Jaymie," she said, matching her friend's emphatic tone, "I think we ought to go over there and make *sure* you locked up, and make *sure* no one got into the place in the meantime. It'll mean checking through every room."

That was what Jaymie appreciated about Valetta; she never second-guessed her, and she was up for anything. They gulped down the rest of their coffee, washed butter tart residue off their hands and bolted out the back door, leaving a confused Hoppy whining and staring after them.

Jaymie crossed the newly sodded valley between the two cottages, as Jaymie pointed out what had happened and how.

She led the way to the Redmond patio and back door, keys in hand, and turned to Valetta. "Look, I know what we're doing is wrong, and I don't want to drag you into it. Still, I'd love you to have a look around, just to see if anything makes you wonder?"

"I'm *in* already," Valetta said, looking around anxiously. "Now hurry up and open! Garnet could come home at any time."

They entered and prowled, ending up in Ruby's bedroom. Jaymie pointed out the letter on the side table. Valetta stopped and looked around, making a full circle. "Something is not right here," she said finally. "I would bet my mortgage money and my life's savings that Ruby Redmond never slept in this room."

❊ Twenty ❊

"**W**HAT DO YOU mean?"

"Just what I said. Look around. Dust on the side table, except where the letter has been placed. The bed is perfectly made up."

"Maybe she's just ultra neat. C'mon, Valetta, just because *we're* slobs who don't make up our beds every morning doesn't mean she is, too."

"Speak for yourself!" Valetta retorted, hands on her hips. "I make my bed *every* morning, and put the vintage chenille bedspread on, and the bed dolly my aunt made for me when I was twelve. But it never looks *this* neat, and there's just . . . Don't you feel it?" she said, turning around. "It feels . . . stagnant . . . unlived in."

Just then, the sound of the key in the front door lock made them both bolt from the room. It was too late to leave the cottage, so Jaymie led Valetta to the kitchen and flicked the sump pump switch. It choked and garbled as Garnet entered the room. She flicked it off.

He looked exhausted, gray, almost, the lines on his face deeply grooved, his jowls sagging, his jawline blurred with gray whiskers. He stood and stared at them, blinking and frowning. "Jaymie, Valetta. What are you two doing here?"

"Uh, Valetta came over to the island this morning to help me work on the cottage interior. It's real dirty after the week of working on the leaching bed. I told her I was worried about how your, uh, sump pump sounded, and asked her to come over and have a listen."

He flicked the switch, and it grumbled to life again; then he switched it off. "It always sounds like that. There's a nut loose in the housing." He slumped down into a chair, his face in his hands.

"How is Ruby?" Jaymie asked, crouching by him. "What happened? Has she said how she ended up in the river?"

He shook his head, wetness seeping out from under his hands. "I don't know. I just . . . I don't know."

Jaymie hesitated; should she point him toward the suicide note? What did it mean? Why hadn't Zack stopped him, or talked to him yet? Shouldn't Garnet have a chance to figure out what was going on with his sister? She vacillated wildly between thinking he was a conscienceless murderer to believing he was an innocent party in the whole affair; there didn't seem to be any middle ground.

"Garnet, has Ruby been upset lately about anything?" Valetta asked, hovering over them.

"We've all been upset over Urban's murder." He shot a look at Jaymie. "You, too, right? I mean, it's awful that his body was right here, outside our back doors." He wiped the wetness away from the pouchy bags under his eyes. "In the end, it didn't really matter."

She watched his eyes. "What do you mean, it didn't matter? *What* didn't matter?"

He shrugged and looked out the back window.

He wasn't going to say anything more. This was a Garnet Jaymie had never seen, a gaunt, gray man with watery, worried eyes. Ruby was afraid her brother had committed the crime, but surely she wouldn't think that if the argument over the sail was all there was to it. Maybe, since Ruby had shared her fears with Jaymie, she and Garnet had talked and he had told her the truth, that he *did* kill Urban Dobrinskie. That could be what weighed on her so badly that she felt she had to do away with herself. Jaymie considered it; if she knew her sister, Becca, had committed murder, how would she feel? She'd be horrified, and yet she'd feel the need to protect her sister, but she wouldn't be suicidal. Was the conflict just too great for his sister to bear? "How *is* Ruby?" she asked again.

He sighed. "She's still unconscious," he said, repeating what Zack had said, "but the doctors say she's going to be okay. They're hoping she comes out of it later today."

"Have you talked to Zack Christian?"

"I did last night, but I missed him this morning; I guess he was there at the hospital all night, but I was in with Ruby and asked not to be disturbed. He left a message on my cell phone, but I didn't want to talk to anyone. I'm just back to get some clothes and night things for Ruby; then I'm headed back to the hospital. I'll talk to the detective then."

"Do you need some help with that? Getting things together for Ruby?" Valetta asked, exchanging a significant glance with Jaymie. "You might not know what a woman would need."

Jaymie watched Garnet's face; he considered it, but then his gaze shuttered and he shook his head. "No, thank you, Valetta. The nurses made me a list," he said, pulling a scrawled piece of ripped paper from his pants pocket. "I'll be okay. I can buy any . . . any personal item she needs in Wolverhampton. No need upsetting her bedroom."

Interesting response. "It wouldn't be any trouble, Garnet," Jaymie said.

"It's okay. Look, I'm going to shower, shave, and put on some fresh clothes, then gather my sister's stuff," he said, standing, his expression set in grim lines. "You two run along and get down to what you have to do. Ruby will be fine. It was just an accident. Fell off the dock, or something."

There were no excuses left to hang around. They couldn't delay any longer, and the women left. Both were silent for a few minutes, as they descended the slope. On the way up to the Leighton cottage, Jaymie said, "He didn't want us looking through her stuff."

"No, he did not," Valetta said. "Why?"

"He was afraid of what we would find, and it was not the suicide note, because he hasn't seen that yet."

"That we know of, anyway."

"If he had seen it, he wouldn't have left it where it was. But what if he sees it and gets rid of it?" Jaymie fretted. "I've already told Zack about it, and he's going to get a warrant now, and ask about the note, and Garnet will know I found it, opened it and read it." She shrugged as they entered the back door, to Hoppy's explosive joy. "Oh, well. Can't do anything about that now!"

She quickly called Zack to let him know where Garnet was, but got his voice mail, so she left a message. It was all a dark blot in her mind, but she really couldn't change it now that she had done what she had done. She and Valetta spent the next few hours deep cleaning, then broke for lunch just as the phone rang. It was the company moving her new patio furniture; they were at the dock and wanted to bring it up to Rose Tree Cottage.

"Perfect," Jaymie said.

Valetta made sandwiches as Jaymie directed the men, who hauled a dolly cart with her new/vintage furniture to the house, and carried it back, piece by piece. There was the white-painted metal table with wrought iron hairpin legs and iron roses, and a set of six wrought iron chairs, missing the chair pads. She'd have to make or buy something before anyone could use them. There were some extra chairs and small side tables, and the antique-looking double glider chair; it was a reproduction, but she was fine with that.

It was a start.

Jaymie made a quick call to Cynthia Turbridge and gave her some ideas for the Cottage Shoppe kitchen; then she and Valetta ate in the shaded copse, after hauling a few cushions out to pad the wrought iron seats. Jaymie had a clipboard with her, and was making a list of things that had to be done before the families descended on the cottage for the dinner. But she just couldn't stop thinking about Ruby's mysterious plunge into the St. Clair. She tapped her pencil on the clipboard.

"I keep thinking about what you said, Valetta, that Ruby's room was unused. What does that mean?"

"I don't know."

Valetta didn't say anything else, and Jaymie looked over at her. Her forehead was wrinkled, and she stared up at the Redmond cottage.

"What's going on in your mind?" Jaymie had known Valetta a long time, and behind the quirky, gossipy, eccentric spinster façade, the woman was a smart, capable, deep-thinker.

Valetta sighed and glanced over at Jaymie, but then looked away. "I'm just ashamed of the way my mind is working. I can't reconcile two thoughts. Ruby doesn't sleep in her bedroom; someone sleeps in Garnet's. Where is Ruby sleeping? Either she has a secret lover or . . ."

Jaymie waited, but her stomach was twisting. Finally, she said, "Or she's sleeping with Garnet."

"That's impossible, right? I mean, it just isn't possible."

"Unless . . ." Jaymie paused and thought. "Wait just a minute; maybe there's a third possibility. We've always believed one thing, but if that *one* thing isn't true, then . . . Valetta, what if Garnet and Ruby are not brother and sister?"

Valetta's mouth hung open. "Geez, Jaymie, you're right!

I've been looking at it all wrong. We only have their word for it that they are sister and brother. But why——?" She wrinkled her forehead, deep in thought.

This was something Jaymie had already considered, with the pair. "They're hiding from something or someone."

"Witness protection, maybe?"

"I never thought of that. I guess it's possible. But that's pretty rare, right?"

"I guess. How do we find out for sure?"

"I think Zack might already know the truth," Jaymie mused. She set her clipboard on the table and leaned back, putting her feet up on one of the other chairs. "I felt like he was keeping something vital to himself. Of course, I don't expect him to tell me everything, but it sure would keep me from jumping to conclusions!"

"So maybe it doesn't mean anything, ultimately, in relation to the murder?"

"I didn't say that," Jaymie answered. "Just because Zack has known the truth about their secret all along, and hasn't arrested them yet, doesn't mean he's dismissed either one of them as suspects."

"True. But is the suicide note on the level, then, or suspicious?" Valetta fiddled with her bead bracelet and grimaced.

"If you were going to leave a suicide note for a loved one, wouldn't you leave it where it was likely to be found, not in a room they wouldn't go into?"

Valetta nodded. "And the unused bedroom isn't likely. That could only be the work of someone who, if we're right about the Redmonds, doesn't know their secret. So, who put the suicide note there? And if it wasn't Ruby's handwriting, whose was it?"

"But that's just the thing," Jaymie said. "I would *swear* that was Ruby's handwriting. It's pretty distinctive, a kind of loopy script. But . . . hey, is there another way to take that, the note, I mean?" She explained what Lisa had said

about the money Ruby had taken out of a bank in Wolverhampton. "I thought it might have been blackmail money,
or something, but what if she *was* planning to take off, like
Lisa surmised, and that was cash to go on for a while?"

"Makes sense. Maybe she was even heading out when
you saw her slip away from the restaurant."

Jaymie pondered that, as she glanced around for Hoppy.
She called to her little dog and he came lurching over from
a spot in the taller grass near the Redmonds' terraced garden. "Maybe she was sneaking out because she didn't want
Garnet to follow her, or worry about her or . . . but that
would work if she was the killer, too, right, and was running
away? It doesn't look good, unless she was scared."

But why would Ruby then say she thought Garnet might
have done it? That part didn't fit. Unless she was deliberately
shifting the blame onto him. If they weren't brother and
sister, then maybe their loyalty had fractured. She thought
back to the note contents. Ruby had said something about
trying to make it work, and that she had hoped everything
would be all right, but that it wasn't. And she said she was
scared and unhappy. Scared of what?

Jaymie relayed the contents of the note as well as she
could recall.

"She said 'I love you' in the note?" Valetta asked. "Wow.
So, if they aren't brother and sister, then they're . . . lovers."

"Lovers." Jaymie thought of all the romance novels she
had read, but she couldn't think of one where the "lovers
with a secret" theme had them playing brother and sister.
That was a new one. "So what are they running from? Zack
hasn't arrested them. If he knows the truth and hasn't arrested
them, then their secret is not about something criminal."

"He hasn't arrested them *yet*," Valetta said. "What you
said a minute ago still holds, that just because they haven't
been arrested yet, doesn't mean they won't be."

Jaymie drew in a breath. "Look!"

From their spot in the shade, they saw uniformed police

surrounding the Redmond cottage, and Zack Christian executing his warrant. Garnet was long gone, of course, back to Wolverhampton. Zack banged on the door and shouted that he had a search warrant, and was going to enter. Two uniformed officers, one of them Bernie Jenkins, accompanied him. One busted the lock on the door, and they went in, and that was all Jaymie and Valetta could see from their vantage point for the next while.

She and Valetta went back to work, but Jaymie was antsy the whole time, watching out the back window, trying to figure out what was going on. This was all on her; Zack had gotten the search warrant because of her call about the "confession" in the suicide note, the note that she was now not even sure was a suicide note. Had she done the right thing? She may well have interfered in a very private matter between Garnet and Ruby, but how was she to have known that?

Finally, the cops left, and Jaymie had to stop obsessing about it all. It was done; she could not now go back and undo it. She and Valetta had one last cup of tea, then, after cleaning themselves up, headed for dinner at the Ice House. Jaymie felt like she practically lived there now, but she had her reasons this time. Valetta and Marg had gone to Wolverhampton High at the same time, and were old friends.

The restaurant was not as busy as normal, the result of it being midweek, and a rib festival starting in Wolverhampton. Jaymie knew all about that because basket rentals were down this week, too, but would hopefully pick up after the festival. It was her first summer, and she frankly didn't know what to expect with her fledgling business.

Lisa was not working, and in fact they had only one waitress on, it looked like, but when Marg saw Valetta with Jaymie, she hustled over to them and led them to a table near the window, overlooking the patio, beyond which was the river.

"Sit; have a glass of wine with us, Marg," Valetta said, patting the chair next to her.

The woman agreed, and sat down, bringing with her a bottle and three glasses.

"Have you heard anything from Garnet?" Valetta asked her friend, studiously avoiding Jaymie's gaze. They had agreed ahead of time to act as if they didn't know anything about the search warrant. "We're worried about Ruby."

"Everyone says she's going to be okay," the woman said, her gruff voice softening. "My niece works at the hospital, though, and she called me to say they've put a police guard on Ruby's door."

To protect her or keep her there, Jaymie wondered?

"What do you think happened?" Valetta asked.

Marg, tight-lipped, shook her head and took a sip of the wine. "Not my business to speculate."

Valetta exchanged a look with Jaymie, and Jaymie took the hint. "I'll be back in a few minutes," she said. "I need to go to the washroom."

She went outside and sat on a bench for a few minutes. A rowdy bunch of men and women walked up to the restaurant and started to file in. It would be busy in a few minutes, once they had ordered. She saw Sherm and Tansy Woodrow in the group, and waved at them. Tansy came over and sat down next to her.

"I heard what happened to Ruby last night, and you found her! You must have been so scared. Thank God you were in the right place at the right time, or she would have managed to kill herself!"

"Is that what people are saying about Ruby?" Jaymie asked.

"Why? Isn't that what happened?" Tansy, asked, her eyebrows arched.

"I don't think anyone knows yet."

Another young woman stood nearby, texting someone on her phone. "You coming, Tanse? We gotta eat and get going, if we're going to get to darts on time."

"Yeah, yeah," Tansy said, waving the other woman away.

Sherm came up to the other girl and said, "Come on, let's go in. Tansy will follow. What are you doing, anyway?" he asked, leading her away.

"I still can't get ahold of Barb," the young woman said. "I don't know why she's not here. She never misses darts night!" She went along with Sherm, as he held the door open for her.

Tansy bent closer to Jaymie. "I heard that Ruby filled her pockets with rocks and waded out into the river. Did you hear that?"

"I was there, remember? There were no rocks in her pockets. I don't *think*." Jaymie thought back to the heavy *something* that fell out of Ruby's pocket. It *was* a rock, wasn't it? Had Ruby pulled a Virginia Woolf? Was it a suicide attempt, after all? Something struck her just then . . . If she had been leaving town, would she not have taken the ten thousand dollars with her? Or was that what was in the bag she was carrying? Where did the bag go? She was going to need to tell Zack about the money, and refer him to Lisa. So many questions, so few answers!

Sherm ducked back out. "Tansy, come on! We need to order *now*!"

She got up and hustled back to the door, but paused, before she followed her husband. "I hope you're right, Jaymie. I'd hate to think of Ruby trying to do away with herself. She's so . . . so strong."

Jaymie glanced in and saw that Valetta was now sitting alone, so she entered and joined her friend.

"It was getting busy, so I ordered us both the special of the day," Valetta said, a twinkle in her eyes.

"You got some info out of Marg, didn't you? I was hoping you would," Jaymie said, sitting down and gulping back her wine. "What did she say?"

"Well, I told her we knew they weren't brother and sister."

"That was taking a chance. What if she didn't know?"

"I know," Valetta admitted. "It was a risk, but I had a feeling. She knew, all right, and has all along, I think. When they set up this business, they needed a shield of some sort, is my guess. They found Marg simpatico, and she became a kind of business manager through whom they could do a lot of the financial stuff."

"Did she tell you that?"

"Not exactly. But she was kinda upset when I guessed it. I promised her we wouldn't be spreading it around. She knows me well enough to trust me with that, but she was a little worried about you!"

"So . . . did you ask her why Ruby and Garnet are here using assumed names, and who they really are?"

"I did."

"And? Come on, Valetta, don't hold out on me!"

The older woman, her eyes gleaming, leaned over the table and whispered, "Ruby is actually a mob daughter from Montreal, Canada; she turned her whole family in, and she's been in hiding ever since."

❊ Twenty-one ❊

"THE *MOB*?" JAYMIE hissed.

"The *mob*!" Valetta's eyes were wide and shone with excitement behind her lenses as she sat back in her chair.

Jaymie sat back, too. "So . . . her name is not really Ruby."

"I don't imagine so," Valetta murmured.

"That opens up a whole 'nother can of worms! If she's been running from the mob, then was Urban's murder a warning? Or did he get too nosy? Or did he know something?"

Valetta looked skeptical. "I don't think we know enough yet to figure this out. Besides," she added, "the cops probably know all about Ruby and Garnet."

"And the murder could have nothing to do with their secret."

"Or everything."

The restaurant got noisy, with the darts competitors

eating and laughing and even, at one point, singing. Certainly too noisy to discuss someone's mob connections. Jaymie and Valetta finished dinner in silence, then walked back to the cottage.

"You realize we're only going by what Marg said. Do you really think Ruby's part of a mob family, or was that a cover for something else?" Jaymie asked, as they strolled along the gravel road in the darkness.

"In other words, were Garnet and Ruby lying to Marg? I just don't know," Valetta said. "I mean, if I needed someone to cover for me—you know, to help me hide—that's the story I'd tell them."

"Exactly! Who's going to try to check up on that? How would you, even if you wanted to? Normal people don't have mob connections. And it's a great motive for keeping quiet. No one wants to bring the mob down on them."

"That's what I was thinking."

"So, we're right back where we started," Jaymie mused. One thing was certain: she was going to confront the Redmonds about their story, and see what they had to say for themselves. She'd have to find a way to do it without getting Marg in trouble for spilling the beans, if it was at all possible.

Jaymie and Valetta returned to the cottage, and while her friend got her bag—she was returning to Queensville, since the next day was a workday—Jaymie snapped on Hoppy's leash, figuring she may as well take him along for his evening stroll.

"You don't have your purse. Aren't you coming back to Queensville?" Valetta asked, as they exited the cottage back into the warm, humid evening air.

"Are you kidding? I'm staying away as much as possible. Mom and I get along better when we don't share a roof."

At the dock Jaymie reached out and hugged Valetta, then released her. "I couldn't have gotten so far today without you; you work harder than anyone else I know. *And* you make a valuable investigating partner."

Valetta's laughter rang out through the night. "Just call me Watson!" She boarded the *Ferry Queene*, and as the boat chugged away, she waved and Jaymie waved back, then turned away.

The river was sluggish and silent, slipping past in silky darkness. It was restful living on the island (or would have been without a puzzling murder mystery), Jaymie thought, but she still would be happy when she could go back to her house in Queensville without having to listen to her mother complain about her hoarding habits. Reeling Hoppy in, Jaymie was ready to head home, weary after a long day of cleaning. She would enjoy the sparkling clean cottage for at least one more night, and then her parents could take it over.

She looked up the slight rise to the marina office, where Will was likely just finishing up, before heading home to his wife, who would be waiting for him. It was a week and a half since the murder, and judging by the crowd at the Ice House, another of the biweekly darts nights was on. By now, the league would be over at the legion hall, just as they had been on the night of the murder, and then they would head to the Ice House for after-tournament drinks. Jaymie had been at the bar once, on one of their league nights; the dart players descended on the place about eleven in the evening, raucous and loud, and started drinking, not finishing until closing. Ice House closing was usually about ten or eleven, but if they had a crowd, the bar manager would keep the place open until state-mandated closing at two in the morning.

Darts. Sherman and Tansy played. So did Garnet and Ruby. And Will's wife, Barb. She was not with them tonight, the unnamed woman had said to Sherm Woodrow, even though she *never* missed a night. Odd. She would have been there, though, the night of the murder. If the players went to the Ice House after, for drinks—and as far as Jaymie knew they *always* did—then . . . She stopped in her tracks. Will Lindsay had said that his wife was home that evening. If Barb had gone to darts, didn't that completely blow the alibi Will had been so vocal about? Why would he mislead her about something like that?

The door of the office opened. Will exited, then closed the door behind him. "Jaymie!" he said. "How is it going?"

Hoppy raced over to him and begged for attention. He picked the little dog up. He had her dog, and she had the leash; it was like she was tethered to him. "I'm fine, Will. How is the work on the marina and slips coming along?"

Her mind was working furiously; could what she feared be true? But . . . why? It didn't make any sense. His situation hadn't changed a whole lot since Urban had died, after all, so what had he gained? He hadn't taken over the other part of the marina; nor had he gotten the Dobrinskies to sell it, to him or anyone else.

But . . . they had begun what had been delayed, the dredging of the marina and docks. No one would kill someone over a delay in dredging. Would they? If she had learned anything in the last couple of months, it was that one could not fathom what was important to others. People had depths and needs and wants that others would never suspect.

"It's good. We'll finally be able to encourage boat traffic and build a larger marina on this side, instead of all the business going to the Canadian side."

"The Canadian side . . ." Jaymie squinted into the failing light. "Wasn't Urban trying to buy a marina there?" she said, remembering something Ruby had said to her.

He looked startled, and tightened his hold on Hoppy. The little dog yelped.

"Will, you squeezed Hoppy too hard. He doesn't like that. Can I have my dog, please?" she asked, tension threading through her voice.

"What did you mean by that?" he said, stopping dead, but not giving up his hold on Hoppy.

"What did I mean by what?"

He was turning an unbecoming shade of red. What had she said? Unless . . . Was it Urban's rumored purchase of the

Canadian marina that would threaten *his* marina? Was Urban blocking the improvements to their marina to increase the attractiveness of the one he was buying on the Canadian side? If so, maybe the only way to stop him, from Will's aspect, was . . . death. Stuttering, Jaymie said, "Uh, well, I don't know; it's just a rumor I heard. I didn't really pay any attention to it."

She leaned over to him and tried to take Hoppy, but he held tight. Her heart sank. "Is everything okay, Will?" she asked, focusing on keeping her tone even and her expression neutral.

He began to walk back toward the office, forcing her to follow, or strangle Hoppy.

"Will, let the poor dog go," she said, her voice trembling. Darn; she had to keep it even, light . . . unsuspicious. "What's up? I don't understand what's going on."

"I just want to show you something, Jaymie." He moved on toward the office, still carrying Hoppy. It was weird, because his manner didn't seem panicked or rushed; he was just carrying the dog to his office, and Jaymie was trotting along as if she was the one on a leash, not Hoppy. The Yorkie-Poo began to squirm, and yipped when Will tightened his hold. The poor pup stared back at Jaymie over the man's shoulder, pleading in his eyes.

"Will, let him go, please," she said.

"You know, it's funny. I just called your place . . . I wanted to talk to you. I was gonna ask you to come down here. Then I see you down on the dock! So I waited until Valetta was gone. She is such a snoop."

At the door to the office, he entered and jerked on the leash, which made Jaymie tumble through the open door after him. What should she do? Risk strangling poor Hoppy? Bulldoze past Will out the door, leaving behind her insanely-courageous-but-small-as-a-teapot pup? No. She was *not* leaving Hoppy behind.

Okay, she'd been in tight spots before; she could talk her

way out of this. She turned around slowly, and took Hoppy gently from Will's arms. He locked the office door behind them. So, if she was going to run, she would need to quickly unlock the dead bolt. Bur first, she needed to distract him.

"What gives? I don't understand what's going on here, Will," she said, determined to pretend ignorance, and to get out as quickly as possible. She injected a little peeved puzzlement in her voice . . . or at least she hoped that was what it sounded like. She was no actress. "You said you wanted to talk to me, or show me something; what is it?"

He watched her, his eyes the flat black of a shark's. She'd never noticed that before, how vacant his eyes were sometimes. He had always donned the façade of the genial nice guy, the happy, helpful marina owner. But she couldn't ponder that for too long, or it would show on her face.

He pointed to a map on the wall; it showed Heartbreak Island, and the two marinas, one on the Canadian side and the American side marina that he co-owned. "You see that?" he said, pointing to the one on the Canadian side.

"Yes."

"Where is it?"

She examined the map, though she already knew the answer. "It's . . . it's on the border, pretty much, isn't it?"

"Yeah, on the Canadian side, but on the border, at the other end of the island. And do you know what Urban planned to do?"

She shook her head, bouncing Hoppy on her hip, trying to calm him. The little dog was trembling with tension.

"Sonuvabitch was gonna buy that marina, and build a matching one on the US side. That way the ferry would only have to make one stop on Heartbreak Island, and not two. Goldarn Canadian government is behind it, you gotta know that; makes it easier for everyone if the customs for both sides are in the same spot. Do you know what that was gonna do to me?" He didn't wait for her to answer. "That was going to put me out of business. I need that ferry traffic! Spence leases space," he said, naming the owner-operator of the *Ferry Queene*, "and that's the one thing that keeps us profitable."

"Oh. I'm sorry, Will." She hoped the guy wasn't going to confess to her. In fact, she needed to talk now, to make him think he might still finagle a way out of the spot of trouble without another murder on his hands. "Well, Urban won't be missed, will he?" she said, brightly, focusing on the man in front of her. "Do you know who killed him? C'mon, if you've figured it out, clue me in!"

"I might know," he said slowly, watching her eyes. "But I'm nervous. What if I say something and the killer comes after me?" He pulled a faded blue curtain aside and looked out the window, then made sure the curtain fell into place again, concealing the outside world from the office, and the office from anyone on the dock.

Hoppy wriggled uneasily in Jaymie's arms; he felt her tension. He knew exactly how she was feeling: scared to death, her stomach churning like an antacid commercial. "That's what the police are for, to protect us honest citizens."

"Hah! That's a laugh," he yelped, his voice echoing off the wood-grain paneling. He paced in a circle, glaring at the map as he passed it.

"What do you mean?" she asked, trying to edge toward the door.

"You can't count on the cops, ever," he said, whirling around and fixing her with a beady-eyed stare. "They don't give a damn about the people, unless you're wealthy. I tried to file a charge against Urban once, and they wouldn't arrest him."

"Arrest Urban? For what?"

"Jerk punched me in the nose once. Just 'cause I said something."

"What did you say?" she asked, genuinely curious.

"Told him he was an asshole."

"He had a bad temper; I saw it in action. He insulted

Ruby; then Garnet punched him out. That was the very night he was killed, you know." That was good . . . sympathy and another suspect offered on a silver platter.

"Yeah, I know that Garnet has a temper, too. I saw him and Urban argue a few times. Old Urb hated that the Redmonds are better sailors than him. It wasn't the boat, it wasn't the sail, even though Urb always blamed the equipment. Fact is, I even got Urban to accuse Garnet of buying foreign-made sails. I gave Sherm the hint, knowing the old gossip would tell Urban and that my partner would go after Garnet. I laughed when I heard about the fight at the Ice House!" He chuckled. "Urban always had an excuse, but the truth was, he was just crap at sailing. He had no feel for the water or the wind. His boy could captain the boat better than him, but he kept that kid scared to death." He gave Jaymie a sly look, while he circled the room, locking windows.

Her stomach wrung itself into a knot. This was not going well so far. Her mind churned furiously, as she tried to figure out how to convince him she did not suspect him of the killing. "I always—" Her voice choked off. Darn. She cleared her throat and hugged Hoppy to her, inhaling his doggie scent. "I always wondered if Sammy had anything to do with his father's death. You know, it's so good to be able to talk to someone about this," she said, sidling back toward the door. "I can't figure it out. Who do you think did it, Will?"

"But you've been snooping around, little Miss Nancy Marple. And Ruby . . . Now, if she'd *died*, folks may have thought she killed Urban. Some people whispered they were having an affair."

It was odd, this conversation, as if he were searching for someone to blame, but even though she had offered him up a couple of likely suspects, he kept probing. "I'm so glad she *didn't* die," Jaymie said. "I like them both. But Garnet, now . . . Maybe *he* killed Urban."

He watched her. "Maybe. You know, Ruby and Garnet, they're not who they seem."

She swallowed. "What do you mean?" Her gaze flicked away, toward the door. It was close. Real close.

"I mean, they aren't really Ruby and Garnet Redmond."

"Who are they, then?" She paused, interested, in spite of her situation, in what he knew and how he knew it. When he didn't answer, she said, "Look, Will, I'd love to chat some more, but I have to go. I really do." She turned and moved quickly toward the door, reaching out for the dead bolt.

"Stop, *now*! You're not fooling me for one second," Will said, leaping across the room and shoving her out of the way. Hoppy fell to the floor with a wild yip of fear. He skittered under the desk and barked. "Shut up, mutt!" the man yelled. He lunged to a battered wooden desk, yanked open a drawer, pulled out a gun and waved it around, as pens and paper clips clattered to the tile floor. "Shut that goddamn dog up, or I'll do it for him!"

"Hoppy, quiet! *Now!*" Jaymie said, in her firm, no-nonsense tone. The little dog calmed, but growled and grumbled, ducking his head and watching Will from under the desk. There was no avoiding it now. Will had taken a step that proved he was not willing to let her go easily. But what did he plan to do next? She glanced at the open drawer and recognized the bag Ruby had been carrying the night before.

"What gives, Will?" she said, her voice throaty with fear, but not quavering.

He rummaged around in his desk, still, while waving the gun at her vaguely. He seemed disturbed, and mumbled, "Why can't women just leave well enough alone? Never met a woman who could just . . . What is it? Am I difficult? I don't think so. Not *me*." He pounced on something and said, "Aha!" It was a pad of paper with what looked like a list on it.

"I hate dogs," he said, squinting his eyes at Hoppy, who growled and bared his teeth from under the desk. He waved the gun at the dog, and Hoppy barked.

"Please, Will, don't!" Jaymie said, her voice now

trembling with fear and anxiety. "Don't hurt Hoppy. He's just scared. You've frightened him!"

"Oh, it's all *my* fault, right? That's what my wife always said. '*Will, don't shout! Will, don't be so angry. Will, you're hurting me!*'" He mimicked a woman's voice with a savage, sarcastic falsetto. "Well, she pushed me over the edge and now she's paying."

Jaymie's breath started coming in quick huffs of air. Paying? How was she paying? Did she dare ask? "What do you mean?" She swallowed, her throat dry and a lump clogging it.

"You'd like that, wouldn't you?" he sneered. "Just like all those stupid cop movies; you keep me talking, I spill the beans, and you cleverly figure a way out, right? But no, you and I are going to take a little walk, and you're going to do something drastic. You've been involved in all these murder crimes lately. Little Miss Nosy. Well, now you're going to go over the edge and commit one yourself. Gonna go *crazy*!" he yelled, waving his hands around in the air.

Hoppy barked frantically, then retreated and growled up at Will from under the desk. Jaymie's stomach roiled, and she felt light-headed.

"That time of month, right?" Will said, pacing, his face getting red and sweat popping out in beads on his forehead. The sweat gleamed faintly in the sickly light of the overhead fluorescent lights. "Gonna get your crazy bitch hat on and come to my home and start to accuse me of doing things." He shot Jaymie a crafty look. "Then you're going to shoot my wife, and I'm gonna have to kill you, and explain it all to the cops. Self-defense! You're a nut job, while I'm calm, cheerful, never-hurt-anyone Will. It was *you* all along."

"Me?" she yelped. "They're never going to believe that! Why would *I* have killed Urban?"

"You've been under a lot of stress lately, with that family of Daniel's," he said, eyeing her. "And dead bodies everywhere lately, right? Sent you over the edge."

She knew right then that he was working out a story in his head, some explanation that he thought might work. But she latched on to something he had said earlier. "What's wrong with your wife? Is she . . . Is she dead?"

"Not yet," he said. "Didn't I just say that you were going to kill her?"

"No one would *ever* believe I would kill someone."

He looked conflicted, unsure. "Isn't that what the relatives always say in the paper, though? 'She was such a nice girl, never a day of trouble in her whole life.'"

"You know deep in your heart that it won't work. No one is ever going to believe that I killed Urban, and it's even more impossible that anyone would think I'd kill your wife, especially with a gun!" she said quickly. She could see the doubt etched on his forehead, and continued. "You'll end up in prison for a triple homicide. If you turn yourself in now, you've got dozens of witnesses who would say what a despicable character Urban Dobrinskie was. You probably won't even be arrested for his murder! Call it self-defense. He came at you; you had to stab him. I won't say a thing. He was a nothing, a jerk, someone who bullied his son and wife so much they were afraid of him. And he was cheating on his wife, right? Everyone says so. In fact, don't say anything at all! *Anyone* could have killed him."

He sat down, tears coming to his eyes. "I can't stop now. My wife . . ."

"She's still alive," Jaymie said. "If you let her go now, she might file charges, but you've never done anything wrong. You'll get off with a suspended sentence, and your life can just go on."

He shook his head, his expression one of a lost soul, someone who doesn't understand how they got where they are. "I have to do this. My wife knows I killed Urban, and she's going to go to the police."

"You don't *have* to do anything, Will. Let things play out. Or you could just leave on the ferry tonight, and be out of the state . . . out of the *country* before anyone knows you're gone."

His face twisted into anger. "You'd all just love that, wouldn't you? Convenient for my wife, convenient for you, convenient for the cops! Well, I won't make it easy for anyone."

She'd set him off. Damn! He paced, and grumbled, while Hoppy growled at him from under the desk. "Calm down, Will, it's okay!" she said.

He turned, slowly, his expression thunderous. "Don't *ever* tell me to calm down!"

Oops. "Okay, Will, calm . . . Uh, it's okay!"

"No, it's *not* okay. We're getting out of here and I'm getting this show on the road. I've made up my mind."

It was dark out. What time was it? How long had she been in the office? The last ferry ran at ten o'clock, and if it arrived, she could maybe get someone's attention, if the timing was just right. He glanced up over her head, and waved the gun at her.

"You sit right where you are," he said, "and don't make a sound. You make any noise and I'll pop you." He flicked the light off.

What was going on? All she could hear in the dark silence was her own heart pounding. Then she got it; he had been looking at the clock. She could hear the jolly toot that meant the last ferry was disembarking at the dock. Voices floated on the night air, cheerful shouts of "Night, Spence" to the ferry operator. Then the thrum of the ferry motor as it chugged away to the Canadian side, Johnsonville. Her last hope was gone.

A few minutes later, Will flicked the light back on. "And now we're going to put my little plan into action. I'll tell you how it's going to go. You are going to hold on to the leash of that little monster, and we're going to walk to my house. You're going to be slightly ahead of me, and this little number," he said, caressing the short stock of his gun, "will be in your back. Move, and I'll shoot. I don't have much to lose now, so you can bet I'll do it. March!" he said.

"I don't know the way to your house," she said, rising, grabbing Hoppy's leash, and moving toward the door.

"Just start; I'll tell you."

"But what if we meet someone we know?"

He paused. She shouldn't have said anything. He might just put her back in the office and tie her up until later that night. Darn it! But he was too antsy to wait. "We won't meet anyone. It's too late and too early."

She knew what he meant. Folks who walked down by the river to walk their dogs or watch the sunset would be gone, and those who would go for a walk to cool off and sober up from the bar wouldn't be out yet. She complied with his directions to head out, toward the cement steps that threaded up through a wooded glade to a lonely spot on the dirt road that circled the island. He and his wife lived in a winterized cottage at the end of the road, just beyond the top of the steps, he told her. It had to be the lonely cottage she had often seen from the ferry, the one perched atop the highest point on the island.

As she mounted the dark steps, slowly because of her uncertainty, her heart pounded. There was one yellowy light about halfway up, and she climbed toward it, worrying that she was going to feel a bullet in her back. What would it feel like? Would it hurt, or would it be like a pinprick, and then nothing? But she couldn't focus on dying; she had to focus on living. As they reached the landing halfway up, Hoppy whined.

"What's wrong with that mutt?" Will muttered.

"He's tired. He's only got three legs, Will. I'll have to carry him, at least up the steps."

"Yeah, okay," he said. "But hurry up about it!"

She bent over to pick up Hoppy, and looked backward down the dizzying stretch of steps, lined by an old wrought iron railing on one side. How could she use the stairs to her advantage? Did she dare take a chance? It was an awful risk, but Will was behind her; if she could give him a shove backward without losing her own balance, then he would tumble all the way down to the bottom, maybe knock himself out.

"Get moving!" he yelled, and she felt the gun barrel nudge her backbone.

If she dithered about it forever, she'd lose her chance. She began to mount, step by step. Thirty or so steps to the top. When should she do it? When she was near the top, she decided, so she could push him down the stairs, and jump up the last couple of steps. Her heart was pounding, not just from fear, but from the long stairs climb. She could hear Will panting behind her, too. He was as out of shape as she was, it seemed, neither one of them good at such a long flight of stairs.

"So you killed Urban. You must have planned it carefully," she said, "to have thought of stealing the wheelbarrow the night before from my backyard."

"Clever, right? I was gonna bury Urban in your leaching bed. I figured you'd all be asleep, but no, you and your damned dog had to be awake, and up. Had to change plans quick. That's why I tried to make it seem like Garnet was the one shouting."

She didn't say that that was the one thing that made no sense to her; why, if he was intending to point the crime at Garnet, did he fake the man shouting, "Get off my property"?

"Not only that; I got you to hare off in all different directions!" he chuckled. "Told you Garnet was badgering me to buy the Dobrinskie half of the marina. Hah! I'm the one who offered it to him, then told him no way. Knew he'd make a fuss, but man, it was timed perfectly! Made him look like a hothead, right in front of you. I was just hoping *someone* would hear him threaten me, like I knew he would."

Jaymie thought back to many instances when Will had subtly pointed her in different directions: he had defended Urb's character, making it seem like he didn't have a beef with the guy, and he had subtly pointed out Garnet's temper, then implicated him in Ruby's near drowning. She had been manipulated, and it made her mad. "I'm out of breath; I've got to stop for a second!"

He didn't object, and she could hear his breath coming raggedly.

"Why Ruby, though?" Jaymie asked. "Why did you try to kill Ruby? And how did you get her note?"

"She trusted me, and told me she was leaving. Thought someone from her past was after her, or some such nonsense. You know, I always thought there was something fishy about those two; that's why I threatened them, the night I did old Urb in. I had them both running around like chickens with their heads cut off! Made sure Garnet was out of the restaurant a good long time. He stood down on that dock waiting for his mystery caller, the one who never arrived on the ferry." He chuckled.

"You were the one calling them that evening!"

"You betcha! Anyway, Ruby asked, could I just make sure Garnet knew about the note she had left on the kitchen counter. So I asked her to come wait for the ferry in my office so no one would see her, and I drugged her iced tea with some of m' wife's sleeping meds. Then I put some rocks in Ruby's pockets, put her in the water, went up to her cottage, and read the note; if it wasn't right, I was gonna rip it up, but it was perfect. I moved it to her room."

"But . . . why? Why Ruby? What did she ever do?"

"Why do you think?" he yelled. "You kept snooping around, and I've heard about those other cases, the ones you'd solved. I figured between you and the cops, you'd dig and dig and dig and sooner or later, you'd get to me, so I figured if you all thought Ruby had done it, and then committed suicide, you'd just damn well leave it alone! It's all your fault; she lived, and that spoiled that, so this is Plan B. Now, *move*!" He jabbed the gun in her ribs.

She started up the stairs again, almost to the top. She had

to steel herself. A half measure would be worse than no try at all. If she just managed to push him down one step, all it would do was piss him off. Was he holding on to the railing, she wondered, and glanced over her shoulder. Oh Lord, he was! That complicated matters. She paused.

"What's wrong now?"

"My shoe is undone. Can I see with your flashlight?" she asked, tucking Hoppy under one arm.

"Geez, like it matters!" he complained. "Keep going."

"I can't, Will. I'm . . . I'm afraid of falling."

"Cripes, what a baby."

It was as if time stilled; she saw him let go of the railing, and switch the flashlight on, pointing it toward her slip-on shoes. If he'd been more observant, he'd have known she didn't have laces. She turned and, with her one free hand, shoved him, hard. He began to flail his arms, going back.

❧ Twenty-two ❧

SHE BOLTED UP the last step as Hoppy barked and
squirmed. Will yelped in dismay, and there was a clatter
and a grunt, then silence. She could taste a metallic tang in
her mouth, as she paused at the top and panted, bent over,
not sure she could move another step. Some scuffling from
below warned her, though, that she may not have solved her
problem. Had Will grabbed the railing and saved himself?
She wasn't going to stick around to find out.

"C'mon, buddy, we have to run," she whispered, as she
put her little dog down and took off, threading through
the trees along a dimly perceived path, illuminated by the
one weak light at the head of the steps.

Will shouted, "Come back here!"

He was close, too darned close! Even with three legs,
Hoppy was faster than her. She paused, unclipped his lead,
and screamed, "Run, Hoppy," as a paralyzing stitch in her
side shot a bolt of pain through her. She began to run again,

but Will wasn't far behind, and he shot; somewhere close to her the bullet found a mark with a *thunk*.

"You'd better stop," he yelled, "or next time it'll be square in your back."

She stopped, terrified. Hoppy was running, but he paused and looked back at her, barking. "Run, Hoppy, run!" she shrieked. For once the little dog obeyed, and took off like a shot, his loping, wobbly gait making him weave.

"I'll shoot that friggin' mutt!" Will yelled. They were on the edge of the wooded area, on the lonely loop of dirt road that rose and dipped on a bend.

Hoppy was somewhere ahead, out of sight, barking as loudly as a dog so small could. She turned, shivering, to see Will, gun stuck out, emerging from the shadows.

"You almost ruined everything," he said, panting. "Almost, but not quite. The dog doesn't matter. March, and stay quiet, or get a bullet in the back. My house is just beyond the bend."

She stilled, evaluating her options. She could still hear Hoppy barking somewhere, and someone yelling for him to shut up. If she screamed, if she *dared* yell, "Help," how long would she live? Would he really shoot her, or would he just run? She didn't like her odds, which she would have placed at fifty/fifty. The road was enclosed by shadow, the light from the few yellowish streetlights illuminating the leaves and casting a weird greenish glow all around them. Could she make a break for it?

"Walk! *Now!*" he hissed, coming up and pushing the barrel of the gun into her back.

She did as she was told, looking around, trying to figure whether she'd have time to dive into the bushes or not. He jabbed again, so close behind her she could hear his grunting breaths. Something rustled in the bushes close at hand. She hoped to heck it was not Hoppy, who had now stopped barking. Damn! Was her brave little Yorkie-Poo stalking his prey? Yorkies were little dogs who thought they were big dogs, and poodles had long ago been hunting dogs, before they retired to the laps of the chic. So she had a lionhearted little pooch who was a hunter at heart.

"Will, please . . . think about what you're doing!" she said, her voice thick with fear. "This is not necessary. Just let me go, and we can talk. I'll give you a head start. You can take a boat and leave!"

"Shut up!" he growled. "This is gonna go my way or not at all. We're gonna walk to my house. You'll shut your mouth, or take a bullet in the back. We'll circle to the back of my house, and go in. I'll stage the scene, and then you'll kill my stupid wife." He sobbed. "It wasn't supposed to go this way! Why did Barb have to ruin everything? I had it all under control."

"So why should I go along with this?" she asked, her voice trembling. She turned slowly under one of the weak streetlights and met his gaze. "If you're going to kill me anyway, why should I go along with it?"

He smiled, and shrugged. "Anything can happen, right? I could change my mind. My wife might have escaped. Who knows?"

He was right; given the choice between eventual death over immediate death, she'd take eventual death every time. "Where are we going?" she asked, resigned to going along with him until she could figure a way out.

He pointed up the lonely road, which rose to a peak. There was a rustic cabin there, Jaymie knew, from her walks around the island. That must be Will's home. It was perfectly situated to look out over the river, and she'd always thought it must have a great view. She doubted she'd have a chance to check that out.

"Walk," he commanded.

She did. It was dark, and he flicked on his flashlight, playing it over the ground in front of them. The road rose, but they were coming to his house all too soon. It was a kind of ramshackle cabin, with redwood siding. It looked like nothing from the roadside, because all of the windows were concentrated on the other side, overlooking the river, Jaymie knew from boat trips along the St. Clair.

Her mind worked furiously. Was she going to have a chance to ditch him? Was there a spot of uneven ground ahead, or someplace for her to dive into protection? But the front of the house was barren, no porch, no trees, nothing. Maybe at the back, then. She knew one thing: she was not entering that house, because to go in was to give up and die.

Her heart pounded, and her senses became preternaturally aware. Every sniff of wood smoke, each rustle of the wind in the treetops and noise in the bushes, every voice at a distance: it all was music, a tune she was using to figure out what to do. If she could just get away from Will, she was not that far from people, folks she might even know and who would help her.

She took deep breaths, willing herself to be calm. She had been in tough situations before, and had come out of them because she was willing to do whatever it took to stay alive. There was clearly no reasoning with him; she'd tried that and failed. So she was going to have to be patient enough to wait for the right opportunity, and gutsy enough to take that opportunity when she saw it.

It was darker near his house. That was good and bad. Good, because it gave her some hope of hiding, but bad because in the dark she could stumble and or fall, and because he had the flashlight. The flashlight. She needed to knock that out of his hand, if she could. Grabbing it was no good. Carrying it lit would make her a target. It would be quicker if she just knocked it away from him. He might even lose time looking for it.

"There . . . go that way, along the path to the back of the house," he said, playing the swath of light from the flashlight along the side of the redwood cottage.

Soon, soon, soon, her heart thrummed in beat with her muttered repetition. Soon. He was right behind her, the flashlight in one hand, the gun in the other. Which was which?

She glanced back. Gun in his right hand, flashlight in his left. Good. The flashlight was in the hand that was farthest from the house wall.

She waited, but as they reached the lip of a dip that would then rise up to the back of the house, she knew it was the moment, maybe her last chance. She whirled and chopped awkwardly at his left hand, giving it every bit of force she could, and he let out a surprised *Ugh* and a yelp of pain. He staggered, but didn't lose hold of the gun or the flashlight. But it was just enough of a distraction, and she hopped down the small rise and darted into the wooded ravine that ran close to the house. Branches scratched at her legs and she tripped, flying into a pile of dead wet leaves, her leg caught on a branch.

But then a miracle happened, and she heard a shout.

"Will Lindsay, drop your weapon and put your hands up! You are under arrest for the murder of Urban Dobrinskie!"

It was Zack's voice, and a moment later she heard another welcome voice. Garnet said, "Go find Jaymie, Hoppy! Go on, boy!" And her little dog yelped.

Weeping, Jaymie cried out, "Hoppy, I'm here, sweetie. Come on!"

A moment later her Yorkie-Poo was leaping wildly around her, as a flashlight played into the woods, and Garnet's voice came to her. "Jaymie? You okay? Say something!"

"I c-can't," she wailed. "Hoppy keeps sticking his tongue in my mouth!"

A shot rang out.

"Damn!" came Zack's voice.

"You okay, Zack?" Garnet yelled through the woods as various voices came toward them with cries of "What's going on?" and "Was that a gunshot?'" and "Yeah, thought I heard one earlier. What's going on?

"I'm okay," Zack called out, "but Will Lindsay is dead. He shot himself."

"Zack, Will's wife is inside the home," Jaymie yelled.

She scrambled to her feet. Garnet reached her, Hoppy leaping around her feet, and with her friend and neighbor's help she shakily found her way through the woods and out to where Zack stood, his service revolver in one relaxed hand, over the dead body of Will Lindsay. The killer still had his own gun in his hand, but his face was bloody. Jaymie turned away before she could see too much, a sob in her throat, as Hoppy sniffed curiously at the body. She reached down and picked her little dog up, turning her back on the scene and hugging her pooch to her.

"I think Barb Lindsay's alive—at least Will said she was—but she might be tied up," Jaymie said, a sob tightening her throat. "We've got to help her!"

"One second," Zack said. He pulled out his cell phone and with the keyboard glowing faintly, made a call. He muttered tersely, then clicked it off. "Garnet, can you stay here with the body? I've got backup coming. Jaymie, you don't know Lindsay's wife, but you're a woman, and she must be terrified. Will you help me?"

She looked up into his brown eyes and liked what she saw. He was finally comfortable with her, enough that he trusted her judgment. "I will," she said, proud that her voice trembled only a little.

THE HOUSE WAS dark. Zack knocked first, hoping the woman may have freed herself from her constraints. When that didn't work, he said, "I have reason to believe she is in danger . . . Who knows how he left her? So I'm going to have to do this." He placed one well-aimed kick at the lock near the doorknob, and the door ripped open with a loud scraping noise.

When Jaymie entered behind him, she heard whimpering close by, and let Hoppy loose. The little dog dashed through the dark and barked. Jaymie followed, as Zack, behind her, searched for a light switch. Hoppy was sniffing intently at a pantry door in the kitchen. She was there; Jaymie could hear her frightened whimpering.

"Barb Lindsay," she said, loud enough to be heard through the wood door. "Just hang on. My name is Jaymie Leighton, and you're safe. I'm with the police, and everything is going to be all right. You're safe now." She didn't think it would help to tell the woman her husband was dead; not at this point, anyway.

She tried the knob, and found, to her relief, that it was not locked. She opened it, and there, on the floor of the tiny pantry closet, was a dark-haired woman bound with zip ties, and with duct tape over her mouth. The wide, pleading eyes made Jaymie sob with relief that they had found her in time.

"Just relax," Jaymie said. "I'll get some scissors or a knife or something."

Zack came back from searching the house, and stuck his gun in the back waistband of his jeans. "It's good . . . There's no one else here."

Jaymie cut the zip ties as Hoppy danced around, happy now that the tension was gone. She then sat on the floor next to the woman and said, pulling at the edge of the duct tape, "This tape is going to hurt if I take it off. Do *you* want to do it?"

The woman nodded, trembling and rubbing her wrists, easing the cricks out of her shoulders and back. She got hold of one end of the tape and wrenched it off, crying out in pain, then sobbing in relief. "Where's Will?" she cried, as dots of blood oozed on her upper lip. "Has he been arrested?"

Jaymie looked up at Zack, who nodded. For her own peace of mind this woman needed to know the truth. "I'm sorry, but . . . Will is dead."

Ten minutes later she had made Barb Lindsay a cup of tea, and both women sat at the kitchen table. From being horrified at the outcome of her husband's crimes, she calmed, and now seemed resigned. The police swarmed her home, searching, now that they knew Will was Urban's murderer.

Zack was in command of the scene and didn't tell her to leave, so Jaymie stayed, as he and Will's widow chatted. Gently, he led her on to her story about Will's downfall.

"He wouldn't tell me what was going on," she said. "But I think he's been in money trouble for a while. When we married, I made sure to keep my finances separate, so I don't actually know."

"How long have you been married?" Jaymie asked, remembering Will speaking of his high school sweetheart.

"Only a year and a half. We've known each other forever—since high school—but I was married for a long time. When my husband died, I was just so lonely, and Will was a good friend so . . ." She shrugged. "We got married. I knew almost immediately that it was a mistake, but I decided to try to stick it out."

"What was wrong?" Jaymie asked.

"He was so secretive. I don't think he was used to being married. He already owned this house, so I moved in." There was a hint of steely resolve in her brown eyes when she added, "And I made sure we had wills, leaving our estates to each other. Life was hell after my first husband died, with his family fighting me at every turn, so I said I was never going to go through that again." The steel melted and she sobbed, "I didn't think I'd have to do this again so . . . so soon!" She put her head down in her arms and sobbed.

Jaymie rubbed her back, saddened by the woman's ordeal.

Zack cleared his throat. "I'm sorry to have to go through this, but I really need to get a handle on this whole thing. I've been looking into Lindsay's movements for a week, but I couldn't find any proof that he was involved in his partner's death. How did you figure out he was the one who killed Urban Dobrinskie?"

The woman launched into the story.

Urban had been dragging his feet on the marina and harbor dredging. It required both of their signatures on loan documents, and Urban kept saying he wasn't sure they should be investing that kind of money. Will was in some kind of financial bind, and needed to prove to investors that they were moving ahead with expansion. She suspected that he had overextended himself business wise, since she had no cause to think that he was gambling his money away, or taking drugs, the usual cause of money woes.

But then he came home one day, ranting that he had found out Urban was making a secret deal to buy the marina on the Canadian side of the island, as well as some land on the US side near it. He was furious. She overheard him arguing on the phone with Urban one evening, and making a time to meet down at the marina. She left to go to her darts club evening, and was out until one or two in the morning, since the league went for drinks at the Ice House, and it ran late, as it often did on league night.

"When I heard about the murder . . ." She shook her head, tears welling in her eyes. She shivered, despite the warm evening air that flooded in the open back door. "I wondered. But I convinced myself it couldn't be true. I mean, we had our problems, and he wasn't always kind . . . In fact, he wasn't the man I married, or at least . . ." She trailed off on a sigh. "He wasn't the guy I remembered from high school."

She cried a bit, then continued. When she finally confronted him just that day, he broke down and told her the truth, saying he did it all for them. He found out that Urban had no intention of going through with the dredging of their marina and harbor, because he was going to put all his money and energy into the one he would soon privately own and the other he would be building. Once he was done, the *Ferry Queene* would only have to stop at Urban's new marinas. It would have ruined Will.

"That's what he said to me, too," Jaymie said to Zack. "It would break him, financially. I think he tried to work it out with Urban, but Urb probably taunted Will with his plans. That's the kind of guy he was."

"Anyway, he told me this evening that he then stole the wheelbarrow from one of Robin's leaching bed digs," Barb continued, "stowed it, then had the discussion with Urban, asking for a late-night meeting at the marina to hash it out." She shook her head and sighed. "He says . . . He *said* that Urb got physical. He said Urb hit him, and he had to kill him in self-defense. But . . . I knew that wasn't true! Why would he have stolen the wheelbarrow beforehand? And the ice pick . . . He pocketed that the night of Urban's confrontation with Garnet outside of the Ice House."

"Really?" Jaymie cried. "How did he do that?"

"We were there having dinner that night," Barb said. "We saw it all. I think Will managed to manipulate Urb somehow so he confronted Garnet about that stupid sail."

Zack narrowed his eyes. "Okay, I'm just guessing at this, but when Garnet left the bar to go after Urb, maybe he left the ice pick on the bar? That *has* to be when Will got it."

"He really planned ahead," Jaymie mused. "He meant to implicate Garnet."

"Will never really liked Garnet. He . . . he thought the guy was shady," Barb said, tears welling up in her eyes.

"Is that why he left the body in my backyard?" Jaymie asked. "He wasn't too clear on that."

"It wasn't your backyard, I think, that he intended. It was Garnet's."

"Zack, it was Will who called the restaurant all evening, in between all the other stuff he was doing. He told me so."

Zack nodded. "We've ordered the phone records, but don't have them yet. I just yesterday set a team investigating Urban's business dealings, because I just had a feeling that had something to do with his death. In another day or so, if this hadn't happened, we would have had Will in for questioning."

"Detective!" one young officer said, coming into the kitchen. "I think we have something." He held up a cell phone. "This is one of those prepaid phones, like, a disposable, practically."

"Is it yours?" Zack asked Barb.

She shook her head, looking mystified. "No. I have mine in my purse, and Will had a dark blue cell phone. I've never seen that one in my life."

"Where'd you find it?" Zack asked.

"Desk in the spare room with some loan papers."

"I'll bet it's the phone the calls to the restaurant came from," Jaymie said. Hoppy begged to come up, and she cuddled her little dog on her lap, hugging him close.

"Maybe," the detective said. "Bag it, Trewent." The officer nodded and went back to his work.

"I tried to tell him it wouldn't do any good to pin the blame on me," Jaymie sniffed. "As if you'd believe it!"

The detective suppressed a smile, but Jaymie caught it. Barb's smothered sob sobered them both.

"He went off the deep end," Barb said. "I'm so sorry for all the harm he caused! I wish I'd turned him in, but until tonight I only had suspicions!"

Jaymie was exhausted, but her nerves were frayed like the raveled edge of a piece of silk. She hugged Hoppy to her, burying her nose in his fur, sniffing deeply the outdoor scents of their evening's adventure.

Zack had been glancing at her for a few minutes, then finally said, "Jaymie, we're going to be at this for a long time. Why don't you go back to Rose Tree Cottage, and I'll see you in the morning."

She nodded. "I have a lot more to tell you," she said. "Lots that I've guessed, and some that Will told me."

"It would help if you wrote it down, just to keep it all clear."

"Okay." She stood, and reached out her free hand to Barb, touching her shoulder. "Will you be all right? I'll stay, if you need someone."

The woman took in a deep breath. "I'm going to be okay. My mom was coming over tomorrow anyway, and I'll get through tonight. Thank you, Jaymie. I'll never forget hearing

Hoppy, and your voice saying everything was okay. I'll *never* forget it!" Her eyes teared up and she stood, reaching out and hugging Jaymie and Hoppy, who licked her face.

The cottage was welcoming. She hadn't seen Garnet since the incident, but it was too late to go over. She'd see him the next day, and thank him for his part in her rescue. Zack told her that Hoppy found Garnet, thanks to his autopilot familiarity with the Redmonds, and when Garnet saw Hoppy off leash and alone, he felt something was up, and followed the excited little dog. He saw Zack on his way—the detective's cottage was not far up the road from the Redmonds—and asked him to follow. That was how they came upon the scene, and saw Will, with the gun, just as Jaymie had dived into the bushes near the Lindsay home.

Jaymie gave Hoppy a handful of treats; he deserved that and much, much more for virtually saving her life. She made a cup of tea and sat, clipboard in hand, at the kitchen table, trying to organize her thoughts.

She was pretty sure Will did not know the truth about Ruby and Garnet, but he thought there was something suspicious there, enough that he managed to imply, in anonymous phone calls, that he would expose them if Garnet didn't meet him. Of course, all he'd wanted was to get Garnet out and alone at an important time, to be able to throw suspicion on the restaurant owner in Urban's murder. Had he used that same technique the night Ruby almost died?

Garnet and Ruby would have a lot to clear up with Zack, but that was none of her business. A tap at the back door startled her. Hoppy barked. She got up, and was surprised to see Ruby waiting on the back deck. Hoppy went crazy, of course, as she let her neighbor in. Ruby tossed Hoppy a treat from her shorts pocket.

The two women stood staring at each other for a long moment. "Do you want a cup of tea?" Jaymie asked, not sure what to say. They retired to the front porch with their tea. It was late, close to midnight, and everything was silent but for the breeze that tossed the tops of the pines across the road.

"I'm so happy you're okay," Ruby said, her voice quiet in the still night. Hoppy jumped up with her and snuggled close, snuffling at her pocket, where the treats lived.

"I'm grateful Garnet did what he did," Jaymie said, fervent in her gratitude.

"We knew something was up. Hoppy wouldn't have been off leash like that if there wasn't something wrong." There was silence for a few minutes; then Ruby started talking. "I grew up in Montreal, Canada. Such a beautiful city; sometimes I dream I'm back there."

"What's your real name?"

"I don't tell anyone that. There is no good reason to endanger anyone else. I am Ruby Redmond."

"Is it really that dangerous?"

Ruby sighed. "Yes. I got married young to an associate of my father's, and I saw them both murdered by a rival, first my husband, and then my father. I testified, and that sealed my fate. I can never go back to Montreal."

They were silent, as Jaymie digested the strange truth of the case. "How did you meet Garnet?"

"He was a cop once, and then private security. My father hired him to look after me ten years ago, after Laurent's death. Laurent was my husband; I was going to leave him anyway, divorce him. I just couldn't handle the violence anymore, the corruption. When Garnet came on board as my bodyguard, he was so different from Laurent. I'll never know why my father hired someone from outside to look after me, but once Pop was killed, I knew I had to get out. I testified against the men who killed my father, but then left."

"With Garnet?"

She nodded. "We fell in love, and got married, just a quickie little ceremony in front of a Justice of the Peace, but it meant all the world to me. Garnet and I went to Florida for a while, but they found us. So we changed our names and came here."

"And you thought you'd been found again."

Her dark eyes welled. "I was so scared!" she whispered. "I couldn't take it . . . those phone calls . . . It was like the last time. That evening there was one phone call for me, saying that he 'knew all my secrets.' And I knew Garnet was getting weird phone calls, too, but he wouldn't tell me what the guy was saying! I was so mad, and upset. I argued with Garnet, but he was trying to protect me and wouldn't tell me what the guy had said. After the murder I began to wonder if the calls were from Urban. Had Garnet met Urban, and . . . and killed him to protect me? It didn't make sense but I wasn't thinking rationally."

"You were really scared," Jaymie offered, still trying to come to terms with what this quiet woman had gone through in her life. Whatever ease she now had, in her fifties, she had earned with decades of turmoil and fear.

"I decided to leave. If Garnet didn't kill Urban—and I decided it was impossible, because he sure wouldn't leave the body in the backyard—then maybe there was someone after me, someone who had killed Urban and planted his body there as a warning. I left Garnet a note and took off, down to the marina with just some money and clothes in a bag. And then Will was so nice . . . He invited me to wait for the ferry in his office, and even gave me a cup of herbal tea. I think . . . I *think* I asked him to tell Garnet I'd left him a note, but I'm not sure. I don't remember anything else except for some foggy impression of being dumped in the water."

If only things hadn't sped along, Jaymie thought, fueled by Will's paranoia and her own presence that evening. Ruby had regained consciousness just that day, and she told the cops everything about being drugged in Will's office. Given another few hours or a day or so, they would have found her bag in the marina office and may have had enough to arrest

Will on the charge of attempted murder on Ruby, and probably would have then been able to tie him into Urban's murder. Zack had been on his trail, but it would have taken a few more days more.

"Will made those phone calls," Jaymie said. "I think he thought you and Garnet were . . . I don't know, fugitives from justice or something."

"I know. In retrospect, the caller didn't make sense, but I was scared out of my mind! We told the police everything right after the murder. I knew if they started to look into our past, there would be questions."

After a few moments of silence, Ruby said, "I think the cold water woke me up a little, because I tried to swim, and then tried to get to shore, but all I could do was hang on to a pier." She shivered. "I could have died. Would have, if not for you!"

"Well, I could have died if not for you and Garnet. And Hoppy! Actually, Hoppy was the hero in both cases. If he hadn't been stubborn and made me look in the water, I wouldn't have found you. And if he hadn't run off and got Garnet to come after him, Will would have found me in the woods and shot me!"

"He's a good little pup," Ruby said, taking another treat out of her pocket and feeding it to the Yorkie-Poo.

"So now you know your secret is safe, right?" Jaymie said.

Ruby nodded. "Only Marg knows, and now you and Valetta."

"We won't say a word."

"I think we'd better make sure folks know we're not brother and sister though. I know there was some gossip about me, and I want to put an end to that, but I just don't want my past getting around."

"I think it'll be okay."

"So, now what, Jaymie?"

Jaymie looked off into the dark, across the road into the

dark pines that lined her road. The island felt peaceful to her again, and she reflected on all the work they had done to make it perfect. "Now I face dinner at Rose Tree Cottage with my family and Daniel's parents. Thanks to Valetta, I think the cottage is as ready as it'll ever be. At least I won't be ashamed of my island home."

"When does the big dinner take place?"

"Day after tomorrow. Then my article comes out in the *Howler* the very next day. I don't know which one makes me more nervous."

"Good luck, hon," Ruby said, reaching over to squeeze Jaymie's hand. "You remember what I said about Daniel. A good man like that is hard to find. I didn't get mine until I was into my forties."

❧ Twenty-three ❧

SAMMY DOBRINSKIE WAS on Jaymie's cottage doorstep the next morning, clipboard under his arm, his expression troubled.

"Sammy! Didn't expect you this morning," Jaymie said, holding the screen door open for him. "C'mon in. Do you want to have a coffee down at the new patio?"

"Uh, sure, okay. I guess it's real early, isn't it?" he said, his cheeks reddening. He pushed his lank hair back and clutched his clipboard to his chest.

Jaymie had on her pajamas, but at least that was, this time of year, a pair of cotton shorts and a sleeveless T-shirt. No bra. "Just go on down, and give me a minute."

It took her ten minutes to change, brush her hair and teeth, and assemble a tray of coffee cups, the carafe and milk and sugar. As she descended the lawn, she saw Garnet and Ruby sitting out on their patio, overlooking the joint ravine lot. Garnet waved. Jaymie called out hello, then continued on to the patio. Sammy was pacing, but as he saw her approach, he dashed to pull out a chair for her and help her with the heavy tray. *Nice manners,* Jaymie thought. He'd do well with girls once he got over his shyness.

"I'm s-sorry for butting in," he said, in a rush of words. "I get thinking, and forget how early it is, and then just rush out and do stuff. Sometimes when I realize how early it is, I'm at the doors of a Home Depot that's not, like, open yet."

"It's okay, Sam. What have you got there?" she asked, and poured a cup of coffee for each of them.

He laid the clipboard down and showed her the finished sketches of her landscaping. "I had some other ideas, and wanted to show you before we take off. Mom and I are driving down to the school this morning to find a place to rent near the college. We'll only be staying there overnight, and I know I'll be seeing you again, to take pictures of the landscaping, but I wanted to get this done."

She looked at his sketches, while he added four spoons of sugar and lots of milk to his cup. He had elaborated on the themes he had already introduced, of "living areas" on the cottage property, and they discussed his ideas for a half hour. Some, they decided, were too complex unless the family decided to modernize and expand the cottage, something Jaymie was not in favor of, though it would make the property more rentable. But there were still a couple of ideas she liked very much, including a barbecue and fire pit area, for families to hang out with their kids and toast marshmallows.

"Do you want to come back tomorrow after I've set the whole thing up for a meal . . . I mean, *before* the family supper? Will you be back in time? I want you to be able to photograph all your hard work in its best setting."

He looked relieved and grateful. "I would. I was kinda afraid to ask, after everything that went down. I know you've been super busy. But it will look its best if I do it with the area set up for use."

"Don't be silly. I'm really sorry about your dad," she said, touching his arm briefly, "but it must be good for you and your mom to know who the real culprit is, isn't it?"

He nodded. "I, uh, wanted to tell you . . . My mom, when she lied about that night, about being home, and all, and me being at a sleepover . . . I knew she went out. She followed my dad, but lost track of him. She ended up on the Canadian side, thinking he was going to visit some woman there."

Jaymie was silent.

"He, uh . . . He had a girlfriend. But the woman dumped him before he got murdered, from what the cops told us Anyway, that's all that was; my mom was scared they'd come after me if they knew I was home alone that night."

Jaymie knew the rest about the night of the murder, that Will had called Urban to meet him at the marina, where he actually murdered him, stowed him in the office, then, under cover of darkness, moved his body using the wheelbarrow. Will then took the wheelbarrow back to the marina and dumped it in the river.

"Are you guys keeping the marina?" she asked.

"Yeah, for now. Mr. Redmond is buying out Mrs. Lindsay's half, I think, and he and his . . . Uh, Ms. Redmond are going to manage the marina while we're gone."

Jaymie bit her lip, and glanced over at him. "You know, Sammy, that they aren't really sister and brother." Garnet and Ruby were fine with folks knowing that much, they just didn't want her past associations gossiped about.

He smiled and tossed his lank hair back. "Yeah, I know, but it's hard to think of them as . . . as a couple, after all these years." He turned pink again, subject to the same problem with blushing that Jaymie had always had. "Y'know what I mean? I'll get used to it. Eventually."

Jaymie did know. It would take a while to let it sink in that they were husband and wife, on the run from her father's mob buddies. As much as they had wanted to keep it secret, there was a very real threat that the whole island would soon know about Ruby's past. The news chain was mysterious and efficient. It wouldn't come from her, though. "Garnet will make a good co-owner for you and your mom. How is she doing?"

"Mom went to see Mrs. Lindsay this morning, and I think it made her feel better. Did you know that Mrs. Lindsay is putting her house up for sale?"

"I heard something about it."

"Someone is looking at it today, some rich folks from out of state."

"Yuck. I hope they don't ruin it. It's got the best view on the whole island."

DANIEL CALLED, AND she spent a half hour on the phone with him, reassuring him that she was just fine, and downplaying the actual sequence of events so he wouldn't freak out on her. She then had to do the same with her father. He wanted her to come home right then, but she told him that she still had work to do, and she'd be home later.

She then worked all day to get the place just right. Later that afternoon, Zack came over and grilled her on everything she knew, thought, or conjectured. By the time he was done, she was exhausted and ready for him to leave. He didn't look so attractive through the jaded and exhausted eyes of a woman on the brink of telling him off.

She took the ferry back to Queensville, had a satisfyingly long gossip with Valetta at the Emporium, checked in on Cynthia at the Cottage Shoppe—it was almost ready for its grand opening; Cynthia had taken Jaymie's suggestions for the kitchen, but had bought up a lot of the enamelware dishes, so Jaymie kept all she had won at the auction—and returned home. Her mom and dad were out to dinner, so she had the house to herself. She got an email from Nan confirming that the article was indeed going to be in the paper, along with a couple of photos. Her blog was still lonely, with just three followers—Valetta, Dee Stubbs and Becca—and a comment or two.

She slept like a log, and awoke early, as nervous as a kid on the first day of school. Becca had called to say she and Kevin wouldn't make it for the actual dinner, but would come the next day to meet Daniel's parents. Jaymie had been counting on her big sister's help, and it made her crazy that she would have to bear the brunt of all the stress herself.

Her mother fretted over Jaymie's hair, her clothes and every other little thing about her. Jaymie had put on too much weight. She couldn't wear shorts; wasn't she going to wear a skirt? And she wasn't just going to put her hair up in a ponytail, was she? Why didn't she curl it for once?

Finally fed up Jaymie escaped, heading out to the island early with a loaded Red Flyer wagon full of vintage tableware and linens. Her parents were coming out later, with the Collinses. The two mothers had actually—unexpectedly, amazingly—gotten together and made all the food, so for once, Jaymie didn't have to worry about them.

As she disembarked the *Ferry Queene* and hauled her wagon along the dirt road toward the cottage—no Hoppy with her today—she saw Zack jogging along the beach, looping back from the dock. How often did he do that? It seemed like she saw him twice a day jogging! He saw her and trotted up beside her. Today he again looked relaxed and casual, not business-suit-all-work Zack as he had been the day before.

"Hi," she said. She was shyer around relaxed-Zack than business-Zack, for some reason.

"Hey, so today's the day, right? The family dinner at Rose Tree Cottage. Let me help you with that." He took the handle of the wagon and started off, with her trotting behind.

She struggled to come up with conversational fodder, but he was keeping too quick a pace anyway, so it had to wait until he hauled the wagon up to the front porch and picked up the heavy vehicle, easily lifting it up to the porch. She would have unloaded it at the bottom and taken three or four trips to get all the china and silverware unloaded. He helped her get it inside, and then plopped down at the kitchen table while she unloaded it onto the counter.

Real vintage china, she had decided, not paper plates. It was the environmentally sensitive thing to do, and besides, she had some nice summery patterns that she wanted to mix and match with plain china. And silver . . . She was going to use her grandmother's Leilani pattern, because it was so pretty . . . light and floral. Zack fidgeted. She glanced up from wondering about her "Vintage Eats" article in the *Wolverhampton Howler* to find him staring at her, an intense look on his face.

"You're going to a lot of trouble for this dinner. You must really want to impress Dan's folks."

She frowned and looked down at the flowered china in her hands. Did she? She hadn't thought of it that way, but she did feel the tension that comes from hoping someone likes you. "Not impress them . . . Well, maybe. I don't know. I want them to like me. That's natural, right?"

"Yeah, it's natural to want your boyfriend's parents to like you. I guess I'd better get going," he said suddenly, heaving himself up and heading for the front door. "I've got to get to work. Got a lot to do today."

"Okay. Bye!" she called out, as the screen door slammed behind him. What was up with him? Men always said that women were unfathomable, and all the while they walked around being a mystery wrapped inside a puzzle within an enigma.

For the next several hours she was too busy to worry about it. She hadn't had time to make new cushions for the outside chairs, as she had planned, but she had made a very quick trip to a design store and bought some inexpensive cushions that worked nicely for the time being. They were yellow floral chintz, and they glowed in the shade of the alders. She set the white wrought iron table with the floral china, softly burnished silver, and butter yellow damask napkins, and piled some tarts and petits fours on a raised china tray in the center.

After finishing up, she gave Sammy a call, and told him to come on over. He came with a professional-looking camera and took a couple of dozen photos, awed and grateful at how the work looked, given that with his design and her flourishes, the setting now looked like a landscaping magazine layout.

He took off, since he and his mom were heading back to the college that very afternoon so they could finalize the arrangements for their apartment near the campus. Jaymie dressed in the shorts and nice blouse she thought appropriate for a casual family dinner. She didn't know what to expect. She had left the menu and food to the two moms, and hadn't really had a chance to check in on them. It would have been presumptuous, she thought, to have even tried.

When the two older couples arrived, Daniel and the dads doing all the carrying, Jaymie was thrilled that it was all so well organized. Mrs. Collins had made sensible choices for their cottage picnic menu: sliced ham, red potato salad, creamy coleslaw, green salad, sliced tomatoes. It started with a cold soup, a kind of gazpacho that was spicy, but really tasty. Good thing she had brought pretty china bowls along with the plates and dessert dishes.

"This is amazing, Jaymie," her mom said. They sat in the cool shade as the sun began its descent after a hot August day, the men chatting about golf and politics, while the women had gone over—lightly, not in detail—Urban's unfortunate demise in the ravine. "I would not recognize the ravine, the way you have it fixed up." She turned to Mrs. Collins, and said, "Alan and I spend a week here every summer, and I'm really looking forward to it this time. I can bring my book down here, to the shade, and lie on a chaise lounge."

Jaymie beamed with pride and her dad squeezed her

shoulder. "The real praise has to go to Sammy Dobrinskie," she said. "That kid is going to be a talented landscaper. He already is, in fact!"

After, when the men offered to do the dishes, Mrs. Collins suggested that Jaymie show her around the island a little.

"Go on, honey," Jaymie's mom said, with a wink. "I'll supervise the fellows so they don't break any of your vintage china."

So Jaymie walked off with Daniel's mother, leading her down to the beach, then up the road, shivering a little as she passed the Lindsay home. Debbie Collins eyed the house, but Jaymie kept up a line of chatter, talking about the island and about Rose Tree Cottage, how her great-grandparents had built it a long time ago as a retirement residence. Finally she fell silent, though, noticing that Debbie Collins lagged behind.

"Can we just sit for a few minutes?" the woman said. "Maybe down on the beach at that picnic table."

They had made a loop, and were now near the beach again, so Jaymie led her down the path to the sandy spot where the picnic table was. The sun was red gold and hanging low in the sky, just beginning to touch the western horizon behind Queensville.

"My Daniel is a very special young man," the woman said, and left it hanging there, like a question.

"He is," Jaymie said. "Everyone here has gotten to know him this summer, and everyone likes him." It was true; even Mrs. Bellwood, Queensville's annual Queen Victoria, and one of the oldest members of the heritage association, had admitted that he was a very nice young man and a great host of the annual Tea with the Queen at Stowe House. His donation to the association of money and a good computer—with all the software necessary for the association to keep on top of things like its website and accounts—had helped, but his own personality and easygoing nature had done the rest.

"I will admit he seems happy."

It was grudging, and Jaymie frowned into the growing darkness, wondering why.

"Happier than he has been for a while," she went on, after a pause. "I won't see him suffer again."

"I . . . beg your pardon?" Jaymie stared over at the older woman.

Debbie Collins's round face was set in a grim expression. "I don't know how much you know about that . . . that Trish creature, but she hurt him so badly, I felt like murdering someone for the first time in my life."

She said it with a quiet, cultured voice, but there was a faint growl that reminded Jaymie of a tigress defending her cub. It began to dawn on her what this walk and talk was all about. This was a chance to probe Jaymie to see what her intentions were! Was she supposed to be in the position of the dangerous young men who were often the heroes of the historical romances Jaymie loved to read? Was Daniel being cast as the young innocent, whose heart and honor needed to be defended by a parent or guardian?

With wide eyes, Jaymie examined the other woman, trying to figure out what was behind that placid exterior. She felt like she was stuck in the middle of *Pride and Prejudice*, being warned away from Darcy by the dreadful aunt.

"I won't see him hurt like that again," Mrs. Collins said, steel in her polite voice. "Unless you can promise me that you won't do the same as that . . . that *girl* did to him, I will do all in my power to break this thing up before it goes too far, and I have the tools, believe me."

Jaymie had a hard time finding her voice. Really? She was being warned away from Daniel? "How do you think your son would feel, hearing you say that?" Her voice was stiff with anger.

"I don't care," she said. "I won't have him hurt."

A cold knot centered in Jaymie's stomach. "What if I told Daniel what you've said?"

"You won't if you're smart. If you make him choose between you and me, I'll win. I have before."

This was a new wrinkle, but there was no way she was going to be manipulated like this. "Mrs. Collins, don't get me wrong, I mean no disrespect, but Daniel is not a teenager." She got down off the picnic table and tugged at the legs of her shorts, which had ridden up. She faced the woman, her cheeks flaming red with fury, and said, "I would never purposely hurt Daniel, but I can't predict how things are going to go between us. Right now we are friends . . . close friends. We're taking it slow. I was badly hurt, too, not even a year ago, so I'm in no hurry to get serious."

In fact, it was Daniel who had been pushing her for more of a commitment. But she decided against telling the other woman any of their private life. She would just use it against Jaymie, probably.

"Good," Daniel's mother finally said and got down from the picnic table, dusting off her skirt. "Let's go back."

They were silent during the walk toward the cottage, and Jaymie's anger was chilling to frigid as they walked. She didn't even notice until it was too late that Zack Christian, dressed in a gorgeous gray summer-weight suit, was walking toward them with a big smile on his face.

"I'd know who this lady is even if you two weren't together. Jaymie, you didn't tell me how much alike you and your mother look. Mrs. Leighton, can I just say what a wonderful daughter you've got?" He put his hand on Jaymie's shoulder and squeezed, his smile intimate. "She's not only beautiful, but intelligent and caring. You must be proud."

There was shocked silence for a long minute, and Zack's expression turned to puzzlement, as his gaze flitted between the two women.

"I am Mrs. Debra Collins," she finally said, her voice hard. "Mother of Daniel Collins, Jaymie's boyfriend. And who, *exactly*, are you?"

He didn't explain, but beat a hasty retreat with a look of

apology cast toward Jaymie. She sighed. Well, if the woman needed ammunition, she now had it.

Daniel seemed to sense some tension when Jaymie and Mrs. Collins got back, and he anxiously corralled her, taking her aside and saying, "Did she upset you, Jaymie? She didn't say anything, did she? She can be a little overprotective of me, but she means well."

"Can you take a little walk with me?" she asked.

"Sure," he said, with a worried frown.

She steered him away from anywhere she thought they might meet Zack—though judging by the detective's clothes, he was working, maybe even questioning some of the islanders about the murder—and so they ended up down by the Ice House restaurant. It was dark, but there was a pool of light now on the patio. She plunked down on a bench and ordered an iced tea from Lisa, while Daniel ordered beer.

"What's wrong, Jaymie?" he said, his voice tense. "What did my mom say to you?"

How to handle this? The first heat of anger had burned off. "To be fair, she's worried about me, and I don't blame her. She loves you, and doesn't want to see you hurt." He started to talk, but she put her hand up. "I'm not going to share our conversation, and I'm not worried about it. But something else happened that upset me, and I want to tell you about it before your mother does." She told him what happened with Zack, and how he mistook his mom for hers.

He laughed out loud. "Wow, you know, I guess she does kind of resemble you, vaguely. More than your own mom, in a way." When she didn't join him in laughing, he noticed, and said, more soberly, "Look, I'll handle my mom."

She glanced over and examined his beaky profile, and the hank of sandy hair that always brushed the tops of his glasses. "I don't want her to take this the wrong way. Zack said I was . . . He kind of said I was intelligent and beautiful, and as my mother, she should be proud. That's *all*, but . . . he kind of touched my shoulder, and I saw her expression . . ."

She saw on his face that he was now taking the whole thing more seriously. This was going badly.

His voice was tense as he said, "Why would she take it the wrong way?"

She had decided to not tell him about how paranoid his mother was on his behalf, and how she had invoked the name of his ex-girlfriend who'd hurt him so badly, but maybe she *should* tell him all of it. "She's your mom, Daniel, and protective; it's her way, probably, to evaluate your girlfriend and see things where there's nothing."

He squinted through his glasses at her. "This doesn't sound like you, Jaymie," he said. "What are you *really* worried about?"

She sighed and took a long drink of iced tea, staring out over the river. She just couldn't tell him that his mother had as good as threatened to break them up; it wasn't fair to put that between them. "We'd better get back. Your folks will want to get back to Queensville soon. I shouldn't have left all the work of tidying up for everyone else, anyway."

They walked back, arm-in-arm. But before they got to the cottage, he stopped her in a shadowy spot and kissed her. "That's nice," she whispered, leaning into him. He held her close, stroking her hair and rubbing her back. It was a lovely reminder of all of his good qualities, not the least of which was that he was a very good kisser. They strolled slowly back to the cottage, his arm around her shoulders.

The four parents were chatting on the front porch when Jaymie and Daniel got back. The two men were talking golf, of course, and the two women were comparing notes on the meal.

"It was all so good, Mrs. Collins," Jaymie said sincerely, sitting on the top step of the porch stairs. "There was something a little different in your potato salad."

"Curry powder," she said, with a sharp nod. "It's Martha Stewart's recipe."

"Jaymie, Debbie was just telling me the most wonderful news!" her mom said, brightly.

Jaymie's heart thumped. News? What news?

"She and Roger have bought a cottage here on the island. Isn't that wonderful?"

"Cottage?" Jaymie's mind was blank.

"Yes, the Lindsay one; we passed by it on our little walk, but I didn't want to say anything just then. We were . . . talking about other things," Debbie Collins said, her face composed and blank. "Poor Barb Lindsay is anxious to sell, after that hubbub the other day, and so it's unofficially official. That fellow—Brock Nibley? Is that his name?—saw to it, and they've already drawn up papers."

"But . . . how . . . Why . . ." Jaymie shook her head, looking from one of them to the other, and landing on Daniel. He shrugged. "How did you find out about it?"

"Brock Nibley," Debbie Collins repeated. "He called us this morning, saying it wasn't on the market yet, but would be, and did we want to see it?"

She had known Brock was cutthroat as a real estate agent—he scanned obituaries and attended funerals to get first jump on listings—but this was swift even for him.

"Seems like a nice enough spot," Roger Collins piped up. "We spotted it last week during a river cruise and thought it had a great view, but that all that potential was wasted. It is so badly looked after, you know. And if our boy is going to be here a lot, we thought we'd have a little nest here, too. 'Sides, Debbie is just longing to work on the place; all this gardening has her inspired."

"We had better get going, Roger," Mrs. Collins said, standing and smoothing her skirt down.

Jaymie was going to go back to town with the Collinses, leaving her mom and dad to enjoy the cottage for a week, which was why she had left Hoppy in the house in Queensville. She *had* been looking forward to returning to being alone at the Queensville house, but the ferry ride was awkward, to say the least. No subject seemed safe, and she and Debbie Collins exchanged glances but did not speak.

Daniel drew her slightly away and said, "Are you angry that they bought the cottage?"

"It's none of my business, but I am surprised. It seems so casual to buy a house in a place you never before wanted to live!"

"I've done that lots of times," he said.

It was like an unexploded bomb had landed in her lap. "What?" She watched his shadowy profile. "What do you mean?"

"Just what I said; I've done that lots of times. Besides a house in Bakersfield and one in Phoenix and Stowe House, I own houses in . . . heck, seven states? Maybe more?"

"Eight . . . You bought a house in Alabama two years ago," Roger Collins, who sat nearby, said.

Didn't his family have any boundaries? Daniel's dad had been listening in the whole time. She kept her mouth tightly closed, then said a tepid good-bye to Daniel by the dock, saying she'd talk to him the next day. She returned home to Hoppy, who had been kept in the house in Queensville all day and was wild to get out.

Once he had fussed over her, and Denver slunk out to rub up against her arm, the warmest his affection ever got, she sat on the back step in the darkness while Denver prowled and Hoppy sniffed around and piddled. Daniel owned, what? . . . Eleven houses? *Eleven!* And she had had no clue. Eleven houses sprinkled over the United States like croutons on a salad. It was ridiculous. What kind of wing nut buys houses on a whim, she wondered. A rich wing nut, she supposed.

It left her feeling kind of tilted over, like something had moved, and she was left off-kilter. Wasn't that kind of major? And Daniel had said nothing about it. Was Stowe House and

Queensville just another temporary stop for an eccentric multimillionaire?

She headed to bed, finally, and tried to read, but there was a knot in her stomach. She supposed it had something to do with all of the fuss with Daniel and his parents, but it was more than that. It was fear, plain and simple. Tomorrow her first "Vintage Eats" column would come out in the *Wolverhampton Howler*, and she was ready to upchuck over it.

The next morning after a fitful sleep she rose, and went to her computer. The Vintage Eats blog she had started was still moving sluggishly along. She went on and wrote a piece about the excellent potato salad she'd had the day before, and the surprising ingredient, and mused about how sometimes you learn new tricks in the most unexpected places.

She was interrupted twice by phone calls, first from Valetta, congratulating her on the column, and then by Dee Stubbs, with the same message. She wasn't sure whether she was most nervous or anticipatory over looking at her column, so she delayed going to the Emporium to get a copy until she published that day's blog column.

But she couldn't delay any longer. She was afraid it would be sold out, something that occasionally happened, if she didn't get over there. She walked Hoppy over, put him in the puppy pen with Junk Jr., and took the few steps up to the Emporium with a hop. She went in to the jangle of bells, like her nerves, and grabbed a *Howler* off the pile, leafing to the Lifestyles section.

There was her "Vintage Eats" column, cute little vintage graphic and very brief bio accompanying, and a black-and-white version of one of her picnic photos, and one of the sandwich loaf. It looked good. Mrs. Klausner looked up from her own *Howler*, and nodded slowly, majestically, at her in approval. Valetta wasn't working today, so there was no reason to linger. After a quick look at the basket rental book, and making some notes on what to tell the cook at the Queensville Inn to deliver for the Saturday and Sunday rentals, she headed home past Cynthia's Cottage Shop, scheduled to open the very next day.

She logged on to check her email, and at the same time checked out her blog. There were . . . wow! There were seventeen comments, and eight new followers! She hopped in her seat and yelped. Hoppy came bounding up the stairs and stood at the office door looking at her.

"Hoppy, people are reading it! They're reading the column in the paper, and coming to my blog! People are reading *my* column, *my* writing!"

He danced around and barked and she laughed out loud. The phone rang and she picked it up on the first ring.

"Congrats, Jaymie! I'm so proud of you," Daniel said.

She got a warm trickle in her tummy. "Thank you, Daniel. I'm so happy with it!"

"Do you want to go out to Ambrosio tonight, just the two of us, and celebrate?"

"I'd *love* to! Kevin and Becca are coming over, but they'll want to spend some time with Mom and Dad today at the cottage."

"Pick you up at eight."

The next call was from her mother. "Honey, it looks so good! I've had half the island reading it already. Congratulations on your column. We're going to take a copy up to your grandma next week."

She hopped in her chair, and said, "Thanks, Mom, that means a lot!"

"So, now that you're writing, you'll be able to stop running around doing all kinds of jobs, right?"

"What do you mean?"

"Well, you've got a real job now."

"It's only every other week, Mom, and they're not paying me for it." Oops.

"They're not paying you for it? Why not?"

It was about to go rapidly downhill, but she was not going

to let her mother burst her happy bubble. "I gotta go, Mom. I've got to . . . to, uh, go next door."

"Oh, yes, please check in on poor Pam and make sure she's doing all right. I can come back if she needs me."

Jaymie hung up. It took a moment, but she got her happy mood back, went over, helped Pam out of a jam, and returned home. Twenty-six comments, fifteen followers, and mounting!

The phone rang, and she picked it up.

"So what are you doing for your next piece?" It was Nan Goodenough.

This time Jaymie was ready. "Well, since Garnet and Ruby Redmond were cleared in the murder on Heartbreak Island, I'm going to go ahead with the piece on them, and the icehouse tools, and making ice cream, just in time for Labor Day!"

"Great. Have it ready in a week." And she was gone, a dial tone replacing her brisk voice.

Jaymie sat back in her chair as another comment popped up on her blog on cooking from vintage recipes. She could do this. It was going to work. She'd get a few cooking articles under her belt, keep blogging, and then begin to work on some other exposure to build her resume as a cooking authority. She'd write more pieces for the cookbook, and eventually, she would be taken seriously by a New York publishing firm, either Adelaide Publishing or someone else.

In the meantime, she'd try to figure out her relationship with Daniel. She liked him. A lot! And she was not willing to let his mother destroy it; nor was she going to let a few quirks of personality—collecting houses was surely an eccentricity, at the very least—turn her away from someone she liked so much.

"C'mon, Hoppy. Let's go for a walk to see if Cynthia needs any help before the Cottage Shoppe opens. I've decided I'm going to give her the rest of that enamelware for her cottagey kitchen after all. Maybe she even has some old cookbooks for me!"

FROM JAYMIE'S VINTAGE KITCHEN

Hello from Heartbreak Island! As everyone knows by now, I love cookbooks and recipes from bygone eras. Oftentimes the recipes aren't very practical or require too much work for my liking, though. They *can* be time-consuming, but if you have to bring something to a bridal shower potluck or summer party, you don't mind the extra effort for something truly worth it. This is my take on one that keeps popping up in cookbooks from the middle of the last century.

Frosted Layered Sandwich Loaf

This is a standard from the 1950s, and I'm thinking about making it for the bridal shower *someone* will have to throw for Heidi Lockland, since she's marrying my former BF Joel. She's really into midcentury modern, so this would be perfect. The recipe is something you kind of have to experiment with and add your own twist to, but I'm providing basic instructions.

One loaf of unsliced bread and three of your favorite fillings. I used ham salad, egg salad, and a layer of cream cheese with chopped olives for the middle, but you can use any combination: egg, chicken, roast beef, turkey, tuna, salmon or ham salad; your preference. These salad ingredients need to work together. You *could* get adventurous here, though, or make a vegetarian version: if you enjoy some particular kind of filling, like hummus, diced cucumber or tomato in mayo, then go ahead . . . This recipe is all about *fun*.

Slice all the crust from the bread, then lay the loaf on its side and cut it into 4 even slices. Lay three of the slices down on the counter and spread your filling choices on each. You can use butter first, if you like; I would advise that you do, if you are using a fairly wet filling like the diced cucumber or tomato, as the butter will seal the bread and keep it from getting soggy. Then carefully stack the slices, topping with the last naked slice of bread.

FROSTING
One or two 8 oz. packages of cream cheese, room temperature or it won't cream.
¼ cup mayo
2 Tbsp. cream

Note: you can flavor the cream cheese if you like, but the fillings are the star, so don't go too crazy. You can also add some food coloring if this is for a party that has a color scheme, but I'm not sure anyone would eat a green sandwich, so be careful! Plain, yellow or pink would be best.

Cream the ingredients together. You'll have to use your discretion when it comes to the amounts, because it depends on how thick you want the frosting, how high the loaf is, etcetera. You want to thin the cream cheese until it spreads smoothly, and frost the loaf as you would a layer cake. Then comes the fun part: decorating! I used sliced olives to make flowers, but you could go wild here, with carrot curls, radish roses or grated carrot as a garnish.

Serve in pretty slices! This is a versatile recipe, and I know I'll make it again for a tea party or bridal shower. Next time I *may* try a dessert version, using a store-bought loaf cake, with diced fruits as the filling and sweetened cream cheese as the frosting!

Hope you enjoy it!

Jaymie Leighton

PS—Hoppy says he enjoyed the leftovers a lot! Also, if you'd like to see some photos of these made by great cooks, just do an Internet search using the words "vintage recipe—sandwich loaf." You'll get lots of interesting hits!

Becca Robbins is happy to help research a farmers' market and tourist trading post—until she has to switch her focus to finding a killer...

AN ALL-NEW SPECIAL FROM NATIONAL BESTSELLING AUTHOR

PAIGE SHELTON

Red Hot Deadly Peppers

A Farmers' Market Mini Mystery

Becca is in Arizona, spending some time at Chief Buffalo's trading post and its neighboring farmers' market to check out how the two operate together. She's paired with Nera, a Native American woman who sells the most delicious pecans—right next to a booth with the hottest peppers money can buy.

When Nera asks her to deliver some beads to Graham, a talented jewelry maker inside Chief Buffalo's, Becca is grateful to get a break from the heat. Little does she realize that the heat's about to get cranked up even more—because Graham has been murdered, and she's the one who finds his body. She soon discovers that Graham was Nera's cousin, and that her uncle was recently killed, too, after receiving a threatening note. Becca begins to think the murders may have something to do with the family's hot pepper business. Now she must find the killer, before she's the one in the hot seat...

Includes a bonus recipe!

paigeshelton.com
facebook.com/TheCrimeSceneBooks
penguin.com